LAZARUS

BY SARAH CAWKWELL

Lazarus by Sarah Cawkwell
Cover by Neil Googe
This edition published in 2022

Zmok Books is an imprint of

Winged Hussar Publishing, LLC
1525 Hulse Rd, Unit 1
Point Pleasant, NJ 08742

Published under agreement with Wayland Games Limited

Copyright © Winged Hussar Publishing
ISBN PB 978-1-950423-94-1
ISBN EB 978-1-950423-95-8
LCN 2022940520

Bibliographical References and Index
1. Science Fiction. 2. Dystopian Age. 3. Wild West Exodus

Winged Hussar Publishing, LLC All rights reserved
For more information
visit us at www.wingedhussarpublishing.com

Twitter: WingHusPubLLC
Facebook: Winged Hussar Publishing LLC

For Bubba, Steve, Dudge and Jeff the Ref - who raced the rest of us to Valhalla and won.

Sarah Cawkwell

WELCOME TO THE

DYSTOPIAN AGE

From the Badlands of North America to the icy realm of Antarctica the world of the Dystopian Age is a wild and dangerous place. It is a generation since the end of the American Civil War and Queen Victoria has been on the throne for over forty years. While Louis-Napoleon builds an alliance in Europe, the nations of the Far East are roused to action against the growing threat from the West.

Combining the newly discovered Element 270 with a limitless power source known as RJ-1027, a global scientific and engineering technocracy called the Covenant of the Enlightened have ushered in an age of phenomenal advancement; bringing to reality projects and ideas that were the stuff of dreams only decades before. This unearned and disjointed scientific progression has, however, come with neither morals nor safeguards and the world has been plunged into a Dystopian Age.

This is an era where individuals can make their mark with opportunities for personal gain as well as the national interest to defend. Whole regions have been devastated by conflict, and yet others are relatively untouched, transformed by the massive expansion of industry and technology into hives of activity that feed the fires of this terrible struggle. Worse yet, it appears that the world itself is changing as if the roiling conflict is enveloping the natural order as well as that of humankind. Bizarre weather events erupt with increasing regularity, mighty storms blow up and then suddenly vanish. At sea and in the air, ships and flying craft mysteriously reappear miles off course, their crews having no recollection of the missing time.

The Union of Federated States has emerged traumatised and hardened from a bloody and protracted internal conflict known as the Ore War. It now tries to brutally enforce its rule across the sprawling and lawless land claimed by the proud Warrior Nation, all manner of Outlaws, wild creatures, and elements of the Enlightened. The cities of the East Coast of the Union are austere and distant places compared to the rapidly expanding and vibrant towns that have sprung up across the West. Towns like Red Oak, Tombstone, Deadwood and Retribution rival each other for attracting the most exotic and deadly of the inhabitants that call the frontier home.

While the inhabitants of the Frontier are not ignorant of the larger world around them, it has little immediate impact as the Union serves as both protector and oppressor; isolating the Frontier from the wider world except for those few agents that slip through the ever-tightening net. There is much more to be found in the West than just a plot of hard-earth and the scrabble for gold. With so many vying for power and influence; the Frontier is truly a place where a man or woman might not just make their fortune but become a legend. A legend to be remembered, a legend to be feared.

Sarah Cawkwell

Lazarus

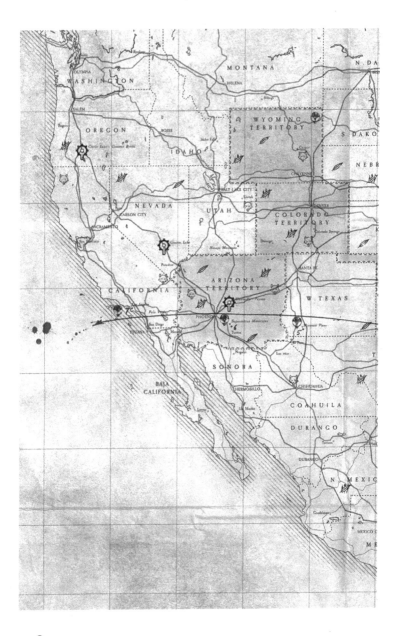

PROLOGUE

The sky was aflame.

Above the mining town of Provenance, a magnificent sunset was beginning, at last, to fade into peach tones instead of the deep orange it had been for the past quarter hour. Normally people didn't bother to look up at the sky, busy as they were with their lives down here on the ground. Tonight, though, had been different. Tonight's sunset had been so spectacular that people had stopped to marvel at it.

One budding young artist had been trying desperately to capture the inherent beauty, mixing his colours with a desperation bordering on lunacy. To his immense satisfaction, he caught the amber sliver through the clouds *just right* and as his brush dragged the watercolours across the canvas, he felt satisfied in the knowledge that he was working, at last, on the masterpiece that would take him out of Provenance and on to far greater things.

A crackly, artificial-sounding trumpet blast echoed from the far northern edge of the town, where the lumber mill was announcing that business was done for the day. Situated, as it was, next to a ragged, sparsely populated copse, Provenance was one of the few places in the territory where a lumber mill was lucrative business. Ranchers and prospectors from miles around bought building materials here, adding to the ever-growing income that the town council had swelling their coffers. Talk on the street was that the whole town would soon be alive with RJ-powered lighting. The main thoroughfare was already benefiting from the money that the town was making.

Now, as the colour faded from the sky and dusk settled over the town, those lights were beginning to come on, flickering at first, but quickly sputtering into crimson-tinged illumination. There was, if you cared to listen for it, a faint hum of the RJ-1027 generator that served the town. Demand for power was growing swiftly; during the day, the sawmill drew heavily on its reserve with a dozen automated saws and twice as many conveyors that made the whole lumber process infinitely more productive. It was without question that the town would need to invest in a second generator soon. The thrum of power in the cables that ran beneath the street's dusty surface and on poles overhead was something that had long become a part of the Provenance background. The residents considered the modernisation of their town as a point of pride.

An iron-coach rumbled over the road's surface with a snarling motor chugged its way into town bringing yet more people with it. There would be a crowd in the saloon that night and the town was fast running out of houses to board the influx of miners, engineers and eager young things desperate to carve out a life for themselves.

The young artist, having been robbed of the spectacular colours of the evening sky packed up his things and carried them into the saloon where just like any number of the other young male inhabitants of the town, he intended to sit nursing a beer and enjoying the company of his peers, his elders and – if he was lucky – the pretty kitchen girl whose eye he had caught the previous night.

Provenance was a young town, as these things were measured, and it was growing swiftly. It was home to perhaps three hundred and fifty people, with more arriving weekly. It was a town that was alive. It was a town that was thriving. It was *special*. And people knew it.

In just a few short hours, everything would be gone.

* * *

"Provenance Lumber Supplies."

Hywel Rhys, the owner and manager of the sawmill read the name out loud and sighed, shaking his head. "The Provenance Wood and Lumber Company," he tried, writing down another attempt. Yes, that one was much better. Until three days ago, everyone had been happy enough to refer to it simply as 'the Mill', but he wanted something grander. He was the owner of a going concern and he wanted that reflected in the new signage he had planned for the mill's exterior. Who'd have thought that naming his officially registered new company would be so difficult?

Rhys was a prosperous man, the top employer in Provenance and he was also a generous man. Thanks to his self-proclaimed wise investment in the Covenant of the Enlightened and the scientific and engineering advancements they offered, he was now the most valued contributor to the town's prosperous growth and rapid progress. Because of his business acumen, he had secured the deal that brought the generators into the town and brought it bang up to date. The fact that his mill production had doubled and made him a very rich man was, of course, merely a by-product. Whisper and rumour abounded and every single person in town was confident that Hywel Rhys was going to win the mayoral election that in three days' time.

He turned his thoughts from the company name and tried something else to distract himself. Mayor Rhys. Yes. It sounded good and so he tried it aloud. He'd garnered quite the reputation for talking to himself.

Rhys raised an invisible top hat with exceptional grace and made a mental note to get his tailor to look into making a new suit come morning. He would need to look the part, after all. He put the non-existent hat back on his head and beamed.

"Good day, ma'am, I'm Mayor Hywel Rhys." He nodded in satisfaction. It sounded excellent. He had *such* plans for Provenance. He was going to divert more of the mill's income to the town hall, to pay for better education, for another lawman. He paused there. That might have to move further up the agenda, because the situation in the town was beginning to change. Wherever there was prosperity, criminals were never far behind. Some of the young people were verging on the unruly, but a resident sheriff would soon put paid to that, he was sure. Yes, Hywel told himself, in five years, the town would be bigger and better even than Tombstone.

The mere thought of such a thing caused Rhys to puff his chest out in pride. He sighed contentedly and leaned back in his chair, patting the pocket of his waistcoat to locate his matches. He put the cigarette in his mouth and after several attempts, managed to light a match. He set the flame to the tobacco and closing his eyes, inhaled deeply. Yes, sir, it was good to be alive at a time like this. When a new town was on the rise, when his own star was in ascendance...

There was a knock on the door of his office, and he started, the chair coming dangerously close to tipping over and depositing him on the floor. He coughed to cover up the sound of his flustered squeak of alarm. "Yes? I mean, come on in. Come right on in." He stubbed out his half-smoked cigarette and got to his feet.

The woman pushed open the door and glided into the room, preceded by a waft of a heady, slightly sickly-sweet perfume. Rhys sniffed without meaning to and pulled his handkerchief from his waistcoat pocket. There was a heavy base of jasmine in the scent, and it set his nostrils tingling. He sneezed loudly. The woman smelled as though she bathed in the stuff.

"Bless you," said his guest, her voice a low, throaty murmur that set other senses tingling. The refined southern accent made her voice so enchanting that it didn't matter that the sincerity content was non-existent. Rhys blew his nose and waved at his guest to sit down.

"Thank you. Please. Please. Take a seat, ma'am. Can I get you a drink?"

"Water will be just fine, Mister Rhys." She settled herself down in the chair, her long skirts sweeping the floor. Every time she came into his room, she brought a touch of colour with her. She favoured bright, bold colours and the dress she wore this evening was a shade of golden, sunshine yellow that set her apart from the endlessly drab greys and browns of common, functional clothing.

Rhys poured a glass of water for her, noting as he did so that the new pumps and purifiers that had been installed only days previously were working even better than the engineers had promised. The liquid in the glass was almost entirely free of sediment, something that had been far too common before their installation. He poured himself a shot of whisky and carried the drinks to the desk.

"I'm hoping you're here to talk about taking an extended lease," he said, getting straight down to business and not allowing himself to become bogged down in formalities. He'd learned that she was a shrewd negotiator and did not appreciate small talk. "I'm assuming things have been going well for you?"

"Extremely well, Mister Rhys." She took a delicate sip of water and smoothed out her skirts. "The facilities are certainly adequate for my needs. But I am goin' to need to hire some more of your young men an' women to help me. I declare that I am just *so* busy."

Every time. Every single time they spoke, he yearned to ask what it was she was doing in the old mines. He knew that her people had set up a small, but secure camp at the minehead. He knew that they did not like strangers snooping around. He knew also that they came and went freely around the town and that not one of them engaged the locals in conversation. They visited once a week for materials and supplies, moving the goods on growling powered carriages and kept entirely to themselves. Yes, every time they talked, he wanted to ask her what it was that she was actually *doing*. She had not wished to divulge when they'd agreed to the contract, saying that it was important research and that if Rhys asked no further questions, he'd be heavily compensated for the fact.

Every time, he remembered that heavy compensation and kept his mouth firmly closed.

"More of my young workers? But, dear lady..."

"I will compensate you most generously for the inconvenience, of course, sir." She lifted her eyes to meet his and there was no coquettishness or flirting in her expression, only desire to get what she wanted. Rhys had the feeling, very deep down, that she usually achieved exactly that. "Ain't I brought a flare of modernity to your quaint little town? Did I not bring the generator with me? Who lit up your streets when the light is gone from the day? People are comin' here all the time. You won't miss, say, a dozen or so workers."

"I understand, I do. And I – and of course, the citizens of Provenance – are extremely grateful, but..."

"Is my money not good enough for you, Mister Rhys? Because I *can* take my business an' my research elsewhere."

"No! No!" Her money was not only good enough, but it was also *very* good enough. And if there was one truth in this entire matter, it was that Hywel Rhys was easily swayed by money. If He couldn't fund the ongoing growth and continued construction – well, the simple fact was that not another soul would want to come to Provenance. The dreams he had for the town turning into something startling, would go up in smoke.

The thought process made him remember his half-smoked cigarette and he patted his waistcoat pockets to find his cigarette tin. He took it out and opened it, offering his guest one. She declined politely and tipped her head to one side. "Is there a problem, Mister Rhys?"

"No problem! If more bodies are what you need, dear lady, then more bodies are what you shall..."

As he spoke, he got to his feet, fumbling with a cigarette. He put it between his lips and dashed around the desk to look out of the window at his dream. It took him a full minute to connect the orange glow in the distance with the actuality of the situation.

A crisis situation brought the best out of Hywel Rhys. And right now, as he looked at the eastern quarter of Provenance burning, flames licking up into the night sky, he was in a crisis situation.

The cigarette fell, unlit, from his lips and he stared. Then he coughed politely and turned to his guest.

"I suggest we continue this discussion later," he said, his voice the epitome of calmness. Inside, a part of his soul had just died.

* * *

Provenance, like so many towns of its ilk, was constructed largely from wood and the fire took hold quickly. The east quarter, a warren of scaffold and half-finished residences was already burning fiercely, the inferno fuelled by pitch and fresh lumber. By the time Rhys reached the saloon, bursting with his news, people had already become aware of it. He knew only the vaguest sense of irritation at having had his thunder stolen from him, but he immediately began organising a chain of water carriers from the protesting town pump to the growing inferno.

An engineer rushed to the sawmill and began frantically attempting to modify the powered coolant hoses to direct water from the mill's water-tower toward the blaze, but a full understanding of Enlightened engineering was a mystery to even those who claimed to know most about it and he was left frustrated and desperate.

For three hours, the people of Provenance attempted to contain the fire in the eastern quarter. Into the dark of the night it burned, the sky once more aflame – only this time not with the glory of a sunset. The town's firefighters were joined by most of the men – and a fair few of the town's womenfolk as well – who joined the efforts to contain it. It was a relief that the fire had started in this uninhabited part of town; it was allowing that vital space to keep it under control. The fires were slowly and gradually extinguished and from his vantage point toward the back of the water-carrying chain, Rhys lifted his eyes briefly to the sky and thanked his lucky stars.

"I think we're winning here," he observed to his neighbour. "We'll have to do a lot of work to get things back to where they were, but it'll be worth it. Maybe this is some sort of divine intervention. I'm telling you; we need to be thankful. Think how much worse it could have been!" He injected enthusiasm and encouragement into his tone. At least that's what he was aiming for.

The other man grunted. He'd carried four buckets to every one of Rhys's and was weary to the bone. He was not seeing any positives in the night's actions whatsoever.

When the last of the fires was doused, the tension began to ebb from people's shoulders and the atmosphere became immediately more relaxed. A handful of prospectors stood together actually *laughing* about the experience, clapping one another on the shoulder and congratulating themselves for their heroic deeds here that evening.

Rhys drew in a deep sigh of relief. If they had not been able to get the fire contained, he dreaded to think what might have happened. He swept his hair back and looked affectionately over at the sawmill, its huge, brooding presence something for him to be proud of.

Then the sawmill's generator exploded.

With a resounding *boom* that shook the very earth on which they stood, the heart and soul of modern Provenance blew apart in a storm of fire that fountained debris hundreds of feet into the air. People were thrown to the ground, rocked by the sheer force of the explosion and panic began anew as fresh, crimson-tinged flames washed from the ruins of the mill in a ravenous wave.

Rhys stared in abject horror. The pinnacle of his career, his future... the town's future... his mayoral achievement... all of it was going up in smoke. The empty bucket he held in his hands clattered to the ground and he was rooted to the spot. A handful of the townsfolk were rushing towards the sawmill with fresh buckets of water, but then a second explosion, even more powerful and louder than the first sent them flying. Blazing wreckage fell like rain, lighting up the sky like a vision of Hell and igniting buildings all across town. Several people close by were struck by the streaming embers, the ruddy flames hungrily leaping from the dry timber to the fresh kindling afforded by human clothing. They were spared immolation by quick-thinking companions who pushed them to the ground, smothering them in dust. Luck by this point, was extremely relative, but the folk who might otherwise have burned alive took it anyway – and the scars that would go with it.

That did it. That unstuck Rhys's feet from the ground and, in a rare demonstration of capability, certainly far more than enough to have won him the mayoral election, had such a thing been remotely likely at this point, he turned towards the horrified people of Provenance.

"We have to evacuate," he said, his voice loud enough to capture the attention of those closest. "Get yourselves out as fast as you can. Don't stop to collect anything other than your families and children. We can't stop this from happening now." The doom of Provenance was an inevitability that broke his heart and even as he took control, even as the people obeyed without question, tears began to stream down Hywel Rhys's face at the waste. The horrible, horrible waste.

The sounds of wailing and swearing filled the night air in equal measure as people who until that moment had been coping admirably lost control and panicked. Something of a crush began as the town in its entirety stampeded in all directions. Controlled and orderly was not foremost on their mind and who could honestly blame them? Hywel Rhys oversaw everything as best he could, but chaos had taken hold of his beloved town and it would not allow itself to be controlled or contained. His thoughts, his attention and his misery were focused on the tragic and untimely demise of the newly christened Provenance Wood and Lumber Supplies Sawmill. Everything he had worked for... for his entire life...

A third explosion signalled the destruction of the kerosene and gasoline fuel tanks with their accompanying RJ fuel injectors. This time, the sky itself seemed to catch fire. The slick of liquid flame that rained from the blast was red-tinged, evil and exceptionally flammable and wherever it landed, things burned faster and hotter than before.

Arthur Fitzsimmons, the town's engineer, wept at the disaster which was rapidly consuming the place he had come to call home. Over the past months, that generator had become the very focus of his life. Of course, he was more than used to explosions and usually he was the one behind them. He was a smart, clever man, in possession of a soot-smeared, cheerful face and engaging personality. But he also possessed something of a propensity for what he called 'experimentation'. That was *his* term for it; others called it 'dangerous game-playing with volatile chemicals and things he clearly does not understand'. He was more than tempted to rush to the sawmill and recover any part of that glorious generator and it took three men to hold him back.

Only a few, short minutes after the initial detonation, the entire town was aflame, fire licking up the side of buildings, fuelled by the aggressive addition of RJ accelerant. All thoughts of heroism fled from the thoughts of the remaining people, and they ran as well.

By dawn, all that remained of Provenance was a town of ash and cinders beneath a choking pall of smoke. Here and there scorched husks and skeletal buildings defiantly remained, blackened stumps like corpse teeth standing in the pale light. The water tower presided over the scene, its legs burned and slightly askew, an ironic thing when so much had been consumed by flame. The tower stood as silent, scarred witness to the death of Provenance. Whatever had caused this tragedy had done its job thoroughly.

It was a miracle, they would say in a day or two, that nobody died.

It was poor comfort.

And it would be a long, long time before Hywel Rhys would suddenly wonder at the fate of his lady guest on that terrible night and wondered what became of her supposed grand plans and important research.

By then, though, the world would have become a very different place.

Sarah Cawkwell

PART ONE – OPENING GAMBIT

Arizona, April

The Spirit Priest had not yet been dead for a full day and already his replacement was wondering whether it was possible to petition the Great Spirit to exchange places with the deceased.

All eyes were on him and that made him desperately uncomfortable.

He was young to be pushed into such a powerful position, a truth that was impossible to deny. But among the People of the Warrior Nation, Stone Fur had been considered a man for many years. Since the day he had hunted alone in the wilderness and returned with the skin of a coyote, a wily creature he had managed to bring down with stones from his sling, the boy he once had been was subsumed into the man he had become. The mantle of manhood settled on his shoulders, and he wore it well. But it didn't mean that he felt any more comfortable.

The recently deceased Priest's name had been *Sewati* in the language of the People, which translated loosely as Curved Bear Claw. He had died in the early hours of that morning, an old, old man whose former majesty and aura of wonder had melted away to be replaced by a tiny and wizened creature swaddled in an outsized bearskin cloak. Stone Fur, still deeply upset by the intensity of a dream that had dragged him from slumber in the watches of the night, had tended to him in his final hours, bringing him water that would barely pass the cracked and dried lips and simply providing companionship and comfort. As an apprentice, Stone Fur had seen many deaths in his young life. Curved Bear Claw though, had been determined to cling to life. It had made those final moments painful for them

23

both.

The old man had drawn a rattling breath into his failing lungs before letting go in one long, slow sigh. He had gone to join the Great Spirit, an event celebrated by the People and yet despite knowing this, Stone Fur had still shed tears.

The two had shared deeply private words in those precious final hours. Stone Fur had been orphaned and taken in by the Spirit Priest when he had been only four summers old. He had graduated from adopted son to apprentice at six. The man had been teacher, confidante and father for so long and Stone Fur had loved him.

"You will bring the word of the Great Spirit to the People, boy. And you will fill the void of my passing. Let the Spirit guide you and all will be as it should be." The voice was a wheeze, squeezed out through his mouth by lungs that were failing. Ancient fingers closed round Stone Fur's hand, nails digging into the tender flesh of his palm, and he had known grief like nothing else. "All will be well, my son."

So had Curved Bear Claw spoken in his final minutes. Stone Fur would take up the mantle of Spirit Priest and he would guide the People as his predecessor had done for so long. The old Priest had passed through the veil secure in the knowledge his protégé would take reins with ease. He knew it, all the People knew it, *everyone* knew it. Apart from, it seemed, Stone Fur.

He had seen eighteen summers come and go. He had hunted and provided, he had fought many and varied enemies and he had assisted Curved Bear Claw with many ancient rites. He had been ready for this task for years. He had wisely made preparations for the funerary rites for days, knowing that the old Priest's time was short.

Yet now the moment had arrived, he had forgotten every word, every gesture. He had forgotten everything.

And all eyes were on him.

The morning had passed in a blur. He had brought news of the Priest's death straight to the leader of their community. Loud Thunder was imposing when he was not angry, and the passing of the Spirit Priest had woken a deep anger in his heart. Fury flashed in his usually impassive eyes and the great hands had balled into fists of rage.

Stone Fur hurried away to tend the preparation of Curved Bear Claw before the old man was committed to the Great Spirit. There were observances and traditions that must be upheld. He would be laid to rest with his medicine bag, still filled with the herbs of his trade – medicinal and recreational – and the carving of his spirit totem. Once anointed and prepared, Curved Bear Claw's body carried with great respect and reverence taken to the Hollow of Sighs where the final elements of the ritual would be conducted. He would be raised up and committed to the Sky Mother and to the Great Spirit. In due course the life that was once granted to him by the Great Spirit would be returned, the circle closed once again.

The circle.

It brought Stone Fur back to the here and now and he focused his attentions on the people gathered in a ring around him. Loud Thunder stood in his rightful place, at the northern-most edge of the mourning circle, watching the boy in the middle closely. The anger and grief at the loss of a mentor and friend had passed. He was here – they were *all* here – to pay their respects to a loved member of their community. More, a *leader* of their community.

Let the Spirit guide you and all will be as it should be.

Curved Bear Claw's final words floated over the anxious young Priest and he knew, suddenly, that he was going to be alright. A sense of deep calm washed through him and carried his fears away. He knelt beside the shrouded body and drew in a deep breath. His heartbeat slowed to a steady pulse, and he took control. He raised his head to the azure skies of the Arizona afternoon. When he spoke, he did so with confidence and clarity, no sign of the nerves or anxiety that had plagued him. He did not see Loud Thunder's nod of approval.

"Great Spirit, hear my words," he intoned. "I am Stone Fur, Spirit Priest to the earthly-bound and your voice among the People. Your servant, Curved Bear Claw has drawn his last breath. He flies to you now, and to those that have gone before. May he be welcome around their fire and take his place among them."

Still kneeling, he placed his forefinger on the lips beneath the shroud. "His words are our memories to carry." Both hands came down to touch the temples. "His thoughts are our memories to carry." Stone Fur finally brought both hands to rest on the body's chest, over the stilled heart. "His life is ours to remember down the ages." At this, he stood.

Amongst the People, Stone Fur was a physical anomaly. He was tall and slender where most were stocky and robust. Like many other Spirit Priests, his eyes were not the dark sloe of most of the Warrior Nation, but they were instead a deep, compelling navy blue. Among the People, such physical differences were not considered a curse. They were considered to be blessings, direct markings from the Great Spirit. So it was that very few Spirit Priests chose their own calling.

He wore a simple tunic made from doeskin, with a belt around his waist from which hung any number of pouches containing herbs and spices of all kinds. As well as delivering the Will of the Great Spirit, many Priests were also healers and tended the sick and wounded. Stone Fur had shown great aptitude in this area and despite his comparative youth, was already well respected and loved. Still within spitting distance of childhood, he had delivered four of the community's newest members.

He stepped toward Loud Thunder and reached up to touch his leader's forehead. It was necessary for the big man to stoop slightly to allow for the height disparity. "Loud Thunder. Curved Bear Claw spoke his final words to me, and he named me his successor. In accordance with our traditions, do you accept this Naming? Will you place your faith in Stone Fur? In this mortal vessel through whom I will give you my teachings and guidance?"

Loud Thunder's dark eyes studied the youth before him. The moment of anger that had so animated him that morning had long passed and once more the veil of stoic indifference had fallen.

"Curved Bear Claw was my oldest friend," he said. His voice was ponderous, each word considered carefully before it passed his lips. "I trusted his guidance beyond imagination. It makes my spirit weep to think that no more will we speak of our younger days. It makes my soul ache to think that no more will we watch another dawning of the sun. And it brings me sorrow to think that when tomorrow comes, he will be gone. Is it right that the sun should rise in the east whilst Curved Bear Claw's body lies still and cold? That it will make its journey across the sky without caring or knowing of our grief before it sinks once more below the western horizon?" His finger pointed to the western sky where the light still held sway before the encroaching night.

Loud Thunder stepped forward and moved into the circle. He turned, looking at each person gathered there. "Is it right that the stars will come out tonight and watch over us whilst Curved Bear Claw's physical self is taken from this plane? And is it right that we will step from this circle when the rite is complete and celebrate his life with joy?"

Silence followed these words; a ritual silence that was right and proper and Stone Fur lowered his head in respect for his leader's grief. Loud Thunder drew a breath and continued.

"Yes, it is right, for it is as it should be. All things must pass over into the great unknown and Curved Bear Claw enjoyed a good adventure." A rare smile touched his lips and Loud Thunder placed his hand on Stone Fur's bowed head. "Great Spirit, I welcome you into this body. I accept the Naming. In accordance with our traditions, in accordance with the Will, I pass the mantle to Stone Fur, of the Warrior Nation."

And so it was done.

Afterwards, Stone Fur found it difficult to admit, but there was something anticlimactic about the whole thing. His life since the age of six had been building up to this moment but he had not felt any different. He had not suddenly felt all-knowing and all-wise. Rather, he had been made uncomfortable by the number of people who suddenly came to him to receive a blessing from the Great Spirit whilst it was still bound to its mortal vessel.

Stone Fur was the last to leave the Hollow, a part of him hating the idea of abandoning the body of this wonderful man to be returned to the earth. He lingered until the very last of the light finally sapped out of the western sky and he returned to join the people in celebrating the life of one of their own.

The communal fire was larger and brighter than usual. In the spring months, the People tended to keep the fire lower in order to enjoy the extending light of day. But tradition demanded that each member of the community who felt they owed something to the celebrated dead feed the flames with an offering of their choosing. Most of the time, these offerings were small, hand-made dolls, effigies of the Great Spirit as an individual saw it. It was the way of Stone Fur's People to think of the Great Spirit as the creatures of the plains and so any number of straw and dried mud creatures could be discerned through the flames.

Stone Fur settled before the fire, accepting a bowl of hot juniper tea from one of the young women of the tribe. He fought down the urge to smile that all of a sudden, the women were treating him with newfound respect that did not just border on awe and admiration – it completely crossed the line. It was easy, he thought as he sipped the bitter drink, to let such things consume you.

There was little alcohol consumed among this community. That was not, of course, to say that the occasional bottle of bourbon didn't find its way in from the nearby settlement. One such bottle was being surreptitiously passed from young warrior to young warrior, each daring the other to pretend they liked the acrid taste of the alcohol. Stone Fur watched, something between amusement and longing in his expression. Once, he had been able to engage in games like that.

Now, though...

Now... he had responsibility.

The weight of it all briefly touched on his shoulders, and he felt the sheer oppression of the task he had to perform. As a Spirit Priest, he would be looked upon to perform rites for the dead, for the newborn, to bless and prepare hunting parties... to perform marriage ceremonies, to call forth the blessings of the Great Spirit when and if the People went to war... somewhere in there he would also be expected to continue the contributions he made to the community in the form of hunting and trapping game.

There was no lack of equality amongst Stone Fur's people. The women and men hunted and fought alongside one another and often, marriage bondings came about as a result of two young people forced into hunting as partners who found their kindred spirits.

There will be no kindred spirit for me, mused Stone Fur. *Only the Great Spirit. That is all I will ever need.*

Some of the People were now dancing before the fire, working out their grief for the loss of the old Priest with shameless abandon. Tears streaked the faces of many, and Stone Fur kept his head held high as he watched the outpouring of grief take on a new form. The sorrow at Curved Bear Claw's passing became unashamed joy at all he had been, and tears prickled behind the Priest's eyes. Tears of affectionate pride.

A zephyr kissed the bared skin of his neck, behind his ear and despite the comparative warmth of the April night and his proximity to the fire, the Priest shivered. A hand came up to scratch at the now itching spot and when he brought it away, it was covered in blood.

Leaping to his feet, Stone Fur whirled to confront his assailant. Pallid, blue light coiled around his forearms and shone from his clenched fists before coalescing into a pair of curved, smoking daggers. The firelight reflected weirdly in the substance of the blades and the trails they carved in the air. He was aware, briefly, of the sensation of being slammed in the gut as though something was attempting to pass clean through his body. He let out a gasp at the suddenness of the attack and then he was falling through nothing into a distant abyss that only he could see.

Stone Fur's mouth opened to scream, but no sound came out.

And then the vision came.

Darkness. Heat.

Lightning cracks the night like lit cobwebs trailing across the sky.

A sudden, percussive boom of thunder. All his senses are tingling. He is absorbed into the vision completely.

A scene of violence is illuminated in the frozen, monochrome moment that exists in the space between light and sound. A figure, a huge figure in baroque armour, its hands locked around the throat of a vast, bleeding horror. There is a broken sword. There is a woman on her knees between them, her flesh laced with cuts and the tears flowing from her eyes a cascade of gemstones.

The darkness splits and cracks again.

The plains stretch away in all conceivable directions and in dimensions that he cannot even begin to comprehend. Those plains are vast and empty, but they are very much alive. He hears the sound of hooves. Rain. Wind through dry, cracked canyons. The bark of a coyote. Horses, once more.

Lazarus

Then the plains tear apart. Tar bubbles up from the wounds and spreads like blood from ruptured veins. Men of bronze are seated atop horses that are not horses. A mountain breaks from the earth and rises up, its peak disappearing into cloud. The rockface yawns wide, forming the visage of a man. Then that face melts and runs like wax into a screaming, monstrous maw into which the men of bronze ride, sabres flashing.

All the time, there is the crash of the thunder; a constant, endless background roar and the lightning a pulsing, eye-aching strobe. A raging torrent of scenes goes on and on, too fast. Too fast, too much.

Massive, angular giants with graven faces haloed in flame.

A man of iron with blood of poison.

An army of corpses marching from the very bowels of the earth.

The stars falling. A laughing angel with the heart of a devil.

Multi limbed horrors with rotting flesh and no awareness behind the eyes.

The world is cold and lifeless.

The world is bathed in light.

The eagle soars.

And then, without warning, he topples. He falls. He is falling.

Falling.

Cool, blue spirit-fire. All cleansing. He feels the peace of that flame and yearns for its embrace.

There is a word, a single word.

He wakes.

Sarah Cawkwell

Lazarus

INTERLUDE

Extract from 'The New York Tribune', April 5th by Minerva Bly

Rumours abound over the fate of the mining town of Provenance, AZ. Three days ago, the town went up in smoke. Everything was burned to the ground and the population of three hundred and sixty-four people fled. This reporter had the opportunity to sit and talk with one of the town's refugees, a Mister Arthur Fitzsimmons, a self-proclaimed 'man of science'.

"It was like the sky itself burned," he said. "Nobody has any idea what started it or how it got out of control so fast. It was the strangest thing... the fire started in the New Quarter, and we thought we'd put it out. Hell, we were ready to crack open the whiskey at that point. Then the generator exploded. It went up good and proper and the town just... couldn't take it. That's not the problem now, though. The problem is finding homes for all these fine people. Thank God we got out of that place alive." His voice drops to a barely audible whisper and horror fills his eyes. "Crimson," he mutters. "Crimson flames. And there was blue, too. Never seen anything like it."

Mr. Fitzsimmons is counting his blessings, it seems and rightly so. Nobody enjoys a disaster more than us here at the Tribune, *and that's the truth – but neither do any of us want to linger on how much worse the burning of Provenance could have been. After all, this reporter is just a humble investigator and has no right speculating.*

Sarah Cawkwell

No doubt our most illustrious and learned will be sending teams to investigate what could have caused such a tragedy, likely spending our hard-earned dollars on what is most likely to be an accident. We need to ask ourselves if we want to see our taxes repeatedly spent in this way, by people who claim to be 'men of science' – but who have yet to produce even so much as a cure for the common cold.

Ask yourselves. Would you prefer your children to receive a free education, or do you agree that these pointless 'investigative expeditions' are truly worth it? When do we ever see the results of these clandestine operations? Maybe it's time we had those discussions more openly. Maybe it's time we did more to protest against the regime. Maybe we need to start asking more questions of our elite.

Guess I'm in danger of being too political (again), so let me reassure you fine folks that the fire that razed Provenance to the ground claimed no casualties. That's surely a blessing, although does seem deeply suspicious to this reporter. You can, of course, claim the town's salvation to be the work of a divine power.

Whatever helps you sleep at night.

Whatever your feelings on the matter, it can't be denied that there are many strange things afoot in the world in which we live. There's those who trust the development of the progress that seemed to have come out of nowhere. They embrace it, revel in all the luxury it brings. Why, who doesn't yearn for the days when we all have lights that come on and off at will? Who doesn't want vehicles that can run for miles and never get tired?

Believe you me, there are plenty of folk out there who don't want these things. The old ways, they say, are the best ways. Is that right? It isn't for this reporter, hand-writing this very report to be hand-set on a printing press later today to comment – you make up your own minds.

In tomorrow's edition, we investigate unlikely claims that Lincoln's death has been greatly exaggerated, and a review of the latest edition of 'Unlikely Tales', that penny-dreadful that has become so popular among a certain mindset.

I say there isn't anything those dime novelists come up with that is anywhere near as strange as the world today.

- *M.B.*

Sarah Cawkwell

Howling Rock, Arizona

She loved these long trips. The opportunity to get away from towns and the ever-changing cities of the east and to return to the world she loved to be a part of. The two men who rode with her were less delighted with this task that was taking them deep into the frontier, but Major Willa Shaw cared little for their feelings. Besides, they were struggling just to maintain pace with her as she drove the 'Horse forward.

She had a stop scheduled at the next town so that they could all refuel – literally and metaphorically – and to hopefully find a cup of the bitter coffee that seemed to the casual observer to be the thing that kept her going. It was said, although never to her face, that for Willa Shaw, coffee was the human equivalent of RJ-1027. Like her vehicle, it was not a luxury. It was life.

Her Iron Horse had been customised for efficiency and comfort to enable her to range for hundreds of miles on a single tank of gasoline, but the modifications had not been cheap, and the engine work was complex. The RJ injection manifold blended the fuel to burn far more efficiently than a conventional engine but not everyone could afford such customisation and so her companions had to make regular refuelling and rest stops at the waystations along the trail. She found it frustrating and frankly, would have preferred to take this journey alone. It had been suggested that her preferences were not important, and two soldiers from her company were detailed to accompany her: Joseph Sweeney, a hoary veteran of the Ore War and Zachariah King, a rookie not long out of Camp Goddard.

Provenance was still a good sixty miles to the west, a short hop considering that they had ridden over a thousand miles already, but Sweeney and King had started grumbling that they needed another break, more to rest their bruised and tired bodies than for refuelling. Against her better judgement, she agreed, less than favourably, to the diversion.

So it was that the three soldiers rode into the town of Howling Rock at dusk. It had been a long time since Willa had experienced the dry heat of the Arizona desert and it made her reluctant to remove her riding mask. Her eyes scanned the long street of the small town, and it was the same as every other place they had stopped over the last few days. A general store, a furrier, a farrier, a fixer, and a saloon. The last was open to the street and six men sat on the porch, lounging, chewing tobacco and watching the newcomers' arrival with unashamed interest.

Beneath the mask, Willa's nose wrinkled. She'd much rather have taken another night out under the stars, but her men deserved a break. And to be fair, the skin of trail dust that caked both her and her uniform was beginning to itch. A bath was a tempting proposition. In fact, the more she thought of submerging herself in water, the more attractive the idea became.

You can take the girl out the city...

She forced Jimmy's unwelcome voice out of her mind and dismounted from the Iron Horse. Her joints were sore from riding in the same position for so long, her fingers tired from curling around the handles of the vehicle. She stretched herself to her full height – still diminutive – and rolled her shoulders to release the tension. There was a balmy heat to the evening that was quite pleasurable, and everything at least seemed quiet here.

Her gloved hands ran across its surface, seeking any imperfections in the fairings, hoses and fuel tank. Damage to a 'Horse's volatile systems had been known to lead to catastrophic and spectacular disaster in transit and nobody wanted that, least of all the people who had to attempt identification of an immolated body fused to a saddle. Satisfied that all was well, she dusted the palms of her hands together and turned to her companions.

"Hit the saloon, boys," she said to her men. "I'm right behind you. You get the first-round in."

She removed the mask then and breathed deeply of the evening air. The dust and arid heat crackled in the back of her throat, and she coughed inadvertently, becoming suddenly thirsty. Coffee would not be enough tonight, she realised.

The saloon, which proclaimed itself to be the *Whistle Stop,* apparently offered 'quality liquor, good food and poker'. Someone had hand-written at the bottom of the sign 'Best dancing boys and girls in the state'. She brushed the worst of the dust from her coat and reached up to rub at her jaw thoughtfully as she studied the sky. The weather, at least, was predictable in these parts. Back east, you never knew from one day to the next what the skies would bring. Cloud, rain, all these things seemed like distant dreams. Arizona didn't have weather; it had a climate. It was predictable.

But oh, the stars out here. Those clear skies, unmarred by any sort of light pollution which stretched as far as the eye could see and presented the glories of the night sky in its true, unadulterated form.

And this, she reminded herself as she lingered in the street, staring up at the glittering, untainted heavens, was why she had taken this investigation. There were Union folk a-plenty in these parts, she knew that.

But they were always busy on one errand or another. Besides, following up this lead had been too good an opportunity to pass up. Every heartbeat brought her closer to Jimmy's killer and the thought of treading that road had ensured this was an easy decision.

"Hey there, little lady. You needin' a gentleman escort to the tavern?"

Willa remained where she was, looking up into the sky and became aware of a figure stepping into the space on her right. He was tall – but then Willa Shaw was just a little under five and half feet. The slight heel on the boots she wore thrust her upwards an inch or so, but even so, she was close enough to the ground that almost *everyone* was taller than she was. This newcomer was probably rugged and handsome – she knew the type well enough. Hadn't she encountered them in every town between here and home? Sometimes they even used the same lines.

Willa Shaw was beginning to wonder if there was an original man left in the country. Thus far, her conclusion was that there was not. In her opinion, the last truly unique man had died two years earlier and there would never be one of his like again. She sighed inwardly and replied.

"Why, you gonna find me a gentleman?" She refrained from punctuating the question with a scathing insult. He'd just been polite, that's all. She moderated her attack. "I'm just fine, thank you," she replied, without doing the man the courtesy of looking his way. "Just enjoying the stars."

"There's plenty you could be enjoyin' that's a darn sight more interestin' than a bunch of lights in the sky, ma'am." There was the sound of a match striking against the building and flame flared briefly between cupped hands as he lit a cigarette. "An' I reckon as I'm the man to show you."

You're a confident son of a bitch, I'll give you that.

Give him one more chance.

She didn't turn, instead continued enjoying the view. Her hand idly traced over the eyepatch she wore over her left eye.

"C'mon, darlin', at least throw me a bone here. I'm doin' my best!"

Last chance blown.

Willa turned to look at the local at his last words. He let his eyes range up and down her frame and took immense satisfaction at watching his cocksure expression slide into pure alarm as he realised, she wore the uniform of a Union officer. She wondered, with idle amusement, what he'd make of the major's stripes she wore on the jacket beneath her coat. She assessed him, her one-eyed gaze every bit as bold as his own.

Tall, check. Rugged, check. Quite handsome, in fact, if it hadn't been for the scar that screwed up one side of his face. Much to her own annoyance, she felt a surge of curiosity. How had that happened? Looked to her like an explosion to the face. Her hand came away from her eyepatch in annoyance. How *dare* he share her misfortune and have something in common with her?

It doesn't matter. Don't ask about it. He'll think you care. Anyhow, he probably deserved it, the arrogant bastard. Mentally, Willa brushed aside the thoughts and resumed her stocktake. Unconsciously, her hands balled into fists and came to rest on her hips, an aggressive stance that made the man take a hesitant half-step backwards.

Willa's gaze took him in. Well-groomed and neatly presented, check. Cigarette between the lips? Check. Attitude, tailored coat, hat... all present and correct. She narrowed her eyes at him. He was ticking a lot of boxes. She didn't like that. There was a fault somewhere and, on a hunch, a faint memory flaring brightly for a moment, she allowed her gaze to move down to his boots.

I knew it.

They were filthy; unpolished and tatty. Never trust a man who doesn't take his boots seriously. Now who was it had told her that? Oh yes. *Him*. Less thought of, the better. Nonetheless, he'd been right, as he so often had been. Willa's arms folded beneath her breasts. Her hip jutted to one side in a posture of indifference and tilted her head to one side. Her one good eye bored into the man, openly assessing him and weighing his value as both a partner and as a human being. He shifted, made faintly uncomfortable by the woman's scrutiny. Then she laughed, without humour. The man's ego popped and deflated. He wasn't used to women laughing at him unless he was deliberately seeking to amuse.

"Well, I sure as heck can't imagine what you're talking about," she retorted. "'Cos I can't see *anything* here that's caught my attention more than the star dust up there. Ain't interested. Move along. Go find some other girl to hit on." She turned to walk away, to catch up to her boys and go grab a drink in the *Whistle Stop*. Her long, braided hair whipped out behind her. In a moment of spontaneity, the would-be suitor reached out to catch her arm. It was not intended as a threatening gesture; he had simply found her interesting and was hoping to explore this a little further. He was unprepared for the intensity of her response.

Willa Shaw *loathed* being touched by *anybody*. It was common knowledge that she didn't even like to shake hands with her superiors, although it didn't mean she did not do it. Not for her the easy hugs and back slapping of camaraderie that existed among Union troops. So to have a complete stranger lay hands upon her... well. Men had been sent to the infirmary for brushing against her when she was not prepared for it.

The world held its breath.

It seemed that luck, as well as stars, was shining down on the increasingly bemused and formerly overenthusiastic soul. She glared at him, a look that had cowed recruits into fearful silence, and took a long breath. Anger flashed in that expression and pulsed in her temples, but she wrestled it into obedience before it could sour into violence. She snatched her arm free and fixed him with a simmering, imperious scowl.

"You get a free pass this time," she said in a low, warning tone. "Touch me again, and you'll not walk right for a week. I might be damn near a foot shorter than you are, but the toe of my boot in your pants will still achieve the desired effect. You hear me?"

"Woah there." The man put his hands up in mock-surrender. "I didn't mean any offence. I was jus' tryin' to be... *friendly*."

"Well, you go be 'friendly' somewhere else. With some*one* else. We clear?"

"As crystal, ma'am." The man touched the tip of his hat in a polite gesture of defeat and watched as the feisty woman shoved her way past him and stormed into the saloon. Two of his companions sitting on the porch snorted with laughter at the open rejection.

"You never do learn, do ya, Sam? Them Union gals ain't the kind ya wanna start messin' with."

Sam watched the woman as she flung open the saloon doors and went inside. Yep. No doubt about it. He was in *love*. Willa Shaw had that effect on many men. Not that she'd care, or even notice. If she knew how admired she was, she'd likely have been embarrassed.

"Now there," he said with an over-theatrical sigh, "goes the woman of my dreams."

* * *

The dreams lingered.

Stone Fur was tired. No, he was *exhausted*. For the past two days, he had not rested well at all. Since the night of Curved Bear Claw's life celebration, his sleep had been interrupted by that same disturbing dream that left him shivering and gasping in a cold sweat. At first, he had wondered if he was simply falling victim to one of the illnesses that occasionally flew through his people, but he was otherwise fit and healthy.

He had very little recollection of those first moments after his waking vision. He'd had such things before, but never one that was so very tangible. He'd not just visualised the things the Great Spirit had sent him, but he had *felt* them. He'd felt his skin crisp from his proximity to the fires raging before him, smelled the cinders on the air. Heard the screams. He'd smelt the storm in the air, heard the thunder of hooves and felt the hot, dry wind of the plains on his face.

Whenever the Great Spirit chose to send visions of such intensity, there was a black period following them. It was difficult for the Spirit Priest to disconnect from the otherworld and to re-engage with the

real one. As such, the elder had given him a grace period of several days before visiting. Stone Fur sat now,
sipping on a bowl of tea, and listened as Loud Thunder,
seated opposite him, quietly told the story of what had
occurred.

"We were caught up in the tales of Curved Bear
Claw. For they are many-fold. And in time, the tales of
Stone Fur will grow to be as glorious. Your greatness is
yet to come. We watched you, Stone Fur. As the Great
Spirit took possession of your heart, your mind, your
words."

Loud Thunder's storytelling was always compelling. Despite the usual powerful boom of a baritone
that had given the warrior chief his name, a voice that
could be heard clearly across a battlefield, he could
deliver personal stories in a lilt and cadence that was
quite captivating. When he spoke now of Stone Fur's
apparent possession, his voice was filled with a level
of awe and respect for the youth that felt vaguely uncomfortable.

"I thank you for your words, Loud Thunder."
Stone Fur offered up a tremulous smile. "My soul has
no recollection. Will you tell me what happened?"

The chief inclined his head.

"You stood. No, you did not stand. You *threw*
yourself upright. You loosed a cry that brought weapons to your hands. They burned with the fires of the
spirit. I have not seen your weapons before. Before his
passing, I admit that I expressed a concern to Curved
Bear Claw that you were not strong enough to forge
your will into stone. I was wrong. Your blades blazed
with a light and potency I could not have imagined and
dispelled my doubt." The big man shook his head ponderously and sighed heavily. "Will the Spirit Priest forgive me?"

"Of course." Stone Fur was impatient to hear more of the tale, but Loud Thunder was not a man to be hurried. He reached out to ladle more tea into his bowl and offered the chief the same. Loud Thunder nodded and accepted a refill. It was good tea; life-giving and bright of character, a brew of young leaves that could only be harvested this time of year. "Please, Loud Thunder, continue."

"You saw Curved Bear Claw deliver the Will many times, I am sure. You know, then, how we could not understand your first words. They were in a tongue not familiar to any of us. You stared about yourself wildly, the daggers in your hands slashing at unseen horrors. We worried you sought to hurt yourself. But we could not take the weapons from you. We knew that."

No, indeed: a Priest's weapons were as much a part of them as their own limbs. Enemies of the People had tried, many times, to pry blade or bow from the hands of a Priest only to find them as insubstantial as air, yet as keen as a razor. Even when removed through violence they vanished like so much morning mist. Stone Fur nodded, wishing that Loud Thunder would tell his tale with more efficacy. He bit back words of frustration and took a long, slow breath before asking his next question.

"I did not hurt any of the People, did I? Whilst... not myself?"

"No, you did not. Your eyes lost focus and you raved at the warriors beside the fire. Your words... still not clear. But then you spoke of the stars falling and the world bathed in light. It was as if you saw that which is to come and that it was terrible. You said that all would fall to ashes and dust. You spoke of many things that made no sense, but we all heard that the world would burn in light. You were... fearful."

Ashes and dust.

The phrase echoed around the Spirit Priest's skull repeatedly. Three words that, the second they were repeated back to him, brought part of the Great Spirit's vision flooding back. He gulped back another mouthful of his tea ignoring how the tea spread a warm wave throughout his torso as if he was sitting in a sweat lodge. He bowed his head and, setting down the bowl, pressed the tips of his fingers together, steepling them as a rest for his forehead. He gathered his thoughts together and spoke.

"I have not settled since that night," he said, quietly. "It is as though the Great Spirit's words are not yet finished. I feel there is more that I must know. But I have tried to reach for it. It will not come." He looked up then and shook his head. His expression was fierce and angry, his face drawn into a scowl that distorted the whorls of dark ink around his eyes. It took his countenance far from its usual benign expression into something of the warrior that beat beneath the chest.

Stone Fur's nature was a gentle one, as was befitting a student of Curved Bear Claw. The old Priest had been a kindly soul, imbued with the wisdom of the ages and of the owl spirit who had chosen him. Any apprentice was likely to adopt that same attitude and Stone Fur, despite a deep ferocity inherited from a long-dead mother, was rational and logical. Loud Thunder saw great potential in him, more perhaps than the youth realised.

"There was more," Loud Thunder said, when the bloom of angry colour had once more drained from Stone Fur's cheeks. "We listened to the Will. You need not concern yourself, Stone Fur. We heard and we understood. These things of which you spoke will not come to pass. Those things that deny you sleep, all the things that you have seen and which you fear, we will deny them. This is why you have been granted this gift. This is why you hear that which to others goes unheard."

There was a pause of several heartbeats while Stone Fur absorbed this news. He opened his mouth to ask the question he was dreading, but Loud Thunder pre-empted him, laying a weathered hand on the young priest's shoulder.

"You need not speak of this beyond those who bore witness, Stone Fur, my friend. My brother. Ghost Wolf does not need to know. We have taken steps and we will attend to it. He has his own Priests and other matters to attend."

Loud Thunder's blunt proclamation should have reassured him. But it did not. Instead, he did the only thing he could do. He accepted the situation and gave it no further thought. 'Life is as a river,' Curved Bear Claw had often told him, 'It may twist and it may turn but it does not halt its course because a pebble is placed in its path. It will always finish its journey.' The memory elicited a small smile and brought a measure of ease. His duties would demand his attention as soon as he felt well enough to attend them.

The People needed their Priest.

* * *

Willa Shaw was absolutely feeling the benefits of the suggestion that she and her two companions take rooms at the *Whistle Stop*. It wasn't because it would be pleasant to have a comfortable bed for a change instead of a bed roll under the night sky, because frankly she would have preferred that. It wasn't even the fact they had a choice of food that wasn't whatever animal they'd been able to trap and cook that day.

No, it was this. This most simple and wonderful things. A *bath*.

She sighed luxuriously and allowed her entire body to slide under the surface of the water. She'd not expected to find anything as remotely glorious as a bath filled with still-warm water where she could rinse off the travelling dust and muck of the past few days. It did mean sharing space with six partially clad young dancers who had been more than happy to let her use their facilities – for a few coins, of course. Everyone in this part of the country was out to make a quick buck. Willa had paid them their fee and brought them drinks as well and they'd welcomed her with open arms into their silk and lace covered bosoms. She pushed aside her vague sense of annoyance at their giggling and silliness and just relaxed.

Her dark red hair floated in the water like a cloud, and she remained under the surface for several moments until one of the girls started squealing loud enough to make her ears hurt, even protected as they were by the bathwater. She surfaced, spluttering and ran her fingers through the mass tangle that was now her long hair.

The eyepatch had been removed, revealing the scar that ran across her left eye where it had been burned in the explosion eighteen months ago. The orb remained intact, but it was as sightless as a rock. The eyepatch was preferable because even Major Shaw had a *little* vanity.

"I thought you weren't gonna come back up," said the girl, a scrawny little dot of a thing, probably no older than sixteen, if she was even that. "I thought you'd drowned, and we'd have to call in the lawmen!"

More giggling followed this exclamation. "Ain't such a bad thing," said one of the other girls, who Willa had learned was called Millie. She was a beautiful, exotic creature with a face that looked as though it had been carefully chiselled from some flawless precious stone. Dark, intelligent eyes studied the world around her with a faint hint of superiority that made her seem other-worldly and exotic. "Some of them lawmen are downright delicious if y'ask me." The tip of her tongue ran over the line of her beautifully shaped lips in a suggestive manner. "An' they got a lot of stress to work out, if you know what I mean."

Oh, yes. Willa knew precisely what Millie meant. Many of the lawmen with whom she'd had any contact in the last few years had been angry, brooding types and lone wolves who seemed oddly unsuited to a life serving the law. She considered Millie thoughtfully. Beside the woman's tall, sinewy-limbed frame, Willa had initially felt raw-boned and awkward. But it had been Millie who'd boldly eyed her in the saloon bar and invited her to make use of the facilities.

The lewd comment about the lawmen set off another chain of squealing and giggling among the girls and it was like someone dragging nails down a board. Willa winced inwardly at the sound. She'd never been that good at feminine, pretty things; the curse, perhaps, of growing up as one of seven – and the only girl with three brothers either side of her. Still, the dancers had been under no obligation to let her use their room for her own purposes. She was grateful and so she could be gracious and put up with a little giggling.

"I can hold my breath for a long time," she informed the girl whose alarm was still apparent in eyes that were too large in an under-nourished face. "And I can swim well. Don't you worry about me, honey, I'm just fine under the water. Besides, I gotta get all this dust off. Ain't had a bath since I left to head out west days ago."

"Where you from?"

"I started out in Napoleon."

A new conversation ensued. Not one of the dancing girls had a clue where Napoleon was and when Willa elaborated, explaining that a few days before she'd been in the state of Arkansas, they looked none the wiser. *So provincial*, was the withering thought before Willa remembered that she was one of the lucky ones. She was one of those who got to travel the country, where others didn't ever get that chance. The majority of people, women and men the same, were born, lived and died in the same small town.

She sat up in the tub, her arms over the side and leaned back, closing her eyes and letting the chatter wash over her. They were still on about the lawmen and the Lord knew that Willa Shaw had definitely had enough of the conversation for a while. She cracked open her right eye when someone nudged her, offering a shared bottle of liquor. She hesitated, then accepted, taking a healthy gulp of the fiery liquid. It burned down her gullet and into her stomach, warming her from within.

"So, what is it brings you to our little town, ma'am?" Millie's deference was pleasant, but unnecessary and with a smile, the Union Major waved aside the formality.

"My name in this room is Willa, honey. Don't feel you gotta stand on ceremony when I'm lyin' here in front of you, naked as the day I was born." Her grin was wicked and infectious. She waved a languid hand at Millie's barely clothed form. "You have the advantage, that's for sure."

"Willa." Millie nodded, committing the name to memory. "What brings you here? Is it business or pleasure?"

"Business. No offence, Millie, I'm sure your town is lovely. But you don't get to do much for pleasure when you're in my kind of position." The words set off a chain reaction of annoyance. When *had* she last done anything for herself? Probably while Jimmy had still been alive. She shook off the negativity and resumed enjoying the moment. "Business. I'm just passin' through."

In due course, she dragged herself reluctantly out of the now-tepid water and used it to rinse out her travel-worn boots and blues. She'd not brought that much in the way of additional uniform; she and her squad tended to prefer travelling as light as possible. The Iron Horses moved faster with a lighter load, after all, and fuel consumption reduced accordingly. Nonetheless, she'd fetched a clean shirt and pants and as she dressed in them, she was grateful, feeling less of a buttcrack nasty. She hung up her wet things with the rest of the clothing that was hanging in this comparatively tiny dressing room and smiled to herself at the contrast of the navy military wear hanging alongside silk stockings and well-mended dresses.

The entire changing room was something of an obstacle course; Willa had to duck frequently to avoid getting tangled up in the clothes lines and every step was one of great caution in case she trod on something frilly that lay wherever the girl wearing it had discarded it during a costume change.

Four of the girls filed out of the dressing room into the bar to perform for the gathered masses. The noise from the common room was startling when the door opened; early evening had become night-time and all the people of Howling Rock had, it seemed, gathered in one place. Willa heard the cat calls and whistles as the dancers sashayed their way into the room and she smiled again. No gunfire. That, at least, was a small mercy. Maybe Howling Rock was one of the *better* towns.

"You're makin' that look like hard work, honey. Here." Millie offered her the bourbon again and Willa accepted. The dancer held out a hand for the comb which the major was using, without much luck, in an effort to sort out her tangled hair. It had become a mass of unmanageable curls after its days of being so tightly braided and then being submersed. Every drag of the comb was bringing fresh agony. Millie took charge of the situation and as she carefully separated the tangled strands, she sang softly, barely audible, but Willa could hear it.

> *"Out where a fresher breeze is blowin',*
> *Where there's laughter in every streamlet flowin',*
> *Where there's more of reapin' and less of sowin'...*
> *That's where the West begins.*
> *Out where the world is in the makin'*
> *Where fewer hearts in despair are achin'..."*

"That's where the West begins," said Willa, speaking the words aloud. She sighed, softly. "You have a pretty voice." Mille shrugged one slim shoulder. It was not a gesture of indifference, merely a quiet acknowledgement that she knew. Willa continued. "My husband... he used to sing that song." His voice had been less like that of a nightingale and more like that of an angry cockerel, but it had been a sweet song, nonetheless. Ironic, too, given that to the best of her knowledge, Captain James Shaw had never been further west than Arkansas.

Women are astute, perhaps more so than men when it comes to matters of the heart and soul and Millie paused only momentarily in her task after Willa spoke. A brief hesitation was filled with a question that was more loaded than the major's pistol. "What happened?"

"He... died," she said, and it was clear from her tone that she wanted to discuss the matter no further. Feeling at ease for once in these surroundings, Willa didn't flinch as Millie placed a hand on her shoulder. Willa was grateful, suddenly, for the kindness of a stranger. Not for the first time, she was glad to be out here in the western states, where nobody knew her business, but everyone cared that she was alright.

"I'm sorry."

"Why? Wasn't your fault he died, was it?" The major's voice grew momentarily sombre and then she laughed warmly and with a sense of humour that her stern demeanour and requirement to be in charge often denied. Millie laughed as well although there was something faintly confused behind it.

The moment of levity dispelled any tension that may have resulted, and Millie resumed combing out Willa's long hair until not a tangle remained. During this peaceful and oddly relaxing process, the two women talked little, having struck up a camaraderie that didn't need words.

She welcomed the peace and quiet for once and let it soothe her troubled soul. She'd initially been keen to come and engage in this investigation, but things weren't quite as engaging as she'd imagined. But regardless, orders were orders and if Willa Shaw was good at anything, it was completing tasks that were set out for her. As long as she was free to do so on her own terms, then everything was just fine.

When the crashing started in the saloon bar not very much later, everything stopped being fine.

* * *

The saloon beyond the sanctity of the girl's dressing room was less of a relaxing place. Everywhere there were bodies. Most of the town found its way in here of an evening and tonight was no exception. The press of human flesh was claustrophobic, the smell of rank, unwashed flesh permeating the atmosphere in an unpleasant fug, but the beer was good and the bourbon better.

Willa's two men, Joseph Sweeney and Zachariah King had managed to squeeze in at a table and had joined in a hand of poker. Both soldiers were aptly demonstrating impressive skills at losing repeatedly. Stakes were low on their table which given their gaming ineptitude was most definitely for the best. The mood was pleasant, the talk bawdy and humorous and both men were enjoying themselves immensely.

Half hour later when Millie and her dancing girls came out and brought music and elegance to the room, they couldn't believe their luck. They'd expected nothing out of this two-bit little town and here they were practically in the lap of luxury, being entertained by pretty girls in frilly dresses and with feathers in their hair. It was, as Joe said to Zach, too good to be true.

It was.

Two tables along from where the Union soldiers sat playing sat a man drinking alone, a bottle of the bartender's cheapest whiskey open in front of him. He'd long since eschewed drinking from the shot glass that had come with it and was now swigging openly from the neck of the bottle. The flush of his cheeks gave away his level of inebriation and he was repeatedly stabbing at the wood of his table with the tip of a wicked-looking serrated blade. The noise of the metal thudding into the table was beating out a steady rhythm, and it was this faintly menacing tattoo that drew Joseph's attention. He glanced over at the drunk and narrowed his eyes.

"Who's that?"

One of the other members of their game looked over and shrugged a shoulder with supreme indifference. "That's Teverson Marsh," he said. "He's an idiot and a troublemaker, but he ain't caused any bother for a while. Used to ride with a posse who just up and left him. What was that name, Pete? Who was that crazy outlaw wench who came out here and tried to make trouble?"

"Aw, I don't remember. You see one of them outlaw posses, you seen 'em all. Ringo's been causin' touble of late, an' that li'l rat. Billy the Kid, they call him. Word is that he hates everyone an' everythin', even his own friends. Teverson's just like they are." Pete lowered his voice conspiratorially. "Reckons the world owes him an' he's out to collect. Mean enough that half those folks just refused to ride with him. They made him turn in his colours an' he was booted out before they could decide to shoot him. Been driftin' for a while."

"When even the bandits and cutthroats don't want anythin' to do with you, then you know you ain't good for nothin'. So few weeks back, he came into town, crawled into a bottle and ain't come out since."

"Not to mention the Pep."

Sweeney raised one eyebrow. "Pep?" He sought clarification and the man shrugged again.

"Yeah, Pep. It's what the young 'uns call it. They say it's more addictive than laudanum. Also heard it called somethin' else." Pete thought for a moment or two, seeking the word he was looking for. His grizzled face twisted with the effort of thought, and he expectorated into the spittoon. "Lazarus," he said, eventually. "Like from them stories the preacher loves to tell. Some kid, risin' from the dead."

Sweeney and King exchange brief, grim glances, but said nothing. Pete slapped his hand down on the table, making the both of them jump. "Now, you gonna meet this stake or you gonna crash out?" Sweeney's gaze swung once more to the unfortunate man who was allegedly so unpleasant or incompetent that even an outlaw as notorious as Johnny Ringo would have nothing to do with him.

Marsh, apparently suddenly aware that he was being scrutinised, lifted his head and stared right back at the Union man. His face was a mass of scar tissue, distorting what were fairly plain features to begin with into something bordering on nightmarish. His lip was pulled into a permanent sneer and the blade with which he was stabbing at the table fell silent. Somehow, that was more ominous than the noise.

Light grey eyes, largely devoid of anything that Joe Sweeney recognised as intelligence, but which most definitely contained a deeply buried malevolence bored into him, charring his sense of contentment into a feeling that left the taste of ash in his mouth.

"Somethin' you wanna say, friend?" Marsh's voice was a low, bass rumble and each syllable deliberate and carefully spoken. Joe shook his head.

"No, not at all. Sorry there, friend."

Joe turned his head away from the man, unable to shake the feeling things were going to head south and looked down at the cards in his hand. The feeling of unease grew instantly deeper as he stared at the cards therein. Two-pair. Two black eights, two black aces and the Queen of Diamonds. Just... something about that hand gave him the jitters.

It was less than a minute later that the chair slammed into him, knocking him clean off his own and onto the saloon floor. Joe went down with a crash, taking the table with him. Cards and glasses scattered in all directions as did several of the patrons seated close by. Most of them were well aware of the drill when a fight broke out and the majority very carefully and discreetly made themselves scarce. A saloon brawl would inevitably bring down the lawmen and there were enough people right here who did not fancy *that* particular confrontation.

Zachariah leapt instantly to his feet the moment Marsh's wild swing brought his companion down and reacted instantly, gun trained on the inebriated brute. "You put that chair... uh, I mean, what's *left* of that chair down right now," said the young soldier, with a slight waver in his voice. "Or you are gonna regret it. And neither of us want that. Right?" He wasn't sure himself whether he addressed that last word to Marsh, in an assertation of confidence or to Sweeney in an attempt to confirm he was handling the situation correctly. The hand that held the pistol was steady, but he was anything but confident he could take on Marsh. Standing, the man must have been a good six and a half feet tall, with shoulders as broad as a steer and arms with muscles thick as tree trunks.

"Put it down, friend. Look, I'll even buy you a drink. Set things right. How about that? Doesn't that sound like something you would like?" Zach tried again; his voice stronger this time. In response, Marsh dropped the chair and swung for Zach with a ham fist that connected with the boy's face like a hammer blow. Cursing for being so slow to fire, Zach attempted to duck, but unused to the rhythm and cadence of fist fighting, his timing had been appalling.

"I ain't your friend," said Marsh, leering as the punch landed. The sound of the man's huge knuckles meeting Zach's jawbone resounded with a distinctly uncomfortable *crack* and the young soldier staggered backwards, letting out a string of cuss words. His hand automatically came up to his jaw and without even re-alising it, he pushed the abused bone right back into its socket. There was a second, uncomfortable *crack,* followed by the crash of Zach King falling ungracefully into another table as he saw stars of pain explode before his eyes.

Somehow, the act of undoing the jaw dislocation had been more painful than the original blow. The unfortunate young soldier rolled through a pool of spilled whiskey, hand groping for his dropped pistol. A number of the *Whistle Stop's* patrons backed away, unwilling to pick a side, or simply curious to see how a Union man would handle himself in a one-on-one fight against a thug like Marsh.

Zach had passed his basic training with flying colours, all his superiors commenting on just how well he deported himself, how he was able to manage under great stress... but right now, every shred of that training went out the window as a deep, scarlet rage bubbled up like a geyser. He launched himself with great gusto at the solid block of muscle in front of him. It was like running at full pelt into a sweaty brick wall. The foul stench of the man's body odour made him gag, but that proved very swiftly to be the least of his problems. Marsh picked up the youth as though he were a child and hurled him, with considerable strength, into the next set of tables. Several bottles smashed on their way down and Zach landed heavily, breaking another table in half.

Sweeney recovered his senses a little and swung the stump of a broken chair at Teverson's ankle. The blow connected with an audible crunch – whether of bone or of wood was less clear – and the big man toppled like a felled tree, his ugly face knotted in a combination of rage, pain and indignation.

"See how *you* like it, you big lug," Sweeney slurred. The soldier scrambled onto the prone thug and landed two solid blows, crushing the big man's nose and dislodging a tooth. Then Marsh, grinning through a mouthful of his own blood, drew his head back and brought it forward in a fluid motion that connected with Sweeney's fist. The sergeant stumbled backward clutching his smashed hand, just as Zach struggled back into the fray. Marsh kicked Zach in the knee, rolled to his feet and grabbed the hapless younger man by the throat.

"You stick soldiers ain't so tough," Marsh drawled. "Y'all break just as easy as..." The rest of his tirade was eclipsed by a crash of glass as King was dragged unceremoniously across the surface of the bar, wiping it clean of any and all obstacles in the process. Marsh began to laugh, an idiotic, manic sound that rang in everyone's ears as he hauled Zach around as though the boy were nothing more than a rag doll.

Veins bulged in his neck like distended crimson hawsers.

Sweeny rose unsteadily to his feet and drew his pistol. The click of the hammer being cocked was suddenly and shockingly the loudest sound in the chaotic saloon. "You had best let that boy go right now, or I'm going to have to put you down. And you know, that is going to ruin a *perfectly* fine evening for the both of us."

More guns were coming out of holsters and the air was filled with the unmistakable sounds of hammers being pulled back. It didn't take an expert to determine that this was devolving swiftly into something uncontrollable. The bartender was already calmly and carefully storing most of the very expensive bottles of alcohol beneath the bar where their chances of being broken were minimised. Millie and her dancing girls lingered just long enough to assess the direction the fight was taking and then the tall, elegant dark-skinned woman ushered her girls back to the dressing room without further ado.

The stage was set. The actors were all in place. The fight was ready to break into an entire new level of violence.

The big man continued to laugh, his eyes wide and turning steadily more bloodshot with the ruptured veins. He tossed Zachariah King aside with a casual indifference and spread his arms wide as though inviting the bullet that would ostensibly end his life. "You? Shoot me? Hah! You ain't got the sand for it, stick soldier." Marsh gargled through his laughter. "The lot of you blue Union bastards. Only good for struttin' around in your perfect uniforms. All fancy, like. The south... oh yeah, the south remembers!"

Across the saloon, Zach got to all fours and shook the stars that were buzzing around his head. There was the unmistakable taste of copper in his mouth, and he put a hand to his nose which was bleeding freely. Sweeney had his gun trained on Marsh, but Zach knew the sergeant would be reluctant to end this with a bullet. He looked around for his own gun but was interrupted by the need to duck a flurry of objects – glasses, bottles, more furniture – being hurled at him by a now apparently fully enraged Marsh. Each projectile smashed into the opposite wall, narrowly avoiding causing any casualties until Marsh ran out of objects immediately to hand and began casting around for anything else he could throw.

The big man was laughing the entire time, like a big, insane and exceptionally violent child.

Where the hell are the lawmen when you want them?

Zach felt a moment's guilt for the thought. He'd never particularly taken to the west's lawmen, finding them uncoordinated and disorganised in a way that the Union had never been. Young and inexperienced though he was, even he could appreciate that the Union had *structure* and purpose, while the loose cannons who purported to uphold the law seemed to just flit from one place to another, answering to whichever of them happened to be the senior at the time.

No lawmen meant that the general public were quite content with the idea of simply letting out a lot of pent-up tension and that was now happening with abandon all over the saloon bar of the *Whistle Stop*. Not in the slightest bit interested in the fracas taking place between the Union soldiers and Marsh the thug, several other pockets of fist-fights had broken out, personal matters that were being settled using the age-old technique of determining who could withstand the most physical punishment before capitulating. Everywhere were the sounds of fighting, of breaking glass and splintering wood. The smell of spilled whisky caught in the nostrils and the back of the throat as it evaporated under the flickering light.

Zach struggled to his feet during a reprieve from the onslaught of items and managed to successfully retrieve his wayward pistol from the floor. He levelled it shakily at Marsh and moved on rubbery legs that were barely supporting him to stand side-by-side with his sergeant. It was evident that in Teverson Marsh they were either dealing with an idiot or a lunatic and it would have been unbecoming of the uniform to simply kill him over a bar brawl. Sergeant Joe Sweeney was definitely not that kind of man and neither, Zachariah King realised, was he.

"Stand down, Marsh," said Sweeney again, although the fact he had a mouthful of his own blood and possibly a broken tooth into the bargain meant that the words came out gargled and unintelligible. *Shtand don March.* The big man just leered at him and continued laughing. He wrenched the serrated blade from its sheath on his belt and brandished it at the soldiers menacingly.

"What say we play a little game, blue boys? I stick my knife in an' we get to see just what..."

Marsh lunged, the blade sharp and quick in the flickering, dim saloon light. It was an unnatural expediency, too quick by far. The kind of attack that no man could prepare against, and Sweeney unwittingly found his eyes close in anticipation of the evisceration that Marsh's attack would bring with it.

A single shot rang out and a retina-scorching spear of scarlet transfixed the thug through the knee.

The joint shattered in a welt of bone chips and cooked blood and Marsh's lunge turned into a stumble and an ungainly sprawl. The silence that followed was, as the adage went, deafening. Daring to breathe again, Sweeney cracked open first one eye and then the other.

Willa Shaw stood in the doorway, her hair still hanging loose around her face after her bath. Her right hand was holding her weapon, which hummed lightly post-discharge, the muzzle glowing deep, cherry red. Marsh lay on the floor whimpering and giggling like a crazed infant.

"Get that heap of flesh out of the bar and into the town jail, Sergeant Sweeney," she said. She turned to walk away, then paused before looking back over her shoulder. "And give the bartender a hand cleaning this place up. I am going to go to bed now and if I hear so much as a glass shatter in this bar after I'm gone, there will be *consequences*."

She departed, a woman whose relaxing evening had been interrupted and whose rage would clearly know no bounds if she was disobeyed. Joe ran his fingers through his hair, then looked down at the prone form of Marsh who had given up screaming and was now just twitching slightly, drool running from his mouth and pooling on the floor in front of him. He sighed and shook his head.

"Give me a hand here, Zach," he said to his companion. No point in risking the Major's wrath. *Nobody* wanted that.

* * *

Despite the brawl, which when all was said and done was fairly typical, it was otherwise a quiet night at the *Whistle Stop*. The saloon never really closed as such, although business died down in the small hours. Howling Rock was small and trusting enough that it worked an honour system when the owner headed to his bed. Besides, Millie and her girls prowled the joint all night anyway, so there was always someone to fetch up another hit of alcohol when it was needed. But in time, most people drifted away to their homes, or to find some other pursuit. Some just slept where their heads fell, snoring into puddles of liquor on the tables.

In her tiny room, on a bed that was somehow less comfortable than bare earth, Willa Shaw was attempting to sleep before the following day saw her and her boys undertake the rest of the journey to Provenance. Already she was missing the climate from home. The Arizona days were dry and the nights were too cool. She never thought she could miss green as much as she did when she came out here. It never failed to amaze her what folks would do to follow the trail left by the money. She fell asleep, eventually, but it was deeply troubled.

In the shared bunkhouse outside, Zachariah and Joseph, bruised and sore, were still brooding over their participation in the brawl and a little ashamed at the Major having to intercede. Despite this they eventually fell into a fitful sleep.

* * *

In those very early hours of the morning, those strange hours between the darkest of the night and the arrival of the dawn, there were still three good-natured poker games going on. Someone was poking at the keys on the badly-tuned piano and churning out the same seven notes over and over. Several people were snoring over a Faro table. The debris from Marsh's fit of temper had been swept up and thrown on the fire for fuel where appropriate.

The night passed slowly, quietly and without further violence or incident worthy of note. There *had* been a couple of women who'd squared up to fight over a man called Pete, but that had died down after both young ladies were escorted from the premises to carry on their conversation outside. The screeching and caterwauling had stopped after a while and the last anybody saw of the two girls, they'd been walking arm in arm together down the street.

Pete, on the other hand, was left abandoned in the saloon, ditched by both his would-be suitors.

Millie and her girls roamed the sleeping masses, picking pockets with great discretion. There were, after all, *some* perks to be had from working in this place. More often than not, folks whose wallets they made a little lighter never noticed. Care. Care and subtlety were the key. A dollar here, a dollar there – it all mounted up and people never noticed. Millie's little criminal crew was well-organised, and her long-term goal was to buy the owner out of his share of the *Whistle Stop*. She knew she could make it into something infinitely better.

She kept an eagle eye on her gaggle of protégés as they worked, diligently collecting glasses and cleaning tables – and pockets – as they went. Jenny approached one man, seated alone in a corner, his long legs resting comfortably up on the table next to a mostly-empty bottle of liquor. His head was down and with the collar of his coat turned up and his hat tipped forward over his eyes, his whole face was thrown into shadow. The man's arms were loosely folded across his chest and his breathing seemed rhythmic and steady. There was a peculiar quality to the sound: a strange hiss and mechanical whirr as though he had clockwork lungs. Closer inspection attributed the noise to the mask that covered the lower portion of his face.

He was still and quiet enough that Jenny assumed he must be sleeping, but as her hand stole towards him, Millie caught her arm. She nodded toward the man's coat, and more pertinently, to the flash of gold he wore at his breast.

"Best leave that one be, honey," she murmured. Jenny backed away slightly.

The lawman unfolded his arms, raised a hand and tipped his hat to her in a polite fashion. His voice, when it came, had a mechanical quality, although it was quite evidently human. Human, and very polite – and despite the amount of alcohol he'd clearly consumed, very sober.

"Much obliged, darlin'."

* * *

Dawn was cool by comparison to the balmy warmth of the previous dusk. Willa knew, from experience and having been out in these parts many times, that the temperature would rise steadily as the morning wore on but wouldn't reach the stifling heat that summer brought to the Arizona desert. A chink of gold in the eastern sky hinted at a pleasant, clear day. She had slept – finally – and she had eaten well on waking. Her stomach was full, her energy was replenished and there were only another sixty miles or so to go. They should arrive at Provenance within the hour, barring any difficulties on the way.

Indeed, Provenance was the only thing currently in Willa's mind that was decidedly unpleasant. She had little interest in the local affairs of an obviously failed Arizona boom town but had reluctantly agreed to take her men there to investigate and investigate she would.

Her uniform was dry and very much cleaner than it had been when they'd arrived in Howling Rock, although there were any number of stains on the fabric that would need more than a quick soak in a bathtub to remove. Still, she felt fresh and ready for action as she stepped out of the front of the *Whistle Stop* and into the main Howling Rock thoroughfare.

Dawn, whilst not as breath-taking a time of day as the starry night, was still something special out here in the sticks. Back home, far to the east in Gotham, business would already be under way and alive with the sounds of engines, the whistle of steam hors and the general hubbub of industry. Street vendors would be hawking their wares in the markets even as it was unloaded. The smells wafting from food stalls set up by enterprising young people who worshipped at the altar of commercialism. Early morning in Gotham was an assault on the senses. Early morning in Howling Rock was...

Quiet.

Yes, that was exactly it. It was a peace that allowed for clarity of thought. The street was completely devoid of life, apart from Willa Shaw and her two soldiers. Millie had served them breakfast this morning and if Willa hadn't known better, she'd have guessed the woman had not slept at all. The food had been plentiful and delicious: bacon, eggs, hotcakes, fresh bread and strong, bitter coffee to wash it down with. That had been *good* coffee and the thought of hitting the trail again and resuming drinking the cheap stuff they carried with them...

Major Shaw, as she was once again after that delicious hiatus of being just plain Willa last night, courteously thanked Millie for her attendance and tipped her generously. Millie had looked at the notes in her hand and seemed on the verge of saying something. Instead, she just gave a half-smile and inclined her head graciously.

"You stop by here again sometime, ma'am," she said and touched her hand briefly to Willa's shoulder. The major wasn't entirely certain how, but she realised she had made herself a friend in the elegant dancer with the big ambitions.

The Iron Horses had been chained up, although it was nigh on impossible to imagine anybody in this part of the world trying to steal one of the Union vehicles. They certainly weren't likely to pick one up and run for the hills. They had the name 'iron' for a reason.

"Did you recharge the fuel cells?" Willa turned to Zachariah who nodded. He was young, barely out of his teens, and eager. Sometimes, she could slap him for it. Still, she knew from experience that time would shape some of that childish enthusiasm.

"Yes, ma'am, I did, ma'am. Got up extra early to make sure we were raring to go!" He snapped a smart salute and if she had been feeling slightly more caustic than the delicious breakfast had left her feeling, she would have rolled her eyes at him. Still, he was a good lad and good company when they camped for the night. Zachariah King's stories were a delight and he'd had her in peals of laughter more than once.

Sergeant Joseph Sweeney was a sharp contrast to the youthful energy that Zach brought to the small unit. An Irishman by birth, he was entering his late thirties and gave the impression that not only was he much older, but also that everything had left him weary. Every setback he encountered was met with a deep, philosophical sigh, an utterance of some Irish curse or other and then he would roll up his sleeves and get on with it. They were a study in contrasts, and she liked and trusted them both with her life.

"So, tell me what you boys learned last night," she said, pulling on her gloves. She looked from the one to the other. "Who exactly was that hunk of flesh you were attempting to wrestle?"

"Someone even the outlaws wanted nothing to do with, Major." Sweeney responded, his tone thoughtful. He was pulling on his own gloves and moving to his vehicle. Like the major the previous evening, he gave the Iron Horse a thorough once-over, waving to King to do the same. "But I don't reckon as it was anything to do with personality. Suggestion was that he's on the Lazarus."

Willa paused, her heart sinking. Rumours of a new narcotic had been circulating for some considerable time now, but nobody yet knew anything about other than the name it had acquired. The Union generals had turned their attentions to the west more and more frequently of late, a move which had unsettled the US Marshals quite considerably. The two separate factions were rubbing along causing a high state of friction and she sensed problems ahead.

"So that's around here too," she said and sighed. She shook her head and turned her attention to the Iron Horse.

The vehicles had been left uncovered and were lined up next to one another in an orderly fashion outside the stables. There were flesh and blood horses in there; the major could hear them as she approached. Her nose wrinkled at the unmistakable stink of animal.

It looked as though one of the horses had slipped his stall and she glanced up as it moved into her line of vision. She was not a great lover of horses, although she appreciated them as a practical means of transport, if only for local journeys. However, she was prepared to set aside that indifference, because this animal was, for want of a better word, *magnificent*. It was huge, for a start, with the sort of solid, muscular build that suggested it had been carefully bred for such a result. A flash of sunlight glanced off its rear quarters and she could appreciate that its dark chestnut was gleaming with a beautiful, healthy shine. White patches on its legs did nothing to detract from its appearance. It looked well-groomed and evidently well cared for.

It – no, as it moved, it became apparent that the animal was very obviously male – *he* was examining the dusty ground for non-existent grazing and was showing no sign whatsoever of being interested in the three Union soldiers who watched him. The stallion gave a harrumph of irritation as he singularly failed to find anything worth eating.

"Do you think we should be putting that animal back in his stall?" Zachariah asked the question with doubt in his voice. He didn't have a clue how one went about collecting a horse.

"He doesn't look particularly bothered," observed Joseph. "And he's not our problem, right Major?" He sighed one of those sighs that suggested he would do it if ordered, but he'd rather not if you didn't mind.

"Right," said Willa, her eyes still on the beast. As she watched, the horse suddenly paused in his endless investigation of the dusty ground and swung his great head towards her.

The eyes.

The heavens above, the *eyes*.

If a human's eyes were, so the saying went, the windows to their soul, then Willa Shaw was presently gazing into an equine abyss. It wasn't that the orbs burned with some kind of brimstone, no. But the longer her eyes remained locked in that dark brown spell, the more she felt sure that she was going to be dragged screaming into the deepest pits of hell. She'd never before encountered an animal that was *judging* her. And this horse was weighing everything about her. She felt the strangest urge to repent. Something. Anything. Just to stop the staring.

She broke the spell first and tore her gaze away. "Let's just get going," she said and mounted the Iron Horse. Her spine complained briefly as she adopted her familiar riding position: she had spent too long stretching it out and now she was forcing it back into her riding hunch.

The two soldiers followed their superior's lead and after a few moments, all that remained of the Union in Howling Rock was their exhaust trail, dissipating on the lethargic breeze that barely stirred in the air.

The stallion watched them leave. If he had been in possession of human shoulders, he would have shrugged indifferently. As it was, he merely whickered softly and turned away to resume his fruitless search for something to eat.

Some things, after all, were important.

* * *

Provenance, Arizona

It was the same as any other mining boom

town she had encountered over the years. The little town had come into being approximately a year ago and within the first few months had boasted twenty cottages and small cabins and around eighty residents. The early success of the mines had quickly drawn prospectors, fortune hunters and business interests and Provenance, as it had come to be known, expanded exponentially. People had held their breath thinking that here was another Tombstone, another town that would be too tough to die.

That presumption could not have been further from the truth, Willa thought as the 'Horses sped towards the still-smouldering ruins of Provenance. Their trip here had been remarkably uneventful but had taken them sixty or so miles through some of the most spectacular countryside that any of them had ever encountered. Even the endless stoicism of Joe Sweeney had been knocked out of him and temporarily reshaped into something approaching appreciation.

Like so much of this part of Arizona, the predominant colour was the burnt orange of a sunset, and it was everywhere the eye strayed. Oranges, umbers, browns and swirls of lighter, pinkish tones that gave shape and pattern to the outcroppings. Odd formations stood as though an artist had begun a project only to be distracted by something else.

The landscape was a patchwork of dry, dusty plains, watched over by rocky, cyclopean plateaus. The entire area was riven with labyrinthine valleys and narrow gulches that scarred its surface. Clumps of tough, scabby grass eked out an existence from the desiccated earth alongside the weirdly majestic cacti. Yet despite such bleak emptiness, life endured here, hiding itself from the heat of the sun as best it could. Life hid also from the ever-watchful eyes of the raptors drifting lazily above their heads in the rising thermals.

The tenacity of the stubborn flora and fauna was every bit as impressive as the hardiness of the people who lived out here and for Zach, who'd never travelled this far west before, a sort of grudging respect was birthed for the difficulties faced by the frontier men and women for whom every day was a struggle.

The heat of the day was still bearable, but a breeze had picked up. At first, it was rather pleasant, leaving a freshness in the air she breathed in through the riding mask. But after several minutes, the ochre dust was joined by a clinging layer of ash which coated everything with a thin film of muck. Goggle lenses, clothes, the 'Horse itself... By the time they slowed the vehicles through the smoking gates of Provenance, any pleasure she'd taken in the cleanliness she'd gained last night had long disintegrated into annoyance at once again being caked in filth.

"Someone was sure thorough about this, huh major?" Zach's habit of stating the obvious kicked in and Willa glanced at him in annoyance.

"Rumour has it nobody died here, King. But we don't know that for sure. So until we're satisfied we aren't going to find people who've lost their lives... keep a little respect on that tongue of yours."

"Yes, ma'am. Sorry." Zach quieted, suitably berated. Nodding, the major shut off the power and dismounted from her vehicle. Her feet kicked up a cloud of dust and ash as she stared at the razed town.

"There's nothing sadder than seeing a new town fail," she murmured. On their long journey west, they'd encountered more than one so-called 'ghost town', but never anything on the scale of destruction that had claimed Provenance. In pop-up towns that happened all over the country, the use of wood in building brought the obvious risk of fire, but usually these things were contained. The design of the towns even allowed for raging infernos to burn out before they touched the next group of buildings.

It was obvious just from looking that whatever had happened in Provenance had been both thorough and absolute.

"There's something even more tragic about a failed town that might have been destroyed intentionally," she added and indicated to her men that they should similarly dismount and follow her. She was yet to be convinced, but the death of Provenance seemed entirely too complete to have happened without casualty and not be deliberate.

The three of them walked slowly down what had clearly been the town's main street. *Provenance*, they called it. A name selected by some crazy prospector who wanted to convey that it was a town of hope. A place of new beginnings. What high hopes and dreams he must have carried on his shoulders. Given the current state of the place, the name had proven an unfortunate and ironic choice.

Prior to their departure, Willa had done a little research into the town. She knew that the remains of the street they now stood upon had been known as Anderson Street, named for the first family who had taken up residence here. She had seen a few photographs, blurred and indistinct, of a number of ramshackle huts that had grown into larger properties.

There was not a single building still fully intact, although some walls were clinging on for dear life. Ash covered the ground and smoke wisped everywhere, coiling thinly from the ruins either side of the main street. Here and there the scorched and blackened remains of store front signs could be made out.

It was bad enough in the heat of the near-noonday sun, but walking in the furnace-like heat of the town's smouldering remains made things even more uncomfortable. It was like the inferno had been baked into the soil which was, in turn, intent on retaining it for a long as possible. The deeper into the devastation that Willa and her men moved, the more she yearned for the cool greenness of home.

"Let's get to it," she said, squinting up into the sky. "Pick a direction, boys. See if we can find anything at all that seems out of place. Anything that suggests this isn't a terrible accident." Anything to report to the superiors who had sent her out her chasing invisible monsters.

Willa picked up the corner of a scorched sign that had once declared this building to have been the saddlers. Opposite, an open-faced building was the only one mostly intact and the smith's forge was still there, the tools hanging nearby.

Still holding the sign in her hand, she stooped down and picked up the remains of a leather saddle. Iron Horses were used across the country, but they did so cling to the older ways out here. That wasn't to say they shunned anything to do with juiced gear, no: the ruptured hulk of a generator still belched fumes into the sky, the last of its fuel sizzling and spitting as it boiled off. The sad, wilted poles that lined the street proved that Provenance had boasted RJ-generated lighting which made it practically sophisticated by Arizona standards.

Her boot caught on something, and she dropped the sign, crouching down and picking up a painting of Provenance. She wondered, vaguely, why the artist had chosen to paint it in a uniform shade of grey but realised that it was just the surface layer of ash. As she carefully brushed it off, she was rewarded with a beautiful scene of a Provenance sunset. She shook her head regretfully at the waste and set the painting back down again.

Willa turned the piece of heavy saddle leather over in her hands and her mind absently strayed to the horse they'd seen that morning. It had been a monster of the species, and the intelligence in those eyes had been disturbing. No, not for her. Definitely not for her. She dropped the saddle beside the painting and moved on.

Everything was the same, burned, scorched, broken and destroyed. Thus far, they'd found no evidence of inhabitation, or that anybody had been injured or killed in the fire. It had been reported in the *Tribune* several days ago and the fact it was still burning in places spoke volumes for how ferocious RJ-fuelled fires must have been.

"Major."

Willa looked up at Sweeney's voice. He was pointing to the road that led into town. Her gaze followed his finger and she scowled. Thinking about the damn thing had clearly summoned it forth. The horse from the *Whistle Stop* was walking into Provenance although this time, it was not alone. The rider who sat on its broad back was wearing a long, battered leather coat of dark tan, which trailed behind him as the horse trotted into the ruins. Willa's scowl grew deeper as she spied the star on the man's breast, the unmistakable proclamation that he was a lawman. Her finger tapped in irritation against the eyepatch.

"Get King," she said to Sweeney. "Let's present a unified front. We're under orders and he's gonna try to tell us we don't have jurisdiction or some such nonsense." Sweeney nodded and moved off to find where

Zach had gone.

As the horse slowed from a trot to a walk, the rider leaned forward and patted him on the neck. The animal nickered in response and tossed his magnificent mane of dark hair. The rider pulled him up to a complete stop about ten feet from Willa Shaw's position and dismounted. He wore a broad-rimmed hat on his head, with goggles over his eyes and a bandana tied around his face to protect from the Arizona dust and heat.

"You needing something, lawman?" Willa stood firm, her feet slightly apart, her hands balled into fists at her hips. The man turned his goggled gaze toward her and his head tipped to one side slightly. But he made no response. Instead, she heard him make a noise that sounded distinctly like a chuckle. "What do..."

He held up a hand to stop her speaking, then whipped around, coat-tails flapping behind him as he dug into the saddlebags. He pulled out a flask of water and a bowl, which he set down for the horse to drink. As the animal slurped noisily – unnecessarily so, Willa couldn't help feeling – the lawman reached up and unwound the bandana from his face.

"You've come a mighty long way to take a look at this little town, ma'am." His voice was still muffled by the cloth of the bandana but even so, it seemed oddly distorted. As he spoke, something in her blood ran ice-cold, a direct contrast to the boiling heat of the noonday sun. She *knew* that voice. Southern at its core, a soft accent and a cultured, well-educated cant to the voice. The accent had changed a little; the kind of voice that had become altered and affected by moving from place to place for several years. And despite that first bite of familiarity that she yet refused to acknowledge, there was something else, something different. A mechanical undertone that she certainly didn't recall.

She harboured a sudden hope, desperate and futile, that this wasn't who she thought it could be. She looked down momentarily and her heart skipped a beat. Amidst the dust and grime of the desert, his boots were impossibly clean.

Never trust a man who don't take his boots seriously, darlin'.

She looked up again, setting her jaw in an expression of grim determination. The bandana came all the way off to reveal an oddly-styled face mask that covered his face below the nose. It was this mask which had distorted his voice and given it the odd tonal quality. She could hear the click of machinery and a small light on the bottom that periodically glowed red, indicating something enhanced by RJ-1027. When he reached up to remove the goggles, the dust of the day against his face had left white rings where they had been. It was vaguely comical. But seeing those eyes that were now regarding her was not comical. Not even slightly.

He seemed taller than she remembered, but it had been a long time. Perhaps it was just that he was so thin. *Thin enough to hide in a shotgun barrel* as the saying went. She dragged her eyes away from his piercing blue ones and let her gaze travel over him from booted foot to ridiculous hat.

"Well now," he said and began striding towards her. There was an easy swagger in his step, a comfortable confidence and familiarity that radiated from him. "Willa Adams, as I live and breathe. What a sight for sore eyes *you* are, darlin'." The tone – despite the mechanisation of the voice – was warm and pleasant: a friend greeting another after many years apart.

"It's Shaw, now. Willa Shaw. *Major* to you." Her arms folded defensively across her chest, and she looked up at him as he got closer. His presence, his proximity... hell, even the *height* of him irritated her in a way she'd not known in many a year. She tapped her eyepatch again; a gesture of intense irritation that her companions recognised, but which inadvertently drew his attention to her missing eye. His gaze held there for a moment, then he looked down again.

"Hank," she said, and her voice was flat. She automatically chose to use the diminutive of his name that she'd always used. It had annoyed him back then and if she was at all lucky, it would annoy him now.

The lawman waited a moment as though expecting her to finish the greeting but when nothing was forthcoming, he simply chuckled again. "Now I have not gone by that for some time. You just call me Doc," he said. "That's what most folks know me as these days." There was the pause of a heartbeat. "So you're a Major, huh? Well, that is a thing. A fine thing indeed. An' so formal, too. Alright, alright... to keep us on an even keel, how 'bout you, Major Ad... Shaw..." He pointed to her as he said this. "How 'bout you call *me* Deputy Holliday?" He pointed to the star at his breast as though was speaking to a fool.

He studied her with the same sort of intensity she'd just studied him and then he reached up and clicked off the face mask so that he could take a good, long drink from his hip flask. If this was *really* the same man she remembered, she doubted that it was water he had in there. The sight of his face beneath the mask, the way it had changed, disturbed her in a manner she wasn't ready to confront, so she covered her shock with a sarcastic comment.

"What happened to the 'tash, Hank?" He'd been proud of that moustache, and he had easily been one of the vainest men she'd ever known in her life. Even now, he was well turned out and while it had obviously seen better days, his leather coat was a good cut; well-tailored and probably expensive. She made the comment just to be spiteful.

"Had to lose it to accommodate the mask," he replied, wiping his lips and clicking the apparatus back in place. "Glad to see yours is still growin', though." He shifted his weight onto his right hip, his angular body forming an assertive posture, especially as it ensured the gun in its holster became more prominent. "So, what on earth brings three of the Union's finest all the way out to a little place like Provenance? Or at least, what's left of it?" He accompanied the last with a sweeping gesture that took in the ruined buildings and the ash-covered street.

"I don't have to answer to you, *Deputy*." There was such venom in the word that a lesser man would have cowed from this fierce woman's simmering rage. Doc Holliday, however, was not a lesser man. She hardened her gaze. "My orders are from a higher authority. But since you're so keen to know, we're here investigating the reasons behind this tragedy."

"Now that is a coincidence," said Doc and his tone was still infuriatingly cheerful. "I'm investigatin' too. Maybe you an' me should put our heads together an' see what we find, huh?" He gave her a slow, lazy wink that fired her irritation up another notch. He straightened up and turned, heading back to the horse. He patted the monstrosity on the shoulder before unfastening the horse's saddle with practised ease and pulled it loose. Despite herself, Willa found that she was admiring the muscular lines of the huge animal.

Against her better judgement, and despite an acute awareness that Doc was actively baiting her, she continued.

"Nice horse." She managed to say it without gritting her teeth. She was so *angry*. Just the sight of him had stirred up a gamut of emotions that she didn't need to cope with right now. Or ever, for preference.

"Why, thank you kindly. He was a gift." He stroked at the stallion's neck. "He is just a bit on the skittish side, however. Won't let nobody but me ride him and he most certainly knows his own mind." The lawman patted the horse's shoulder with great affection and spoke to him. "He's the colour of the nutmeg. And of the heat of the ginger... he is pure air and fire, and the dull elements of earth and water never appear in him..."

He let the quote tail off, seeing no hint of recognition in the faces of his audience. He sighed quietly. He looked over his shoulder, his body language speaking volumes. He tensed, and he was studying her with the sort of expression in his eyes that defied her to laugh at his next words. "His name is Solomon Smith."

She didn't laugh. She knew him better than that. *Much* better.

"Good name," she said, solemnly. "Solid, strong Biblical name, that. Solomon. And that was *Henry V,* right?"

"*Smith,* darlin'. Solomon *Smith.*" Doc relaxed his posture, looking delighted that she'd picked up on his soliloquy and resumed freeing Solomon Smith of the accoutrements that bound him to human service. The job complete, the man patted the horse on the flank and let him wander off freely. The stallion immediately trotted out of the town and disappeared into the heat haze. Doc watched him go and took off his hat.

He ran his fingers through his unruly mop of dark blond hair and tipped his head to one side. She couldn't see his mouth beneath the mask, but the glint in his eyes suggested he was grinning at her.

"Don't you worry he won't come back?" She suspected that the horse hadn't slipped his stall at all that morning; that Doc Holliday just let the animal roam free.

"He ain't never let me down before, darlin'. Me and Solomon Smith have been together for three years now an' he is the most reliable partner I could ask for." Willa stared at him for a few moments, trying to determine if he was making a joke at her expense. She determined that he was clearly not. The lawman gave her a smile – damned crooked smile that she remembered all too well – and put his hat back on to shade his head from the worst of the noonday sun. "An' he's probably got things he needs to do, so ain't no point my holdin' him back, right?"

Somewhere, it seemed, on the road he'd taken since leaving her, Henry John Holliday had thrown his sanity over the edge of a cliff. Maybe it was his illness, making him crazy. Whatever it was, she'd never expected to see him ever again and now that he was right here in front of her... She shook her head just ever so slightly. He wasn't her problem any more, not that she'd ever really considered him a problem. She pushed back some of the hostility and took a deep breath.

"Alright. Where d'you want to start, Deputy Holliday?"

"You looked over the sawmill yet?" The lawman squinted in the direction of the largest building in town. "Place was juiced up to the hilt. Could well be where this whole sorry mess started out."

A quick check with her soldiers revealed that no, nobody had yet reached the remains of the once-proud Provenance Wood and Lumber Company. Doc nodded and began walking in that direction. "Then I will make my start there. What say we meet back here in... shall we say an hour? An' we can compare notes."

"I don't have to do what you tell me to do. I'm conducting my own investigation."

"Sure, Major. Whatever you say. I fully understand."

He walked off, that same swagger in his stride and she scowled. She looked from Sweeney to King and back again. Both were keeping their faces carefully neutral. Too much so, she felt. It was more than clear to her that both of them were itching to ask her personal questions that she would not answer. She glowered at them.

"We meet back here in an hour. And that's *my* order. You got it?"

They got it.

* * *

She caught up to him as he was heading towards the sawmill, his long legs carrying him in strides that her shorter stature found hard to match. He glanced over his shoulder when he realised, she was there and whether unconsciously or deliberately, he slowed his pace so that she could walk level with him.

Walking this close to him, familiar scents began to permeate her nostrils, awakening long-dormant memories. He smelled now, as he always had smelled; of tobacco, whiskey and soap - cleanliness and indulgence in a single package. There was also another scent in there as well, something with which she was familiar. The fumes of juice-burn, that tell-tale stench of gasoline tinged with an RJ injection manifold. Her Iron Horse obviously gulped through the fuel a lot faster than most RJ-enhanced gadgetry, but even on the tiny scale of Doc's mask, there was an unmistakable odour; a sort of scorched flavour that tingled at the back of the nose.

Peppermints, too. He was fond of the candies, she remembered that. She remembered how, back in Texas where they'd met, the kids of the town had loved the dentist who gave them sweets. *Drumming up business*, was the cynical view. Demonstrating a kindness had been hers. She knew he came from a large family, with an apparent endless swarm of younger cousins who somehow filled the void left after his baby sister had died in her cradle. She'd loved that generosity in him. Underlying all those other scents was a hint of peppermint.

Without meaning to, she took a deep breath and then forced herself to move past the flurry of memories that this olfactory onslaught brought and focused on the here and now. "You been here before, Deputy?" When he replied that strange metallic cant to his voice startled her again, but she kept any reaction off her face.

"Sure have. Provenance was a nice little place. All pleases an' thank yous. It was doin' well for itself." He shook his head and sighed behind the mask. "An' now it is just a smokin' crater. Ain't like anythin' I have seen in my years out west. Not a single body. Not one. You found nothin'?"

"We haven't been here all that long." Willa raised a hand to shield her eyes from the sunlight and squinted up at him. "Only just started searching. But not seen any sign of deaths. Just a tragic accident, you think?"

"Maybe," he said, thoughtfully, pausing in his striding for a moment or two. He looked out over the remains of the town. "Maybe not. I read somethin' about people seein' weird-coloured flames, blue and red, an' that's kinda strange. Not so much the red, I guess, since it looks like the RJ generator went up, but..."

A dark shadow moved, catching Willa's attention and she glanced towards it. The horse, which Doc had let loose, had already returned to the town and was trotting comfortably along behind him. It stopped when they stopped and fixed her with its solemn stare.

"Your horse..."

"Solomon Smith."

"Whatever. Isn't it a bit... *unusual* for a horse to behave the way he does? The whole... following you around like he was a dog or something?"

"Is it?" Doc seemed surprised by the suggestion and looked over her shoulder to where the big stallion was presently standing. "I have got sorta used to him, I guess. He comes and goes as he pleases an' sometimes, we are just usually headed the same way. Ain't that right, Solomon Smith?" The horse shook his mane at being thus addressed and shifted from one great leg to another. Willa shook her head again.

"Why 'Solomon Smith'?"

"That is his name, darlin'."

It seemed that was all the explanation she was going to get, and she let the matter go. They resumed walking, he at a much slower speed than before, and they did not speak to one another. Yet, the silence was not uncomfortable. Both of them were looking around as they walked, seeking out anything that seemed out of the ordinary or even a little bit curious, but nothing presented itself.

The shell of the sawmill when they got close to it was enormous. It had clearly been, when it was intact, a vast space in which the workers would have been kept busy on a daily basis. Willa sniffed the air and frowned a little.

"Juice," she observed. "Place reeks of it." Doc nodded. He reached up and clicked a switch on the side of the mask. The constant hum that accompanied him paused momentarily and she tipped her head curiously to one side.

"Just a pause in the flow," he said, noticing her watching. "Helps me catch scents better than when all my pipes are bein' cleaned out." He sniffed the air deeply and nodded his agreement.

"The owner was proud of his generator," he observed. "But not as proud as the engineer was." He coughed a few times, a chest-wracking hack that sounded painful and, given the way he winced momentarily, presumably was. He cleared his throat and took another, more careful breath. "Didya read the *New York Tribune* a couple days back?"

"I don't read the papers," she admitted and felt a bit ashamed of the fact. He shrugged his shoulders and reached up to click his filter back into place. The hum resumed, a constant, underlying thrum. His eyes closed – just briefly – but enough for her to realise how much respite the machine gave him.

"Ya should," he told her. "Lots of interestin' things in there if you look under the politics." She made a dismissive noise and waved a hand vaguely.

"I get enough of politics back home," she said. He chuckled lightly, letting the matter drop.

"Reckon what you're smellin' there is whatever is left of the fuel. Let's get over there an' check it out."

Behind Willa, Solomon Smith began to shift restlessly. Doc looked up at the stallion's movement and his eyebrows feathered together in concern. "Somethin' botherin' ya, Solomon Smith?"

By way of response, the horse continued to shift uncomfortably, shaking his mane with increasing agitation. Doc's eyes narrowed. "He don't like juice none. He just about tolerates this little thing here..." He touched a hand to the mask. "An' he will put up with a little bit of shootin'. But anythin' more than that, he does not like one little bit." The lawman's fingers briefly rested over the gun in its holster. "Guess he ain't keen on the stuff that's still bubblin' up out of that hole. Can't say I blame him."

"Looks that way," she replied. Here, the burst guts of the generator had caved in the floor of the mill, leaving a deep, fuming crater, melting the metal fixtures and charring everything else to ash.

"Right there, look." Doc pointed a gloved hand towards the blasted hollow. There were still vestiges of energy arcing out from the remaining innards of the thing, filling the air close to it with a fresh, clean sort of scent like the desert after an electrical storm that cut right through the pall of industrial pollutants. It was a strange sensation and the closer the major got, the more lightheaded she began to feel.

"Reckon this is where it started, then," she observed. "All seems kinda obvious. The generator overloaded and started a fire."

"I do not think so," said Doc, shaking his head and studying the hollow shell a little more closely. "In the interview in the *Tribune* engineer clearly stated the explosion came after they started evacuatin'. Reckon it is less a fault of the mechanisms an' more..." He broke off as the horse began to whicker urgently at him. Once again, his eyes narrowed and this time, his gun came clean out of its holster. It rested firmly in the palm of his hand and his sense of unease was infections. Willa also loosed her weapon, although unlike Doc, she did not arm herself.

"Somethin' ain't right here," the deputy murmured. There was a faint creaking beneath their feet, the sound of what remained of wooden floor struggling under extreme duress. It was incredible that anything had survived of the building at all given the destruction elsewhere, but it wasn't that fact that was niggling at the back of Doc's mind. "Whaddya see, Major? What is it that is *different* in here?"

"What?" She had been studying the destroyed generator with a mixture of distrust and curiosity. Like so many, she was increasingly content to reap the benefits that the scientific advancement brought with it, but that did not mean she didn't find it unsettling.

"Tell me what you are lookin' at."

"Why? You gone blind as well as stupid?"

"Tell me." His voice had a sense of quiet urgency to it and she stalled on the vicious counter attack. She turned to examine the generator.

"Well, I am not familiar with generators this big," she said, "but looks to me like it took out most of the south wall there when it went up. Burst its fuel lines, then burned the rest in the blast." She pointed towards the fizzling, crackling crater. "Put that big old hole in the floor. Sounds like the Fourth of July down there. And the thing still seems to be spitting out some sort of power."

"But it is mostly broken, right?"

"Looks pretty bust-up to me. I 'm not an engineer, though."

"So. Broken generator dribblin' out sparks." The deputy's finger pointed in the vague direction of the agitated horse. "An' like I told you... Solomon Smith, ain't happy around RJ-fussin'. But what is comin' outta that hole is just a dribble, ain't any more than he is used to." The horse had backed away from the wreckage pit and was glaring in its direction, eyes rolling in his sockets. "So somethin' else has got him spooked. Any thoughts? 'Cos I do declare that I am comin' up blank."

Willa shrugged one shoulder and said the first thing that came into her mind. "Another generator? Fury or arc maybe? Or some contraption that fell into the hole and is still churning away down there?" The two exchanged looks and Doc nodded slowly.

"Could be... Good thinkin', Major Shaw. C'mon. Let's look some more."

Despite herself, despite that initial desire she'd harboured to slap his arrogant smirk to the other side of his head, the approval in Doc's tone buoyed her enthusiasm still further. They'd fallen into a sense of comfortable investigation and his snappy, short questions had urged her own natural sense of curiosity to the fore. They'd always been a good team and whatever anger and animosity she harboured towards him had been put, for now at least, to the back of her mind. They were here for the same reason and differences aside, working together was always better than the alternative.

She had even grown used, once again, to the pattern of his speech; his slow Georgia drawl, his infrequent use of contractions, his tendency to break into quotes from classical literature. The years that had passed between them seemed to be no time at all.

Here and there were the remains of the logging machines, parts melted and welded into one another where the combined fires of the inferno and the white-hot explosion of the generator had fused them. So much RJ-enhanced machinery in one place was surely *asking* for trouble?

"Imagine if this had happened when the place was full," she said, expressing the inner thought that was niggling at the back of her mind. "It wouldn't just be machines we'd be looking at." She'd seen more than one Iron Horse explode in her time. Seen more than one good soldier fused to their vehicle by crimson fire. Separating man from machine in those circumstances was nigh on impossible.

"True enough," said Doc. "Whatever happened here could have been a whole lot worse. An' it is certainly bad enough as it is."

Beneath their feet, the floorboards creaked again, and Willa felt an inexplicable sense of discomfort. A shudder ran its way down her neck, and she visibly shook herself as though to free the sensation from her limbs. The deputy's eyes moved to look at her.

"Y'alright?"

"I'm fine. I just... you ever have that feeling you're being watched?"

"All the time. An' I am gettin' it right now." He idly waved the gun in his hand. "I did not get this out just to make myself look even more amazin' than I did a minute ago. Okay, here is what I am thinkin'. I reckon as we should meet up with your boys an'..."

Exactly what it was that Doc Holliday thought they should do was forever lost as the shout for 'Major Shaw' filtered through the still afternoon air. Willa and Doc exchanged glances.

"King," she said and didn't wait another moment. She turned, sprinting out of the remains of the sawmill into the street. Standing some feet away from them stood young Zachariah King, his weapon unholstered. He was not aiming at anything, and she noted that he was prepared for trouble rather than engaged.

"What's the issue, King?"

"Over there, Major." Zach waved with his gun, indicating the far end of the street where a lone figure was making its way toward them. "Just appeared from nowhere."

"The old mines maybe," said Doc, exiting the sawmill and coming to stand beside them. "Only thing out that way once you leave town. Get past that, an' then there's just miles of dust an' Arizona nothin'. The mines though... they were closed off right after the new ones opened. Runs right underneath the town here." He glanced back into the ruined mill, thinking of the crater. "Jus' like back home... back in Tombstone."

"People fleeing the fire holed up in the old mines you reckon? Got themselves stuck?" She hadn't missed Doc's correction, how he didn't consider Tombstone to be 'home'. The Holliday she knew was a wanderer, a vagrant. Perhaps he wasn't so changed after all. "Could it be that they've been trapped down there?" What a horrible thing to imagine: running in terror from a horrendous fire, into old mines that could have collapsed in on them. "Report from my seniors said that nobody was missing."

"Plenty of vagrants pass through these towns. Grifters, maybe, prospectors, even. Sometimes, just families down on their luck, lookin' to make a new start." replied Doc. "Nobody cares 'bout them. Maybe that's who this fella is. Ho there! Need help, my friend?"

There was no response, but the figure continued heading towards them. Its gait was strangely erratic; it was not walking in a straight line, neither was it staggering. It seemed merely to be *ambling*, moving without any sort of real purpose.

"Somethin' not right here," said Doc, stating as he apparently liked to do, the bloody obvious. "Why ain't he answerin'?" The lanky deputy swung his long coat to one side, revealing the second pistol holstered on his hip. His fingers closed delicately around the weapon, but he did not take it out. He tipped the brim of his hat back and squinted against the light of the sun. "Looks to me like he's got a head wound."

"You can tell that from here?"

"You get good at spottin' this kinda thing out here, darlin', trust me on that."

"I'll get over there right away." King put his weapon back in its holster and began to head towards the meandering figure, calling out every step of the way. He got within a few feet of the injured man and froze dead in his tracks.

A head wound, the deputy had said. That, Zachariah King thought as he stared at the man before him, was the least of it. Yes, there was head trauma. Definite head trauma. Having the back of your skull missing accurately fell into that description. Rammed into the back of the thing's – King could no longer think of it as a 'he', not now – was a cylinder of some kind, wicked, crimson light seeping from a slit in its side. Its face was distorted, forever locked in a rictus scream of terror. There was no terror in the eyes, however. The eyes were devoid of anything. Feeling. Emotion. *Life*.

Then it turned to face the young soldier full on. King had never seen anything quite so appallingly unnatural as the figure standing in front of him. Besides the horrific cranial trauma, it was missing its right arm below the elbow. The wound looked as though it had been treated and cauterised and there was a metal cup there, the kind that would often be fitted to those who lost lower limbs and had cheap prosthetics fitted. Angry veins pulsed beneath its foul, greying flesh and the distorted head lolled to one side as it considered King with vacant curiosity. A hollow, barely audible wheeze escaped its dry throat, and it began to stagger awkwardly toward the soldier.

King had read and heard of the Covenant of the Enlightened's reconstructed people or so-called *constructs*, but he had never seen one, neither had he ever intended to. Most people hadn't. Thanks to the Covenant's ungodly science and medicine, some at death's door were given a chance of a new lease of life. Well, a half-life at least. People who, for whatever reason, be it the wishes of their family, choice of their own or as some kind of punishment, were... *changed*. They were invariably people who had suffered physical trauma of some kind that would otherwise have killed them. Limbs severed, flesh wounds that festered... they were rebuilt. Repaired. *Renewed*. They were granted an extra lease of life in return for willing servitude to the Covenant or subcontracted out to one of the many nations of the world that would employ such services. Perhaps, he thought, with the sort of flash of insight that came with a moment's intense emotion, they had been working here. Working the mines. Manual labour...

He shook his attention back. From what they said about them in the newspapers and periodicals, the reconstructed were not mindless creatures, devoid of thought or purpose. Yes, sometimes the trauma of the surgery could scramble a man's mind, but they were not the living dead.

"Get back." King raised his pistol, trying his hardest not to notice just how much his hands were shaking. If this *thing* had any sense of reason, it would hear his words for the threat he hoped they conveyed. "Get back, now."

"King!" The Major called his name from further down the road. "What's happening?" She and the deputy were making their way towards him, and he turned briefly.

"Major, you need to get here now. This thing..." He did not end the sentence, instead instinctively squeezed the trigger on the pistol as the monstrosity made a lunge for him. The juiced weapon discharged with a high-pitched whip-crack and shot clean through the thing's torso in a welter of scarred tissue. The Major broke into a run and Doc matched her pace easily, his longer legs meaning that he reached the creature before she did. It was stumbling, listing badly to one side from the injury done to it.

But despite the ragged hole in its chest and freshly exposed ribs, it did not drop.

The shock of the impact alone would have been enough to kill most living things, and even if it didn't, the terrible wound would have seen them gasping their last in a few, short minutes. But Doc, taking in the sight with quick thinking tempered by a healthy smattering of utter disbelief, realised that you could not kill something that was not exactly alive. Both of the deputy's own pistols flashed so quickly to the kill that you could be forgiven for thinking that he'd willed them there.

"Get back, kid," he said to the young soldier who was staring, a confused expression on his face. "Quickly now!" He levelled one of his pistols at the stumbling, walking corpse and fired. His aim, as ever it was, struck true and the high-velocity bullet ripped right through the thing's throat. It made no noise – no noise at all – and that somehow was worse by far than any screaming or gurgling it might have made. King remained standing where he was, until Willa grabbed at his arm and hauled him away from the grizzly sight. Doc fired his second pistol and the horror crashed to the dust of the floor. No blood oozed from its injuries. It was, the deputy suspected, his flesh creeping in horror, fully exsanguinated. He'd seen such things before, but usually the victims had the good grace to stay thoroughly dead. Only given that it had been making those strange rasping sounds that were a mockery of breathing, it was evident that it hadn't *been* dead. Something was holding it to life. A gawkish, horrible parody of life that sickened him to the very stomach.

"I couldn't put it down, Major Shaw." The boy was babbling anxiously, and Doc didn't blame him. As these things were measured, the deputy was an experienced veteran of situations that called for gunfighting. That young soldier couldn't be much more than twenty. Doc felt a wave of empathy for him. "I tried."

"It's alright, Zach. It's done. It's stopped moving, at least." Willa glanced over at the inert figure. "You got any thoughts, deputy?"

"I got plenty of thoughts," he replied, grimly, "but I ain't got a single one that would answer the question you wanna hear the answer to." He hunkered down next to the figure and examined it a little more closely. He reached into a pocket and pulled out a small vial with the tiniest trace of a reddish substance at the bottom. His eyes, behind the mask, darkened. "*This* on the other hand," he said, getting to his feet, "I know plenty about."

Willa's eyes went to the vial, to its contents and she scowled, her hands balling on her hips. "So do I," she said. "Leastways, if it's what I think it is."

"Lazarus," said Doc and Willa nodded.

"Major," said King and there was a faint note of panic in his voice. Willa ignored him briefly, caught up in the discovery of the narcotic.

"There was a fight in the saloon last night," she said. "My boys got into a squabble with a big chunk of stupidity and the locals said that he was likely taking this stuff. It's getting too common."

"Major." King tried again, this time rather boldly tugging at her arm.

"Ain't that the truth?" Doc slid the vial into an inner pocket of his greatcoat and dusted the garment down. "Questions, question. Namely, who was this poor fella, why was he comin' out of the mines an' what in the name of all that is good an' holy happened to him to leave him like that?"

Questions indeed. And Major Shaw did not have a single answer.

"Major!" This time, the young soldier's voice would not be denied and both Willa and Doc turned to look at him, then followed the line of his pointing, shaking finger. Emerging from the dust haze at the end of the street was a shambling, sighing, gasping mob. They were all clad in rags, their eyes grey and vacant and their flesh laced with distended veins. They hobbled on awkward legs, some withered and broken, and grasped at the dry air with emaciated hands and capped, truncated arms.

"Major, what's going on?" The voice belonged to Sergeant Sweeney who had been summoned by the gunfire. He was jogging lightly, which was considerable effort for him. Sweeney was not a man overly given to running anywhere. Willa assessed the approaching figures. Just as the prone figure lying in the dust had demonstrated, they seemed incapable of walking in anything remotely resembling a straight line. She made the grim assumption that here were more of the same.

"We need to put those things down before they find a way out of town. have no idea what they are, but they're unnatural abominations. I don't know what devilry is going on in this place, but..."

"Say no more. Less talkin'," said Doc. "More shootin'." He lifted his guns and aimed at the leading edge of the mob.

Before Willa could even eke out any sort of retort, the lawman had already started firing, fanning the hammers of his pistols with singular skill and unerring accuracy. In a matter of seconds, both weapons were empty, and the shots stitched a line of wounds across the closest members of the shuffling horde. Bodies were perforated and skulls broken in puffs of frothing, pink-tinged matter. Several dropped and vanished beneath the stumbling feet of those behind.

It irritated Willa that even under such dire circumstances, she was able to spare a moment's admiration for the man.

Sweeney, who had barely been able to register the presence of the... whatever it was... that was lying in the dust at the deputy's feet looked up at the sound of renewed gunfire and grimaced, pulling his shotgun free and moving to stand next to the lawman. Doc cast a brief sideways glance and nodded at the sergeant.

"King, you keep back for now," said Willa, drawing her own weapon and preparing to stand beside the other two. She could see how the situation had shaken him and knew that he was more of a liability right now than an asset.

Later, she would be furious with her decision to turn her back on the boy. Even in the cold light of reason, even when everyone else reassured her, she still blamed herself.

The percussive blast of Sweeney's shotgun echoed around the abandoned town and another – *creature* was the only word she could pull up right now – crumpled to the ground. The others seemed not to notice, or not to care what had become of their fellows and kept right on advancing. They still shambled, their stumbling gait slow and awkward, but the gunfire seemed to draw them, give them purpose. Reloaded, the lawman and Union soldier fired their weapons in a surprisingly coordinated attack and again the closest creatures dropped. Another mob emerged from a burned-out barn, their grasping hands tearing through the skeletal structure and breaking it open with a crash of splintering wood. They turned as one and followed the sound of gunfire.

"The *hell* are those things? Where are they coming from?" Sweeney lowered his shotgun and stared at them. "Major?"

"If I knew the answer to that, Sergeant, I'd know what to do about it," snapped Willa. It seemed that the things would just keep on advancing until they were put down, but for everyone they stopped, more appeared. A story briefly flitted into her mind; a tale Henry Holliday had told her once. Mythology, he'd said. A monster in Greek mythology called the hydra. These monstrosities were like the hydra's heads.

"I reckon," the lawman said, lowering his pistols to reload once again, "that we are gonna have to fall back." He looked around, then back at the approaching horde, its enthusiasm to reach them undimmed by the losses. "Reckon we need to find ourselves somewhere much more defensible. Better still, gettin' the hell outta here seems like a pretty good option."

Willa hated the idea of retreat, but the tactician in her ceded that they were grossly outnumbered by an enemy that didn't appear to suffer from the burden of morale. She held back the scowl and nodded. "Pains me to admit I'm agreeing with you here, Deputy, but I think you're right." She gestured and raised her voice to the two soldiers. "Fall back boys. Let loose with covering fire but fall back."

She unloaded her weapon, shooting closest creature in the face as it reached out a grasping hand for her and took a step back. The echoing boom of Sweeney's shotgun told her that her sergeant was similarly following firing discipline. Zachariah King, however, was deathly pale and trying desperately to control the quiver in his hands as he fired his six-shooter. The boy only managed to take one step back before he realised something had a tight hold of his ankle.

"Major!" King cried in alarm, struggling to free himself from the grip.

"King!" Willa admonished the young man through the sound of gunfire. "King, keep up! Come on! I ordered a retreat, not some sort of heroic last stand. Move it! There are far too many of them!"

"I can't retreat, Major!" King's voice rose in a loud wail. He tried again to shake the grip of the cold hand locked around his ankle, the last gasp of the first creature he'd killed, but he may as well have tried to stop the tides. The thin fingers held fast; their grip locked around his ankle. With mounting horror, he emptied his weapon into the arm and shoulder of the creature, decorating the street with pulverised flesh. It was all for nothing; the limb maintained its persistent grip.

"Major!" The young soldier was no longer shouting. Now he was screaming as the horde closed in on him.

"I got him. I got this, Willa." Willa was jostled slightly as the lawman brushed by her shoulder. He holstered one pistol, drew a wicked-looking knife from his boot and without waiting to give any further explanation of his plan, prepared to rush to the aid of the beleaguered Zachariah King.

She caught his arm and he turned to look at her. "Make it fast, Hank," she said. As an afterthought, she added, "Doc." His eyes widened in surprise, but she ignored him. "We're running out of space real fast here and it doesn't look like those things are planning on letting up any time soon."

He nodded and made a dash for it. Doc Holliday reached King just as the leading edge of the mob reached the feet of the fallen enemy. The boy was trying furiously to reload his pistol, but there were more bullets on the ground than in the chambers. That, added to the fact he was shaking like a leaf in a hurricane did not help his situation one little bit.

"Come on kid!" Doc said, hacking at the grasping limb. "Stop playin' with your catch. We gotta get out of here, an' we gotta get out of here now!"

"Help me Doc!" Zachariah pleaded, tugging furiously at his ankle. Something gave; the dry bones in the withered limb gave an audible crack. Something else reached for Doc but the lawman's reflexes were impressive. The creature exploded in a shower of stinking flesh and rotten fluid.

Then something else grabbed hold of the fallen corpse, yanking it into the mob with ponderous, irresistible strength. Zachariah King, still moored to the body by the hand locked around his ankle was dragged with it. King screamed; the sound of a boy terrified beyond words as the grasping hands of the mob took hold of him. Doc rolled away and made a grab for him, his fingers just barely brushing against Zachariah's outstretched hand, and then the young soldier was gone.

The lawman scooted back and got to his feet, smothered in road dust, in time to see the creatures clawing at King. The boy was screaming in terror as the vacant, wheezing things tugged and pawed at him, lacerating his flesh with their splintered nails. His wide, wild eyes locked with Doc's, filled with a silent plea and Doc nodded once. He felt sick to the stomach.

"I am real sorry kid." Doc said and meant it. "*Requiescat in pace.*" Grief welled up in him but did not overwhelm him. Then he shot the boy cleanly in the head and spared him the agony of death at the hands of the unimaginable.

"Get out of there!" Sweeney's shout cut through the swelling anger and Doc Holliday fell back to where Willa and the soldier were waiting.

"We'll talk about this later." Willa said, her expression unreadable, and Doc nodded.

"Yeah," he said. "Later. That is assumin' we all get to have a later to enjoy. Think we can make it to the 'Horses from here?"

Willa looked at the approaching mob, their rapidly dwindling supply of ammunition and then across the empty street to where the Iron Horses were parked.

"Don't see as we have much of a choice. Let's go for it. Move!"

The trio continued their retreat, the shuffling, stumbling mob trailing behind them. They were within feet of the vehicles when another group of creatures smashed through a scorched and half-ruined shop front, cutting off that route of escape.

Willa cursed loudly. Under other circumstances, Doc would have commented on the foul use of language coming from her, but he wisely kept his mouth shut. She spun round to Doc and Sweeney. "They must have spread out through the ruins as they came out of the mine." Realisation dawned. "And out of that damned hole in the mill!"

"Imagine," muttered Doc, more to himself than aloud. "Corpses with strategies." He was aware, on a curiously fundamental level, that they were not fully dead, these things. But they had been tampered with and altered to such a degree that it was easier by far to consider them as such. He wished to *God* he could put a name to what it was that was occurring here, but it was beyond him. Had King lived, he could have shared the theory about constructs.

But there would be no easy answers.

"Now what we are we gonna do, Major?" Sweeney asked the question whilst he loaded the last pair of shells into his shotgun. "I mean, I don't want to be negative about this situation, you understand, but we're rapidly running out of options."

Willa did not have an answer, but before she could even speak, Doc interjected. "There's always that." She looked to where he was pointing and squinted up at the water tower, burned and listing but somehow still standing amidst the wreckage. "Unless we are gonna get all particular about the site of our last stand?"

The mob spilled around the corner, now pinning them between the two groups of clawing, empty-eyed monsters. The luxury of arguing about the situation was very neatly taken out of their hands.

"Fine. Make for the tower." Willa agreed, despite deep-down reservations. It was not much of a plan, but it was a plan and was all that they had.

By some twist of fortune, the ladder that ran up to the narrow platform at the top of the tower was still intact. Doc stopped at the foot of the ladder and snapped a few shots off at the pursuing mob. As Willa arrived, he made an over-exaggerated gesture with one hand. "Ladies first, Major Shaw," he said.

She didn't have any time to argue but treated the lawman to a withering glare as she scrambled up the ladder. She was closely followed by Sweeney, whose bigger frame meant that it took him considerably longer to make the climb. Doc was counting each precious second as the mob began heading in their direction. Once Sweeney was up, the lawman made his own way up the water tower, gasping into his mask as he pulled himself up the climb. His respirator was good, but over exertion was still a strain.

Sweeney leaned over the edge of the platform as he reached the top and shot a creature in the face as it struggled to work out the ladder below.

"Much obliged Sergeant Sweeney," Doc said to the soldier. "I suggest we best set that ladder free in case our shufflin' guests manage to fire up enough imagination between them to put it to use."

Sweeney nodded and after a few good kicks sent the ladder tumbling into the street. The mob swarmed around the base of the tower, pawing at the supporting legs, their empty eyes turned toward the platform above.

"So," Sweeney said, after a few moments. "Now what do we do?"

"I confess, Sergeant," said Doc, spreading his hands out helplessly, "I had not thought quite this far ahead."

Willa looked out over the ruined town and walked slowly around the rickety platform until she could see the Iron Horses. So close, and yet so very far away. Then she looked down at the horde. A few of them looked as though they were trying, unsuccessfully, to climb the wooden legs. It was a strange scene; it was as though they were acting on a half-remembered memory of climbing, but not quite firing the right parts of the brain to recall how to do it. She most definitely didn't have enough bullets left for all of them. By her calculations, between the three of them they barely had enough bullets left to deal with a quarter of their attackers. That, of course, was assuming they decided to stay dead after a single shot. Thus far, evidence did not point to that being the case.

"Well, this is a pretty mess we've gotten into." Her mutter went unheard and was directed at nobody in particular.

Then the tower suddenly lurched alarmingly to the left and pitched her over the side. She didn't even have time to shout out as she went.

Sweeney managed a horrified, "Major!" but only just managed to keep his feet as the tower lurched a second time. Somewhere below there was an ominous crack of wood giving way.

Doc peered over the edge of the platform to see the several knots of creatures clawing at the tower legs, the dead flesh of their fingers peeling back to the bone but doing nothing to halt their mindless determination. He fired several times into mob, emptying one pistol to little effect. Sweeney fired his last shell for just as little reward.

"You think she's gonna be OK?" Sweeney said as Doc got to his feet.

The lawman looked down at the throng but could see no sign of the Major and while the fall was not so terrible, certainly not likely to be fatal, what was waiting at the bottom most certainly was. But Sweeney was looking at him with such boundless optimism and hope in his face, that the lawman was forced to resort to the thing he did best.

Lie.

"Why, I'm sure she's just peachy. Even now, she is gonna be makin' good her escape. Mark my words, Sergeant, she will be back in two shakes of a lamb's tail an' damn me if she won't have the cavalry in tow."

There was a silence and then Sweeney grunted. "You're a terrible liar Doc Holliday."

"Why Mr. Sweeney, you wound me. Lyin' is my stock in trade."

Sweeney grunted again and returned his attention to the mob. "Well, I reckon that if I'm gonna go out, I ain't gonna go out clawed to death by whatever it is that those things are." He reached inside his uniform and produced a fat stick of dynamite that he held in front of him like a talisman. Doc's eyes gave away his startlement at this sudden revelation.

"I gotta ask. Why on this blessed Earth is it that you happen to have a stick of dynamite in your jacket, Sergeant Sweeney?" One eyebrow cocked quizzically as he asked the question.

"Army needs people who know how to blow things up. I know how to blow things up." The sergeant managed to sound bashfully sheepish about the whole thing. Under other circumstances, Doc might have found it endearing. "I've been saving it for the right occasion." He looked down, then back at Doc. "I'm thinking that there probably aren't many other opportunities going to present themselves to me that are as right as this one."

The lawman looked down at the mob and then back at Sweeney and nodded slowly.

"Well alright then." He checked the last remaining rounds in his second pistol then offered his hand. "Sergeant Sweeney, it has been an honour, and should we somehow manage to walk away from this absurd endeavour then I will *gladly* buy you a drink. Possibly two."

Sweeney smiled grimly before shaking the lawman's hand. "I'm gonna hold you to that Doc." He held the fuse to the hammer of Doc's pistol and waited. Doc gave the soldier one last, meaningful look and fired. The shot took the top of one of the creatures heads off and ignited the fuse with a flash. Sparks immediately began travelling hungrily toward the explosive.

The tower lurched again, and Sweeney lost his grip on the dynamite which bounced once and, just like Willa Shaw only moments earlier, tumbled over the edge of the platform.

For a long, terrible moment, nothing happened.

Then the world exploded.

Wood, dust, stone and body parts flew in all directions, billowing into a plume that reached into the sky. The tower, already compromised, toppled majestically into the street with a tremendous crash, spilling a deluge of sun-heated warm water into the hungry earth. The tiny platform shattered, sending Sweeney and Doc Holliday sprawling into the carnage, the latter's respirator being torn free and sent flying, disappearing into the debris. The lingering echo of the blast seemed to take a long time to soak into the empty Arizona sky, but the silence that followed once it did, was as deafening as the explosion had been.

Sweeney rolled a dead, unmoving body from on top of him, paused a moment to check it was not Doc – which it was not – and spat out a mouthful of dirty water. Then he sat up and looked around. Where the tower and the clamouring mob had been there was now nothing but a smoking ruin. All that remained of the tower legs were shattered stumps, thrusting upward like broken teeth, and the mob was a scattered mess of severed limbs and lifeless bodies. There was a wheezing cough to his right and the soldier reached for a shotgun that wasn't there.

Doc Holliday pulled himself from beneath the sodden flotsam, brushing water and splinters from a hat that had inexplicably remained on his head throughout the entire fracas. He looked over at Sweeney and gave him a sickly, but unmistakable crooked grin. "Well," he said hoarsely, "if it isn't Sergeant Sweeney. That was quite the ride, eh?"

Something else moved amidst the wreckage, something that shouldered broken wood and beams aside as it struggled from beneath the debris. Sweeney and Doc turned to watch with mounting horror as one of the unliving things dragged itself upright. It was missing an arm and its flesh was ragged and torn, but the dark veins beneath its skin writhed and pulsed with unnatural life. It jerked and spasmed as if palsied and its mouth opened wide, the jaw distending into a soundless, cavernous scream.

Doc instinctively reached for his guns but found the holsters empty while Sweeney seemed unable to tear his gaze away from the transformation taking place before him. The throbbing veins swelled and thrashed, filling with a deep, lambent crimson. The dead flesh expanded, ballooning on one side and filling the creature's intact arm until the bulging knuckles dragged on the dusty ground. Its skull distorted weirdly, the jaw sagged open into a vile, gaping maw and the lid of one eye peeled back as the grey orb filled with yellow and bulged out of its socket. With a cracking of bones, a twisted vestigial limb popped from the ragged shoulder and pawed at the air with idiot curiosity.

It let out a bubbling, keening cry and stumbled toward the two men, its flesh still growing and running like wax. It only got two steps when the insane wailing was eclipsed by a screaming, metallic roar.

The beast jerked and danced like a marionette as it was struck by a torrent of shells and Doc glanced over his shoulder to see the welcome sight of Willa Shaw sitting astride her Iron Horse. Smoking brass casings chugged from its weapons like rain and the high calibre shells tore chunks from the bloated creature. It staggered, wailed again and attempted to shield its face with its giant arm. Willa did not relent and continued to fire, the cannons first demolishing the offending limb and then obliterating what remained of its head. Then the monster exploded in a welter of flesh and red-black fluid that painted the street in every direction.

Silence fell, broken only by the tinkle of brass casings as they came to rest. Doc wiped a streak of gore from his eyes and treated Willa to his best smile. Then, in a strange echo of their original meeting, he spoke.

"Willa Shaw. Why ain't *you* a sight for sore eyes."

* * *

They found what remained of Zachariah King buried beneath dust and wood and it was Doc Holliday who dug him out, without being asked for assistance. He did not even offer; he just got on with the grisly task and recovered the body of the fallen soldier. When he was finally clear, the lawman covered the boy with his coat whilst he hunted around the town's remains for a shovel so he could give the kid a proper burial. All the while he had to pause, struggling for breath for without his respirator, he could barely manage to fill what was left of his lungs. The first search for his mask had proved futile, but he'd insisted on dealing with the burial of Zachariah.

Until now, none of them had spoken of what had occurred. The abused bodies and chunks of flesh were grisly and horrible, and Sweeney was sorting through the remains, seeing if there was anything at all that might answer some questions and hoping that he would locate the Doc's respirator.

Willa studied the young soldier's face. His death had bothered her greatly, in part because it was never easy to lose someone under your command, but also because she had made that harsh comment to him on arrival in this place to avoid speaking ill of the dead. And now he was one of them. Provenance had claimed at least *one* victim who had a name to put to him.

"He was a good kid," she observed. Sweeney glanced over at her.

"He was, ma'am. And he died fighting. That's the best most of us can hope for." It wasn't strictly true, and they both knew it, but they would honour his memory accordingly.

Doc re-appeared, a shovel in his hands. The wooden handle had splintered and broken, but it was serviceable enough. He nodded towards the body.

"Where d'you want him puttin'?"

"Just outside the town," she replied. She'd already given it some thought. "Where we left the Iron Horses. Softer ground there." Doc nodded and, heedless of the staining to his clothing, gathered the boy's body up in his arms. Sweeney stepped forward as though he would take up the burden, but Willa put out a hand to stop him.

"No," she murmured. "Let him do it. It's important to him. He never did like to be party to someone's death if he could've helped it."

The deputy's anger and rage after the battle had been directed at nobody but himself and he'd had to end the tirade when a coughing fit had rendered him next to useless. It made her wonder just what other horrors Henry John Holliday had been exposed to in the years they'd been apart and she found a new – grudging – level of respect for him.

"Are you alright, Major?" Sweeney's concern for her stemmed from the look of intense thought on her face. She glanced at him and smiled, but there was no heart in it.

"I'll be fine," she said. "Let's get Zachariah laid to rest and pitch up for the night. Patch up our own injuries, take a breath. Ain't a lot more we can do."

"What about if there are more of those... *things*?" He asked the question that had been on her mind and she shook her head.

"I think we'd know by now," she said. "Get the distinct feeling that we made enough noise to summon anything from miles around."

"I'll stand watch anyway," insisted Sweeney and Willa nodded.

"Good idea."

They continued working together in silence for a while, both sifting through the bits of body and broken buildings until Sweeney let out a crow of triumph, holding aloft the deputy's respirator. It was scratched and looked a little dented, but was otherwise whole. "I'll get it right to him," said the sergeant and Willa nodded. She didn't think she had the heart to deal with Doc right now.

Sweeney made his way over to where Doc had been working at digging a grave. He'd needed to stop, wearily sitting on the ground next to King's body, his body shuddering now and then when he coughed. Sweeney approached hesitantly.

"Take a break, Deputy Holliday," he said. "You look half-dead." He offered up the respirator and the young lawman looked up.

"I ain't dead. Not yet." He reached out, taking the device from Sweeney, gratitude plainly etched onto his thin face. The sergeant did his best not to let his gaze linger on the gauntness of the young man's appearance; the shadows beneath the eyes, the hollows in the cheeks and lips that were presently stained scarlet with blood coughed up from mangled lungs. Doc examined the respirator carefully, then sighed, clicking it back into place. He closed his eyes for a moment or two, silently willing it to work.

A tense moment passed, during which it seemed uncertain as to the continued functionality of the device, but then the light resumed its soft arterial glow and a cocktail of drugs and pure, precious oxygen was diffused directly into the lawman's respiratory tract. The relief was immediate, was immense and was very, very welcome. He nodded once, and his eyes opened again.

"I ain't dead yet," he repeated. "Just appears that some parts of me are eager to stop livin' before other parts are quite finished." Sweeney flashed a grin. He liked the self-deprecating style of the lawman, liked the man's moxie and readiness to put himself at risk for others. He reached over and took the shovel up. Doc looked like he might protest, but Sweeney shook his head.

"Let me," he said, simply and Doc, recognising a man who would not be swayed, nodded. Sweeney glanced over at a movement and pointed. "Well now," he said, and his tone was amused. "Looks like we got one more for dinner." Solomon Smith, who had fled the town at the emergence of the horrors was casually walking back in again as though he had been there for the entire time.

"That horse," he said, "is the strangest animal I ever did see."

He got to work.

* * *

The heat of the camp fire, its gentle glow and the welcome warmth it gave out was soothing and Willa Shaw allowed herself to drift into a light daydream. The sudden reappearance of Henry Holliday back in her life had thrown up a lot of feelings and memories she'd far rather not have thought about, but the most overwhelming images that came into her head were those of her dead husband. Doc had asked no further questions about her married name and she was not inclined to divulge any further information.

She had, as a direct result of the day's activities, suddenly realised just how much she missed her husband.

Their marriage had been solid. Jimmy and Willa Shaw were made for each other, everyone had said so. She had loved him to distraction and although they were only granted a handful of years together, they lived every moment to the full. After his death, her career was all that was left to her and she threw herself into it with grim focus. She became obstreperous, and more than a little reckless, but never insubordinate. She hadn't seen *this* man for… what would it be now? They'd parted company about six years previously. He would be just into his late twenties by her reckoning – already older than his diagnosis had predicted.

Such a short time, but so much has happened.

Water under the bridge, so the saying went. Holliday was a memory from another time, something best left forgotten and swept under a metaphorical rug. They had both been young, he particularly so, and most definitely foolish. They'd engaged in a liaison that had been as much a match of intellect as it had been physical attraction – and there had been plenty of that from both sides. It was bordering on scandalous – a Union soldier and an antebellum Southerner.

To look at him now; haggard, gaunt, half the man he'd been, it was hard to recall how he had been. But then, six years had aged her more than she might have liked to acknowledge, too. Time was rarely kind to any and she, at least, didn't have Doc's illness to contend with.

A log tumbled on the fire a cracking loudly, starting her out of her reverie. She realised that without intending to, she had been staring at the deputy for the past few minutes. She cursed inwardly, forcing her eyes downward.

The silence between them continued and it was eventually palpable and uncomfortable enough that even the ever dependable and stoic Joseph Sweeney got to his feet. He dusted down his uniform and shifted from one foot to the other.

"Well, I'm just about done in, major. But I'll go out on the perimeter. Take watch. Maybe you or the Deputy there could come relieve me when you're ready? In the meantime," He lowered his voice respectfully, "Stop worrying over Zach's death and get yourself some rest."

"Good job, Sweeney. Thank you." His concern was touching, but she suspected 'worrying over Zach's death' was going to be something that would keep her awake for several more nights to come.

"Yes, ma'am. Good night. Good night to you too, Deputy Holliday, sir."

The lawman flipped a lazy salute in the soldier's direction. "Take it easy, my friend. Sleep tight. Don't let anything that shouldn't bite you bite." The words were made that much more ominous by the mechanical wheeze of Doc's mask.

"Sure, I'll remember that." Sweeney's discomfort was obvious.

As he departed, his heavy tread grew quieter as he walked away, the dusty ground crunching beneath his booted feet. The noise ebbed and died, leaving the major and the lawman alone. *Properly* alone for the first time since they'd clashed wills in the scorching heat of high noon.

Like this, sitting opposite one another, their faces were both lit by the flames of the campfire. She took a moment to study the play of light and shadow on the harsh planes of the mask he wore. In this light, his hair glinted with the odd copper highlight, and it was so tousled, so untidy, that a long-forgotten part of her yearned to reach over and smarten him up. Right now, they were close enough that she could have done that – but there was no way she could start to cross the gulf, the yawning void that this silence put between them. A silence that teased the minutes into long, unbearable stretches of time that she was fairly certain would drive her mad.

On the far side of their makeshift camp, a big, dark shadow moved as Solomon Smith snorted his contempt for the spot in which he had chosen to bed down and got up. It distracted both Willa and Doc and they watched the stallion discontentedly wander for a while until he once more settled.

After another indeterminable length of time had passed, and the sound of the sleeping animal's heavy breathing had become just another noise in the background, there was a rustle. Doc Holliday turned from his deep contemplation of the fire and angled his head to one side as he considered her.

"So... are we gonna do this, then?"

Doc had broken first. Mentally, she felt a crow of triumph rush towards her lips, but she had long outgrown games of one-upmanship with Henry. *Keep the advantage, Willa. Don't give him the upper hand.* She chose to feign innocence, whilst knowing full well to what he referred.

"Do what, Hank?" She took a sip of the coffee in her mug, but it had long since gone cold. She pretended not to care.

"Please," he said, and this time, it was just ever-so-whiny and plaintive. "Call me Doc."

He reached up and with a *click*, unfastened the respirator. He took a gulp of air and inhaled deeply, relishing the pure air that sped into his diseased lungs. Whenever the apparatus came off, in those first few moments, his olfactory senses were heightened like they'd never been before he'd started wearing it. He closed his eyes and revelled in the pleasure of it all; the dry, gentle breeze that carried the scents of the Arizona night; the wood smoke from the fire, the leather of Solomon Smith's saddle against which he leaned, the metallic flavour of blood in his mouth that never seemed to go away...

He dug into the pocket of his coat and coughed into the kerchief he drew out. In the darkness, it was hard to tell, but the cloth that returned to his pocket came away smeared with scarlet. He cussed softly, then took a few moments to compose himself.

The major found that just as before, when he'd first arrived, she was once again disturbed by the sight of his naked face. His skin seemed too tight, stretched over the fine bones of his face and his pallor was nigh on alabaster white. A fine layer of sweat added to the look of illness that permeated every pore. Without the moustache she remembered, he looked so much younger. There were traces of stubble on his face, but no more.

If she tried hard enough, she could remember him. The handsome, vital young man he had been back when they'd met in Texas, but it was hard to piece those memories together and all but impossible to overlay the recalled face over the emaciated shell he had become. She was not sure whether to feel pity for him or not.

She thought of her eyepatch and whether he was curious about her own physical changes. But just like questions about her marriage, he said nothing.

"Alright," she said, reluctantly conceding this round to him. "Doc."

"Thank you, darlin'." There was a rasp in his natural voice that was filtered out by the mask; a suggestion that he spent too much time coughing. Once, Henry Holliday had loved to sing. Now, he'd be lucky to croak out a chorus. He spoke so quietly with the respirator removed that she had to strain to hear him. She broke the silence again.

"You aren't a practicing dentist now, though?"

He laughed. "Hell, no. You really think there's call for a dentist who coughs all the time? It does not make for steady work. It got so I was breakin' more crowns than fittin' 'em. Besides, this place is full of criminals needin' the law bringin' down on their heads. I got skill with my gun, an' the willingness to stand up for what loosely passes as right in these parts. Call goes up, I answer.." He leaned back against the saddle and looked up into the endless expanse of the night sky. "Man's gotta do his duty out here, otherwise, what do you have? Nothin', that's what. Usually it's Wyatt who gives me my orders, keeps me busy. This time, another lawman has me deputised. Leastways for now. An' he has largely given me freedom to roam. Bass Reeves. You hear of him?"

"Maybe." She didn't want to break the subject now he had brought it up. She chose not to laugh with him as he chuckled and her tone was curt, dismissive, aiming to sting and hurt. "So we've established that you don't want to give my teeth a check over. So tell me. What is it you *do* want to do?"

He let his hands drop into his lap and looked up at her, a half-smile on his face. "Y'ever hear of the phrase 'discussin' the elephant in the room'? Honey, there's a veritable *mammoth* right between us right now. If we are gonna work together on this thing, then we gotta work through this problem."

"This problem?" She leaned backwards and studied him. "Not my problem, *Doc*." She put an emphasis on the syllable, injecting as much disdain as she could possibly manage. He visibly winced. Score one point to Willa Shaw. "It was *never* my problem."

"Fine." He shrugged his shoulders. "You don't wanna sort it out? That's fine. But do me a favour, huh, darlin'? Get the hell off your high horse, 'cos if you don't, why, that fall is surely gonna hurt." His voice raised slightly as his temper began to fray. He'd spent a large part of the day caught up in this constant bickering match and it was wearing. The fight, coupled with the temporary loss of his respirator had been physically demanding, but dealing with Willa Shaw had drained his emotional reserves to their limit. He was exhausted, but too proud to acknowledge it. He took his hipflask out and knocked it back, savouring the burn of bourbon as it soothed the omnipresent pain in his chest.

Pride, so the preachers liked to remind him, was a sin (just another, he figured, to add to his ever-growing list) and these two, the major and the deputy, why, they both had it in spades. Sinners both, their paths to eternal damnation were assured. Fast-tracked to an eternity of suffering. The Express Train to Hell had become his mode of transport.

"Don't you dare presume to lecture me, Henry Holliday. You *left* me." Her hands clenched into fists of rage and he saw. He looked down at her balled hands and sighed softly. Even that was an effort without the mask, but he had wanted to have this conversation as naturally as he could manage. He wanted to be *himself*, not the half-machine. He spread his hands in a semi-mock surrender and shook his head.

"Is that true? Wouldn't you have left me anyway in the end? After the diagnosis? After it became clear I would be nothin' but a burden?" The accusation was not unfounded, but it didn't lessen the hurt of the words.

"I..." Damn him. That wasn't the *point*. "We'll never know, will we, because *you left me!*" She was far angrier about an act from her past than anything else she'd experienced in the past twenty-four hours.

The bar brawl. The sudden and forced re-acquaintance with a man she'd rather have forgotten. The mine filled with whatever the hell they'd been, and the death of young Zachariah King. She was fuming and Doc was an easy target. "You left me," she repeated and there was venom in the words.

"I was dyin', Willa."

"I wanted to *help* you!" The rage, the feelings of impotence and helplessness that had come when he had been given the terminal diagnosis all came flooding back, multiplied by the intensity of her current mood. He had been young, too young to receive such news. He ignored the earlier symptoms, denying the fact that his mother had died from the disease before him. *It's just a winter cough I can't shake off, darlin'.* She heard those words now as though he'd just spoken.

The disease had progressed faster than anybody could have anticipated and that doctor back in Fort Worth had told the young man gravely that he shouldn't start making any long-term plans.

Willa felt a second surge of pity for him, then remembered how much he hated being pitied. That, she expected, would not have changed. "We could have seen doctors..." Her hands were clenched so hard that her nails were biting into the skin of her palm and even as the words left her mouth, she realised the pointlessness of it all. Doc shook his head. One hand moved as though he would reach for her, but he reconsidered.

"And let us be honest now. The conclusion would have been the same. Why, thanks for givin' us every last penny of your money, my friend, but the prognosis is still the same. You are gonna die. Your time's measured in months, maybe. But hey! Don't you fret none! For another few bucks, we can keep you in laudanum 'til your time comes..."

"I wanted to help you." She interrupted the flow of self-directed bitterness, but the harshness of her tone had softened. Some of the anger began to flow out of her and she stared over the fire at him. Her fingers relaxed once more as she opened out her fists and the blood flowed back to her hands painfully.

"Nobody coulda done anythin', Willa."

"So you just left." She sneered at him. "You ran away." It was cruel, certainly and if she had been seeking to fell him with another cheap shot, she succeeded. He couldn't hold that look, eyepatch or not. Another silence fell, but this one was contemplative, not awkward. He sighed, softly, his thin shoulders drooping with the motion. Any fight he might have had left in him tonight seeped away.

"You can *not* run away from dyin', Willa. That kinda thing has a habit of followin' you." He picked up a stick and poked at the fire listlessly. It popped and crackled angrily at this sudden treatment, then flared into a stronger light. "But if it makes you feel better... yeah. You got it right. I tried to run away. I came out west. Some said the climate would be good for my condition. It helped, for a while. I even got a little better."

"You can't tell me that was because of clean living." When they'd parted ways, he'd already become overly fond of alcohol and she'd picked that lingering scent of liquor up on him earlier. He chuckled at her comment.

"No, ma'am. Nobody could ever accuse me of clean livin'. When you know each day on this good earth could well be your last, you may as well enjoy it. I smoke too much, I drink too much liquor. I spend all my hard earned money on Faro an five card pick up..." He threw the stick down on the fire and his eyes took on a shadowed, haunted look. "As for the bein' well thing... sadly, that did not last. I got *really* sick. Wyatt – Wyatt Earp. You heard of *him*, right?" When she nodded he barked out a laugh. "Yeah, figures. Mention Bass Reeves an' everyone's none the wiser. Mention Earp's name an' the room lights up. Everyone knows that son of a... well, we ain't speakin' right now. We got what you might call a *complicated* relationship."

"Your speciality."

"True enough." He gave her his smile, as crooked and charming as she remembered it. Without the moustache, without the respirator, the scar on his upper lip, something he'd acquired in childhood but which he never spoke about, was quite clear. He couldn't smile any other way if he wanted to.

Somewhere beyond the camp borders, an animal let out a feral howl. Both Doc and Willa's hands automatically went to their weapons, but relaxed when they realised there was no imminent threat. Doc had another drink and continued his tale. "Whatever I might think of Wyatt Earp at the moment, I cannot deny he saved my life. Him and some people he knows. Got me this." He held up the mask and turned it in the firelight. "It saved my life. *Earp* saved my life." The bitterness in his tone did not come close to expressing the anger he felt towards his friend. "I hate admittin' he's right. When you got pride as prickly as mine, Willa, ain't an easy task to swallow it."

'Really sick' had been his first true run-in with the grim reaper. He'd tasted death that night as his body rebelled and he all but choked to death on the blood frothing up from his ruined lungs. Delirium had taken him down and when he'd recovered, Earp had been sitting over him, grim-faced and speaking in half-riddles about debts and how it hadn't been Doc's time to die. That had been as far as the lawman would be drawn on the matter.

Somewhere in the world, Wyatt Earp was building a very long list of debts. Sometime in the future, people were going to come to collect. Doc had been a gambling man most of his adult life. He *knew* how that worked. But from what little he knew of the people with whom Earp had treated, he didn't think that breaking a limb as payment would suffice. The two men's relationship had suffered. Doc had been enraged that Earp saw fit to force this choice and Earp had not been able to express how he'd not been prepared to lose his friend. Willa shook her head and when she spoke, she pulled the deputy from his momentary reverie.

"I'd have come with you, if you'd asked me. You know that, right?" She was speaking more gently now, stepping down her attack. He took another long pull from his hipflask and scowled as he realised it was now empty.

"Sure I know it. Why d'you think I didn't ask you? You had your eyes on that career. What were we gonna do if I stayed? Settle down an' marry? Your family woulda loved that, huh? You takin' on a dyin' man five years younger than you? An' a Georgian to boot? Imagine the scandal." His blue eyes met hers and there was regret there, yes, but there was also resolve. "I said nothin', 'cos I did not want you to throw your life away on a dyin' man. Look at you now, darlin'. A Major, nonetheless. No, you were better off without me. An' we both know that is the truth of it."

"And now? Are you still a dying man? That mask, the RJ-contraption..."

"The fear of death follows from the fear of life. A man who lives fully is prepared to die at any time."

His response was eloquence itself and she tipped her head to one side. He smiled, a little sadly.

"Mark Twain. We are all dyin', Willa. I am just sittin' in a body that's more eager to win that particular race." He turned the mask over and over in his hands, long, slender fingers caressing its metallic surface thoughtfully. "It ain't a miracle cure. The consumption ain't gone, but this thing? It holds it at bay. Don't you be tellin' Wyatt this, but in a way, I am mighty grateful for it." He clipped it back into place.

"An' frankly, Willa, if holdin' death at arm's length is the best I got, I admit it. I will take it. This life I got ain't much, I know. I got my gun, my horse an' I got a purpose. An' I am not ready to let it go yet." He got to his feet, stretching out his lean frame, ironing out the knots in his shoulders and spine. "I am turnin' in. I will take the early mornin' watch. Tell your man Sweeney not to kick me too hard when he wakes me. I am a delicate specimen, y'know."

After he'd left her, she remained alone by the fire, revisiting old memories that maybe, just maybe were best left buried.

* * *

With Doc taking the early morning watch, Willa had been able to get a little more rest than usual and despite her constant misgivings about the lawman's presence, she was grateful for that. What she was not grateful for was the horse, presently snuffling at her ear and nudging her awake. She wished quite powerfully that he had stayed gone after he had fled from the fight yesterday.

"Can't you control your damned animal?" She sat up and made vague swatting motions with her hands. Solomon Smith whinnied and backed up, moving away from the major with what she suspected was a smug expression.

"Solomon Smith goes where he wants, darlin', ain't my place to tell him what he can an' cannot do." He patted the horse's neck. "Although sometimes, he does what he's told. C'mere, you lummox."

The big horse trotted over to the lawman and Doc reached up to pat its neck. "See?" He fumbled in the saddlebags and extracted a curry brush and began grooming dust out of the stallion's tangled mane.

Willa rolled her eyes and moved to the fire where a pot of coffee was steaming. She poured herself a cup, sipping with immense gratitude on the bitter liquid. Everything would improve after a coffee. Zachariah King would still be dead, but that was yesterday's tragedy. She walked away to find Sweeney, who was kneeling on the ground by his Iron Horse, checking it for damage.

Seeing her approach, the soldier immediately got to his feet and saluted. "Good morning, ma'am."

"Sweeney. Did you get any rest at all last night?"

"Lawman relieved me like he said he would. I had a couple of hours, but..." The shudder spoke volumes and Willa inclined her head in an understanding kind of a way. Her rest had not exactly been without nightmares either and neither wanted to be the first to admit it. Instead, she steered the subject towards the condition of the Iron Horses and found herself considering what they would do with the one that Zach had ridden. She sighed and sipped more at the coffee as her eyes wandered back to where Doc stood.

He was talking to the horse as he worked the brush across its body, his voice low and inaudible.

While she could make out no specific words, the tone was lilting and soothing, unmistakably gentle. As she watched, it struck her for the first time that Doc Holliday and Solomon Smith were complete polar opposites in terms of their physicality. The horse was huge, a prime example of his species: well-muscled, young, strong and full of bright vitality. His skin practically gleamed wherever Doc's brush touched it and the morning sunlight caught and glinted off his chestnut magnificence.

He held his head up high as though fully aware she was watching him and when he turned his head slightly to fix her with what she could only describe as a withering stare, she felt deeply uncomfortable and suddenly became enormously fascinated by the contents of her now-empty coffee mug. When she felt it was safe to look up, she did so and resumed her observation.

Compare the splendour of that animal to the man holding the brush. He was thin and sickly, that permanent film of sweat visible on the flesh beneath the mask. He relied on that thing just to keep him breathing. He was young – the only characteristic he and Solomon Smith shared – but the cruelty of his consumption had made him old before his time. His progress with the grooming was slower than it might have been had he been at full health.

They were so different, it seemed unlikely that they should be a partnership but it was evident from watching that Doc had a deep fondness for the animal, whilst the horse for his part simply stood, submitting to this grooming without a fuss demonstrating patience she'd not thought him capable of demonstrating.

A thought flickered into her mind and she struggled to dismiss it. It was, she fancied, as though

Solomon Smith *understood* the delicacy of the deputy's health and was making concession for it. He was *taking care*. An unexpected wave of sympathy for the man welled up in her stomach and she grimly forced it back under the rug of not giving a damn.

The thought was ridiculous. It was just a horse.

"There you go, Solomon Smith!" Doc tucked the brush back into the saddlebags and stepped back to admire his handiwork. "Y'all are set. We got a long journey ahead of us, an' some rough country to cover."

The horse harrumphed in response to the lawman's words and Willa moved a little closer. The man seemed oblivious to her presence and just carried on talking to the horse as though it were another person. "I know, Solomon Smith. I know." He patted the stallion's neck and tightened the last strap. "You ain't keen on long journeys, an' neither am I. But this is important. You understand?" Much to Willa's slightly cynical amusement, he actually held up a finger and wagged it at the horse. Solomon Smith leaned down and bit the hat clean off Doc's head.

"Hey! Enough! Give that back!" The lawman snatched his hat back from the horse's teeth. "Stop it. Now listen. You gotta stick with me an' not jus' up an' leave the way you usually do when we talk about this."

Almost as if hearing the lawman's words somehow gave Solomon Smith licence to wander off, the horse hesitated for a moment and did precisely that. He tossed his head in an impertinent manner at Doc and trotted off out of the gate of Provenance. Doc made a grab for the horse's reins as he went but was far too slow. He began following the horse, breaking into a run. He was swiftly outpaced, and the stallion disappeared in a cloud of dust, heading off at a full gallop as soon as he got out of the town.

"Your horse just left you," Willa observed helpfully from her vantage point. There was an opportunity to make a scathing addition to that comment. A phrase along the lines of 'and now you know how it feels', for example... but to be honest, she had no bite this morning. After watching the lawman and his horse, she was feeling mellow and the words he'd spoken last night, while they were hard to digest had not been unkind.

She was also acutely aware that he was shouldering the burden of guilt around Zach's death. She decided to cut him a break. She actually *smiled* at him, even though it annoyed her somewhere on a basic level. He looked at her, clearly feeling sorry for himself and tugged the chewed hat down on his head.

"Yeah." The deputy shook his head and unclipped his mask. He sipped at his own coffee – lacing it first with the contents of his hipflask which he'd evidently replenished. "He does that."

"He'll be back though, right?" The stallion had wandered off and back several times since they'd arrived, and Holiday hadn't shown any hint that he was bothered.

"Maybe. Depends what mood he is in."

"You know something? I think I hate your horse."

"Trust me, he's well aware of your feelings."

"Don't be stupid. He's... it's just a horse."

The deputy studied her for a moment after she said this, something unreadable in his expression. It was a peculiar exchange and she cut it short by turning her back on Doc and pouring herself another coffee, and one for Sweeney. He was grateful for it and thanked her, but she just shrugged it off. Her arm was stiff and half-numb from where she'd been lying on it and as she sat up, she was acutely aware that her hair had come loose from its braid in the night. Suddenly very conscious of how she looked, she attempted to impose some order on her presentation.

Doc stared after his vanished horse with a forlorn look in his eyes. Apart from one small bag which he was carrying over his shoulder, Solomon Smith had just left him without transport, without any changes of clothing, without maps and without companionship for the journey he had to make.

"I got a theory," he said, heading toward the fire to the coffee pot. He picked it up and discovered it was empty. He couldn't even offer to make any more as his bag of grounds had just galloped off to who-knew-where.

"Feel like sharing?"

"Sure." He reached into the pocket of his greatcoat and took out the vial of Lazarus. "I thought 'bout somethin' I said to you in passin' yesterday. About how vagrants an' travellers an' such wander through these boom towns an' nobody ever really knows where they are from one day to the next."

Willa thought back to the horrors from the mine. Their clothes had been mismatched and ragged, certainly, but until now she'd not considered the implications of that at all. Now she was starting to get an inkling of where Doc was going with his thoughts.

"Takes money to buy Lazarus, though, right?"

"That is right enough." Doc looked at the vial. "Either money, or someone handin' it out like I used to give peppermints to the kids. I have been lookin' into this stuff for a while now, learnin' what I can an' piecin' together where it is comin' from."

Willa's eyes narrowed slightly, and she decided, spontaneously, that she would throw caution to the four winds. "You ever hear of Annabelle Hamilton?"

The way Doc's eyes showed immediate recognition, she had her answer before the single word even left his lips.

"Yeah." She kept her face comparatively neutral and guarded, not wanting to elaborate until she knew the extent of his questions. "Why exactly do you have any sort of interest in her?" Rather tentatively, she reached for a reaction. "Has it got something to do with the Lazarus?" After all, that was part of the reason the Union had her name on their list.

"Not particularly. Truth be told, I have taken more of an interest in the activities of her brother. Goes by the name of Ben. He's apparently got himself in with a rum lot an' I'm curious to find out what's happenin'. Again, I am just followin' up on rumours. Nobody likes to tell us lawmen anything which is why local town gossip is always worth listenen' to. I had heard a rumour his sister had taken space in the sawmill. Somethin' about it seemed off to me, but I couldn't place it. Then the fire happened and I came by to check it out. Why do you ask this now?" Willa nodded and opened up to the deputy.

"Sources have theorised that she's got something to do with Lazarus. That she developed it. We obviously want to follow this up, because we don't want this stuff spreading through the ranks." Lazarus's known effects as a street narcotic were the dulling of the senses, an effect not dissimilar to that of laudanum, but much more potent. It was also extremely addictive. Secret service agents had been tracking its passage across the country for quite some time and intelligence had brought them here, to Arizona.

Maybe this hadn't been a wasted journey after all.

"Looks like we got somethin' else in common then, Major Shaw."

"Yes," she said. "Annabelle Hamilton. Now we have to find out if she *was* here and if so, where she was going. And naturally, what she's doing. And while we're at it…"

"…we can ask her where her brother is. Good thinkin'! We should head back to Howlin' Rock and ask around."

"It's a long walk. You'd better get started. Maybe you'll catch up to your horse on the way."

"Yeah. Sixty miles or so. I certainly cannot hope to make that journey in a hurry." His eyes were filled with hope, and she simply sipped her coffee. Doc tried a different tactic.

"S'pose I can sit out here. Wait to see if Solomon Smith decides to come back."

"I suppose you could, at that." She smiled, tipped out what was left of the coffee and began busying herself with putting things away. A brief side-glance granted her the satisfaction of seeing him visibly deflate, but that satisfaction was tinged with just a tiny bit of guilt.

"Right. Well, I had best start walkin', then."

"Best had. If you start now, you could be at Howling Rock by nightfall. Tomorrow. Maybe the next day. I'd go for that." She smiled properly, then. Her brightest, sweetest smile and he lit up enthusiastically.

"Hope is a fickle mistress," he murmured, then tipped his hat to her.

He waited for just a little longer, but no offers were forthcoming. He gathered up his meagre belongings and glanced up at her. "You stayin' put for a little longer, or you want me to put out the campfire?"

"We'll check things out a little more," she said. "Safe travels, Deputy Holliday." The man nodded, dejectedly, then stood, dusting down his coat. He peered out across the plains, but there was no horse.

"Well, been good seein' you again, Willa. Sweeney, take care of yourself an'... I'm sorry 'bout the kid." He lingered a moment, then hoisted his bag over his shoulder, reconnected his breathing apparatus, tipped his hat again and began walking.

"How long you going to give him, Major?"

"A few minutes longer. Ssh, Sweeney, you're ruining my moment."

He was still walking away and she waited a minute or so. Then she said, loud enough for him to hear, but maintaining a conversational tone, "or you could, you know, bite down on that spiky pride of yours and just ask if you could use the spare Iron Horse."

He stopped walking. "Y'know," he said, then turned round. "I had not even *thought* of that."

She'd been worrying about what to do with Zach's vehicle since she'd woken that morning and now, here was an opportunity to do a favour for someone in need – even if that someone *was* Doc Holliday – and to ensure the vehicle wasn't left out here for scavengers. As he walked back, Sweeney smirked at her. This was a side to his commanding officer he'd never seen, and he was quite taken with it. Doc reached them and his eyes were lit with enthusiasm.

"You done saved my hide, Willa Shaw," he said, then caught himself. "Major."

"You fought well yesterday. Zach's death wasn't your fault. No, don't look at me like that and shut up before you speak. I know you're wading around in a pool of guilt right now, but don't. None of us are fools. We all know what we've signed up for.

He knew the risks. We *all* know the risks. The 'Horse is yours until such time as you can turn it in at a Union camp. You ridden one before?"

"Sure have. For local trips though, I prefer Solomon Smith."

"What about if your horse comes back?"

"Oh, he will find me, he always does." Doc dropped his satchel into the panniers on the back of the Iron Horse and scrambled onto it. It somehow suited him less than the stallion, but his posture was good, and it was clear that he knew what he was doing. Reluctantly she stepped back.

"On your promise now, Doc."

It was the first time she'd used the name without hesitating whilst talking to him and he glanced up at her, surprised. Then those blue eyes of his softened and she knew, although the mask hid it from her, that he was smiling.

"Cross my heart. I would add 'hope to die', but I imagine you would like that too much."

"We'll take it easy for a few miles so you get the hang of it. You take care of that vehicle, you hear me?"

"Darlin'," he said, mischievously. "It's just a 'Horse."

Sarah Cawkwell

INTERLUDE

Extract from 'Unlikely Tales'

The darkest swamps of Louisiana are home to some unlikely creatures. Alligators, with jaws that can take a man's limb clean off. Biting mosquitoes that will fill your blood with poison soon as look at you. And worse still are *them*. Those who practice an old and ancient evil that only ever gets spoken about in whispers. Nobody trusts them.

Legends claim these folks strike deals and bargains with the helpless and the innocent, but that there is also good that they do. They – most of them are women, or so the rumours say – often act as midwives to those who can't get no succour and help from anyone else. Unwed ladies and such-like. Because out in the swamps of New Orleans, there isn't no sense of decorum, no sir.

So runs the tale of one lady, Constance Lacroix-Layman whose husband died serving the Confederate army in the Ore War. Why, that girl was cut to a thousand pieces on the death of her beloved husband, Robert Layman, and she couldn't get no sleep. She stopped eating and turned instead to drinking for comfort. Her nightmares plagued her even when she was not resting. Rage took hold of her and would not let her grieve for the man she'd loved. She took poorly because of it and it took her house servant, Jenny, to point her to the lady who could help her.

Her name was Mama Marie, and that was all Constance knew. Nobody knew how old she was and there weren't nobody going to ask her. Jenny made the arrangements for Constance to meet with her and that was that. She was going into those swamps whether she liked it or not and was she ever frightened? Of course, she was frightened. Constance was a town girl, born and raised, and as she made her way through those dark, spooky pathways, pitch black as tar even at midday, why, she was deeply frightened.

"Don't you worry none, Miss Constance," Jenny reassured her. "Ain't nothing for you to take fright at. Mama Marie, she see you right. She help you get the sleep you need. She help you with that pain you got in your heart."

She lived out from the swamp paths, in a bayou in the south side that was accessible only by stepping very carefully on rocks. Jenny leaped like a goat, nimble as you like, from stone to stone while Constance wobbled and whimpered her way across. She was led out to a ramshackle old wooden shack where Mama Marie lived and she forgot, for the tiniest moment, her fears. The shack was barely standing, the swamp cypresses beside it indicating a strong prevailing wind that should have taken it to pieces long since.

"Mama, it's Jenny. I done brought that lady I tell you about." The house servant knocked thrice on the door – no more, no less, traditions have to be upheld – and a voice from within called out a vague word of greeting. Then Connie, scared as ever she had been, was led inside. The woman within was half-hidden in the shadows and sat on a huge chair that was more akin to a throne than it was to anything else. High-backed and decorated with animal pelts, there were pouches of herbs hanging from it like decorations. When Constance entered the hut, her eyes began to water slightly from the smell of whatever herb was burning over a fire in the corner. It filled the air with a sweet scent that left her feeling a little light-headed – but then a week of being drunk and eating next to nothing had that effect anyway.

"Sit you down, girl, an' let Marie take a look at you." The woman removed the pipe from her mouth, the scent of the tobacco smoke wafting from her lips as she spoke and adding to the odour of the shack.

It was hard to resist the words. The woman had some sort of strange power and Constance thought on that as she sank down on a comfortable pile of cushions and blankets opposite the woman. The poor girl suddenly felt tired. Weary and old before her time and her posture slumped under this strange woman's scrutiny. She felt tears fill her eyes and looked down at the floor as they overflowed and dripped to the floor.

"Poor chile. It hurt bad, don't it?" Marie got down from her enormous chair and moved across the room, her body graceful and lithe, her movements fluid and delicate. She got to her knees in front of the young widow and held her close. Constance could only nod and sob into her shoulder, grateful for this very human contact that she had been denied through estrangement from both her own and Robert's families.

"What you need in your life is a chance to start over, girl. You'll know your Bible stories well enough, I'll wager. Tell me, darlin', what you know of the tale of Lazarus, risin' from the dead."

It was a shame Constance was thus distracted, for had she but paid attention, she might have realised that the shadows playing on the wall behind Mama Marie in the flickering light weren't what she might have thought to see.

No, they hinted at something entirely more terrifying. And if only Constance Lacroix-Laymen knew in that moment what she found out to her great cost later, she'd never have gone into the swamp. And she would have understood, with great clarity, the significance of the question of Lazarus.

PART TWO – THE MIDDLE GAME

The train rattled through the Arizona countryside, but she was not in the slightest bit interested in viewing the scenery as she went. Frankly, she'd had quite enough of the Arizona Territory for now. In a few short hours, she would be in Utah, where the people were infinitely more civilised than those she had just left behind in the *pathetic* little town of Provenance.

Lady Annabelle Hamilton idly waved the antique lace fan that she took everywhere with her. It mostly served to waft the hot air around and resulted in making her even more uncomfortable than she had been to begin with. She did not like the climate this far west, but the information that had brought her out here had been sound. She'd been promised plenty of subjects, plenty of pond-scum who would take up the offer of Lazarus and that she'd found to be quite accurate.

Nonetheless, she was a Georgian by birth and while she was used to sultry, humid days in the summertime, nothing had prepared her for the relentless dry heat of the Arizona deserts or the primitive lifestyle existence on the frontier had forced upon her. She yearned, more than anything else, for a long, cool bath.

Provenance had gone up in flames, taking much of her hard work with it and yet she was unable to find it in her to care one iota about it. Incineration was the best thing that could have happened to the place. Indeed, it had probably improved its appearance radically.

Irritated, she closed her fan with a loud snap that made the other passenger in her compartment, an elderly fellow with long, white handlebar moustaches, jump bolt upright. He looked over at Annabelle and his eyebrows knitted together in disapproval at her interruption of his precious afternoon nap. He could feel his gaze take her in. The long dress, the perfect makeup and then the elegant mechanical arm she had in place of her left limb. While such augmentation was not uncommon in the world these days, to see it so brazenly displayed on a lady of refinement was unusual. But her traveling companion had focussed on the steel of her limb, not realising it was nothing compared to the steel in her mind and soul.

She looked back at him.

Nobody could hold Annabelle Hamilton's gaze for long. There was something bewitching about her eyes. The dark green irises were banded by a ring of amber, almost copper and the effect was at one and the same time haunting and compelling. She was quite beautiful, of that there was no question, but those who looked into those intense eyes for too long found themselves made deeply uncomfortable.

She gave the old boy his due: he managed a full three seconds before he picked up his newspaper with a loud *harrumph* and hid behind it. The game had been over too quickly and all too soon, the familiar sense of boredom settled in. She turned to look out of the window for a moment, but it was still more of the same. In that instant, she hated the frontier with a passion.

Several more minutes passed and, extracting an exquisitely beautiful timepiece from her bag, she realised that she still had hours to go until Salt Lake City. She pouted prettily and catching a brief glimpse of her doll-like reflection in the glass of the train's window, preened for a moment. She *did* look marvellous today. That shade of cornflower blue was her best colour, no doubt about it, but so rarely worn. A shame that the

Union had ruined most such shades for her with their association with the colour.

She had mastered the game of self-adulation as a child in defence against parents for whom nothing she ever did was good enough. *This is why we don't allow you to choose your own clothes. That dress is* quite *the wrong cut for you. Your hair is out of place. See, but don't be heard.* Lacking praise where she sought it, she simply awarded it to herself. But, as it always did, the game palled after a while and she snapped open the fan again, lazily waving it as she contemplated. This would not do, it would not do at all. She needed some company. Some intellect. Someone to flatter her outrageously. Fortunately, she had someone like that close at hand.

"Lieutenant." She lifted her gentle, fluting voice with its lazy Georgia drawl. "Lieutenant Mackeye, would ya come in here?"

The man who entered the compartment was clad in a grey uniform, spotless and neat as a pin. His long hair and moustaches were well-groomed and perfect in every way. He bore his first lieutenant's stripes with evident pride. The old man lowered his newspaper momentarily and studied the newcomer with one eyebrow raised archly. It was rare to see anybody sporting a uniform that was not one belonging to the Union and to see a Confederate Officer state his allegiance so openly was nothing short of shocking.

"Ma'am." Mackeye snapped the smartest of salutes and clicked his heels together efficiently. Lady Annabelle tipped her head on one side at her aide.

"I'm bored, Lieutenant," she said. "An' thirsty. Get me a glass of water, would ya? An' I mean the proper stuff, out of our own supply. None of that vile stuff they call drinkable in these parts. That'd be darlin' of ya. Thank ya."

Despite the lack of 'please', her manners and graceful style were undeniable. Mackeye saluted again and spun on his heel. Lady Annabelle glanced over at the old man again and his paper raised up very quickly.

She smirked.

Mackeye returned in short order with a glass of clear, pure water. He'd even had the kindest of thoughts and popped in a slice of lemon for her. Her smile was so broad it threatened to split her face in two.

"Well, ain't *ya'll* the thoughtful one today?" She waved vaguely at the seat opposite. "Sit down, Lieutenant, all that standin' around is makin' me tired. Sit down. Keep me company for a while."

"It'd be my pleasure, ma'am." Mackeye was an Alabama man, so stiff and upright that you'd be forgiven for thinking he had a steel bar instead of a spine. He sat opposite her, ramrod straight and turned to look out of the window. His slight sneer suggested that he felt much the same way about it that she did. He turned around again and relaxed by the tiniest of amounts. She fanned herself for a moment or two, sipping on the lemon water and decided to treat Mackeye to a little less aloofness. He *was* a very dear man in his own way after all, and his loyalty was not to be questioned.

"This trip has been..." She hunted around for a suitable word and settled on "...irksome, Lieutenant. Frustratin' to say the least. Things were goin' so well an' then that fire happened. All that work. All that precious *research*."

"We were lucky to get you out of that place safely, ma'am," he said. "But I have to admit, I don't think I'm going to miss the place." That was not a complete truth on the Lieutenant's part: there were more Southern sympathisers in the western States than you might have thought and he his own conversations with various locals had not been entirely unproductive. As her main go-between, Mackeye's actions in various saloons and the seemingly endless mining camps that had sprung up along the silver trails of Arizona, his task had been many-fold. He'd enticed and provided those who showed interest with the Lazarus. He had brought them, with rumours of wealth and promises of easy fortune, to Provenance. And it had been Ross Mackeye who had ensured Lady Hamilton's safety when the fire had broken out.

On the whole though, he *really* wasn't going to miss the territories either.

"We were doin' good works, Lieutenant, an' I am most vexed by the way things turned out. Most vexed indeed." She fluttered the fan and pressed the glass up against her cheek as a means of cooling herself down. "I was ready to move onto phase two an'... yes? Can I help ya, sir?"

The last was directed at the elderly gentleman who was making a poor show of pretending not to listen. He looked uncomfortable at being put on the spot and fidgeted in his seat. Her eyes continued to fix on him and even the Lieutenant swivelled round to stare.

"No, ma'am, I'm right sorry." He squirmed under that stare, and she revelled in it for a moment or two.

Her smile was sweetness and light and she cocked her head onto one side. "There's plenty of space in the next carriage, y'all might be more comfortable if ya head through there. Lieutenant Mackeye, maybe ya would help that *nice* man with his bags an' take him through next door?"

"My pleasure, ma'am." Mackeye got to his feet, smoothed out the front of his uniform and indicated to the poor man, who by now was slack-jawed in disbelief that he should get up and leave. The gentleman found a shred of dignity and began to protest that it was a public train and he could sit where he wanted, but it was to no avail. Mackeye picked up his bag and waited patiently.

"*So* lovely meetin' ya," said Lady Hamilton, shining her most glorious and benevolent light on him. "Enjoy the rest of the trip. Bye-bye now." She waved, a dainty little gesture that contained not one shred of sincerity. No longer able to avoid the inevitable, the elderly man got to his feet, and muttering the entire way, was led from the carriage. Lady Hamilton watched him go, the rictus smile fixed to her face.

Mackeye returned in due course and at a gesture from his mistress, drove home the bolt that separated the two cars.

"I can't believe they allow people like me to ride the train with people like *that*," she complained. "Ain't no good ever came from such things." The pout reached her lips again and Mackeye slid back into his seat.

"I'm sure you're right, ma'am," said the Lieutenant mildly. He was used to her displays of blatant snobbery and thought nothing of them. She was landed gentry. It was her right to act in a superior manner to those around her, because she was, in fact, superior. He accepted it with military stoicism. "Still, he's gone, now."

"Good." She drained the last of the water from her glass and shook her head when the officer made to stand, clearly intending to fetch her another. "No, I'm fine. Where were we?"

"Provenance, ma'am."

"Yes! *Aren't* you clever?" She tapped him lightly with her fan and let out a single, silvery laugh that absolutely broke his heart. "Those constructs were provin' to be *quite* the advance for the drug. Do ya think we shoulda stayed around to see what happened?"

"It was too dangerous. I swore to protect you."

Their eyes met for a moment and, if as-yet unwritten – certainly unproven – theories about parallel universe were true, a million different versions of Annabelle and Ross seized the day. They *carped* that *diem* completely and lived out their lives in peaceful harmony. This was not one of those universes. She looked out of the window again and the moment, the chance, the *opportunity* was gone.

"Probably all burned down, and those constructs were rendered useless, anyway. So sad. I *so* wanted to see the effects of long-term usage of Lazarus... ah, well." She sighed, theatrically and flicked the fan open once more, resuming the mechanical movement that kept her cool in this sticky heat. "Let's talk instead about what happens when we get to Salt Lake City." All the pettishness had gone now that there was nobody else present and the sharp, intelligent woman that Ross Mackeye had become accustomed to emerged once more. She waved a hand imperiously. "Read me Benjamin's wire again."

Mackeye withdrew the telegram from the pocket of his jacket and smoothed it out. As these things were measured, it must have been an expensive communication.

RECEIVED YOUR SPECIFICATIONS STOP INTRIGUED
STOP HAVE PROTOTYPE READY FOR YOU TO TEST
STOP SALT LAKE CITY, UTAH TERRITORY STOP BE
GOOD TO SEE YOU STOP BEN

"Our first task," said Lady Hamilton, obviously meaning the Lieutenant's first task, "after ya find me a *nice* lodgin' place, preferably with bathin' facilities, will be to track Benjamin down. It's all very well him givin' us a destination, but an address would've been handy." She clicked her tongue against the roof of her mouth. She had not seen her brother now for some time, but they had remained in touch. A year or so previously, their paths had diverged, their loyalties had conflicted and despite their great love for each other, the Hamilton twins had separated for the first time.

"I am sure that he has his reasons for secrecy, ma'am." Mackeye, ever placating, folded the telegram back up and dropped it into his pocket. "I took the initiative and sent word ahead to one in my former unit who I know has settled in the Salt Lake City. If fortune favours us, then we will already have leads. And I have already arranged a hotel room for you in a fine establishment." He had clearly thought ahead to the next stage of their journey. He knew her well enough to anticipate her needs and had delivered. Like he always did.

"I love ya, Lieutenant," she said, beaming at him. "Always so *organised.* I don't know what I'd do without ya." She gave him a dazzling, sunshine smile and resumed fanning herself. The gesture meant that she missed the wistful expression that came across the officer's face. He smoothed it away before she lowered the fan again and noticed.

First Lieutenant Ross Mackeye's life was to serve; it had *always* been to serve. When he'd joined the army, he'd done so to defend a way of life he believed in. He had struggled to get to the rank of Lieutenant. He'd not been born into privilege like so many other officers, no. He had earned his rank through hard work and heroism beyond the call of duty. He was fearless in battle: cool-headed and capable. He was bright and sharp, able to think his way out of a crisis when others would resort to violence and when he had met Lady Annabelle Hamilton, three years previously, he knew that he had found the love of his life. Life in the army and his career had always taken precedent over marriage, but things were changing as he sped through his thirties, heading rapidly towards what could be considered middle age.

Unfortunately, Lady Annabelle had not noticed the officer's ardour and when she had appointed him to serve her as a personal aide and *de facto* bodyguard, he had hoped that she might finally become aware. Of course, she was some ten years his junior, but that was a normal age difference among the young ladies of the south. They looked for older, more experienced men to protect them. Even if those older men hadn't been born into the same level of privilege as them. His background was not a bad one. He was a good, eligible option for marriage.

In that duty, Mackeye was bound. In that duty, he found a strange satisfaction. And in that duty, he found himself incapable of expressing his feelings. This bold, brave officer who had fought the enemies of the south, sometimes single-handedly, in terrible battles found that he simply could not tell this Southern belle how he felt. It was not, of course, the gentlemanly thing to do and propriety was a gift that was fast dying out.

He'd accepted his lot in the end, of course, resigning himself to the fact that she would never notice him, and threw himself into his new role with great gusto.

Those early yearnings never truly went away, though.

"I do my best, ma'am," he said and the faintest of smiles lifted his moustaches upward. He had learned to compartmentalise his feelings for Lady Annabelle. He hoped that time would see an end to them.

* * *

"Have there been more dreams, Stone Fur?"

The question was simple and straightforward enough but the answer dizzyingly complex and convoluted. The young spirit priest looked at Loud Thunder.

"Yes," he said, in his soft, quiet voice.

"And yet you barely sleep. You have not eaten in two days. How do you feel this will help your people? You should sleep now, my brother. I will guard your repose." The older warrior would clearly not take 'no' for an answer and fully entered the tipi, settling himself down in front of Stone Fur's cold hearth. He busied himself by laying a fire and looked up only once. He waved a hand at Stone Fur.

"You sleep now."

Since the night of the powerful, heart-stopping visions that had terrified him so much, he had been spiralling in a loop of sleeplessness and anxiety. Too afraid to fall asleep in case he witnessed them again, too tired to concentrate on the matters at hand. This, he knew, was Loud Thunder's attempt at an intervention.

"I am not tired," he lied. Loud Thunder chuckled.

"The circles beneath your eyes make a lie of your words. You will sleep, now. I told you I would guard your rest and I will do so. The people need your services, and your weariness robs them of you. He would not be pleased."

He. Loud Thunder meant Curved Bear Claw, whose death Stone Fur was still struggling to reconcile. The words hit their target and the spirit priest curled his fingers briefly into fists before relaxing. He bit back an uncharacteristically sharp retort that rushed angrily to his lips and with a heavy, long-suffering sigh, he curled up, allowing his eyes to close. Loud Thunder did not mean to wound with his words but wound they did.

It was an exercise in futility. He could hear Loud Thunder as the older man worked on building the fire. He heard the strike of flint and tinder and that was the last thing he remembered before exhaustion took a tight hold of him, dragging him under the surface of sleep and into the ethereal world of unlikely dreams and visions which had been plaguing him for so many days now.

There was darkness. Then there was light. The two states flickered between one another as though an electrical storm rampaged across the desert at night, each forked crackle of lightning outlining everything for the blink of an eye. Such weather was considered sacred to the Warrior Nation. It was a time of deep magic that nobody understood but everyone yearned to harness. The People knew that there was inherent power in lightning. They just did not know what it was.

Through the scene, Stone Fur walked or at least, his spirit walked. He moved behind the figure outlined in rippling blue fire that he recognised as himself. The shape shifted frequently from human to something else; something he vaguely recognised but which his confused thoughts would not allow him to acknowledge.

"Stone Fur."

The sound of the voice that he loved and missed so much brought the sting of tears to his eyes. Momentarily, he knew wonder. I dream, and yet grief still touches me, falling like beads from a torn necklace. Where his tears fell, tiny flowers bloomed from the barren ground.

"Stone Fur. My son."

Curved Bear Claw. His mentor. His father-figure. The words seemed to come to him from all places and from no places. He yearned for the comfort of the old man's wisdom, the reassurance of a friendly hand to the shoulder, but it was not real. He knew the vision for what it was. Yet he reached for the formless voice, and another figure shimmered into being; intangible in the flickering gloom, a scrap of shadow in the monochrome strobe of the lightning. Stone Fur's fingers closed on nothing but air and the frustration was deep.

"Curved Bear Claw, my world is darkness." He thought he spoke the words aloud, but his dream-form remained silent. Instead, the hazy image of himself took on texture and substance and its corona of azure fire danced as if it were animated with life itself. Weird, scattered shadows cavorted around him, curling into half-recognised and half-seen images of warriors, animals and soaring birds. Thunder boomed, clear, crisp and imminent "I do not understand what is happening to me." Despite the strangeness of the translation of his words to dream-form, he knew he must seem petulant, like the child he had once been.

When the reply came, it was thin and sighing, the growl of a distant storm or wind through tall grass. Stone Fur had never known Curved Bear Claw to seem so frail, even at the end of his days.

"The earth lies wounded, my boy, and corruption has seeped into the wounds. A corruption that

works to poison it further." Stone Fur moved toward the disembodied voice. A ray of crepuscular light pierced the storm and brought sudden, shocking life to the formerly empty plain. Grasses, tall and rippling in a phantom wind. Trees; chestnut, maple, ash. They flowed and ran together like a painting of living oils. Stone Fur's shadowed dream-form brightened, warmed by the velvet tones, the deep rich umber that filled the air when it spoke, punctuated by other colours of the Earth; hazels and dapple-greys, the rich blue of the sky, the sharp yellow of an eagle's curved beak. He reached the pool of shifting sunlight, passing through a cloud of iridescent butterflies that coiled around him before fluttering out of sight in a dazzling display of colour. The dancing shadows that had surrounded him retreated and left their abstract life.

Stone Fur heard the words and while he could not fully understand, a deep grief and yearning filled his heart with a terrible pain, an awful sorry. "All that our People stand for is in danger of falling into darkness, a darkness that is poison to all that it touches. But also, to light... to a terrible, scouring light that not even the deepest places of the earth can hide from. These are powers beyond care. Powers beyond our ways to understand. They take. They consume. They give nothing back. Life, Stone Fur, is balance. Darkness and light must exist in harmony in a way that only the People can truly appreciate. As you truly know."

As the ephemeral voice of Curved Bear Claw sighed and whispered, the flowing patch of vibrant life first blackened into a grotesque parody of nature and then burned away to ashes once again leaving an empty, barren plain.

"Curved Bear Claw, please. I... I cannot manage riddles and visions any longer. My mind is lost. I

fear the madness comes for me. I am afraid. So afraid."

The sky turns blood-red and taints the lightning. Red. Even in nature, the hue is the colour of danger.

"You are right to fear, Stone Fur." Curved Bear Claw's voice, so stern, so stiff in life was beginning to fade, as though the impossible gulf between the two was growing greater. It was a voice filled with equal parts instruction and compassion and Stone Fur's tears streamed from his fire-limned eyes, trickling unchecked down his face. *"The darkness comes for me, like a tide of claws and wings and razored feathers. It is cold. Cold like ice, sharp as a blade and hungry as a wild bear. I am lost, my son. Lost. But all that we know might yet be saved."*

"What do you..." Stone Fur's train of thought stopped dead in its tracks, and he realised in a pounding heartbeat that he knew exactly what it was that the spirit of Curved Bear Claw was saying. *"I have to wake up now, don't I?"* He hated the thought. He wanted to stay here, in this beautiful, terrible, shifting landscape with the presence and security of his mentor. But that presence was a ghost of a whisper now, fading and leaving nothing but an aching sense of terrible loss and fear. It was a sense that grounded him firmly back to the real world; a binding tie that only death would sever. A world to which he knew he had to return. *"I have to wake up."*

"You do." Stone Fur reached once more for the dissolving tableau of colour, reaching for a reassuring touch, but his hand met nothing but air. *"Wake up, boy."*

"Stone Fur. Wake, up, boy."

The transition was seamless; from Curved Bear Claw's kindness and benevolence to Loud Thunder shaking him on the shoulder. The young Spirit Priest surfaced into consciousness groggily and blinked at the big elder.

"You weep, Spirit Priest. I thought to put an end to your sorrow by waking you. Forgive me if this was poor judgement on my part."

"No, no, it is good, Loud Thunder." Stone Fur sat up and rubbed at his eyes. The light outside had faded to a clear dusk, with the first stars of the night just visible in the night sky. He had slept for perhaps two or three hours. It surprised him; the meeting with Curved Bear Claw on the spirit planes had felt much longer.

Curved Bear Claw.

The Spirit Priest moved from half-asleep to fully awake before Loud Thunder could even take a hand from his shoulder. He rose to his feet and a look of grim determination affixed itself to his face.

"We need to go to the Hollow of Sighs," he said. "Curved Bear Claw's eternity may depend on it."

Such was his quiet intensity that Loud Thunder didn't question Stone Fur's words. He simply nodded. "Then that," he said, "is where we will go."

* * *

Willa and her small group arrived back at Howling Rock a little over an hour after departing Provenance, the deputy looking around eagerly for any sign of his horse. His optimism and sense of insistent loyalty was not rewarded and the look of disappointment in his eyes came close to inducing sympathy in Willa Shaw. They brought the Iron Horses to a stop beside the saloon that they had left only the previous morning. Had it been only a day? Truly? So much had happened in such a short space of time and she knew that she was still processing the horrors. She shook off the sense of grief that threatened at the edges of awareness and focused on the present.

"Plans," she said, snapping her fingers at both Sweeney and Doc. The sergeant did not so much as blink; he was used to this approach from his commanding officer, but Doc's eyes grew wide with surprise as her fingers clicked in his face. He put out a hand to brush her arm aside and she glowered at him. They held the pose for two, maybe three seconds and she conceded, dropping her arm. He nodded.

"There are a handful of refugees from Provenance still in town," said Doc, dismounting first. "This was the closest town, so many of 'em came straight here. Probably be sensible to ask around, see if we can figure out if Hamilton was there or not, an' if so..."

"...where she is now." Willa finished his sentence and nodded. "I need to get a telegram to the barracks. Report in. How about I head over and do that and you and Sergeant Sweeney work together on finding out what you can?"

"Seems good enough." The deputy shrugged his bony shoulders, a gesture his thin frame was well suited for. "As long as you say please."

Willa's head whipped round at the sound of a daring snort of laughter from Sweeney and he instantly fell silent. She narrowed her eyes. She did not appreciate being made fun of and yet that was precisely what was occurring her. She spun on her heel and marched off toward the post office on the edge of town.

Sweeney pulled down his bandana and took a breath. It was like inhaling the sun directly. The Arizona afternoon was still, with barely a zephyr to stir the air. It hit the back of his throat and made him cough briefly.

He glanced over at the deputy who was not struggling with the ambient air at all. He supposed the respirator did most of the work for him. Doc Holliday was watching Willa Shaw as she strode purposefully down the street. Sergeant Sweeney knew the look, but he opted not to comment on it. Instead, he took a tactful approach.

"Well then. Where should we start, deputy?"

Doc's eyes lingered on Willa for a moment longer, then he glanced at Sweeney. He studied the sign outside the *Whistle Stop* saloon with undisguised longing in his eyes. Then his gaze shifted next door to the boarding house where some of the refugees had been put up. "There," he said, pointing at the latter. "Gonna stop by the general store first. Pick up a daily paper. Might be something in there that could be useful. Hamilton's pretty well known, so if she has shown her face anywhere, it would get reported. Also..." Here, he became visibly sheepish. "*Unlikely Tales.*"

Sweeney burst out laughing. "I didn't have you pegged as someone who enjoyed that terrible fiction stuff!" Doc shrugged one shoulder.

"Everyone needs an escape from cruel reality," he said, cheerfully. "And that is how I get mine. There's a great story runnin' right now an' I am lookin' forward to seein' exactly how it plays out. All about New Orleans..." In his Georgia drawl, it came out as *Nawlins*. He quelled his enthusiasm sheepishly. "Well, there is readin' those stories and liquor of course, but even I am prepared to concede that the hour is way too early to start hittin' the tables. I'll leave it another thirty minutes at least." He winked. "Let's go get the papers."

A trawl through the daily news sheets brought them no joy whatsoever and after Doc had folded up that week's edition of *Unlikely Tales* and put it securely in an inside pocket for perusal later, they made their way back across the street to the boarding house. There was no sign of the major, but then it could often be a lengthy process to send a telegram, especially when the queue sometimes stretched out the door.

"Why, sure I can point you in the right direction, darlin'," said the housekeeper of the establishment, a cheerful looking woman in her forties. She might have been pretty, once, but a hard-working life and time had eroded away the maiden's beauty. Still, her eyes were bright and intelligent, and when she smiled – which she did frequently – her cheeks dimpled in a most attractive manner.

Her accent was not local and again, Sweeney marvelled at the mix of people who had gravitated away from their homes to start new lives here. Despite being a Union man, he was not unsympathetic to the fact that a lot of those migrants were originally from the Southern states that had been hardest hit during the Civil War. "Hywel Rhys. Owned the sawmill there. Such a lovely man. He's still here, sortin' out all sorts of paperwork. Has his own booth set aside in the saloon."

"Thank you kindly, ma'am." Doc tipped his hat to her courteously, taking her hand in both of his. Had he not been wearing his respirator; it was clear he would have raised her hand to his lips. For the very briefest of moments, she was no longer an established, locally respected businesswoman and housekeeper, but a shy, coquettish girl made bashful by the attentions of a stranger. Then she laughed warmly.

"Get outta here, Doc Holliday," she said, pushing the deputy a little. "You ain't gonna win me over and Lord knows you tried enough times."

"If you ever get bored of that hard-drinkin', no-good husband of yours, ma'am, you know where to find me."

"I do indeed! Probably in the saloon, drinkin' with him! Now shoo!" She picked up her porch broom and waved it threateningly at him. Laughing, Doc and Sweeney made their exit from the porch onto the dusty front street. It was late afternoon now and some – not all, but some – of the day's heat had settled into a more bearable temperature.

"You like that with every woman you meet?" Sweeney had been quietly impressed by Doc's geniality and flirtatiousness.

"Mamma Holliday did not bring her little boy up to be rude to a lady," came the reply. "Manners cost you nothin', Henry Junior', she used to say to me, 'an' mean everythin'. And she was certainly right." His eyes glinted with youthful mischief and amusement. "An' yes. I am. With every single one. C'mon. Let's find this Rhys fellow."

Military rank and a tenuous assertion of it being an emergency only got the Major so far ahead of the queue in her quest to send a missive. Thus, it was that when Willa Shaw finally managed to escape the close air of the communications office and the associated irritation of sending a simple telegram to the barracks a little further up north, she found her man Sweeney and the incorrigible Doc Holliday were already ensconced in the *Whistle Stop*.

* * *

The hotel in Salt Lake City had been open for barely a month and was so new that the smell of paint on the walls was still ever-present. The room that Mackeye had secured for her was large and light and – bliss – airy, with a front elevation looking out over the street which at this late hour was busy with people heading out for meals. It was a great deal more sophisticated than the Arizona territories, but it still wasn't home.

She immersed herself in a bath properly for the first time in days while Mackeye was out tracking down her brother and enjoyed a cool, crisp white wine whilst she did so. Stepping out of the bath she reattached the mechanisms of her prosthetic arm to the stump of her left shoulder. Flexing the delicate fingers to test its functionality, Annabelle began drawing a brush through her long, dark hair. She studied her reflection in the mirror and frowned. All that time in the Arizona sun, squinting against the daylight, had ruined her delicate complexion. She had *freckles* on her face. Freckles, destroying her beautiful peaches and cream skin! Still, she'd learned a tip or two over the years and was presently daubing lemon juice across her cheeks in an effort to make them fade. Add to that all the squinting against the sun which had left permanent creases in the corner of her eyes.

Arizona. Hateful place.

She looked out of the window at the fading light of the Salt Lake City day.

Utah. Hateful place.

But then, Annabelle struggled to find anywhere that she felt truly at home. Her earliest efforts to win the approval of her parents had been rebuffed and despite her best efforts at pleasing them, she had never managed to do so. They envision a life for her that did not fit with her own plans. Ben had been her champion, of course. Her twin brother, gifted with a mind of quicksilver that rivalled her own, had been lauded for his success, but Annabelle's keen interest in the excitement was met with scorn and comments that it was nothing but a passing phase and that ultimately, she would embrace the life of a lady.

She had done *better.* She had found a way to embrace both of those lives and her mother was no longer alive to disapprove.

Annabelle felt a brief pang of regret for the lost years and the opportunity to fix bridges with her mother. But there was no time to linger on the past, and the death of Daddy was still an all-consuming well of pain to her if she allowed herself to dwell on it for more than a moment. She had more pressing problems right now and the *very* least of these was her appearance. Such trivialities were easy to focus on.

All those days in the endless sunshine had brought out lighter shades in her voluminous dark hair and so she pushed aside all the self-criticisms and focused on that instead. Within minutes, she had returned to admiring herself.

There was a soft knock at the door of her room, and she frowned, turning from the mirror. She was presently dressed only in the towel that she had wrapped around herself after exiting the bath.

"It's Lieutenant Mackeye, ma'am. I have news. Are you decent?"

You could say 'yes'. Imagine his face at finding you in nothing but your towel.

She winked at her reflection. She knew she could be cruel, but she was not *completely* without decorum. She adopted her most prim tone. "No, Lieutenant, I most certainly am not. Give me ten minutes an' I'll come downstairs."

He knew that for Annabelle Hamilton 'ten minutes' meant an hour, at least. "Very well," he said and left to go downstairs to wait for her.

She took her time getting ready. She was Southern aristocracy and had been brought up to adhere to the adage that appearances and first impressions were not to be taken lightly. By the time she made her way gracefully down the stairs to the dining room, she was as pretty as a picture and heads turned at her descent. She knew they were all looking, and she soaked up the admiration like a thirsty flower taking a drink of water. Few people could have imagined that the beauty was nothing more than a shell to the brilliant and extraordinary scientific mind that worked below.

The Lieutenant was seated at a table in the dining room but rose to his feet in a gentlemanly manner when he saw her and moved to take her arm. She gave it to him gladly. She was delighted that she had found a man like Ross Mackeye as her bodyguard. He was so well-mannered and understood the societal niceties. She allowed him to guide her to the table and waited as he pulled out the chair for her. She sat, making quite a show of settling the skirts of her long dress around her and waited for him to also sit.

"So," she said. "What news?"

"Your brother is working out of a facility on the north edge of the city," he replied. "I have had a message sent to him that we have arrived. I did not think you would mind if I extended him an invitation to join us here for dinner?"

"I do not mind at all, Lieutenant," she said and treated him to a devastating smile. "He may be a difficult man to talk to at times, what with those insufferable ideas he likes to call his 'values', but he *is* my brother. An' I suppose I am quite fond of him." She sighed contentedly.

"I like it here," she said, confidently. "I am glad we took the trip west, awful though it was. We made good progress. But this here place is *so* much nicer." She looked around the well-appointed dining room. If this had been Provenance, men – and woman – would already have been bickering and fighting. That wasn't to say that there weren't card games going on in the saloon part of the dining room, because there were. But they were quiet, self-contained and civil affairs. Occasionally a voice was raised in anger, but for the most part, this was a peaceful, expensive hotel. Most of Utah's ne'er do wells could never hope to afford the price to cross the threshold.

That suited Annabelle Hamilton just fine.

"So, when should we expect Benjamin?" She accepted a glass of champagne from her Lieutenant, who poured from a bottle that had been chilling for some time. He did not drink alcohol himself, preferring to keep his senses sharp.

"He should be arriving imminently. My contact here was *most* efficient and I know how much you appreciate efficiency in all things."

She didn't reply and he wasn't that surprised. A look of something that could best be described as anxiety flickered into her eyes. She and her brother had not been together for a while and he knew that while she had instigated the separation of siblings, she had done so with great reluctance. The Hamiltons were more than simple brother and sister. They were twins, with all the bonded connectivity that implied.

"Do I look presentable enough?" Her concern for her appearance was touching to the Lieutenant. He had seen some of the things she had achieved over the past few months. Her intellect was spellbinding and here she was, worried about how she might look to the eyes of her estranged brother. He considered his reply and decided he would speak from the heart. He reached over the table and took her gloved hand in his own.

"I have seen many women, from home in Alabama all the way out here to the western frontier and you shine brighter than all of them, ma'am." He spoke the words with such sincerity that a blush touched her cheeks making her even more attractive.

"Such words, Lieutenant," she said, playfully smacking at his hand with her free one. But she was not displeased. She held his gaze for a moment or two longer and before he could speak further, the little tableau was ruined by the arrival of the bartender returning to replenish their drinks.

Mackeye could have punched the man. He released Lady Hamilton's hand and leaned back in his seat, sipping at a cup of iced tea without making any further comment.

They did not have to wait for long. Fifteen minutes passed in a series of awkward pauses and idle talk. At that point, a young man, accompanied by two others entered the door of the hotel. Eyes the absolute double of those belonging to the woman seated opposite scanned the room eagerly and his handsome face lit up when he saw her. He said something to his companions who nodded and returned outside.

Benjamin Hamilton came swiftly across the room to the table where his sister sat. Mackeye rose courteously to his feet, but Ben had only a sparing glance for the man who served Annabelle.

When seen together, the physical similarities between the two were impossible to deny. Those curious parti-coloured irises, the well-defined features and even the smiles were identical. She was looking up at him, refusing to let that smile show on her face, but her eyes danced with delight. Her brother looked to be in good shape; his body more muscled than she remembered, his hair longer and with a stray lock that frequently fell into his eyes. He wore a silvery-grey coloured three-piece suit with a cream waistcoat and a deep, grey and yellow cravat that perfectly matched the colour of the gown she had elected to wear for this meeting. The synchronisation of minds had not, it seemed, been completely severed. He carried, in one hand, a silver-topped cane. It was, she was certain, no more than an affectation rather than a walking aid. He threw his hands out wide in greeting and spoke in a loud voice that carried around the room.

"Annabelle! You look beautiful as always, though I must confess I don't approve of how you accessorise yourself this evening." He had lost a lot of his own Georgian drawl, by design rather than by accident. While she eschewed this obvious hiding of his heritage, she appreciated that sometimes it was necessary to keep one's origins a secret. She was not fully aware of her brother's activities, but she was fully aware of the kind of people he surrounded himself with. She knew that a man in Ben's position couldn't allow himself to be seen as soft or vulnerable among folks like that. If that meant he had to talk like a thug, then that was what it had to be.

She pushed back her prejudices about other people for a moment and concentrated on her brother. Periodically, his gaze was drawn to the wide silver armband she had taken to always wearing above her right elbow and a look of distaste came into his eyes. The engraved band proudly displayed the Confederate emblem, contentious at best in the long years since the Union claimed victory in the Ore War. The reason for the distaste was not the armband itself, per se, but rather the fact that her brother was acutely aware that

Annabelle had crafted the cuff from silver smelted from the plating of their father's own service pistol. The very same weapon he had used to take his own life as their family home burned, like so many other noble houses, at the end of that allegedly 'civil' war.

For Annabelle it was a treasured memento. A symbol of all that she had lost. For Ben, however, it was a macabre token of the worst night of their lives. And he would never, could never, understand why she wore it.

"Benjamin. Why don't you take a seat, darlin' boy? Ya makin' a scene." Her imperious tone cut through the moment, and he pushed his hair out of his eyes. His face shifted into a wolfish grin, in a slightly embarrassed manner. She waved at the other seat set at the table and he slid into the chair, laying the cane against the table. Mackeye waited politely until the boy was sitting and then sat down himself.

"Lieutenant Mackeye, I don't think ya ever had the chance to meet my brother, Mister Benjamin Hamilton. My *twin* brother. Younger than me by some thirty minutes. An' current heir to the Hamilton fortune. Which is in as much ash and ruin as the noble Southern cause these days." There was undisguised bitterness in the tone. Even in this age of so-called social enlightenment, though she was technically the elder sibling, Southern society still preferred to acknowledge a male heir over a female one.

"I have not met him, ma'am. It's a pleasure, Mister Hamilton."

"Ben." The young man waved a friendly hand in the air and then reached across the table to clasp both of the Lieutenant's hands in his own in a warm greeting. He was bright and effervescent, happy, it seemed, to express himself. "Just Ben is fine. I gather you're the one taking care of my sister? Why, sir, I don't know whether to thank you or commiserate with you. She ain't the easiest of women to remain companionable with and that's no lie."

Mackeye's lips didn't so much as twitch. "I manage," he said and tried to ignore the glare this earned him from his mistress. He was already rather taken with Ben. His easy-going nature was refreshing in a time when everyone played their cards close to their chests.

"That's enough with the pleasantries," said Annabelle, her tone severe. "Let's get down to business, shall we? Ya got my plans and schematics, Benjamin?" Throughout their entire life, she had never called her brother by the diminutive that everyone else chose to use. She took after her mother in that regard. *Benjamin was the name y'all were given, boy, an' I won't call you nothin' else.*

"I got them. You *have* been workin' hard, haven't you, Annabelle? I have to say, I was intrigued by the prospect. I have to say, though. There's a lot of people who wouldn't approve of your choice of – ah – *template*."

"Ya mean the nearly-deceased, Benjamin?" She said the words loudly enough that people close by looked around. She clearly didn't care, but Ben looked uncomfortable.

"Well, yes. It's just not the done thing. These ain't just simple-minded folk given new meaning through reconstruction. They ain't the usual constructs like the ones we saw in that Sturginium mine in Denver. These are... something else. Something I'm findin' altogether more unnerving." Ben held her gaze for a moment and then sighed with a shrug. "But... let's save that argument for another day. I've looked over your essays and I've come up with a lot of suggestions and designs that you should be able to incorporate into your..." He hesitated and his voice lowered. "What exactly do you call those things you're making?"

"Things?" She sounded righteously disgusted by the term. "They ain't *things*, Benjamin. They're my *soldiers*. An' when I get them right, when they are as perfect as they ever can be, then they will be my *army*."

The proclamation was nothing short of shocking and even Ross Mackeye allowed his eyebrows to raise in surprise. She smiled sweetly at the men. "An' they will be right at the head of the force that rides to take back what's ours."

"...what's ours?" Ben's question was faint, and he knew the answer, but he wanted to hear her say it anyway. She took a sip of her champagne and, setting the flute down on the table, smacked her lips in a most unladylike manner. Then she regained her composure and returned the sweet smile to her face.

"The South, darlin'. My soldiers – an' let's be clear on this point – who are not 'things' – are gonna be the trump card in the game to take our home back, the plan to return what's rightfully ours again. We're gonna kick out them Union folks and damn me if we don't reclaim the South as our own once more."

She raised her champagne glass in toast and beamed at her brother.

* * *

"A little on the early side for drinking, isn't it? Even for you, Holliday." Willa folded her arms across her chest and glared at Sweeney. He stood from the booth where the three men were seated and threw up his hands in innocence.

"Not a drop has passed my lips, ma'am," he re-assured her. "We're just chatting to Mister Rhys here. He owned the sawmill back in Provenance." She un-folded her arms and grunted her acceptance that her soldier was not drinking. That same courtesy didn't ex-tend to Doc Holliday, who was already three shots in and looking much happier for it. He saw her looking at the shot cup in his hand and he waved it at her.

He didn't stand up.

"Soothes the cough, darlin'," he said. He had removed his respirator for a while now he was out of the scorching heat of the day. "An' Mister Rhys *did* of-fer. Be rude not to accept now, wouldn't it? Tell the Ma-jor what you told us, Mister Rhys."

"What?" The poor beleaguered Hywel Rhys, whose life had taken a considerable downturn since his entire future had exploded so spectacularly, looked over at the major and half-rose from his seat in a po-lite manner. "Oh. Yes. Good day to you, ma'am. Deputy Holliday here tells me that you're enquiring after one Lady Annabelle Hamilton."

"That's right." Hearing Doc being referred to as 'deputy' still unsettled her. He was too erratic, too un-trustworthy to ever wear a deputy's badge. If she ever met the irresponsible lawman who'd given him the duty, she'd give him a piece of her mind. "We have rea-son to believe she might've spent time in your town."

"Why, in that assumption, you'd be quite right. Please, won't you join us?" He waved to the booth, and she slid in to sit beside Doc who was refilling his cup with a cheerful expression on his face. "As I was say-ing to the deputy... and may I say again, Doctor Holli-day, what an honour it is to meet you? I knew Marshal Earp for a time back in Texas..." He caught sight of the major's face and hurriedly continued. "Lady Hamilton spent some time in Provenance. Indeed, she hired some of the space the old mine offered. The tunnels themselves have long since been closed off – safety, you know – but the minehead itself is a marvellous space, plenty of room..."

"I have no interest in renting space from you, Mister Rhys," interrupted Willa and the man's face fell. "What was she doing there?"

"She's a lady of science, you know. Remarkably intelligent. And quite, quite, lovely. Why, were I not a man in my forties..." Doc coughed, spluttering slightly on the bourbon. All eyes turned to him, and he waved a hand idly.

"Excuse me," he said. "You just never know when this cough's gonna take over." He hid the smile in the cup as he drank. Rhys was fifty five if he was a day. The sawmill proprietor nodded his acceptance of the apology and continued.

"She was very eloquent and quite willing to pay me a considerable sum up front for use of the facilities and for the services of some of the working folks around the town as well. She even had several of her own workers shipped in as a form of payment. They were all hard workers, too."

"Yeah," interjected Doc, shooting a glance at Willa. "Yeah, we may well have met some of them."

A silence, awkward and hesitant drifted between the group, then Rhys shook himself to awareness and resume. "We were in negotiation for a renewal of the contract when the fire took hold. Terrible. Just terrible." The man mopped at his brow with a handkerchief. "So many plans. Up in smoke. And after, her nowhere to be seen." He shook his head. "I would have feared her perished had I not heard that all her things had been packed that very morning and taken out of the hotel by her man. I can only assume she had business elsewhere."

"I can imagine. Tell me, Mister Rhys. Have you heard of Lazarus?" The confused look on the man's face answered the question without need for words and she nodded.

"Pep?" Doc offered from his corner. He'd stopped drinking now, to give him his credit. Maybe he really had simply been applying the alcohol in its medicinal form. She would give him the benefit of the doubt.

"Oh, yes, I've heard of Pep. Most popular among a certain... type of customer in the saloons in these parts. Easier to lay hands on than laudanum, so they tell me. But less medicinal and more, well, recreational, I understand. I have no doubt it was on hand among the people of Provenance." It was clear from the expression on his face that he did not approve of such behaviour. Willa nodded and moved the conversation forward, making a bold statement.

"Here's the truth of it then, Mister Rhys." She leaned forward on the table, her expression intense and she waited until she was absolutely sure she had his full attention. "We have reason to believe that Annabelle Hamilton was heavily involved in the production of that particular substance. That she was using your facilities – and perhaps the people of Provenance and its surrounding areas – to further her research."

"Lady Hamilton? No, surely you're mistaken. She is a *perfect* lady..." Rhys waved off the idea, but he looked unsettled, his voice trailing into silence.

"Mister Rhys, I have been following leads on her for some time. My superiors in the Union have intelligence that suggests her activities over the past months have been increasingly worthy of suspicion. I understand that Deputy Holliday has been looking into the situation from a more... *local* perspective." Doc nodded at this.

"I can't believe that fine woman... no, you are surely mistaken. Yes, this is all a mistake."

"Mister Rhys." Willa Shaw's patience was not known to be anything other than short and she snapped across him now. "I suggest that you leave the deducing to those whose job it is to do so. All I want to know from you is this. Do you know where she went?"

Rhys looked startled at her hard tone and visibly shrank, but to give him his credit, he gave the matter some thought. After a moment, he brightened. "Colm Henderson, the former post master in Provenance, lovely man, breeds horses... anyway... he mentioned that her man sent a telegram to Utah a day or two prior to the fire, yes. Salt Lake City, I believe. A stranger place I can't imagine, what with all those Mormon fellows setting up there..."

"You are sure about this?" The Deputy had apparently been taking advantage of the conversation's distraction to refill his hipflask from Rhys's bottle of whiskey and looked up now as he spoke. He screwed the bottles closed, setting the whiskey back down on the table and pocketing his hipflask. If Rhys had noticed the blatant theft of his bourbon, he didn't comment on it.

"Absolutely sure, Deputy Holliday, sir."

"Good. Then if we get movin' now, we can head that way." He got to his feet. "Unless you have another idea, Major?"

"It's a long journey," she said, hoping to put him off coming with them. It had as much impact as a dandelion flower on a horse's flank. He beamed his irritatingly crooked, charming smile at her and clipped on his respirator.

"Then we had best stop yappin' an' get started." He pushed the bottle of bourbon back towards Rhys. "Enjoy the rest," he said.

"Thanks for buying it, Deputy Holliday. Do pass on my best regards to Marshal Earp, won't you?" Willa's little opportunity to bite at Doc was stolen with the revelation that he hadn't stolen the alcohol at all. The fact the deputy was wearing his respirator hid his facial reaction to Rhys's comment, but his eyes narrowed slightly.

"Your best regards. Sure, I will do that."

Outside, dusk had taken hold and the last of the Arizona sun had sunk below the western horizon leaving a sky tinged with pellucid amber hues. Stars could just be seen starting to appear in the night sky and Doc looked up at them, then back to Willa, interrupting her before she could even speak.

"You are a man down," he said, as gently as he could. "I am right sorry about that, an' you know that if I could make a change about what happened back in Provenance, I would do it. But I ain't got any powers over what has been. Let me come with you on this one, Willa. I have seen too many good folks go down thanks to that poison she's spreadin' around. I swear to you I will not interfere with military business. Let's work together. We'll be doin' each other a favour. An' even you gotta admit it looks good. Union and the law workin' together." He held out his hands helplessly and she barely resisted an urge to punch him in his stupid face.

She fixed him with a steely glare, but his words were honest and impassioned and she gave way to him. Just as she always had done. "Fine," she said, "but I'm in command and for the purposes of this mission, you damn well do what I tell you. And the moment I consider what you're doing constitutes 'interfering', you'll be back here quicker than you can say your name. Is that clear?"

"It is." He raised his hand and gave her a lazy sort of salute. She wrinkled her nose in distaste and moved away to get onto the Iron Horse. If they left now, they could cover a reasonable distance before weariness brought them low.

"Glad to have you along, Doc," said Sweeney – although not quite loud enough for Willa to hear it.

"See if you are still sayin' that in a couple of days' time, Sergeant," replied the deputy, swinging his long legs over his own Iron Horse and starting the engine. "See if you are still sayin' that."

* * *

At twilight, the Hollow of Sighs was a place of tranquillity and unashamed natural beauty. The ancient tree, its branches drooping with the weight of centuries, were moved by a light spring breeze that kissed the young Spirit Priest with a warm blessing as he stepped into the clearing. It was the kind of change in the weather that had been imminent for a few days now; a storm was in the air. The People knew better than most the early signs of a change in weather patterns.

It had been such a short time since they laid the body of Curved Bear Claw out for his return to the Great Spirit. It was not unusual for the immediate family and loved ones of a recently departed to visit the site after a sky burial to leave offerings, trinkets, and mementos, but it was not a pleasant experience for most.

Stone Fur was steeled against what he expected to see. The sight would be grizzly and unpleasant, but all the People understood that the flesh was never anything more than a shell. The body was just a skin to be worn during a brief time on the Earth. Who Curved Bear Claw had been in life would live on in the hearts and souls of the Warrior Nation. The old priest's body was meat, nothing more. This was something that Stone Fur understood.

What he saw in the clearing was far worse. What he saw was more unsettling than any corpse, perished or otherwise. What he saw was nothing.

No ruined flesh, no scattered scraps, nothing. Curved Bear Claw's body had simply vanished. There was still a faint outline in the dust marking where the body had been when they'd left it and Stone Fur dropped to his knees to study the ground carefully in the fading light. He had been around nature his entire life and he recognised most animal and bird tracks with ease. Something had most definitely been scuffling around, but the dust was so disturbed that he could not tell what it, or what they might have been.

"Where is he, Spirit Priest?" One of the young warriors who had come with him to the Hollow spoke quietly, more than a little fear evident in his tone.

"I don't know." Stone Fur put a hand to the ground and closed his eyes. *If you want to touch the spirit within, you must become one with all your senses.* He remembered his lessons. He knew how to do this. He allowed his whole body to relax, opening every sense to the unheard song of the earth, to the deep murmur of the Great Spirit as it coursed through the veins of creation.

As he did, one sense at a time heightened, bringing forth the hunter's skill that marked his spirit. He could feel the breath of the wind on his face, the whisper of wings and sleek feathers as they tucked behind him, preparing to swoop on his prey. His sense of smell sharpened until he could smell and taste the pure, clean air of the desert skies. All four of those senses blended and merged, until finally he felt himself connect with his spirit guide.

He could hear, somewhere on the periphery of awareness, Loud Thunder speaking to him, but it was just an incessant rumble and he could not make out individual words. Just the thrumming of the big warrior's deep bass.

Stone Fur opened his eyes and they were no longer his. Gone were the blue eyes of the Spirit Priest, and in their place were the sharp yellow eyes of the eagle.

Now look, boy. Use your senses and truly look.

He was flying. Not his physical form, that remained precisely where it was. But his other self, his spirit, soared above the Hollow of Sighs, looking down and seeing Stone Fur kneeling motionless. It was like gazing down at an image frozen in time.

Stone Fur's spirit heard a distant, far-off screech and he turned his head sharply to listen more carefully and then he spread out wings of pure thought and rose with the updraft. He was carried east, north, then further east. The land below became dry and barren, the air baked and dusty. Then he saw something that even in his spirit-flesh filled him with loathing. Sensing his distress, the eagle let out a sympathetic cry of indignation and circled closer.

There was a flock of... *creatures* was the only word he could find. He could think of no other name for them. They flapped awkwardly through the air ahead of him, their movements staccato and artificial. Pinions of steel held them aloft, their joints creaking and squealing with each movement, a mockery of natural life. They possessed the bodies of men and women, but these were bodies that had been ruined and altered by means so foul that the Spirit Priest could not begin to contemplate their origins.

Grey, sickly flesh clung to limbs that ended in cruel hooks, blades or stubby pistols. Rivets and valves studded their skin and their heads were capped with iron and nests of lenses that entirely robbed them of any identity that they might once have possessed.

Yet most horrifying of all were the steel claws of their feet. Each creature clutched a lumpen burden in its brutal talons. Men. Women. Children. Some still twitched or squirmed with feeble movements, but most simply hung limply in their captor's grasp. Among them, Stone Fur easily spotted the colours of Curved Bear Claw's burial shroud. The monsters had desecrated the body of the old priest, carrying it off for their own vile purposes. Stone Fur had no notion of what the creatures might intend for their victims, be they alive or dead, but the sight of his former mentor in their clutches filled him with absolute fury and revulsion.

The eagle responded.

Stone Fur's spirit-vision plunged and, on the periphery of that sight, he both saw and felt his talons extend, hard and black against the fading amber of dusk. The iron-shod skull of Curved Bear Claw's captor raced toward him, the exposed flesh of its neck a soft target at the end of a long, blurred tunnel. The creature creaked and hissed at one another as he descended, the flock breaking up and snapping at this sudden predator in their midst. Gunfire cracked around him as previously unseen pistols opened fire. A line of sudden, shocking heat creased his back. His target flashed past and the eagle screeched loudly in a combination of pain and frustration at being denied. Kneeling in the

Hollow of Sighs, far from that place, Stone Fur opened his mouth and howled in sympathetic rage.

His vision of the skies blurred once more as the flock of creatures fell away. His senses rushed back into his body with a tangible snap. The young Spirit Priest stood bolt upright and the yellow of his eagle's eye was replaced with curling blue spirit-flame.

"Spirit Priest?" Loud Thunder's voice was tentative. "What was it? What did you see?"

By way of response, Stone Fur let out a roar, and an inferno of cerulean fire boiled out of him, mushrooming into the sky like a beacon. It flooded the Hollow of Sighs, washing around the old tree like a tide. It crawled over rocks and warriors and over every living thing that was there, but it caused them no harm. The gathered people marvelled for a moment at the sight of the pure flames that crawled over them and yet did not burn and then they retreated.

The fire drained back into the Spirit Priest, flowing back into his eyes and mouth like an inhalation that could swallow the world.

He staggered.

The gloaming returned to the Hollow of Sighs.

"Never before have I known such a thing," Loud Thunder rumbled, an edge of wonder in that deep, tectonic voice. "What is it that you have seen, Spirit Priest, that causes Stone Fur to burn so brightly?"

Stone Fur turned to face the other man, the sight of Curved Bear Claw's violation still achingly fresh in his thoughts. "A great and terrible evil," he replied. "An evil that has taken Curved Bear Claw. Thieves of the flesh. They must be hunted, Loud Thunder. They must be destroyed." His fingers curled into a fist of defiance. "They must be destroyed. This cannot go unanswered."

Loud Thunder held Stone Fur's gaze for a long moment before he nodded, once. He turned to face those who had accompanied them to the Hollow of Sighs and raised his staff high above his head.

"War!"

The big man roared the single word and that single word shook the very stones around the Hollow.

"Gather the warriors! We go to war!"

* * *

They rode into the night, the temperature dropping to a balmy, more bearable heat that gave all three of them a fresh surge of energy, even Doc Holliday. He was enjoying the experience of riding out on an Iron Horse for the first time in a while. There was his own Interceptor back in Tombstone, but that was there and he was not.

Doc had any number of reasons for his distrust of Enlightened science and the respirator that kept him living was at the top of that list. While he was, as he had told Willa, grateful that Wyatt Earp had seen fit to provide it for him, he was not grateful for the knowledge that there had been a price. Not money, because had that been the case, Doc would have paid back in full. Wyatt had never expanded on the deal he'd made when Morgan...

Stop thinking about it.

The deputy pushed all the unpleasant thoughts of Tombstone and the most recent argument with Wyatt out of his head and instead focused on the road ahead. They would have to stop soon. Fortunately, the roads that led to and from Utah to Arizona were lined with many makeshift camps and waystations populated by those following the endless lure of silver. Some

179

of those camps had become semi-permanent and even boasted simple buildings. It was one of those to which they were headed now. Little more than a shanty town, but then Provenance had started that way. Even the town too tough to die had once been nothing more than a row of lopsided tents pitched as the result of a single man's dream.

The camp where they stopped for the night was one of the larger ones on the trail to Utah. Two wooden buildings served an encampment of travellers from all walks of life. One building housed the saloon and lodging facilities – where they were able to secure three beds for the night. The other building was pure trade; where furriers brought their quarry, where people bartered for what they could afford to buy and sold their personal possessions in a desperate attempt to survive. An open-fronted workshop with softly glowing lanterns was as civilised as it got.

There were children here. That was not so surprising; developments and new mining opportunities had reached a stage where entire families upped sticks and moved out to the frontier in a hope of making their fortune. Most did not. Many never even made it this far.

The saloon was loud and lively and both Doc and Sweeney eyed it hopefully. Willa was less keen to sample its delights, but options were fairly limited. She thought perhaps to simply go to bed and rest for the night, but when Doc suggested, gently, that it might be nice to have a small, personal wake for a brave young soldier, he successfully pushed all her buttons.

The three of them took a rickety booth and the deputy ordered a bottle of Old Overholt. He poured out generous measures for the three of them and they toasted young Zachariah King. Doc toasted him several times, drinking the lion's share of the rye whiskey. Willa grew irritated with his solid drinking and allowed her attention to roam around the room, watching the comings and goings of all these people. Young, old, male, female, they were all accounted for. She watched the girl behind the bar dealing with the unwanted attention of a drunk drover and nodded her approval as the flat of the girl's palm met the drover's face to good effect.

She seemed familiar in a way that Willa could not quite fathom.

"What do you know about this Annabelle Hamilton woman?" Sweeney's question to Doc pulled Willa's attention back to the here and now and she swung her gaze to him, interested in the answer.

"Lady Annabelle Hamilton." There was mockery in the correction, Doc putting a heavy, sarcastic emphasis on the woman's title. When he was drunk – and given the amount of alcohol she had witnessed him putting away, the man was surely inebriated – Doc's accent grew far more pronounced, and he became harder to understand without paying careful attention. "Why, she is one of the Atlanta Hamiltons. Big ol' family, sprawlin' right across that city. Handful of 'em made their way down to Griffin where I was born. 'Course, the Hollidays were hardly a small family. One thing I never wanted for growin' up was kinfolk. Aunts, and uncles an' cousins fillin' every possible space. Prob'ly a marriage or two between the two families." He laughed, bitterly. "Maybe that makes her my cousin or somethin'. She would be a bit younger than me, I guess. Mid-twenties somewhere. Prime of life an' all that."

"You don't sound that impressed," observed Willa and she took the bottle of whiskey, frowning at the small amount that was left.

"They were big on science, the whole lot of 'em," continued Doc. He reached to take the bottle back from Willa, but she kept it deliberately out of his grasp. They glared at one another for several seconds and yet again, she won. "An' they had a most unsavoury reputation as the kind of people who were willin' do anythin' to stay on top. The ends always justified the means." He shrugged. "I left Georgia when I was twenty-two. Ain't really kept up to date with the gossip."

"So, what you're saying is, in answer to Sweeney's question, you know nothing about her?"

"Got it in one." Damn his crooked smile, even more obvious and pronounced without facial hair. "Although I would recommend caution. If she is indeed behind those things back in Provenance? Then there ain't no tellin' what she's up to. Whoever set that fire was clearly more in the know than we were, I'd reckon."

"Maybe we should have tried harder to work out who that was," she said, thoughtfully. Her attention went back to the woman behind the bar and she felt a flash of something she could only ascribe to *déjà vu*. There was a distinct sense that she had been here before, or encountered this situation before...

"What's wrong, major?" Sweeney noticed his superior's distraction. She nodded toward the bar.

"She seem familiar to you?" She tried to ignore Doc who was now singing quietly to himself, some sort of old folk song that he obviously didn't know very well. Half humming, half singing, he was just annoying. Sweeney squinted over at the girl, then had the decency to look ashamed.

"Honestly, major? Lot of these saloon girls look the same to me." His words brought a roar of laughter from the deputy who allowed the brief explosion of hilarity to back off to a giggle. Both Willa and Sweeney glared at his reaction. He waved his hand vaguely at them and got rather unsteadily to his feet.

"I am gonna go see what local gossip I can pick up on," he announced cheerfully. "See if there's anythin' at all that can help our... whatcha call it. Our cause. Yep, that is what I am gonna do. Help our *cause*. An' I'm gonna do that..." He spun around, a full one hundred and eighty degrees and apparently spied his destination. He pointed with one long, spindly finger at a table where a poker game was underway. "...right there."

"You sure you're in the best frame of mind for cards, deputy?" Sweeney's concern was oddly touching, and Doc patted the big soldier's arm in something approaching affection.

"Ain't you a peach of a fella? Trust me, sergeant, I am in the *best* frame of mind for cards. Drunk enough not to care but not so drunk as to not be able to still pay attention." His grin was charming, and he hid it behind the respirator before he swaggered off, introducing himself to the group at the card table and sliding into a recently vacated chair as though it was his God-given right to be there.

"How in the name of all that's good and holy did that man ever get a deputy's badge?" Willa was scathing. Sweeney shrugged. He was no fool. He'd worked out the connection the two must have had at some point in their past and he refused categorically to interfere. Thus far, he had nothing but praise for the young deputy's courage and acumen. Sure, it was obviously that the man enjoyed his drink just a little too much... but given his personal circumstances, it was understandable, if not forgivable.

"Not for us to decide how the lawmen conduct their business," he said, mildly and Willa scowled. Then she sighed, acknowledging that Sweeney was right. In her years as a soldier, she'd never understood how the structure of those outside the military even held together it was so loose-weave. The sergeant offered out his shot-glass and she nodded, filling it from what was left.

"Zach was a good kid," he said, returning her focus to the reason they'd stopped here in the first place. "If it helps any, I know his older brother. When we have to take the news to his family, I'll do it."

Not for the first time in her association with him, Willa appreciated the solidity of her sergeant. He grounded her when her anger got out of hand. She poured her own drink and shook her head.

"We all have duty to uphold, Sergeant Sweeney, and while I deeply appreciate your kind offer, well, it's my responsibility. I'll do it." She looked up once again at the girl behind the bar who was now sliding between bodies, evidently heading out of the saloon. Her eyes met Willa's and the two women seemed frozen, locked for a moment in what might have been recognition. The saloon girl broke the spell first and hurried out of the building.

Millie?

"I *knew* I recognised her," breathed Willa, pushing aside her drink. "Would you excuse me, Sergeant?" Sweeney waved a hand easily indicating that no, he did not mind at all. She slid out of the booth and trailed the saloon girl outside. The coolness of the evening took her by surprise; she had grown used to the endless heat. Tonight, though, the clouds had gathered and Arizona was experiencing one of its infrequent cool spells. There may even have been the tang of rain

Sarah Cawkwell

in the air. She allowed herself to hope that was the case; a good downpour of rain might quell the worst of the dust for a few days. She did not see the saloon girl straight away, but it was moments before she recognised the slim silhouette moving around the corner of the general store building.

"Millie?" Willa called out the name. The saloon girl hesitated briefly and turned her head a fraction, but continued on her way as though nothing had happened. Willa did not like to be ignored. A spark of annoyance flared and she picked up her pace. "Millie!" More forceful this time.

As she rounded the corner of the building, she was surprised to see that nobody was there. The shanty town was not so labyrinthine that Millie could have disappeared that quickly. In confusion, Willa spun around a few times. She wondered, briefly, if perhaps she was simply so very tired that she had imagined the familiarity of the girl. *Damn Doc and his whiskey*, she thought. Maybe she should have eaten something before drinking anything that strong.

When a rose-scented figure dropped onto her from the building above, she realised very quickly that she most certainly had not imagined it all. Willa was knocked to the floor and sprawled in the dust for a moment, winded.

A loud crack of thunder announced the arrival of the promised storm. Lightning brought her attacker into focus and she was almost certain that it was Millie, the co-owner of the *Whistle Stop* Saloon. What she didn't know was why the woman who had, just a day or two earlier promised friendship was know kneeling over her, with a wickedly curved knife in her hand.

Millie bared her teeth in a snarl. "Why are you following me?" The voice was the same. Terrifyingly

185

the same, though Willa could have sworn in the half-light that her lips never moved. But this could not be the same woman that Willa had met in Howling Rock. She had been sweetness and light, not aggressive like this.

"Millie?" Willa struggled beneath the woman's tight hold, but she was strong. Willa wriggled slightly until she managed to get one hand free. "Millie, don't you remember me? Willa Shaw. We met in Howling Rock."

"That's not my name." The girl relaxed her grip slightly. "You've made a mistake. We have never met."

"No, I'm sure I..." The blade of the knife was back at Willa's throat in a heartbeat and she was afraid even to swallow for fear of that razor edge against her skin. Had she really met this woman before?

"You. Have made. A mistake. You don't know me. Stop following me. Get out of here." The woman leaned in close and there was another flash of lightning, another deafening crack of thunder. In the dazzling light that split the night sky, Willa swore that the girl's dark eyes were entirely gloss black. Before she could process that particular horror, there was the sound of a gunshot. The girl who claimed she was not Millie leaped off her prey and twisted her body lithely so that she was now facing the other way, staring down the small alleyway between the two buildings. Her posture was that of a hunter; crouched and tensed, ready to attack.

Willa took the opportunity to roll clear from the spot where the woman had pinned her and got straight to her feet. She reached for her own pistol and wrenched it free of its holster.

Another gunshot could be heard and Willa tried not to let it distract her from the situation in hand. "What the hell do you think..." The question was driven by anger, but she was having trouble thinking.

"Shhh." The saloon girl held a finger to her lips. "Be quiet and listen. Can't you hear it?"

"I'm getting pretty tired of this charade." Willa levelled the pistol at the girl. "Now you're gonna tell me just what is going on." Thunder cracked directly overhead, both interrupting and startling Willa into immediate silence. Seconds later, the first fat drops of rain hit. They formed tiny craters in the dust at her feet, disappearing into the thirsty ground faster than anything she'd seen.

The woman made another improbable leap, an athletic twist of her body, a kick-off from the wall and landed, cat like and nimble directly behind the Major. "What do you hear?" Her voice was low and breathless and Willa stared at her.

"I heard a gunshot."

"They're always shooting each other in this place. Tensions run high all the time. Angry people. Bitter people. Hungry people. Desperate, terrible people. Never stop being angry with each other. But now *really* listen." The girl lay a hand on Willa's forearm and the major blinked at her, not understanding. "Listen, Major Shaw."

"If you aren't Millie, then how do you know my..."

"Listen."

There was something faintly hypnotic in the girl's voice and Willa found her thoughts taking on a strange kind of clarity. It felt as though someone was guiding her through her own thoughts and senses.

I can hear the thunder, she thought. *I can hear the sounds of people in the saloon... drinking, laughing, arguing, fighting.* Her senses guided her upstairs, to the private rooms above the saloon and colour flushed her cheeks. "Now that," she said, "I do not want to hear."

"Listen harder. Above the sound of human voices. Above the sounds of nature. Can you hear it?"

The turn of phrase struck her as odd, even as her thoughts and senses became sluggish and syrupy. What had she meant by 'human voices? There was no time to dwell on the question because that guiding thought had taken hold of her mind again. She found herself drifting further away from reality and into a strange sort of lucid dreaming. Despite her fine ability to keep a clear head in crisis situations, Willa was helpless against this peculiar power.

The beating of wings. Yes. I hear it. But those are not feathers. That is not the sound of an eagle, or a raptor of any kind. There is something in that sound that seems familiar… a ticking, almost. A mechanical whirr. Seems familiar.

Doc's respirator. That constant clicking that it made whenever he had it active. A flying machine, perhaps?

Worse. Something far worse.

Millie-not-Millie released Willa's arm and shook her head. She leaned in to the major, close enough for her lips to brush next to the major's ear. "You're going the wrong way," she whispered. "When you wake up, you'll know that, but you won't remember this conversation." A flicker of a smile; Willa could feel it on her ear lobe. Millie's soft lips pressed against her neck in a gentle kiss. "Now sleep."

"I most certainly…" Willa crumpled in a heap at the girl's feet, her pistol falling from fingers gone suddenly lifeless. The saloon girl knelt and checked she was breathing regularly before she stood up again, sniffed at the air and ran.

The heavens opened and the rain began to fall in a heavy, steady downpour that quickly turned dust to mud and saturated the unconscious Willa Shaw. By the time Joe Sweeney found her, an hour later, she was drenched to the skin and would not wake.

* * *

If she dreamed, she did not remember it. When consciousness returned to her, dawn was creeping in through the dirty window of the bedroom, touched with that golden, rosy glow that promised a beautiful day. Willa Shaw could not remember a time when her body had felt so *rested*. It was a good feeling and she wondered why it was that she had slept so well. She recalled sitting with Doc and Sweeney in the saloon downstairs and drinking to Zachariah King's memory. Perhaps those couple of drinks had simply done her good. She also recalled that Doc had drunk far more than could be considered sociable and she grasped at the feeling of disappointment she'd tasted when she'd seen him so inebriated.

Still, he wasn't truly her problem any more and whatever he did was none of her business. She closed her eyes again and sighed, softly. A contented sigh rather than the usual expulsion of irritation or frustration.

There was a muffled cough and the sound of someone shifting position next to the bed. She opened her eyes once more and turned her head. As though thinking of him had somehow summoned him, there he was in all his slightly dusty and mud-stained finery. Doc Holliday was sitting sideways in a high-backed chair next to her bed, his long legs draped over one of the arms. In his hand was a slim pamphlet and he was reading it avidly, not so much as looking at her. Other than a slight redness around the rims of his eyes, there was no apparent evidence of his drinking excesses. Despite his debilitating illness, it was clear that his body had become so used to the alcohol that it could shrug off its more unpleasant side-effects.

"Have you been sitting in that chair all night?" She was rewarded with the simple pleasure of him jumping visibly. He swivelled round so that he was sitting properly, like a boy whose mother had just caught him with his feet on the furniture. She yawned lazily, amused for a handful of seconds until something occurred to her. "Have you been sitting there *all night*?" The repeat of the question was not as polite as the first time. "I mean, just... *watching* me?" Another thought flickered into being and she anxiously glanced beneath the blanket. She was still fully clothed.

Small mercies, yes, but she was quite pleased.

"Well, I slept for a bit, to be fair," he admitted, "but otherwise... yes." He was wearing his respirator and the light was winking steadily. "Just, as you say, watchin' you. It has been pretty borin'. Just glad I had my book to keep me company." He waved the 'book', which was little more than a few pages of typesetting held together with string. She caught a glimpse of the cover. *Unlikely Tales.* She snorted in derision.

"I mean, really? A man of your intelligence reading those things. It's just so much rubbish."

"Basis in fact, all of it." He tapped the cover of the slim booklet and nodded assertively. "Fancified with fiction, I will grant you that, but even the unlikeliest story has to start somewhere."

"It's all nonsense."

"You are a nonsense."

"When did you become an idiot?"

"When did you start snorin'?"

Sarah Cawkwell

The clash of wills took over again, but this time it was friendly and light-hearted. The brusque exchange had brought back so many memories of their time together, when sniping arguments had been the norm. She smiled at him and she actually meant it.

"How you feelin', anyway? Your man Sweeney found you outside in the pourin' rain, all crumpled up in a heap. He could not wake you. We checked you over, but we couldn't find anythin' that might have taken you down. No obvious injuries, no wounds... there was a street argument right after you left the saloon, ended in a gunfight. I had to step in." He was nonchalant about the part he had played in that particular entanglement.

He put his book in his lap and tipped his head to one side. "What the hell happened to you out there?" There was real concern in his eyes, all the bickering and squabbling just a front for the depth of care he had for people. She was touched by the expression and sat up, pushing her tangled hair out of her eyes.

"I don't know," she said. "There's a gap in my memory. I can recall leaving the saloon, going outside... but I don't even remember exactly why it was that I did that. After that," she shook her head and held out her hands. "Nothing. I didn't drink that much."

"Maybe you were just exhausted," he said and it was sympathetic. "Y'know. You have been through a lot this last couple days. An' you worry too much. There are a couple of doctors in camp an' if you want, I can get 'em for you. Ain't gonna tell you how to live your life, but if you ain't well..."

"I'm fine, Doc," she reassured him. "Maybe you're right. I guess I was just... really tired. Anyway, I'm good now. Maybe a wash, something to eat and we can get on our way to Salt Lake City."

"Need to talk to you 'bout that," he said. He bent the book enough so that it fit into the inside pocket of his coat and leaned forward in the chair, his hands clasped in front of him, resting on his knees. "Some of the stuff I learned last night? I got a feelin' we are goin' the wrong way. Turns out that..."

You're going the wrong way.

"Yes," she said, doubtfully, interrupting the deputy's flow. "We are going the wrong way." She heard herself say the words, but for some reason it felt as though her voice was not her own. "We don't want to go to Salt Lake City. Even if they are there now, by the time we got there, they would already have left." They? How did she know *that*?

"Oh? An' what makes *you* so sure?" He was affronted, that much was clear. He had worked hard on piecing the information together and he felt, rightly so, that Willa Shaw had just stolen his thunder without so much as a by-your-leave. She gave him a tremulous, uncertain smile.

"A hunch," she said. "Let's call it a dream."

Because I can't possibly start to explain what the hell happened to me last night.

"Let's say you're right," Doc said, without displaying any sign that he disbelieved her. She was not the type to be airy and dreamy. This entire situation had been ridiculous so far – why shouldn't he believe that she had experienced some kind of premonition. "Let's say you're right about this and we're goin' the wrong way. What's the *right* way?"

"Somewhere not too far. I need to look at some maps. Triangulate what I saw in my..." She didn't want to say dream. It had been so *real* "But I think we should go somewhere where I can get more people." She gave him a smile that had no humour in it.

Sarah Cawkwell

"We're going to Fort Wall."

* * *

The plains shook with the thunder of hooves and great plumes of dust blossomed into the clear morning sky. Teams of braves mounted on noble sky stallions charged and wheeled about, whooping and hollering war cries. Still more warriors sat around the cooking fires, their bronzed flesh already painted with bars and wedges of white and ochre. Even a trio of Fire Bringers had been drawn up for what was to come; their multiple barrels oiled; their carriages primed for battle.

Loud Thunder observed the scene from a rocky bluff, his arms folded across his huge chest. Stone Fur stood by his side and together, the pair watched the gathering warband in a companionable silence. A huge Spirit Totem stood upon the site and the young Spirit Priest had already spent the night beseeching the Great Spirit for its blessing in the upcoming battle. The totem remained now, as it had been all night, silent, dour faces unfeeling and unfathomable.

"Will the spirits aid us when we go to avenge Curved Bear Claw?" Loud Thunder's question was a deep rumble, and it was the first time he had addressed Stone Fur directly since the muster began. The unexpectedness of his voice caused the Spirit Priest to jump a little. In the aftermath of his vision, everything had seemed so clear. The need for action, the need for retribution. Those things had been a certainty. But now the host was gathered and the reality of what lay ahead settled in. A gnawing sense of doubt had begun to take hold, subsuming the surety. It had brought questions, some more troubling than others.

What did it truly matter that the body of Curved Bear Claw had been taken? Was that not the purpose of a sky burial?

Not in the way he had seen.

The horrific image of the unnatural things and their still-living cargo came back to the Spirit Priest's mind to haunt him once again. It was not just for Curved Bear Claw that they made these preparations for war. It was for all the victims of those abominations and to punish those who had made them. That was the true evil here and it needed to be vanquished.

"I believe that they will come to our aid," Stone Fur replied after a time. "They will rise to fight beside us when battle is joined."

Loud Thunder nodded and grunted his approval. "Then I should also prepare. Will you perform the rite for me? As Curved Bear Claw always did when we rode to war?"

Stone Fur nodded readily. "It will be an honour, Chief, to walk in the footsteps of the great Curved Bear Claw."

Loud Thunder gave the younger man a brief, but warm smile before kneeling on the ground in front of the totem. Stone Fur, glad for the distraction from the thoughts in his mind, took up a bowl of white paint, mixed from the pale clay of the hills and began to apply it to the big warrior's skin. He sang as he worked, a soft, low dirge that rose and fell with the strokes of his fingers.

"One people, one land.
Blood calls to blood.
Spirit calls to spirit.
An arrow once loosed cannot be returned.
A blow once struck cannot be undone.
Hear the thunder of the drums, the hooves, the heart.

Sarah Cawkwell

Blood calls to blood.
Spirit calls to spirit.
One people. One land."

He stepped away from the chief and Loud Thunder stood, his face and body now painted with bars and wedges that echoed those of the warriors below. "Now, Stone Fur, my Spirit Priest, you will ride at my side." Stone Fur inclined his head, handed Loud Thunder his staff and nodded. The big man continued. "Now we will bring down the wrath of the Great Spirit upon those who would commit such evil. You will be our guide and we will be your axe. Together, we will find the heart of this corruption and together we will cut it out."

He turned from Stone Fur to the host gathered below. He raised his staff to the sky and released a long, ululating cry.

And the plains answered.

* * *

Ben Hamilton's workshop was in a modern, airy unit on the east side of town. After they had dined, he arranged transportation to take his sister – and at her insistence, Lieutenant Mackeye – right to the door. When she stepped inside the stone-walled building, with its spotless surfaces and delightfully clean windows, she clapped her hands together in girlish delight.

"Ya wouldn't *believe* the abject squalor I've been subjected to for the last few months," she told her brother, threading her mechanical arm companionably through his. He glanced down at her and smiled slightly. Dinner had been initially awkward, the two of them skirting around the argument that had been the last real conversation they'd had. But good food and just

195

enough wine had loosened them both up. Mackeye watched the transition with great interest as they went from slightly hostile to warm to acting as though they'd never been separated.

Now she was dragging him around this well-appointed workshop, where all sorts of strange things lay. Mackeye held back, not really understanding the thrust of his mistress's conversation, nor the enthusiasm of her brother's engineering talk. He was feeling decidedly out of place among these highly educated creative types and not for the first time since he'd come into Lady Annabelle's service, he found himself yearning for the company of his fellow soldiers.

"How does the Lazarus work?" The question from Ben to his sister caught Mackeye's attention and he turned his thoughts back to the present. That was something he was particularly interested in himself. Lady Annabelle's skills as a chemist were second to none in the South. She had prepared the powder herself in that ramshackle, makeshift laboratory with the minimal tools available. Imagine what she could have accomplished had she been based somewhere like this?

Early on, she had demonstrated an astonishing ability with pharmacological substances. She had been fascinated by medicines, demanding in a child's voice for Daddy to explain *how* and *why* the laudanum helped those who took it. Wanting to understand why the powdered bark of the willow tree could relieve headaches. So many questions that Daddy couldn't answer.

"Go and look it up in the library," had been his curt reply and so Annabelle had done just that. She had read every book in the Hamilton private library, then devoured everything her brother brought home from his own schooling. She, of course, as the daughter of the family, was home-schooled, but mostly in the classics, in embroidery and in managing a household. There was very little room for science for a girl of Annabelle's breeding.

She resented it.

As she'd grown older, she taken it on herself to experiment. She had acquired chemistry equipment through a gentleman chemist she briefly invited to court her. His bitter accusations that she was more delighted with his test tubes than with his flowery gifts of sweets and jewellery were not entirely incorrect. So, she had the equipment and she had her wiles – and she *studied*. She read, she experimented, and she shamed her parents still further. That innate sense of curiosity had fuelled her for years and even now she could lose hours to experimentation.

Annabelle had been seeking the means to prove herself for so long. Now, with the creation of Lazarus, she had brought forth something *brilliant*. And she was confident in the fact that she could step up onto the world stage of genius inventors and more than hold her own in the face of hard, angry old men who may have been smart, but were without imagination.

Then a decade ago the unimaginable happed. The Ore War ended with the fall of the Confederacy. For Annabelle the life she knew was suddenly torn away in humiliation and unfathomable loss as her Daddy had put his shiny silver service pistol in his mouth as their home burned. It was said that Annabelle's mind had snapped. That the injuries she suffered that terrible night were far more than just the loss of her arm. But Mackeye knew her mind had not broken. Rather it had broken free.

Mackeye watched her. There was a light in her eyes in this space and it was more than just the simple pleasure of being reunited with her twin. She *belonged* in places like this. Despite his misgivings at times about what she was doing, the way it frequently rubbed the fur of his morality up the wrong way, Mackeye couldn't help but be fascinated by the way she operated. He'd been there at the birth of Lazarus. He'd seen its early trials. He'd seen its initially devastating side-effects. He had watched her curse like a miner, cry like a baby and laugh with unashamed delight over the brewing of the stuff. It was *hers*. To every last drop.

"I'm proud of that creation, Benjamin, I surely am." She waved a hand at him, indicating he should fetch her a seat, which he did. It was more than evident that Ben Hamilton doted on his sister in much the same way everyone who came into contact with her did. She was spoiled, petulant and demanding, certainly, but her beauty and charm went a long way. "It's based off Carpathian's 1027, of course. I have been distillin' it down to its component parts and there are some strange elements in there. I have not been able to identify most of them, but I've been experimentin' with what I found. Some elements just evaporate. Soon as it touches the air, it's gone. Ain't yet figured out a way to capture it. But then there was this residue in the test tube."

Ben was listening avidly and fetched himself a seat so that he could be more comfortable. He didn't offer Lieutenant Mackeye the same courtesy. The Lieutenant noted it mentally.

"I ran a few standard tests on this residue an' damn me if some of its properties ain't just like those of laudanum!" There followed a long string of chemical names, the things that made up the Lazarus base and Mackeye's attention began to wane. He let his eyes wander around the laboratory, the workshop, the... whatever Ben had going on here. His gaze came to rest on what looked like a mechanical arm. Curiosity got the better of him and he moved over to look more closely. He could hear Lady Annabelle's voice as she continued to hold court with her intrigued and devoted audience of one.

It *was* an arm. At least, most of an arm. It was constructed entirely from a dull, non-reflective metal that had the look of brushed steel and from what little Mackeye understood of anatomy, was designed in the same way that a real arm was. A ball and socket joint would connect to a shoulder, presumably either of the same artificial design or possibly even to organic bone and the arm would move freely within the limits of its rotation. A brief thought struck him that it might even rotate more if it was not restricted by natural musculature.

He put out a hand and allowed himself to touch the metal. To his surprise, it was not cold. It wasn't warm, not exactly. Not in the way that flesh and blood radiated warmth, but there was a latent heat in the material. Whatever it was, it wasn't anything that Mackeye was familiar with. He glanced over his shoulder. The Hamiltons were still engrossed in their discussion and so he picked the limb up.

It weighed next to nothing. Before the Lieutenant had the time to marvel at the lack of weight to it, the fingers began to open and close of their own accord, reaching and grasping for who only knew what. Mackeye let out a gasp of shock and dropped the limb back onto the workbench, where it continued to claw at the air. The action caused it to scrabble across the bench like an animal in its death throes. It was ghastly to watch.

Ben's head snapped up and he got to his feet, hurrying over to pick up the limb. He took a tool out from the belt he'd strapped on and made a couple of adjustments. The fingers slowly, painstakingly slowly, ceased to move and the appendage was still once more.

"I'd appreciate it if you didn't touch things in here, Lieutenant. Some of it is very delicate." He set the inert prosthetic down. "And as you can see, some of it simply isn't finished. When it's done, it will be marvellous, but until then, don't touch, hmm?"

It was embarrassing. Ben was speaking to him as though he were a child. The Lieutenant, feeling oddly chastised, mumbled an apology, adding that he'd only wanted to look at it and how impressed he was with what he'd seen. It was entirely the correct thing to say.

"Really? You like it? Oh, that's just *marvellous!* Annabelle, this man of yours is very perceptive! Look, Lieutenant, let me show you one of the other hand attachments..." And before Mackeye could even comment, Ben twisted the metal hand on the end of the limb. It came off with a soft 'click' and Ben fumbled about on the workbench. He retrieved something that looked very much like a fan of stiletto knives and connected it to the arm. He held it up, a huge beaming smile on his handsome face, clearly expecting some sort of reaction.

"That's..." Mackeye sought for words. Ben made another couple of adjustments with the screwdriver-like tool in his hand and the blades came to sudden terrifying life, spinning so fast that they blurred in his vision. Mackeye imagined what something like that would do if it met with flesh and a sickening feeling began in his stomach. "That's..."

"Genius?" The prompt was so earnest and hopeful, the parti-coloured eyes so wide and enthusiastic that Mackeye gave in. Damn, but the boy was like his sister.

"That's genius," he conceded and was rewarded with a happy smile. He was also rewarded with Ben Hamilton stopping the blades whirring and for that, he was infinitely grateful.

"Wait until you see what it's like when Annabelle adds it to one of her reconstructed soldiers," he said.

Ross Mackeye had a brief but terrifying flash of what the future might be like in the hands of people like the Hamilton twins and asked himself for the thousandth time whether this was all going to be worth it. Something must have shown in his face: perhaps it was the way all the colour drained from his cheeks, perhaps his usually rigid stance relaxed slightly, but whatever it was, Lady Annabelle came up behind him and touched his arm lightly with her own elegantly fashioned prothesis.

"We do what we must do for the South to rise, Lieutenant," she said, in the kind of soft, gentle voice that he had always hoped she would use for him – but certainly not in this particular context.

Mackeye's blood froze in his veins and, so help him, he did not know if it was with fear or true delight at the prospect.

"Provenance was just a testing ground. A recruitment facility for early experimentation," she continued. "There's a bigger, better facility 'bout halfway back there. Out in the middle of nowhere, where we won't be disturbed. Mind, everywhere in these parts is in the middle of nowhere, ain't that so, Benjamin?"

"True enough, but useful for our purposes."

201

"Now, I'm hopin' that my *darlin'* brother here is gonna come with us an' help me to put some of *his* creations together with *my* creations." She studied her brother earnestly and spontaneously took his hands. "Ya still should come with me, Benjamin. There ain't no place for you with that Jackson fella. Y'all are so much *better* than that."

"He's good to me. And I like his ideals."

"Damn ya for the stubborn bastard ya are."

If Ben was shocked at his sister's use of strong language, it didn't show on his face. "I'll come with you for this experiment, Annabelle. I promised you that. But I have my own duties to attend to. You know how I feel about Carpathian."

"Fine." She pouted prettily. "I'll let ya off with it this time. But I ain't ever gonna stop tryin' to convince ya." She took his hands and leaned forward to kiss his cheek in a gesture of sibling affection. "My Hellions have been busy. Lots of subjects to be found out in the wilds of the frontier. There'll be plenty for ya to do. And if my theory is right, then plenty for me, too."

Ben glanced over at Mackeye, looking a little uncomfortable. "She knew I can't say 'no' to her. Never have been able to," he said, by way of explanation. There was nothing affectionate in that phrase, Mackeye noted. "Let me gather a few things together and we can go and get some work done."

While the Hamilton brother busied himself, Lady Annabelle drew Mackeye away to speak to him quietly. "Ya have to excuse Benjamin," she said, sweetly. "He does get so excited over his work that he sometimes forgets his manners. He don't mean nothin' by the way he is. Don't ya be takin' no offence at him now."

"None taken, ma'am, I assure you. You mentioned the Hellions. I wondered where they had got to." She smiled that same sweet smile again.

"I like to think several steps ahead," she told him. "An' they are *such* good little things. They'll be waitin' for us back in Arizona." She said those last four syllables with extreme distaste.

Mackeye struggled to reconcile what he knew of the Hellions with the words 'good' and 'little'. Only 'things' seemed right. He'd definitely wondered where they'd got to – but he had also hoped that he would never have to see them again. Ever since Annabelle had acquired the Hellion from that psychopath Caym, Mackeye had regarded them with a mixture of fear and loathing. Even now he had to force himself to push aside all the discomfort he was feeling and focus on his task. He had been hired to ensure Annabelle Hamilton's safety and when that had been all he had to do, life had been simple. It was getting more and more complicated by the day. His discomfort must have shown on his face, because Lady Annabelle tipped her head to one side.

"Everythin' alright, Lieutenant Mackeye?"

"I'm good, ma'am. Just a little... overwhelmed by all this science, I suppose. I'm an old-fashioned sort of man."

"That y'are," she said, with deep fondness and she patted his cheek. "An' ain't ya adorable for it."

Somehow, despite everything that he had just seen and heard, the Lieutenant found her words the most difficult to reconcile. She smiled her beautiful smile at him, and he was, as ever, hopelessly lost.

"C'mon, Lieutenant," she said, catching him by the hand and tugging at him, like a child eager for a parent to follow where she led. "Let me show you more efficiently how the Lazarus works. 'Course, what we got here ain't so ripe for the process as what I had on the Slough Pile back in Arizona, but Benjamin's managed to bring us some fresh meat."

The Slough Pile. Fresh meat. The way Annabelle Hamilton spoke about the dying was disconcerting. Mackeye had seen the Slough Pile, of course, back in Provenance. It was the name Annabelle had given to the veritable mountain of the mostly dead and dying. Many were brought in as lost causes: illnesses that could no longer be treated, injuries that could not be healed. They were all kept in dormitory-style accommodations that were poorly kept and it was from those rooms she selected those on whom she would experiment, seeking to forever alter them and 'make them better'.

"Most of my peers don't like to work with the sick or the infirm," she commented as she unhooked a leather work apron from beside the door and moved toward her work area. "My own experiments tell me that too long dead just ain't good enough. There's still work to be done there, I think, but it could be somethin' I accomplish with time. So, for now, for my current purposes, I prefer the slow-dyin', or someone right on their last breath. Anythin' older than that starts gettin' a little bit too ripe even for my sensibilities. I like my subjects weak enough to be pliant, but alive enough to fight back. An' what's even more perfect, are those whose failin' bodies are *prepared*."

"Lazarus, you mean?"

"Mhmm. Ain't ya the smart one?" She reached out and tweaked his cheek with her mechanical arm like he was a child. The metal fingers felt surprisingly warm like that arm had on the bench, though the touch was far from gentle.

Annabelle began to fasten the apron at her waist. "Lazarus at the point of death? Why, that's a miracle cure. It will hold a person in that moment for longer than they were meant to survive. Combine that with the skills of those who build the constructs, or the prosthetics my little brother builds and why, Lieutenant. Damn me if ya don't have a nigh-invulnerable workforce, or army on ya hands." There it was again: her easy talk of raising an army.

There were two bodies laid out on slabs, thoughtfully covered with sheets which she yanked aside to reveal that they were both males, one little more than a boy and the second an older man, maybe in his fifties. She studied them with the practised eye of a coroner, reaching over to one and raising an eyelid. The eyeball beneath was bloodshot and strangely distorted. "Likely brain haemorrhage," she said dismissively. "No good to me. Brain's the important part in this situation. Time will come when I can do more experimentation with those deader than doornails, but that ain't today."

She moved to the other body and repeated the exercise, lifting the eyelids. She clapped her hands together delightedly. To Mackeye's horror, he saw a twitch in the boy's hand. He couldn't determine if it was just a reflexive action or if the youth was still clinging onto life – but then he became acutely aware that the chest was rising and falling – albeit with a judder. He could hear a rattle in the boy's lungs. Pneumonia, perhaps.

Annabelle reached for a scalpel that was laid out with a variety of other tools on a nearby table. She made a deep incision in the young man's body, dragging a line from left shoulder to sternum, then an identical line from the right. Finally, she drew the blade down the boy's abdomen.

Lazarus

The weak, pathetic moan that rose to a scream and then cut off abruptly answered the Lieutenant's earlier query as to the existential state of the boy. He *had* still been alive, even if only barely. Now he was – as Annabelle had worded it – one of the recently deceased.

Dead enough to be pliant, alive enough to fight back.

"Saw," she said and then, when Mackeye didn't respond quickly enough, she barked the word at him as though giving an order. Grimacing, the Lieutenant picked up the bone saw and tried not to let his distaste show when she hacked through the breastbone and snapped the ribs back enough to get to the heart. She put her hand in and drew the organ out through the cavity.

By now, she was covered in gore, despite the apron her delightful outfit now a sodden, scarlet memory of what it had been when she'd dressed. She studied the dead man's heart closely and nodded. "See the swellin' here and here?" She gave a running commentary, heedless of who may or may not be listening. "The product of too much good livin', rich food an' fine wine. Our friend here... why, his heart just couldn't cope any more. He's perfect." She squeezed the heart in her hand, which squished with a most unpleasant sound.

Mackeye stared and forced himself not to wrinkle his nose. He chose his words very carefully as he studied the organ in Annabelle's hands. "Surely even in this new... this new *state*, he will require a heart to continue to function.?"

"Why of course he will." Annabelle's reply was bright. "I just have to make some modifications first. Poor ol' fleshy thing could scarce take the strain otherwise." She produced a vial filled with a reddish substance that the Lieutenant had come, over recent weeks, to recognise as Lazarus. She clipped the vial to a wicked-looking syringe and jammed it into the heart, pressing the plunger until all the contents had been deposited.

"Just a li'l somethin' to get him started and to keep him goin'. An' our new subject here... why, he will be right as rain in no time. Mind, this is truly wasteful, usin' a whole dose like this. Now folks who have been takin' the Lazarus for a while, they build up enough in their heart over time for this process to be more... natural." She smiled sweetly as though immensely pleased with herself. "It's fine stuff. Hopelessly addictive. Folks just can't get enough of it once they get their first taste."

Mackeye could not agree with the idea that any of this was 'natural' in any way, shape or form, but wisely chose to keep his thoughts to himself. He was quiet as Annabelle continued. Then he voiced his thoughts aloud.

"I start to understand now. It's not just the physical experimentation you've been doing – the work with the constructs in the mine, but also researching the effects of Lazarus on those who have *not* become constructs."

"Why, Lieutenant!" She stood motionless, the boy's heart in her hand, blood oozing down her arm and staining her pale yellow gown the colour of fresh meat. "Y'all are *so* much more perceptive than I gave ya credit for!" She was delighted. He was appalled. "Now then, we'll just pop this li'l darlin' right back in here before it gets too excited." Black, throbbing veins had already begun to creep over the surface of the organ. She pushed it back into the open chest cavity and pushed the ribs closed with a wet, unpleasant *crack*.

"Ain't the human body a marvel, though, Lieutenant? With just a gentle push in the right direction it can heal an' mend almost anythin' that happens to it. And with the right engineers to replace what's broken... it's astonishing."

She pulled the abused skin back over the exposed viscera, leaving a ragged Y-shaped slash. As Mackeye watched, a delicate lattice of dark vessels formed around the damaged tissue and partially knitted it back together. Sluggish gore still leaked from several tears, but the body looked as though it was going to hold together.

"It ain't perfect," Annabelle said, studying the corpse objectively. "An' they burn through a large dose like that so very quickly. But when all ya need is foot soldiers, perfect ain't a major factor." Mackeye stiffened at the casual disregard with which she spoke of soldiers. Perhaps sensing his irritation, she gave him another of her dazzling smiles. "Apart from you, of course, Lieutenant. Why, ain't ya just dandy the way ya are?" It was impossible for him to hope to gauge her sincerity and so he carefully chose to accept what she said at face value.

"I'm glad my service is appreciated," he replied, awkwardly.

"Of course it is." She patted him fondly on the cheek, leaving a bloodied smear and then returned her attention to the butchered corpse. "Now then. With just a li'l more work, we will have him back on his feet. But first..." She waved a hand imperiously and raised her voice. "Benjamin!"

Her brother entered the room loaded down with some kind of harness. It was all hinges and straps, folding joints and brass. It dangled loosely, like a flattened anatomical skeleton comically missing its head, but Mackeye knew the Hamiltons too well by now to find anything remotely humorous in the creations that they produced.

"Y'all ready to go once we're done, Benjamin?"

Ben stopped beside the autopsy slab and nodded. "Ready when you are. The generators are running flat out, but with everything else shut down, it will be enough to power the gateway. Now, here's what I've come up with. If you'll just..." He hoisted the harness up and huffed with the effort. "If you will just turn the subject over? I'm eager to see your Lazarus in action."

Annabelle clapped her hands in delight. "Lieutenant, would ya be a dear and turn this young fella over for my brother?" Mackeye could only think of a few things he would enjoy less than carrying out her request, but he nodded stoically and reached across the body, rolling it over. The boy *must* be dead. Nobody could endure anything like that.

"Good, good. Now, then..." Ben heaved the harness onto the motionless boy's back and straightened it out. After a small amount of tugging and shuffling, he fastened it around the body's waist and the remaining hinged pieces lay beside the flaccid limbs. Most disturbingly, the harness sported a segmented, artificial spine which ran from neck to hip. Satisfied that everything was where it needed to be, Ben moved around to the platter of implements and took up a steel-headed hammer.

"This will be so much easier and more efficient when we're at the production facility of course," he said, giving a running commentary as he began to work. "The subjects should ideally be upright during the fitting, but for this demonstration, well this will have to do." Thick rivets protruded from the shoulders, hinges and spine. Ben lined up the hammer and with a single blow, drove one of the rivets into the body, fastening the steel in place with an unpleasant crack of bone.

Annabelle watched in rapt fascination as her brother moved around the table, hammering the remaining rivets into place until the harness was fully attached, complete with a socketed cup that covered the back of the skull.

"Why, Benjamin, if ya hadn't already been called a genius once today already, I'd absolutely be doin' that right now! They'll be so much sturdier like this. Much less of the vague wanderin' around."

Ben stepped back and surveyed his work with a critical eye. "That's the idea, Annabelle. Now then, I've done my part." He gestured to the skull socket. "I am keen to see you do yours."

Annabelle produced another vial from her bloodied skirts, this one much larger and sheathed in steel. It sported a wicked-looking hollow spike at one end and a faint crimson light leaked from a slit in its side. She leaned over the inert body and without so much as pausing, drove the spike into the socket. There was another crunch of bone as the tube pierced the base of the skull.

The boy's eyes opened wide.

Mackeye winced involuntarily and took a step or two back.

"That should do it," Annabelle beamed, evidently delighted with herself. "Just make sure to keep your sabre to hand, Lieutenant. Every once in a great while, one of them gets a li'l, shall we say, *enthusiastic*? Takin' off their heads at that point is the only decent thing to do. Best that before they get too wild."

The creation twitched and jerked a few times before letting out a long, slow exhalation. Then he seemed to undergo some sort of massive seizure, writhing and thrashing on the slab with unnatural animation. Half a minute passed before he once again fell still.

There was absolute silence in the room. All three of them held their collective breaths.

Then, with an awkward staccato motion, the young man slid from the slab and stood swaying in the middle of the room. His jaw hung slack, and the eyes were vacant, but he was undeniably, horribly alive. At least, after a fashion.

"*Now* who's the genius?" Ben grinned boyishly at his sister, and she preened under his words.

"It would be unladylike of me not to accept such a compliment, Benjamin."

"We're gonna do great things together, you and I. Great things!"

"Then we should make a start on that, don't you think?"

"We should." Ben nodded emphatically and glanced at Mackeye as if suddenly recalling the other man was there. "You coming, Lieutenant?"

Mackeye had watched the exchange with the same mixture of admiration and absolute horror that had haunted him since his arrival. While in Provenance, he had been Annabelle's fetcher and carrier, and occasional dinner companion. He had known that she was producing these things, but never once had he witnessed their creation. He was torn by a split sense of admiration and horror.

"Lieutenant?" Ben repeated the question and Mackeye just nodded mutely, following the twins as they left the room arm in arm. He glanced back just once before he left. The newly birthed creation simply stood there, swaying gently, its new artificial joints

211

squeaking. Mackeye knew, with absolute certainty, that it would continue to stand there until the flesh rotted from its bones, watching through its horrid, pale eyes as its own body slowly disintegrated.

Did it know what it was? Did anything of who it had once been remain behind that unblinking gaze?

He recoiled from the thought, hurrying after the twins.

Ben led them to a large basement room where some equipment had been piled beside a massive ring of iron and cabling that stood upright, its upper edge nearly touching the ceiling. The noise was deafening, atrocious, and Mackeye saw no fewer than four generators running at full capacity wired into the device. Ben immediately went to work at a panel of switches and dials. The noise rose in pitch and volume, increasing until it reached nigh-on unbearable levels.

"I tell you Annabelle, if our friends in the Enlightened had sold us this before the end of the war, things would have been very different." Ben shouted above the din of the machine. Mackeye looked at him blankly and Ben laughed with delight at the Lieutenant's confusion. "Ready to head back to the Arizona territories?" he said with a flourish that Mackeye couldn't help thinking was a tad unnecessarily over-dramatic. "Behold, the void-engine! A miracle of modern science!"

He pulled a switch and several massive breakers sparked as the power engaged. The space within the ring blurred weirdly as though viewed through frosted glass and then it darkened, cracked with scarlet-tinged arcs of lightning and fell in on itself. A flat plane of absolutely nothing hung within the circle, though Mackeye was sure *something* moved within it. Whenever he tried to look directly at it, however, it slithered out of view.

Annabelle looked over her shoulder at him and smiled that heart-breaking smile. "Come along then, darlin'," she said. Then, she stepped into the hole and vanished.

While scientists and engineers like Annabelle and her brother made portal travel appear so conventional, to most in the world it still seemed utterly alien. But, to give him his credit, Ross Mackeye hesitated for only a moment before he charged after her.

* * *

There were Union soldiers everywhere, which was only to be expected in a barracks. That knowledge did not serve to make Doc Holliday feel any less uncomfortable, though. The masked lawman had drawn more than one curious glance as the small group rode their Iron Horses in through the gates and more than one of those glances had been, to Doc's eyes at least, outright hostile. He knew it was his imagination.

Probably.

He was uncharacteristically quiet as he followed Willa to the CO's office, set in a white-walled adobe. It was blissfully cool inside, and the young lawman removed his respirator as they entered. It was less a show of respect than it was a need to breathe something other than his own constantly recycled oxygen. After a while, it got stale and unpleasant inside his respirator. He still hated his dependence on it, but when he did not wear it, he felt its absence keenly.

Colonel Hackett was a powerfully-built man in his early fifties, sporting an impressive walrus-style moustache that dominated his face. Age had not diminished his powerful build at all and he looked more than capable of taking on enemies *mano-a-mano.* He looked up at the arrival of Willa and Doc and he studied first her, then the lawman. He noted her stripes and nodded a welcome.

"Major," he said as she snapped a smart salute. "Welcome to Fort Wall. What brings you to our little corner of the Arizona Territories?"

"Lazarus, sir," she replied and the affable expression on the Colonel's face was immediately replaced by one of controlled anger. "We've been investigating a number of leads. Myself and Deputy Holliday here, sir..."

"Holliday?" The Colonel's piercing gaze turned to Doc. "One of Earp's men, aren't you?"

"I like to think I am my own man, sir, but otherwise, yes. That is right enough. Although I am presently workin' with Bass..." The Colonel nodded and interrupted.

"Earp's got a good reputation in these parts, despite his tendency to be... what is the politest way I can put it?"

"Obnoxious? Self-satisfied? Belligerent?"

A smile lifted the impressive moustache above the Colonel's lips and he inclined his head, acknowledging Doc's choice of phrases. "Belligerent, yes. I understand that he has very little trust for us and perhaps we haven't always seen eye to eye with the way Lawmen do things around here." He took on a serious manner again. "Such differences notwithstanding, you are most welcome here, deputy. Why don't the two of you take a seat and tell me what you've learned?"

Doc glanced at Willa. She was all business, all military, all... *Union* in front of the Colonel and he felt desperately uncomfortable. Not only did he not have a military bone in his entire body – he'd ever preferred the looser structure of law reinforcement – but he was among the *Union*. Yes, things were different now, but he was still, when all was said and done, a man from Georgia and old memories ran very, very deep. He came from a large, extended family and many of his ancestral menfolk had lost their lives in old battles.

He became aware that Willa was watching him, and he shifted awkwardly. She nodded, mostly to herself. "Why don't you go take care of the vehicles, Deputy Holliday? I can brief the Colonel with what we've discovered." It was a thoughtful gesture, and he was immensely grateful for it. He nodded to her and to Colonel Hackett and left the cool building.

He'd lived in Arizona for long enough that the wall of heat didn't startle him when he stepped into it, but out of a habit borne of months of living with the respirator, he put the device straight back on over his mouth and nose. It clicked a few times and didn't do what it was supposed to. Removing the respirator again, he studied it without the faintest clue what he was looking at. Since it'd been knocked from his face back in Provenance, it had been intermittent at best.

"Work, you useless piece of..." He thumped it against the flat of his hand and put it back on again. Whether by luck or design, the action appeared to have had a result. It clicked again and then he felt the flow of air into his lungs. He was going to have to get the thing looked at and properly fixed.

As he headed back to their parked vehicles, he ignored the glances he received from the various blue-clad soldiers. His back straightened and he forced his usual swagger into his walk. So what if they were all staring? Let them stare. He could more than hold his own against them, he knew that.

By the time he reached the Iron Horses, the germ of an idea had taken root in his thoughts. By the time he'd finished considering it, the more that idea had taken hold, roots bursting through the surface of his mind, subsuming rational thought and logic and replacing such things instead with the man's more customary over-inflated sense of ego. He straddled the Iron Horse that had once belonged to Zachariah King and checked the fuel gauge. It was still more than half full. By their reckoning, and after Willa had spent some time looking at a map and listening to Doc's descriptions of the area, they'd pinpointed, more or less, where the Hamilton facility was. It was an approximately thirty minute ride east from where the Union barracks were.

He could be there, study the lay of the land and get a feel for what they were up against and be back within the hour. What could possibly go wrong with a quick reconnoitre?

The alternative was to stay here in this camp along with all these *Union* soldiers – he could not help but emphasise the word in his head – and stand around like a spare part. No, being proactive would serve everyone that much better. Mind thus made up, Doc glanced briefly around the barracks and gunned the Iron Horse into life. Not a single soul so much as raised an eyebrow as the lawman raced out of Fort Wall and into the trackless plains.

He'd long mastered the art of finding his bearings by the position of the sun, but as the vehicle had a built-in compass on the dash, it would be rude not to use it. He brought the map of the surrounding area up in his mind. To the south and west lay some of the Warrior Nation grounds and he had rarely had dealings with them. They kept to themselves and that was the way they liked it. Doc rather liked it that way, too.

Hamilton was pushing her luck constructing a facility so close to Warrior Nation territory. If they even got wind of what she was up to...

There was no way in all of creation that Doc Holliday could muster any sort of sympathy for what might happen to Annabelle Hamilton if they got hold of her. He had seen what she was capable of back in Provenance and it had been the single most unethical use of science he'd ever witnessed.

Thoughts of Morgan flashed through his thoughts once again and he bit back his own sarcasm. *Focus, Holliday. Just focus.*

The ride was dry, dusty and almost unnervingly without incident. He drew the vehicle to a standstill atop a ridge that overlooked the supposed site of the Hamilton laboratory. A number of warehouse buildings sat in a rocky basin with crude, corrugated iron roofs surrounding a low, square building studded with some sort of antennae. Thick cabling trailed from its walls and terminated at a mesh fence which completely surrounded the complex. He had no idea at all what they place may have been previously; his best guess was that it had been custom built for Hamilton.

The deputy dropped from the Iron Horse and pulled himself up to a good vantage point atop a cluster of boulders. It gave him a decent enough view across the depression in which the facility lay. There was silence. The valley floor was absolutely still; sheltered even from the lightest of breezes that stirred the warm, heavy air. There was something faintly serene about it and Doc Holliday did not like it. Not one little bit.

He was too cynical and had survived too much – even at his relatively young age – to believe in premonition or predetermination, but he had a creeping sensation that something was not right here. That something was about to go horrendously wrong. What he did not anticipate was the sudden and unexpected beating of mechanical wings that heralded something dreadful.

A shadow fell across the lawman in his hiding spot, and he squinted up into the sky just in time to see the man-sized creature with the vast, mechanical wings settle to the ground in front of him. He groaned inwardly, recognising them for what they were: Hellions. The outlaw Caym had attacked the heavy rail near Tombstone last year and Morgan and Martha had gone to sort it out. He knew how nasty these things could be. Doc Holliday had a justifiably earned reputation as one of the fastest draws in the west and he had his pistols in his hands faster than the eye could conceivably follow.

"Stop right there," he said eyeing the thing and keeping the creeping horror under control. Quite how he managed that, he did not know. It was, like the things back in Provenance, mostly human in form. But it had been so horrendously altered and twisted that he felt bilious just looking at it. Half of the face and the lower jaw had been removed to be replaced with metal plates that gave the flying horror a bite that Doc guessed could crunch right through flesh and bone. It repeatedly gnashed those jaws together in a threatening gesture.

The long, spindly arms ended in heavy talons, with razor-sharp claws that grasped towards him. Rolling back nimbly, Doc avoided its initial reach and discharged first one, then the other pistol directly into its chest. The creature rocked back, a pair of smoking holes in its torso, and the jaws opened wide, emitting an unholy shriek that caused the lawman to drop his pistols and clamp his hands against his ears against its drum-shattering timbre.

The sound reverberated around the valley and to his intense discomfort, Doc heard an answering cry from somewhere down on the valley floor. He could not afford to take his attention off his attacker, whatever might be coming for him, and he scooped up his guns and jumped backward again, firing for a second time. The winged horror staggered, and a spray of pinkish fluid escaped its maw. It simply screeched again, before beating the huge wings at its back, rising with surprising grace given its ungainly appearance. Doc swore furiously as a second creature burst up above the ridge line and swooped down to join the first.

"I ain't gonna go out fightin' a pair of jumped-up damn turkey buzzards," he snarled beneath the respirator. The pair of creatures lashed at him with snapping, mechanised claws, but he wove between them like a dancer, a pistol trained on each. He squeezed off another pair of shots towards them and again, his aim was true. This time, a wound seemed to register as a fist-sized hunk of meat was blasted from its shoulder in a shower of grey tissue and tainted blood. Sluggish arterial gore painted the dry rocks where it gave off a faintly disturbing and certainly unnatural glow. The damaged monster let out another of those cringe-inducing shrieks and dove awkwardly into cover to nurse its wounds.

The remaining creature spread its oddly graceful steel wings and dove at the lawman. He rolled in the dust, the snapping claws of the thing's iron-shod feet closing mere inches from his flesh. He shot it again, to little effect, the slowly oozing punctures where its vital organs should have been inconveniencing it not in the slightest.

If anything at all had remained of its humanity it would have been crippled, doubled up in agony, but it was evidently clear that it was far beyond the concerns of the flesh. In that instant, Doc had his answer. He berated himself harshly, all the time ducking and rolling away from the creature still busily attempting to disembowel him.

"My mamma," he said, to the creature, not caring one bit if it heard him, understood him, or even cared. "My mamma told me that tearin' the wings off things ain't the kind of thing a nice young gentleman does. Ain't it unfortunate for you..." He took aim.

"...that I am not a nice young gentleman anymore?"

He fired.

The shot shattered the intricate joint that hinged its metallic pinions. Rivets and delicate bearings exploded in a shower of shrapnel. With a squawk of what Doc liked to think was outrage, it wheeled out of control, thrashing its wings as hard as it could manage in an effort to right itself. The effort was largely wasted, as before it could attempt a safe descent, Doc shot it again. This one tore through its other wing and the creature shrieked one final time before plummeting to the valley floor in a tangle of limbs. It hit the ground with a satisfying crunch and continued to flail like a broken clockwork toy.

The second Hellion took advantage of Doc's brief distraction to lunge from hiding. It swooped in behind him and ploughed into the lawman from behind, knocking him over the edge of the ridge. Swearing and cussing the entire way, Doc tumbled down the valley side, rolling in the dust and crashing from rock to rock until he sprawled to a halt inches from where the broken-winged creature was attempting to right itself.

All the wind had been knocked out of him causing his respirator to send a fresh burst of air to compensate. He had bitten his tongue on the way down and had, to his dismay, also let go of his guns again. His mouth was filled with the iron tang of his own blood; a flavour to which he was well accustomed, but by that same token, which he had never liked. His world spun for a few moments, and he struggled to his feet just as his airborne assailant swooped into him again. This time, it kicked him hard in the chest, its claws biting into his flesh. The impact flipped him off his feet and he found himself sprawling in the dust for a second time, his face horribly close to the mesh that surrounded the Hamilton complex. There was a faint buzzing in the air that made his gums itch, and he knew, without really knowing, that it would be an *incredibly* bad idea to touch the fence.

Then something hard and metallic hit him in the face and rolled him onto his back. The pain was excruciating.

This is not *the way I'm going to die.*

Such fierce determination had been the mark of Holliday's life. From his early years, when he had struggled with languages until he finally mastered them, through to his education in dentistry, learning to play poker, how to shoot a gun... through all these times, Doc Holliday had demonstrated perseverance and a desperate drive to succeed. And against all the odds, he had.

So, when he told himself that he was not going to die like this, bleeding and torn to pieces by a pair of armoured vultures, a flood of adrenaline dragged him upwards. His pistols were gone, lost somewhere in the dust up on the ridge, but that didn't matter. He still had hands, and he still had his knife, which he pulled now from his belt.

He stood, swaying just ever so slightly, brandishing the blade.

"One step closer, an' I will fillet you."

Whether or not it understood him, he didn't know, but it did pause momentarily at the sight of the weapon. Some strange expression flittered across its malformed face, confusion perhaps? A memory of a life that had come before it had become the thing that it now was.

There was a stand-off that lasted a full three seconds before both creatures closed in on him. He swung the knife in a wide arc, keeping one of them at bay for a moment and kicked a plume of dust up into the face of the other. Even without organic eyes, the monster seemed momentarily blinded. He took the opportunity to bury his blade in the joint of its knee, where flesh and steel fused. The limb went dead, and it crumpled to the ground, howling furiously. The second darted in and Doc buried his knife up to the hilt in its throat. It gurgled unpleasantly, spitting acrid-smelling bile all over the lawman and blinding him temporarily. He reached up to wipe the fluid from his face just as something struck him hard in the gut.

He flew backward again with the force of the blow, but this time, he could not get up. His chest was on fire. He had actually felt something tear in there, a feeling he knew all too well. His lungs, with such poor material to work with, frequently tore at the slightest provocation. Something had broken in his chest, and he could feel his thoracic cavity beginning to fill up with blood. The respirator helped him to breathe, but it in no way cured him of the disease that was ravaging his lungs, and neither would it stop him drowning in his own fluids. That last blow had been too much, and he stumbled into a boulder, legs rubbery with the effort of remaining upright. He slid down it without any hint of grace or élan, coughing desperately behind the respirator. He was drowning. He may as well have been immersed in the Mississippi as far as his body was concerned. The irony of drowning in the middle of the Arizona barrens was not *entirely* wasted.

There was only one way to clear the detritus in his chest at that moment and he hated doing it. But it was either that or slow asphyxiation. He slumped against the boulder, reached up and ripped the respirator from its clasps. He then proceeded to hawk up gobbets of blood, phlegm and frothing tissue. After a second of two, he was able to draw a shuddering, shaky breath that did little to fill his lungs with oxygen. He gulped a few times and then, when he was sure the worst of it was over, he put the respirator back on. Its effects were instant and, to his great relief, the sensation of drowning began to ebb away.

Not today, Doc. It was Wyatt's voice he heard in the back of his mind and just for a moment, he wished his friend were here right now. *It's not your time to go and I'm not going to let you.*

Who are you doing it for, Wyatt? Me, or for yourself?

Suddenly, that old feud seemed very, very ridiculous. If he got out of this situation alive – which given the current circumstances was not looking favourable – he would sort the mess out. He'd fix what had broken in their friendship and he would make every day count.

First, however, he had two marauding monstrosities to kill. One problem at a time, the miasma of fatigue drained from his sight and he realised that no further attacks were forthcoming. He looked up and realised that the things had retreated. They had not gone; they remained hunched a few yards away, but they seemed docile and unresponsive, as though someone had ordered them to stand down their attack.

"Well now," came a voice. Soft, feminine. Georgian, like his own, but stronger and far less tempered by a life of travelling. "If my eyes don't deceive me, ya gotta be Henry Holliday. My goodness me. Look at ya. Ain't you a pitiful sight? What *would* your Mamma say if she were here? Oh, damn, that was right bad of me. She *ain't* here, is she? Now what was it killed poor Alice all them years past? Same thing that's eatin' ya, I guess. Tragic. Truly tragic." There was no sympathy in the tone. It was pure mockery.

The lawman turned toward the voice and the petite, dark-haired figure of Annabelle Hamilton came into view. She gaily twirled an open parasol in her mechanical arm, to protect her from the heat of the day. Her long yellow skirts brushed the dust at her feet and the silk swished as she walked. She came to a stop in front of the injured Doc and tipped her head to one side.

"Ya ain't lookin' well there, Henry. Need a bit of a lie-down?"

"Shut up." Doc's voice was low and had it not been bubbling with blood and rasping from the endless coughing, would have carried a note of danger. Annabelle Hamilton simply fanned at herself with an exquisite lace fan held in her other hand and stepped closer to the stricken deputy.

"The Hamiltons and the Hollidays," she said. "Separated by 'bout fifteen miles, no more. In another world, we would've been contemporaries. But look at what ya done gone to yourself, Henry. Why, ya ain't no good prospect for no girl." She lifted one foot and pushed against his shoulder, sending him sprawling into the dust again. "Why the hell ain't ya dead yet? Ya mamma at least had the decency to let the disease take her when it should. But li'l Henry Junior just keeps draggin' right on, long past his time was up."

"Shut. Up." If Doc had one trigger that was guaranteed to get a rise, it was talk of his mother. He had adored her, and his world had been devastated the day consumption had taken her from him. He thought back, briefly, to the fifteen-year-old boy who had been passed from uncle to aunt, until he had gone to medical school. He could not help but compare that bright, optimistic young man with the broken thing he had become. He looked up at her, his vision still swimming slightly from the attack.

"That ain't no way to talk to a lady now, is it?" She tipped her head on one side and laughed, a tinkling, silvery sound that was full of menace. Doc let his fingers creep to the hilt of the knife that lay on the floor beside him. He was most definitely not beyond cutting this bitch down in cold blood. Whether he could or would be fast enough to accomplish that task was the only thing in question.

"I ain't seein' no lady here," he retorted, and she laughed again. One of her winged beasts took a step forward as though it would end the Lawman right there and then, but she held up a hand to stop it in its tracks.

"No," she said, holding up her delicate mechanical hand. "I'm feelin' benevolent. Let us allow the good dentist here to go back to his friends. Because he's seen, now He sees what we can do an' he knows just how futile anythin' he or his little tin soldiers might try would be." She crouched down in front of him and patted the respirator where his cheek would be.

"Like what ya seen, darlin'? These Hellions,

225

Doctor Holliday, are just some of my beauties an' they are, I promise ya, the very least of what I got to offer. What we have goin' on here, my darlin' Henry, is the future." She indicated the two Hellions with her fan and then she stood. She pushed lightly on the fallen man's shoulders until he toppled, ending flat on his back. With another of those tinkling laughs, she spun gracefully until her heeled, booted foot came to rest on Doc's thin chest. "Whereas y'all can consider that ya very much a relic of a past that's best left on the prairie for the dogs." She considered him, keeping her foot where it was.

"But ya know, I could make ya somethin' *so* much better. Don't ya want the South back, Henry? Y'all every bit as much as a Southerner as I am. We got that in common. Give ya body to me an' I can turn ya into somethin' outstandin'." Her eyes shone with what she probably thought was great passion, but what Doc thought was plain, old-fashioned insanity. "What a team we would make. A Hamilton an' a Holliday at the head of the biggest, baddest army the Union folks won't see comin' 'til it's too late."

That did it. She was, Doc reasoned, quite, quite mad.

"Well?" She pressed the issue. "How 'bout it?" He coughed again and was forced to swallow back another mouthful of blood.

"Why, Annabelle Hamilton," Doc said sweetly, defiant to the last. "I can see right to your petticoats from here." The comment threw her off balance, figuratively and literally and she stepped off him before hunkering down beside him once more. Up this close, she was no less beautiful than at a distance, but there was great cruelty in her face as she hissed into Doc's ear.

"Get outta here, Henry. For the sake of our shared heritage, I'm givin' ya this one chance to turn around an' go back to that one-horse town ya call home. What I'm doin' here ain't none of ya business. So, if ya know what's good for ya, then go."

"Your compassion is duly noted, Miss Hamilton."

His fingers twitched against the hilt of the knife, but he was too exhausted, too weak. He cursed his constitution as she turned and walked away from him. She raised one hand and waved absently. "Goodbye, then, Henry Junior. Don't ya fret none. Y'all be dead soon enough an' then ya can give your mamma my *very* warmest regards." She marched through a gate and back into one of the buildings, her minions shuffling, skittering or limping behind her. She was a monster. A callous, heartless monster.

His last thought, before unconsciousness sucked him under, was that he was truly going to enjoy shooting her smug face off her head at some point.

When he surfaced, thirty minutes later, he was alone. His head was aching, and he took stock of his physical condition. The liquid bubbling in his throat had diminished but the charge in his respirator was all but depleted as a result. It had worked overtime to cope with the additional load to his already terribly burdened body.

The injured deputy took a tentative breath and when the pain was no more than a light burn, he declared himself fit to stand. He got upright and stumbled in the direction of his Iron Horse, managing almost two meters before he fell again. He closed his eyes and drew on the intrinsic strength that his long-term condition had given him. For years, he had lived his life by working out the easiest route from point to point.

Before the respirator, he'd not been able to walk any great distance without becoming breathless. Now he could breathe just fine, but speed was most certainly not an option. Inch by painstaking inch, he somehow managed to drag his battered body from the valley and up the shallowest incline of the ridge.

There was a deep-down voice criticising him with great enthusiasm for his decision to come out here by himself. It sounded, he realised glumly, just like Willa Shaw. She wasn't going to let *this* one lie quietly, he suspected.

By the time Doc reached the top of the ridge he was bordering on completely exhausted and had to lean against the Iron Horse for several minutes. He was light-headed, a roaring in his ears that suggested he might pass out again at any given moment and he *hurt*. He was no stranger to pain, and he focused on the present, putting his thoughts in the moment and dismissing as much of the peripheral pain as he could manage. Eventually the dizziness passed, and he was able to trust himself to ride the vehicle.

The trip back to the barracks was not a long one, but he still opted to take it slow. There was, he surmised, no point in surviving a run-in with Annabelle Hamilton and her little flapping army of weirdness only to fall off the Iron Horse on a short hop. His injuries be damned; he'd die of embarrassment if that happened.

He steered the vehicle in through the gates and knew he must look an absolute sight; bloodied and battered, barely managing to keep upright at all. He knew before he looked up that Willa was waiting for him. He could feel her rage radiating from her at a distance of several feet and, to her credit, the moment she saw the state of him, she let go of the vicious tirade she had armed herself with and was preparing to launch at him. She pushed his obvious condition to the top of her mental priorities.

"Doc!" She rushed over as soon as he shut off the engine and helped the beleaguered lawman down off the vehicle. "What the hell happened to you out there?" She ran a critical eye over his condition. "Come on. Straight to the medic with you." Unbidden, she slipped under his arm and propped him up. It was not the most graceful of positions, with the height disparity, but she'd managed with taller men – and certainly heavier ones. Doc Holliday weighed little more than a child and she felt disturbed by just how thin he had become.

"Annabelle Hamilton happened to me." The answer did not surprise her and she bit back the sharp retort. "She is makin' an army up in there," he told the major as she led him into another low-ceiling building. Despite his current condition, despite an extraordinary amount of pain, the dentist in him couldn't help but approve of the cleanliness. The surfaces in here practically *sparkled*. Maybe he was bordering on delirious, but the place brought a pang of yearning for his old practice back in Dodge City.

"An army?"

"Yeah. I am guessin' it's more of those things we saw back in Provenance. An' I encountered a couple with wings. An' they definitely pack a punch... thank you, sir, I can get on the bench myself..." This was said to the physician who cocked an eyebrow as the weakened man struggled to prove his own words. Lieutenant Phineas Taylor had served at this barracks for only a few short years but had been a military doctor for most of his career. He was used to seeing all sorts of independence among the Union troops so was not even remotely impressed by this demonstration of bravado.

"Major, your assistance, if you would?" He was a big bear of a man, nearing his mid-fifties. His hair was steel-grey and he chose to go clean shaven which showed off his worn, craggy face to perfection. He had a perpetual frown on his face and that was evident now as he cast a quick, critical glance over the lawman. Willa helped Doc out of his overcoat and stepped back as the deputy insisted on unbuttoning his own shirt. As he shrugged the fabric clear, she winced at the injuries on his chest. The talons had raked three deep wounds across his torso and already he was beginning to bruise.

More than anything, though, to see how frail he had become was disturbing. She could count the bones in his ribcage, plainly visible. His skin was practically translucent. She forced herself to give him an encouraging smile as Doctor Taylor fetched cloth and water to clean the injuries. She elected to go for lightening the mood, knowing that was his preferred coping mechanism and made an admirable contribution.

"You look like Solomon Smith kicked you from one side of his stable to the other."

To her immense relief, he laughed. That proved to be a mistake and the doctor paused in his cleaning to let the deputy get his breath back. When he was steady again, he nodded at her. "I wish Solomon Smith had been there, darlin'. He would have made short work of those things." His laughter abated and his eyes grew serious. "I suspect they were just the start. I reckon that this army Annabelle Hamilton is creatin' is gonna have the kind of things that no sane person would ever dream up in their craziest nightmares. Aside, m'by, from Carpathian or one of those A-grade Enlightened lunatics. I – do you mind, sir? You could at least have the decency to warm the damned stethoscope up before you stick it on my chest!" The physician, startled by the imperiousness in the deputy's tone, took a step back in alarm.

Willa decided to take control of the situation. "We made an agreement back in Howling Rock, Deputy Holliday," she said, in what Doc had come to think of as her 'Major' voice. "And part of that agreement was that you are under *my* command. Therefore, I command you to shut the hell up and let Doctor Taylor here do his thing and fix you up. Then you can tell me what's going on and we can deal with it accordingly. Do you understand me, sir? Do you?"

Both Doc and Taylor were staring at her, the barracks doctor with an impressed look on his face and Doc with complete, undisguised admiration. The deputy reached for her hand, studied it for a moment or two and then he pulled off his respirator. He raised her hand to his lips and kissed her knuckles with unashamed affection.

"I understand *perfectly,* darlin'," He looked over at the now completely bewildered Doctor Taylor and waved his hand graciously. "You may proceed."

* * *

In the event, his injuries proved to be largely superficial. Once the deep gashes on the lawman's torso were cleaned and stitched – accompanied the entire time by Doc's very loud and surprisingly creative swearing – Lieutenant Taylor identified several cracked ribs, but none broken.

"Lady Luck smilin' on me again, eh?"

Lieutenant Taylor's quiet assessment that the deputy had lost somewhere between sixty to seventy percent of his lung tissue wasn't quite so convinced in Doc's faith in luck, but he chose to say nothing. The strange respirator that he wore was a remarkable feat of modern engineering, but the deputy seemed deeply reluctant to discuss how it worked. At Doc's behest, Lieutenant Taylor took the respirator to the barracks generator room for recharging and a little repair work performed by the resident engineers.

Those two short hours while he was separated from his lifeline were worse by far for Doc than the injuries Hamilton's creatures had left him with. Those injuries were external, and they would, given time and care, heal. His lungs would never mend themselves. Lieutenant Taylor offered him a healthy dose of laudanum to dull the pain and despite hating the stuff, hating how woozy it left him, Doc accepted it readily, with the eagerness of a man who, before Wyatt Earp had made a gift of the respirator, had been an addict. Sleep, no matter how artificially it might be induced, was very welcome right now and as the laudanum soaked into his senses, he dozed fitfully while Willa fretted.

She did not fret about Doc, not exactly, she knew that he was in good hands. On top of that, she did not care to admit that she was worried about him. No, her concern was for what his ridiculous expedition had brought to light. *An army*, he had reported. The thought filled her with dread. They had barely survived dealing with a disorganised mob of Hamilton's creations back in Provenance. The idea of a full army was nothing short of shocking.

Willa Shaw was an eminently pragmatic woman and an excellent soldier. She was also a great leader of men and women who would flock to her call if she rallied them and moment by moment, she was beginning to realise that was exactly what she now needed to do. She left Doc sleeping and being carefully monitored by Lieutenant Taylor and headed out to the main compound, lost in her own thoughts.

Annabelle Hamilton had made her intentions plain and had struck the first blow. If she was building an army, then Willa Shaw would muster an army of her own to meet it. There was an entire garrison of Union soldiers right here – once she spoke with the Colonel, obviously. But she knew what his reaction would be. Before she had even crossed to the other side of the compound, she had already begun planning her units; where she would deploy them, how they would work, how they would support each other. She began running scenarios through her mind. Airborne monsters would be a challenge, but nothing was insurmountable. Not with the might of the Union army behind her.

For the first time in days, Willa began to feel in control of her own life once again. The idea of leading an army on the offensive filled her with passion and patriotism. Annabelle Hamilton would be thwarted; on that point she was absolutely certain.

She only half-listened to the Colonel as she delivered her report and laid out her plans. At first, he seemed incredulous at the idea of an army of abominations, but once it was pitched as a 'new army of the south', the man became instantly more interested in what she had to say. He was, after all, a career soldier – a veteran of the Ore War – and he would not see the hard-won peace jeopardised by the actions of what could only be described as fanatics.

A few short hours later, the call to arms went out and the barracks sprang to life. Willa Shaw nodded in satisfaction as soldiers and engineers scrambled to arms. The motor pool came alive with activity and the heavy doors of the armoury swung open to begin the distribution of heavier ordinance. The great, armoured tread of the Union moved slowly – but once it was in motion, it was nigh on unstoppable.

War was coming.

Sarah Cawkwell

INTERLUDE

Extract from 'Unlikely Tales'

In due course, Constance's tears ran dry and Mama Marie sat by, studying the widow's tearful face. "It hurts bad, don't it, chile? But all this cryin'? Why, that ain't gon' get you what you need. You grievin' for your man an' I understand that, I truly do." She stood, moving to the other side of the small hut. She took two shot glasses from a shelf and, reaching up above her head, brought down a small, square bottle that was intricately decorated with shapes and patterns that made no sense to Constance.

"Glass of this an' you'll soon be focused," said the poured two glasses of a thick liquid. In the semi-light of the woman's hut, it looked to be the colour and consistency of blood. Constance shuddered at the thought, but when she was handed her glass, she smelled berries. Mama Marie smiled at her. "Raspberries, in the main," she explained.

Constance took a tentative sip. It was sweet and potent as were most alcoholic drinks brewed by those not licensed to do so. It was also quite delicious and following Mama Marie's lead, she tipped the glass's entire contents down her throat in a single move. She did, in fact, immediately feel less grief-filled and calmer. Mama Marie gave her another smile.

"Take another, girl. An' let's talk some about how you can help me."

"I ain't got nothin' to offer, Madame Marie," said Constance, a little sadly as she downed a second glass of the raspberry flavoured drink. She felt a little light headed, but no more than all the bourbon she'd downed since her husband's death had left her feeling. *Keep on drinkin' like that, girl, an' you'll wind up pickled from the inside out*, she'd said to herself in the more sober moments.

"That, darlin', is where you're wrong. So, so wrong. You ain't got no family, have you?"

"No, Madame. When my husband... now he's gone, I ain't got nobody. His parents, my parents are long-since dead and there weren't no brothers or sisters..."

"No children?"

Constance flushed, upset once more by the remark. "No, Madame. Weren't for want of tryin', but for whatever reason, we weren't graced with children."

"An' you gave yourself to just the one man? No lovers?"

"Madame Marie!" Constance was suitably shocked. "Why would you ask such a thing?"

"To make sure you ain't got any ties bindin' you to this life, holdin' you back from what you could become. I mean no offence. If you honestly want a better future, my girl, then you gotta be prepared to embrace it. An' that means letting go. So now you gotta let go."

Again, Constance could not tell if it was a trick of the light, or the sense of wooziness she felt after drinking Mama Marie's liqueur, but there was something in those words that filled her with a deep-seated terror – but it was tempered by curiosity.

The wall behind Mama Marie came alive once again, a writhing, seething mass of repugnance that the young widow failed, once again, to notice. She felt warm and relaxed, the grief of mere moments past now a thing long forgotten.

"You believe I have a future?" Her question was shy and hesitant, and she was unprepared for the laughter that came in response.

"Every life given to me has a future. And your next life will be a beautiful thing, honey." It was a strange thing to say, thought Constance and the last thing she ever heard as a warm-bloodied, living woman was Mama Marie's laughter. She realised, too late, that the nightshade-laced drink had poisoned her. She slid from her seat to the floor, not losing consciousness or awareness and was paralysed, unable to move.

But she could still see. And what happened next was enough to terrify her so much that her heart, already slowed by the poison, tried desperately to pound in fear before it burst in her chest.

Mama Marie's flesh swelled and ran like tallow, her lithe body swelling to monstrous proportions. Her dark skin became slick, mottled and waxy, hair falling away to become nests of writhing tendrils. Her legs thrashed bonelessly and buckled beneath her, swiftly transforming into a skirt of fat, questing tentacles. And her face... her once narrow and beautiful face became something lumpen and bestial. The creature slithered horribly across the floor of the hut and Constance lay helpless as she was scooped up by the grotesque limbs. A gaping maw opened before her to reveal ranks of needle fangs and a long, sinewy tongue that curled about with a life of its own.

The creature drank in Constance's fear and with it, everything that it was to be *her.*

As Constance died, her life and soul seeping from her body, she realised that all the pain had gone and her very last thought before she winked out of existence entirely was gratitude that Mama Marie had taken away the hurt. And she remembered the story of Lazarus.

During her peaceful death, she had not once thought what Mama Marie's words about how her next life would be beautiful had meant. But she would learn soon enough.

Lazarus

PART THREE – EN PRISE

Lazarus

There was a storm that night; a violent, relentless break in the weather that brought most of the month's rainfall in a few short hours. Lightning struck the desert repeatedly and hit a number of small outposts, causing fires and making its presence well and truly known. By dawn, it had blown itself out, although the temperature was cooler than usual for the time of year.

Morning's rosy glow crept over the Superstition Mountains, filling the sky with deep, honey-rich tones and a pinkish tinge to the few clouds that emerged. It was, if you were inclined to look, a day filled with rich promise and potential. Stone Fur, Spirit Priest of the Warrior Nation *was* inclined to look and he gazed upon the morning's omens with somber approval.

The Warrior Nation, under the leadership of their young Spirit Priest and Chief, had been roused to anger and now marched north in the light of the new day. Young Braves rode ahead of the war party, racing their Sky Stallions against the dawn. Manes flew and whooping cries greeted the sun. Stone Fur, now anointed and adorned for battle observed their enthusiasm with mixed emotions.

As he watched the sun come up that morning, the Spirit Priest was certain of victory. To believe anything less would be foolhardy and that was the one thing that Stone Fur was certain he was not. No, he read the omens and he welcomed them with gladness in his heart. Gladness, and a little fear, for the path his life had taken thus far had not been that of the warrior.

For those whose focus was elsewhere, however, the glory and premonition of the sky was wasted.

At Fort Wall, Willa Shaw was preparing herself for a battle of her own. She had closeted herself away for the night with Colonel Hackett and shown the fiery determination that had rightly earned her the reputation she had earned as someone who would not sit by idly when she was able to act.

She sent out six of her best riders to scout out the area. Doc's descriptions had been excellent, but she needed to make sure that Annabelle Hamilton went nowhere. Two hours later, one of them returned and reported that the lights were burning bright in the facility. The others had remained to guard, ready to head straight back to the barracks in the event the occupants evacuated.

By dawn, she had been awake for close to thirty hours and was still not tired. Adrenaline coursed through her veins, keeping her going and if her past history was any indication, she would not stop until the job at hand was complete. It made her irritable and intense and what she really did not need right now was a bruised and bloodied Doc Holliday standing in front of her and telling her his plans.

"I can't forbid it," she said, through gritted teeth. "I am not the boss of you. What I can do is suggest, as your friend..." *That* did not come easily. "...as your friend, that what you're proposing is absurd. They would be crazy to follow you."

"Crazy is as crazy does," he said, shrugging his shoulders easily. "I ain't gonna sit by an' do nothin', though. An', I mean no disrespect, darlin', but I ain't gonna go into this fight at the side of the Union without makin' sure *somebody* has my back. Nothin' personal."

A pause, during which Willa raised her eyebrows and balled her hands on her hips.

"Alright, it *is* personal, OK?" He held his hands wide in a mock-gesture of surrender. "There is a small mining town a few miles from here. Me an' Wyatt, we had ourselves some trouble with a gang of RJ runners down that way. About a year back. Well, folks in that place were none too pleased to find out about those boys an' what they done. Believe me, they were *real* keen to lend the law a hand. Hands, an' a rifle or two. Way I figure it... they're gonna be even less happy to hear about the Hamilton's on their doorstep." He paused for breath, then continued. "So, I am gonna head down there an' I'm gonna form me a posse. *Then* we will go into this fight with you. On our own terms."

For what felt like the thousandth time in a few short days, the two iron wills clashed. This time, they both looked away, an uncomfortable no-score draw.

"Fine," she said, between gritted teeth. "But I am not responsible for what happens to them. And I am not responsible for you anymore. I haven't been since the day you got on that train and disappeared out of my life."

"Willa..." Doc held out a hand, briefly, as though he would catch hers, but she pulled back from him. He let his own hand drop and a million regrets surged to the surface. Instead, he just nodded. "I get it. And, if it is worth anythin' at all to you, I am sorry. I truly am."

Then he turned and walked away.

"So am I," she said to his retreating back, but not so as he would hear her.

* * *

Lady Annabelle Hamilton took great care with her appearance that morning. As she sat in her well-appointed bedroom in a side room of the facility, she studied her expression in the mirror. It was important, she had decided, to wear the correct expression as befit the situation. What sort of face should a well-brought up young lady wear for war? She had tried a look of deep studiousness but dismissed it just as quickly as it just made her look like an old maid. For a while, she attempted stern, but the wrinkles that would bring put her off the idea.

Finally, she adjusted her expression into as neutral an expression as she managed, touching her cheeks with just a hint of rouge. She ran a deep, blood-red lipstick across her beautiful lips and put her hair up into a chignon atop her head. Her choice of clothing for now was based around a lady's riding skirt, allowing her much more mobility than she usually had. She'd chosen her favourite yellow and grey for the ensemble and, as she put the last hairpin into her immaculate hair, she nodded firmly. She would, she conceded, do.

Her outfit, like all the dresses in her wardrobe, was sleeveless, a necessary accommodation on account of the mechanisms of her prosthetic left arm. But just like losing her own limb in that terrible fire the night Daddy died, she had made herself stronger. A Southern phoenix from the flames. Putting such unpleasantness out of her mind, she slid her favourite silver armband up to her right bicep before looking across at the second outfit she had picked out. She would change into that one a little later, because she simply could not do it without assistance. A shame there were no ladies here. One of the boys would have to suffice.

"Annabelle, we need to plan our strategy." It was her brother's voice, and it came from outside her room. She rolled her eyes at her long-suffering reflection. All night long, Benjamin and Mackeye had been huddled together, heads bent close over a hastily drawn map of the valley, discussing 'strategy'. She had grown bored after a half hour or so and retreated to the workshop so that she could play with her toys. It had also presented a marvellous opportunity to distil more Lazarus as well. It had settled overnight and the residual powder that remained at the end of the process was awaiting harvest in the workshop.

"Annabelle! Hurry up!" His tone was wheedling now, and she sighed theatrically.

"Oh, alright, Benjamin. Do calm yaself down, darlin', or y'all gon' go pop or somethin'." She stood, smoothing out the front of the skirt and, giving her reflection a daring wink, moved to open the door. She wrinkled her nose in distaste at her brother's appearance. He had clearly slept in his clothes given how untidy they seemed. His hair was a mess and his chin sporting a dark stubble. His eyes were bright and excited, however, so if he'd slept at all, he'd slept well.

Or had been helping himself to her precious coffee.

"You look terrible," she informed him as he looked up, his face briefly souring as the glint of that hated armband caught his eye, but he said nothing. Instead, his expression changed, and he attempted to smooth his wild hair into some sort of order to please his particular sister.

He offered up a sheepish grin and she waved a hand absently. "So... ya so sure that they're here?" She demanded.

"Absolutely sure. As far as Lieutenant Mackeye and I could determine that dentist fellow you were playing with yesterday went as far as the Union barracks some fifteen miles to the east of here." She began walking toward the workshop and he matched her pace easily, although he had to scurry to catch up to her. "No doubt he's gonna... he's going to get some of those troops all fired up and bring 'em straight here. So, you need to sort out what's ready to fight and get them ready." He grinned at her. "Nothing like putting our collaboration to the test, eh?"

"Mmm," she agreed, attempting to suppress her own excitement at the thought of seeing her Lazarus enhanced creations take the field of battle. She knew that she had much still to learn, but what she had accomplished, with the Lazarus, with the reanimation process itself and what she had gained through an alliance with her own brother was nothing short of spectacular. Carpathian would be delighted with her progress, she was sure.

The idea that she cared about what that old duffer thought irritated her and she let out a snort of self-directed derision. Her thoughts wandered briefly to the respirator Holliday had been wearing. Probably not even an Enlightened design, she figured. It looked more primitive than that arrogant empire of scientists and engineers would manufacture. Though it was still the kind of scientific development that was outside her skill set, much to her annoyance. Assisting the living had never really been her field of interest. She pushed the thought away. It was not a pressing issue. After today, Holliday would be thrown onto the Slough Pile. She'd get to him in due course.

"Good morning, ma'am." Lieutenant Mackeye looked as unshaven as her brother, but it was clear that he was a man more inclined to present himself in a manner befitting a gentleman. He half-bowed from the waist as she entered the vast workshop. He was in full uniform, pristine as ever he was, and were it not for the dark circles beneath his eyes, she would have not known that he and Benjamin had been awake all night.

"Lieutenant," she said, her tone pleasant. "My brother thinks we're goin' to war. Whaddya reckon?"

"Well, I think your brother is likely right, ma'am," came the grave reply. "I am sure that you had your reasons for letting that gentleman go yesterday, and it's most certainly not my place to pry, but the chances are high that he will inform the Union of our activities."

"Good," she said and clapped her hands together like a delighted child. Both Ben and Mackeye looked surprised at this reaction, and she laughed her silvery, tinkling laugh. "Don't ya boys *want* to put the army to the test? Sure, I can't think of any better way to test their mettle by puttin' 'em into a good ol' fashioned fight. Sure, they ain't up to *some* standards, but they're pretty good all the same, dontcha think?"

"Well, yes, ma'am, but to suddenly be brought to battle without spending any time planning... strategizing... or even understanding what the enemy might bring to bear..." Mackeye was apologetic, but his tone held a firmness that made Annabelle pay attention. "As a consequence, your brother and I took the liberty, last night, of putting together what could best be called a plan of attack." He smiled at her frown. Her response was haughty.

"An', pray tell, Lieutenant Mackeye, exactly what part d'ya expect me to play in this whole thing that you an' Benjamin have concocted without me?"

"Why, ma'am, you'll be the general, of course. Every army needs its leader, and nobody here is as uniquely qualified as you are to lead this particular one."

Her ego was stroked, but Mackeye could tell from the look on her face that she was not quite placated enough yet. He continued, his tone soothing and striking precisely where he knew it needed to strike.

"And when you lead us to a glorious victory, why, all the Covenant of the Enlightened will be desperate to work with the genius who created the Lazarus army."

"The Lazarus army?" She turned to consider him thoughtfully, sucking on the mechanical fingertip of her left hand before smiling radiantly. "Yep, I sure do like that one. Peach of a name, Lieutenant. I'm so glad I thought of it."

"Yes, ma'am. You're a genius."

"Ain't that the truth?"

* * *

Stone Fur stood quietly, a small icon of an eagle resting in his hand. It was a beautiful piece, hand-carved by one of the People's many artisans and while it was made entirely of wood, the extraordinary way in which the feathers had been carved suggested the ripple of the wind past its wings. The cruel curve of the beak looked as though it would be razor-sharp if you put your hand to it. And yet it was tiny; small enough to fit into Stone Fur's palm. The detail was truly exquisite.

"The People are waiting to hear you speak, Spirit Priest."

Loud Thunder's tone was deferential, awe-struck even. Since the events at the Hollow of Sighs, the young Spirit Priest's unmistakable leadership skill had come very much to the fore. He had laid out his plan, his vision, and the need to strike back at the corruption whose touch was responsible for the desecration of the sacred burial ground and his voice had never once risen in anger or fury. Everything was explained in a quiet, reasonable tone that compelled everyone who listened. He held an absolute belief that this was the way the Great Spirit guided them, and that belief was communicated to his People with ease.

It was, Loud Thunder told him, because he did not order them. He simply asked them to serve the Great Spirit's will and they did so, eagerly.

He curled his long, slender fingers around the totem staff in his hand, feeling the edges bite into the flesh of his palm. He was one with the eagle, the eagle was a part of who he was. He was ready to rise above the bonds of his earthly existence and carry out the will of the Great Spirit.

"Then let them hear me," he said in his quiet, even tone. He raised his head to the sky and held his hands up to the air. "Let the Great Spirit speak through me and tell them what they must know."

* * *

The frontier town of Little Beam was smaller even than Howling Rock. Barely deserving of the 'town' label, it was a single street lined on either side by rickety, ramshackle wooden buildings. No fewer than three saloons lined the street, along with a general store, a garage, and a gasoline and RJ depot. It was the latter which had given the town any sort of reason to exist at all and was a waystation for vehicles on the journey southwest.

This morning, however, it was ominously quiet as Doc Holliday edged the Iron Horse in past the ragged sign listing drunkenly at the town limit. '*Welcome,*' it enthused, '*to Little Beam*'. Admittedly, it was early and the only people stirring at this hour were the fixers and one or two of the drovers who were heading eastwards. The goggle-wearing engineer raised a hand in greeting, recognising the deputy.

"Bill," said Doc, allowing the 'Horse's engine to back off to idle, a low, throaty sound. "Doesn't anybody get outta bed before noon 'round here?" He inclined his head graciously toward the fixer, who chuckled.

Bill Hawkes was a heavyset man with a thinning head of jet-black hair. His moustache was small and neat in his broad, friendly face and his skin was tanned a dark nut-brown from all the hours he spent out in the sun. His shoulders and arms attested to his profession and while he was not quite six feet in height, he was strong and powerfully built. Those arms had hauled many a drunk out of the saloon at the behest of the owners and, Doc knew, also held and cared for the infant twin sons that he had borne with his tiny little wife.

"That's a fine-lookin' machine you got there, Deputy. You finally trade that crazy horse of yours in for a proper ride? Never thought I'd see the day." The fixer grinned. "You ever need any work doin' on her, you know where to come."

"You do not trade in a horse like Solomon Smith, Bill. In fact, I am pretty sure I could not trade him in if I tried. He'd just come right on back, just like he always does. Probably give me a hard time over it, too." Bill gave a bark of laughter at the notion and the young deputy inclined his head. "Where is everyone at this mornin'?"

"Big game last night, Doc. Surprised you weren't here for it." The deputy switched off the engine and sat for a moment. Then he gathered his resolve and looked up at the smith.

"I need to get everyone together, Bill." The deputy's seriousness was instantly picked up on by the blacksmith who'd formed a part of Wyatt Earp's posses before. "There is trouble brewin' nearby an' I need all the folks we can get together." Wyatt and by extension Doc Holliday did not discriminate. Men and women were equals in their eyes and anybody who could carry and fire a gun, or drive a vehicle was welcome.

"What kind of trouble?"

"Get everyone together, an' I will tell you." Doc took off his hat and ran his fingers through his hair. "All you need to know right now is that if we do not rustle up every weapon and vehicle that this place had to offer, then I declare we will not be alive long enough to regret it."

Bill Hawkes was already running. Doc threw another sentence after him.

"An' make sure you bring Mrs. Kelly!"

* * *

"Most of you have no idea who I am," said Willa, not made remotely self-conscious by all the eyes that were locked on her tiny frame as she stood at the front of the assembled unit of Iron Horse riders. "But for the record, I'm Major Willa Shaw."

At her name, there were a few muttered whispers and despite herself, she felt a swell of pride. Sweeney was standing at her right-hand side, and he too seemed to blossom under the recognition afforded his commanding officer. She gave him a tight, controlled smile and turned her attention back to the troops.

"As of right now, Colonel Hackett has put you under my command and I am here to tell you that we have a fight on our hands the likes of which you cannot begin to imagine. I tell you this. I have fought many things in my time, but the enemy we're facing today is..." She hesitated. How did you describe an army of the animated dead to a group of soldiers, some of whom looked young enough to barely be out of basic training?

Honestly, that was how.

"The leader of our enemy's army is a woman by the name of Lady Annabelle Hamilton. She's one of the Enlightened."

Now *that* got people's attention. The whispering became a clamouring murmur and then one woman put up a hand. Willa nodded at her. "What is it, Corporal?"

"The scientists who came up wit' all the juiced vehicles and weapons and such like?"

"That's right. There's different stripes of 'em all over the world and not all are good. Hamilton has developed some means of keeping things alive that have no right to be."

Whisper whisper whisper.

"Pardon me, ma'am? Did you just say that she brings life back to the dead?" The disgust and disbelief were palpable, and Willa steeled herself.

"Not that. Not exactly, but it may as well be. She dares to call it science, but what I see are husbands. Wives. Children. Dragged from the edge of what should be their rest and forced to walk this land again as slaves to the ambitions of a monster." The more she spoke, the more she warmed to her subject. She balled her hand into a fist and brought it down, emphasising her words and her anger in equal measure. "Have we not already won the war against the enslavement of the people of the Union to the ambitions of the Confederacy? Have we not already bled for this? Have we not already spent the lives of too many sons and daughters of the Union in the name of freedom? To be faced with this is an *insult*! And I say to you all now that it will not stand. It *must* not stand!"

There was a resounding cheer and Willa nodded. She had their attention now.

* * *

"So... let me get this straight. Some gentrified bit of skirt is makin' walkin' corpses?"

It was a simplification of what Lazarus did, of what it achieved, but if it meant this crowd bought into his rhetoric, then Doc would roll with it.

"Yup. Strollin' along, easy as you like, kickin' seven bells of hell outta anythin' in their way." Doc nodded, solemnly. The townspeople were gathered in one of the saloons, as tightly packed as sardines and frankly smelling much the same. The deputy was glad, once more, for his respirator dealing with the worst of it. "That same – ah – gentrified bit of skirt – is also the one behind Lazarus."

Nothing.

"Pep?"

Response. They knew *that* alright. Damn Hamilton and her thriving drugs trade. Couldn't she have left it at that? Why all the weird stuff? Why all the horror? And why, more than anything else, had he ever thought he had what it took to form a posse by himself?

"Anyway, that is what she is doin', ridiculous as I know it sounds. Fixin' up those unfortunate dead folks with weapons an' turning them loose on the world. We ain't gonna sit around and let them come to us, come to where we live, so I figured it was better to pull together a posse to take the fight to them. Anybody up for it?"

"Where's Earp? Ain't he the one who rounds

people up?" Doc wanted to snap at that comment, but instead he kept his expression neutral.

"The Marshal is busy with other things." It wasn't a complete lie. "I got full jurisdiction here an' the task has fallen to me. So, who can I count on?" He looked steadily around the assemblage. They mostly looked steadily back. "Who of y'all has got the gumption to come face these ungodly things down an' get 'em run outta town?"

Apart from the immediate acceptance of the offer by Mrs. Kelly, there was a resounding silence. One man blew his nose loudly. They were waiting for something more and intuition told him precisely what that something was. Doc sighed. "I ain't got anythin' to pay you with, y'all know that, right?" The silence extended a little further and he felt himself start to grow irritated. Motivational speaking was usually something best left to Wyatt, who had a leader's skill. Doc's job was to stand at his side looking determined and serious, not to give the speeches. He had the 'trusty sidekick' thing down pat. Standing on the upper plinth was not as easy as Wyatt made it look.

Someone coughed, a noise of intense embarrassment. Doc sighed and rolled his eyes. It was time to draw the metaphorical big guns. "Look," he said, in as reasonable a voice as he could manage. "Who is up for a righteous brawl an' a reasonable amount of shootin' at bad folks? Come with me an' I swear I will pay for the first round when we get back."

If we get back.

There was scattered cheering. Doc nodded. He had their attention now.

* * *

Her brother was exhausting. His energy and enthusiasm for the project was quite wearing, but Annabelle had to admit that she was starting to develop great excitement as well. The first real test of her army would come here, in this dusty desert valley and she knew that the reports of their success would buy her great favour in the eyes of those who really mattered. She watched her twin brother out of the corner of her eyes as he worked.

Ben Hamilton was wearing an apron over his clothes, and it was covered in a combination of blood and bodily fluids, of oil and grease. Some of those stains had made their way to his face and into his hair and as he sawed at limbs and screwed in metal fixings to hold the assortment of weaponry he had developed; she had never seen him so happy.

"I miss havin' ya round, Benjamin," she said to him. "Ain't this some kind of wonderful? The two of us workin' together. The way we should, don't ya think?"

He looked up at her and smiled, small dimples forming in his cheeks. "We're good together, you're right there. What you've achieved with this army is nothing short of incredible and I'm so proud of you."

"We could make the arrangement more permanent, ya know," she said. "Y'all could come back home with me an' work for the people I'm workin' with now." Her brother's work paused momentarily, but he did not stop. Neither did he answer. She pressed the matter. "Benjamin, what ya even *doin'* hangin' around with that no-good piece of human waste, Stonewall Jackson? What's he got that I can't bring ya?"

Ben wiped his hand across his nose, smearing the oil and grease in a long streak. "Can we not have this conversation? I agreed to help you and here I am. Helping you. That's good enough. So shut up, let me work and go check the soldiers are ready."

"Don't ya *dare* talk to me like..."

"Annabelle."

"What?" She was incensed at Ben's attitude, not for one second considering that her constant nagging of her brother might well have been instrumental in him leaving her side in the first place.

"Shut up. I'm busy. We'll talk later. But now, I gotta work. If I'm right, this place is gonna come under attack before the day is out. So..." He put his head on one side and gave her a disarmingly sweet smile. "Less talking and a whole lot more doing."

Her mouth fell slightly open at this newfound confidence he was demonstrating. He gave her another sweet smile and made a shooing movement with his hands. She tilted her head up in the air to register that she was deeply insulted and flounced out of his way. He watched her go and shook his head. She wasn't going to let it go and he knew that later, there was a long, uncomfortable discussion to be had.

Ben Hamilton loved his sister. But he did not love some of her ideals and did not subscribe to her particular vision of the future. When this was done – and he was only helping her *because* she was his sister, not for any other reason – he would be leaving. Oh, no doubt she'd cry and pout and be petulant at him, but since he had struck out on his own, he had flourished.

And, he reasoned as he took up a razor-sharp blade and carefully inserted it into the weapon socket of one of the idle bodies, he would continue to do so without her.

Annabelle seethed and sulked all the way from Ben's workshop to her own half of the vast space. Her glorious soldiers, her *children*, she supposed, were dormant at this time. They had all been treated and

257

prepared for activation and when the time was right, she would engage the charged implants that would ensure their potential was realised.

She moved through the massed army, a silent, motionless horror of bodies in various stages of their construction. Some had been stitched back together by her own hand, a neat, even stitching that connected flesh to flesh, sinew to sinew. She could do nothing about the corruption that blackened their abused tissue, although when they were activated, with the correct stimulation and the active Lazarus buzzing in their system, some of that discolouration would fade. The army would look, from a distance, normal.

At this distance, they were anything but.

"My beautiful creations," she murmured as she stopped in front of one of the fresher bodies. "So glorious. Such an achievement. When this day is done, everyone will know the Hamilton name. My skills are gonna be the top of people's wish lists." She put out a gloved hand and stroked it down the cheek of a young man who had been quite lovely in life and had retained some of the beauty in death. She looked down at his hands, which Benjamin had converted into cruelly hooked blades.

The youth's face was set in a rictus grin of horror, the very expression he had worn in the moment of his death. She knew him as one of the vagabonds who had passed through Provenance and her moment of reflection became something else. For all she had loathed that place, the mining town had brought her the great breakthrough which had led to the successes she now enjoyed. She had been granted access to a herb, local to the Arizona mountains, that she had studied and incorporated into her brewing. She had managed to get more, but it had piqued her curiosity.

What other marvellous properties did local flora have?

There was another plan in effect there; one which would have immense ramifications that she had not even remotely considered. She would find them out soon enough.

A pity, she mused, patting the soldier on his cheek, that Provenance had burned to the ground. But strengths, her father had taught her from an early age, came from adversity, and sacrifices must be made in the name of progress.

"Lieutenant Mackeye!" She called out the soldier's name, suddenly acutely aware that her man was not by her side. "Where are ya? I need ya here."

"Be right with you, ma'am." The officer's voice floated across the space, and she smiled in satisfaction. Her brother may have developed a mind of his own, confound him, but at least she could trust to Lieutenant Mackeye to be reliable. When he appeared, she was briefly taken aback by his appearance.

He had cleaned and polished and scrubbed and buffed everything about his uniform. The fabric was immaculate, the buttons and boots polished to a shine in which she could perfectly see her reflection. He was immaculately groomed, his hair and moustaches clean and neat. The unsheathed sabre he wore at his waist had a gleaming edge that she suspected was the result of a long session with the whetstone. He was every inch the cavalry officer and she found herself admiring him for a moment.

"Why Lieutenant, dontcha look handsome this mornin'?"

"Just because we are going to war, ma'am, doesn't mean a man can't look his best. My old commanding officer would never have let a unit of scruffy, unkempt soldiers out on the field, and it does no harm to maintain standards." He snapped a smart salute. He kept his gaze locked firmly on her, not once letting his eyes stray to the horrors that surrounded her. He'd come to the conclusion that the best way to deal with this unlikely situation was simply to not look at it. If he couldn't see it, it was far easier to believe it didn't exist.

"I like your attitude, Lieutenant. Very gentlemanly." She patted him on the cheek. It was fortunate, perhaps, for Lieutenant Mackeye, that he did not know it was the same gesture she'd made, a few moments ago, to a motionless creation.

Ross Mackeye was not fundamentally a bad man. He was, however, loyal to the core and had, over the course of the last day or so, had considered his moral stance in this whole affair. The mechanics of what was occurring horrified him at a fundamental level. But he had sworn an oath to Lady Annabelle's father that he would ensure her safety at all costs.

In his days as a soldier, Lieutenant Mackeye was renowned for his fearlessness in battle; acknowledged for the decisiveness of his actions. He was man of rare focus and he brought that to bear now. Something of the old steel sprang into his spine and he caught Annabelle's hand, very gently removing it from his face. She didn't acknowledge the symbolism of the gesture, but it was there.

"I am yours to command, ma'am," he said, quietly.

"Good," she said. "I got a job for ya that's gonna test every ounce of ya strength."

* * *

A breath of wind eddied in the valley, forming a dust devil that skittered and danced across the dirt. It petered out and died before it reached the hardpan track that led to the Hamilton facility, but it was a herald of a cold silence that descended. The calm before the storm.

The tempest was heralded by the march of boots, squeak of mechanised joints and the throaty growl of RJ-injection gasoline engines labouring in the Arizona heat. Four full units of soldiers, resplendent in their Union blues formed up behind Willa Shaw's cavalcade of Iron Horses, their rotary rifles and cannon pods gleaming with oil in the high sun. Spurred by the Major's words, the Colonel had mobilised the garrison, including the latest additions to the armed forces. Running ahead of the army in long, loping strides, several armoured K9 automata units sprinted to the top of the ridge and scanned the valley below with softly glowing lenses.

The artificial hounds were minor marvels compared to the heavy tread of the GI bots marching beside their flesh and blood counterparts. Their armoured bodies, though tarnished with dust from the journey, wore fresh coats of fresh paint and the heavy cannons at their sides looked new and unused.

At the rear of the column, Joe Sweeney rode in the cupola of what he laughably referred to as 'the support'.

The Major halted the body of her force a mile north of the Hamilton facility, waiting for Doc Holliday to arrive. They had agreed the meeting place and time and she knew his timekeeping habits of old. He would be here almost precisely seven minutes early. *It's pathological,* he had told her once. *Even when I try to arrive late for things, I still show up exactly seven minutes early.*

Seven minutes before the hour, she heard the throaty sounds of other Iron Horses approaching. Doc Holliday led the way on the borrowed Iron Horse, bringing with him what had to be the most mis-matched, disparate group Willa had ever seen. The age of Doc's posse ranged from an eager-looking teenager who carried a pair of old-fashioned pistols to a woman astride a patched-together Iron Horse who looked to be easily in her late fifties.

When the latter pulled down the protective dust-scarf and lifted her goggles, Willa was struck, as she always was, by the hardiness of the women of the western frontier. Iron-grey hair was bound tightly back from a face lined and prematurely aged by the relentless Arizona climate. She wore a long-barrelled shotgun across her back, with the tell-tale red glow of an RJ chamber that was fully primed. She had that sort of wiry strength Willa always associated with old cow drovers.

There were fifteen of them to Willa's military unit that numbered over fifty. Her heart sank slightly but she had not expected a vast turnout.

"Major," said Doc, formally greeting her as he pulled up the Iron Horse beside her. All the frivolity and geniality had gone from him and he was prepared for battle. The former Georgian dentist carried himself with a cool gravitas that she found appealing and of which she approved enormously. "This here is the posse I pulled together from Little Beam. Not many of 'em, I grant you, but good people to a man. An' to a woman, of course, Mrs. Kelly, no offence, darlin'." He nodded his head towards the woman who had caught Willa's attention. She inclined her head at his acknowledgement, and he tipped his hat. There was an air of fading aristocrat about her. Doc chuckled softly.

"Mrs. Kelly took over the family business when her husband passed. She is one hardworkin' gal. The town's undertaker. Nothin' fazes her. Everyone said that it weren't right, a lady takin' on such a task, but they didn't have no kids an' she said she knew the business better than her dead husband ever did. Proved everyone wrong. She was first to sign up. May have been the free drink I offered... but nonetheless. Mrs. Kelly's the gal for this job, take my word on it. She's the deadliest shot for miles around, tough as they come. Maybe tougher."

There was real pride in Doc's voice and a warmth toward the older lady that she sensed came out of a deep respect. It occurred to her that he probably knew every single one of the people he had brought with him; knew their names, their stories, everything about them. Her unit was made up of mostly strangers. Maybe it wouldn't have hurt to get a few names. But Doc had always been like that. She'd found, over the years, that most Southerners wouldn't just say 'good morning' and pass on by. They'd stand next to one another in a queue and learn their mutual family histories. Such a languid, easy attitude had always been beyond her reach.

The two groups, the Little Beam posse and the Union forces, remained apart from one another, eyeing one another with wariness. Willa chewed at her lip for a moment. She had no idea how they were going to work together, but she was going to have to hope that any potential misunderstandings could be avoided by running everything through Doc. Not that it seemed a much better option, but then she knew that there was a least a *chance* that the Lawman would pay attention when she started giving orders.

"They might not look like much next to your pretty folks, darlin', I freely admit that. But damn me if they ain't good at what they do. An' they got nerves of steel, which I am thinkin' they're gonna need out here."

Willa and Doc shared a look, then, a look of shared knowledge of what they faced. Memories of the fight in Provenance, the loss of young Zachariah. For a fraction of a second, they connected, just as they always had connected. She was grateful when Doc broke the moment by pulling papers and tobacco out of one of his belt pouches.

"Alright, Deputy, here's the plan." It did not take much for her to fall back to her natural tendency to command, and Doc did not seem inclined to steal her thunder. As he fiddled with the fixings and rolled his cigarette, he watched her carefully, evidently taking in every word she was saying. She had rarely seen this professional side to him outside of those days back when he still occasionally practicing dentistry and she liked it very much. For the first time, she understood a little of why he had been granted a Deputy's badge. She was suddenly extremely glad of his support, small though his posse may be.

"My 'Horse riders and I are going to take the road, roll right up to their front door, and if your riders are happy to ride alongside us, then that's where they should be," she said. "From what you reported, this is a box valley, banked on both sides by high ridges." When he nodded, she continued. "Sergeants Regan and Wallis?" Two men stepped forward and saluted smartly. "I want you to take your men up onto the west ridge. Covey and Weis? The east."

"Understood," Sergeant Covey said. "Our primary role is covering fire, yes?"

"Exactly that."

"The ridges are high, but the one I fell down was not too hard on the boots," Doc said, thoughtfully. "If needs be, you can come down and bail us out if we get into a situation."

"Only if it becomes absolutely necessary." Willa interrupted the Deputy's flow. "Most of the 'Horses have gatling cannons. Two have flamethrowers." Their eyes locked for a moment and he nodded his understanding.

"So. Mutilation of the walkin' dead is the primary objective? Death dealin' to the dead. Catchy, huh?"

"Do you have to always be so crude about this stuff?"

"Why of course I do. It is my copin' mechanism, darlin'." He winked slyly.

"Orders ma'am? The Indestructibles are ready to do their duty." The voice was tinny and synthetic, like a scratchy gramophone recording being played through a loud hailer. Doc turned to find a hulking, armoured simulacrum of a man standing to attention. On one shoulder were painted sergeant's chevrons and where its eyes should have been, was a softly glowing slit.

"What in the name of *thunderation* are you?" The words were out of the Lawman's mouth before Willa could address the thing's question. He'd seen GI bots before, of course he had, but he had been caught unawares and his tendency to distrust walking, talking engineering spilled out of him unbounded.

"We are Union UR-31E General Infantry Automata. Unit designation IR-1, sir!" It snapped off a startlingly smart salute. "You may call me Irwin."

"*Irwin*?" Doc's incredulity was comical, and Willa watched the exchange with a moment's much-needed amusement.

"Correct, sir. Sergeant Irwin of the Indestructibles."

"Irwin's Indestructibles!" The unit of mechanised soldiers standing behind the unlikely sergeant all chorused at once in their synthetic voices.

"Sergeant Irwin and the other 31Es are a masterpiece," Willa said, feeling that she needed to explain the automata's remarkable manner. "His difference engine programming is extraordinary. Like all automata his speech is really just pre-recorded phrases played when needed. But he's part of Tesla's newer generation. Teslabots, they call them. These sergeant models have ten times as many phrases as the old GI-Bots did. I'm told they can even splice parts of the recordings to give more appropriate responses. The job of these Indestructibles..."

"Irwin's Indestructibles!"

The GI-bots chorused again, and Willa tapped her finger against the side of her mouth thoughtfully. "Did *you* order them to do that, Sergeant?"

"Yes, ma'am."

The teslabot almost sounded pleased with itself that she let it go.

"Well, sergeant, your job is to hold the road. Close the door behind us, as it were. If anybody, or any*thing* tries to break out of the valley and it is not wearing a Union uniform, or is not one of Mr Holliday's posse, then I want you to halt their passage."

"With extreme prejudice, ma'am?"

"Yes. Absolutely. As extreme as it gets."

"Understood, ma'am!" The mechanical man saluted again, the sound of his hand against his metal head a hollow *clang*. "For glory! For the Union! Irwin's Indestructibles, muster!" He turned and walked away to a resounding chorus of *Irwin's Indestructibles* from his compatriots. Doc chuckled.

"You know, I think I *like* him." He paused for a moment. "Indestructible?"

Willa sighed. "'Tesla's latest design? Well, we can hope. The primary objective is to make sure none of those horrors leave the valley. Secondary objective is to take Annabelle Hamilton into custody so that she can answer some questions that some folks are going to be just *dying* to ask. So tell your people to make sure she's taken alive. If it really is a closed valley, then she and whoever else she's got stashed in that building aren't going to be going anywhere and I'll wager she's going to use those things as a moving shield to get out. We remove that option, she's nothing more than a cornered aristocratic rat."

"Why, Willa, such a pretty turn of phrase. Never knew you could be so vindictive."

"Shut up. Now, for our tertiary objective..." She squinted her eyes against the early morning sun. "We burn that place to the ground." There was a deep, bass rumble and the earth vibrated as the support finally arrived. The vehicle rolled along on two sets of huge, iron-shod wheels, the larger pair biting hard into the baked earth. The prow was almost entirely dominated by a wedge-shaped plough the sat below a rotary cannon, two vision slits and the yawning maw of an enormous turret gun. Fumes belched from the boxy rear of the machine where yet more weapons bristled, and a grinning Joe Sweeney sat in the cupola looking down at them. Glancing over her shoulder, she shot a quick, tight smile at the Sergeant. "That's his department."

"So I noticed back in Provenance. Hey, Joe." Doc tipped his hat. "New toy?"

"Doc." The Sergeant beamed at the Deputy. "The engineers tell me it's a Rolling Thunder Mark

Three Armoured Fighting Vehicle. But around these parts we just call it the Rolling Thunder. Felt I might need to pack a little more than dynamite this time."

"You know, Mister Sweeney, I think you might just be right."

"Enough, you two." Willa was taut and on edge and her command came out as a bite. "Let's get introductions done and get your people and my people talking to each other." She nodded over at the two disparate groups. "We begin the attack in fifteen minutes."

* * *

"Count is at least one hundred- and fifty-foot soldiers in various stages of upgrade and a dozen Hellions," announced Ben Hamilton ambling over to his sister's side. "There would have been another, but it took too much damage yesterday. I've thrown it onto the Slough Pile for you to do whatever you want with. I..." He stopped speaking and stared at his sister. She had changed out of her dress and was wearing a most un-ladylike set of leathers, the kind worn by those who rode Iron Horses on a regular basis. Sensible, he acknowledged, but he'd never seen his sister wearing anything except one of her opulent dresses. The fact she was in possession of legs genuinely appeared to surprise him.

The top half of the outfit was a harder leather than the rest, designed in the style of a corset and the whole ensemble, a dark, rich chocolatey-brown in colour had clearly been designed with freedom of movement in mind. Sleeveless as always, the gleam of her mechanical arm and her brightly polished Confederate armband stood out along with her pale skin.

"I ain't so pleased with the Hellions," Annabelle commented, ignoring the look from her brother. "There's so much more I could've done to improve them. Still, guess we all must start somewhere. But I s'pose we just ain't got the time to do any more work on 'em. Lieutenant, come on. Ya takin' ages to do this job! Pull tighter, darlin', ya ain't gonna hurt me."

The last was said to Lieutenant Mackeye who had been lumbered with the job of tightening the leather corset. This, it transpired, was the job that was going to take all his strength. He was doing so with obvious uncertainty, having never actually had to perform such a task for her – or indeed for any other woman – before. Such an intimate and such a very feminine thing was so far removed from everything he had ever experienced, and it was making him deeply uncomfortable.

After a few moments of pulling half-heartedly, sure he must be squeezing every breath of air out of her lungs, she swung her arms and confirmed, with a cheeky grin, that she 'wasn't in danger of fallin' out any time soon'.

"Annabelle!" Ben was scandalised by her choice of phrase, and she pointed at him and giggled. Her spirits were high; the thought of the upcoming battle was fuelling an energy and eagerness to put her creations to the test. High spots of pink showed on her flawless skin, a sure sign that she was excited. She squeezed her brother's arm with her own flesh and blood limb and raised up onto the tiptoes of her boots to plant an affectionate kiss on his grease-smeared cheek.

"When'd ya get so *sensitive*, Benjamin? Let's get to armin' ourselves then. We're gonna have guests shortly." Now that she was more appropriately attired for battle, the genteel Georgia lady was gone, replaced by a cold, hard woman of war. She strode with purpose towards the small armoury that she and Mackeye had been gradually building up for several months.

The Lieutenant and Ben exchanged glances as she began picking through pistols and rifles of all kinds. She considered a grenade for a few moments, then rejected it. She was mildly annoyed that they could only field one hundred and fifty worthy warriors. There were corpses enough on the Slough Pile to make so many more. If only that wretched dentist hadn't come along and found them...

Thinking of what she could do to the consumptive gunslinger once she had his dying body on her workbench brought a modicum of comfort. The first thing she would do would be to rip out all of the teeth from his head, because nobody loved irony more than Doc Holliday.

A siren began wailing somewhere and Ben looked away from his sister towards the noise. It was an artificial howl; low, low and atonal and he wrinkled his nose at it. "Is that what I think it is?"

"Somebody is at the door," she replied, without looking back at her brother. She picked up a rifle and sighted down the barrel, hefting its weight on her shoulder. She lowered the weapon, resting it against her hip before turning to the two men, beaming a huge smile at them. "Sounds like our test subjects have done gone arrived right on cue. Gentlemen? Shall we dance?"

* * *

Five minutes until the attack began and the Union soldiers were almost in position.

Before any kind of conflict, Doc Holliday always experienced an intense rush of adrenaline that he welcomed. It brought every sense to heightened levels, leaving his body feeling as tightly strung as a well-tuned instrument. Whether it was a simple shoot-out with a lone gunman or a full scale battle like this one – well, that didn't matter. The outcome was the same. The sense that he could take on the world intoxicating; so different to the sense that he was simply existing, living through each day with no real knowledge if the disease would claim him before the sun went down. When he was fighting, Doc felt more alive than he usually did.

You got a death wish, Holliday?

People other than Wyatt Earp had asked him that question and he had to concede the point that perhaps it did look that way. After all, he was always eager to throw himself into the fray, heedless of the dangers. No, it wasn't a death wish, not exactly. But it wasn't heroism, either.

Riding with Willa at the head of the column, he had a clear view ahead into the valley. The facility seemed quiet and there was no sign of activity at all. Only the telltale crimson glimmer of RJ cannisters and the ever-present low hum of the fence hinted that there was anything happening within. Well, the Deputy thought grimly, in a handful of minutes, there would be *plenty* happening.

Two minutes.

He glanced over toward the east ridge and could make out the shapes of some of Sergeant Covey's unit, belly-down in the dust. He glanced over his shoulder at the cavalcade of riders behind him, a motley crew of Willa's own cavalry and Little Beam residents. Most of the civilian vehicles were not armed, their riders relying on personal arms to defend themselves, but the Union Iron Horses all sported reassuringly heavy cannons.

He loosened the holsters on his pistols, ready to draw at a second's notice. He had been taken by surprised by that accursed flying thing yesterday and he'd be ready if it happened again.

One minute.

There was a throaty roar as the riders gunned their throttles and spread out into a loose 'V' formation, kicking a huge plume of dust into the mouth of the valley. Weapon feeds clattered as they fed ammunition into breeches and Doc could make out the unmistakable whine of a juiced rifle powering up. Even above the engine noise, it was a sound that stirred him. There had been no agreed signal for the commencement of the battle. With that extremely obvious – and loud – approach, there was no need for it.

"Well, boys an' girls," Doc yelled above the din, his tone as cheerful as ever, "looks like this is our time to shine." He didn't know how many of the riders heard him, or whether they were even listening, but as the distance closed it felt right to share a few last words. He wracked his brain for something encouraging to say and struck gold. "Good luck. All of you. An' remember the adage, the thing that a friend once taught me. Fast is fine… but accuracy is everythin'. Make those shots count!"

He was rewarded with whoops and cheers of approval. Wyatt's words, not his – albeit with a little flourish - but they were as accurate and appropriate now as they had been when he had first heard them. Doc briefly unclipped his respirator, taking a long and appreciative pull of bourbon from his hip flask. He inhaled as deeply as his feeble lungs would allow and slowly let out the breath. The closest building loomed ahead, its faded walls obscured by the high, thrumming fence. He slipped the mask back into place just as Willa thumbed the trigger on her 'Horse, opening the cannons up in a bellow of sound and fury.

A torrent of shells streamed from weapons and were joined a heartbeat later by the following riders. The snap and crack of smaller arms was largely drowned out amongst the din. The fence danced and twitched under the assault, shedding fat, crimson sparks as it weathered the storm. It tore and sagged in a few places but remained largely untouched by the onslaught. The same could not be said for the nearest building. It rattled and shook as the blizzard of shells chewed fist-sized holes out of its walls, perforating it with munitions and touching off something flammable within.

It seemed unlikely that anything living within could have survived and Doc wondered for a moment about the previous order to take Hamilton alive and just how rigorously that instruction would be adhered to.

The 'V' of machines broke off their assault as they approached the fenceline, the formatting splitting apart to circle east and west creating a cordon of vehicles and choking dust.

In the saddle, Doc hadn't even been aware he'd been holding his breath until the shooting stopped. When he let that breath out, it brought a coughing fit with it. All the years of practice and coping with his illness meant that the moment passed swiftly and although there were tears in his eyes from the effort, he forced himself to focus. To find that moment of clarity in which men lived and died. The attack would surely not go unanswered. If the Hamiltons were in there – and he had no reason to doubt the Union scouts – then there was every chance that more of their abominations were in there with them.

There was a heavy, metallic sound and a crash of machinery nearby, followed by several popping detonations. Thick smoke began to pour from buried charges and Doc's eyes streamed as he zipped the Iron Horse through one of the plumes. His heart leapt into his throat as he emerged from the other side to find that the ground had fallen away to reveal a dusty ramp. He leaned to one side, heaving the Iron Horse over, gliding over the hole. In that horrible, frozen moment as he stared into the abyss, the abyss stared right back at him.

The first wave of enemies emerged from the smoke seconds later, an unruly mob of sagging jaws, stitched flesh and grasping hands. To Willa, at the head of her unit, it looked as though they had simply been pointed in the direction of the enemy and released. That would have been comical as a strategy if she had not already witnessed just how effective it was. These things differed from those back in Provenance: they appeared to have been modified. Some were wearing rigid body frames while others had limbs replaced with hooks, barbs or scything blades.

And guns.

One of them turned in Willa's direction and raised a limb terminating in a stubby pistol. It fired without aiming and the shot glanced from the armoured faring of her Iron Horse, drawing a string of expletives. Ahead of and to the left of her, another shambling body lurched into one of the Little Beam riders, mashing the unnatural thing into unrecognisable parts, but also sending the man and his machine tumbling end over end in a fatal crash.

"Check your firing lines!" Willa yelled the order as something loomed up at her out of the smoke, claws grasping. She jinked the 'Horse to one side, lashing out with an armoured boot which cracked against the monster's skull as she passed.

The things seemed to be everywhere, and the combination of dust and smoke was now working heavily against the riders as the infantry could not hope to see in order to provide supporting fire. Willa gesticulated at the nearest riders and raised her voice again in another order.

"Spread out! Give the rifles some room!"

They clearly heard, because they began to break formation. Before the leftmost rider could break free of the smog, however, several rattling shots chewed up the side of his vehicle and touched the fuel tank. Machine and rider blew apart in a shower of parts and scarlet fire. Willa squinted ahead and saw a bulkier construct with a rotary cannon firing indiscriminately into the smoke. The Major gritted her teeth and hit the throttle, her fingers poised over the trigger.

"I'm already on it, darlin'!" The voice came from beside her and was filled with a grim sort of joy. She knew the tone well.

Willa glanced over to see Mrs. Kelly standing up on the pedals of her machine, throttle opened full and iron-grey hair flying loose. She had her rifle tucked in against her shoulder and sighted down the barrel at the cannon-wielding corpse as it blasted away. As if sensing an approaching threat, the creature turned, churning up the ground with gunfire. Several shots narrowly missed the undertaker, but she neither swayed nor flinched. Her surety of balance was astonishing and even in the heat of battle, Willa could appreciate a skilled rider when she saw one.

The cell on Mrs. Kelly's rifle pulsed and narrow lance of red light momentarily transfixed the abomination. Scant seconds later, its head came apart in a spray of bone and vaporised tissue.

The old woman sat down in the saddle, sliding her weapon onto her back in a single smooth motion before she winked at Willa and guided her 'Horse out toward the edge of the conflict.

"Cavalry, break off! Let the shooters on the ridge do their work!" Willa motioned with her hand and the Union riders followed her lead, followed by the Little Beam posse as they understood what was happening. The circle of machines expanded and disengaged.

A wall of shambling horrors followed them out of the smoke, hands and weapons clawing at the empty air. Any assessment of numbers was impossible as the rising dust and drifting, choking smog obscured the emergence tunnels. But they advanced without fear, their faces fixed in silent, slack-jawed screams. In other places, to become a construct was a noble sacrifice. It brought security to a family in financial difficulties. It meant a life of servitude – but it didn't mean a loss of dignity. What the Hamiltons had wrought here was shocking.

They were met by a rippling volley of gunfire from the infantry on the ridges, the soldiers picking their targets and shooting in disciplined ranks. The Lazarus-fuelled constructs jerked and twitched as they were struck, losing limbs and chunks of flesh. But most continued their advance, seemingly stoically bearing wounds that would have felled most.

Willa realised, to her dismay, that it was ammunition that could eventually cost them the victory. Cannons, rifles and pistols could run dry, but these creatures might well keep right on coming. A single shot could cripple a living soldier, but it was taking six or seven times that much to make the enemy stay motionless.

A K9 unit loped past her, its limbs a blur of motion. It leapt at one of the constructs, bearing it to the ground and fastening its iron jaws around the monster's head. The soldier stabbed at the artificial hound with bladed limbs to little effect, while the canine maw closed down with vice-like strength. There was a sudden, wet crunch and thrashing limbs went still. The K9 worried at the body for a few moments in an eerily organic, feral way and they bounded off into the gloom.

The dogs, at least, had no concerns about ammunition.

Doc could see that the valley was beginning to fill with the horrors and a brief flash back to Provenance, the relentless assault and seemingly endless influx of new threats. That had been at a makeshift facility that had been abandoned. This was... something else entirely. Who knew how many more of those things Annabelle Hamilton had stashed beneath those buildings?

He had retreated from the immediate threat and found himself riding alongside a handful of the Little Beam posse who had followed him out of the smoke. He looked over at the wall of advancing dead and then back at his fellow riders. "Grenades," he said. No need for him to bark his order. He simply raised his voice a little. The manner in which he spoke the word seemed to stop just short of adding 'if you please'.

The explosives had been distributed among the Union and civilian riders in the interest of saturation, a decision that now seemed increasingly wise. Three of the men produced softly glowing canisters which they twisted and lobbed towards the approaching creatures. They did not react to the threat, simply stumbled over the explosives in their midst and continued their approach. The resulting detonations echoed throughout the valley and rained dirt and dead flesh in all directions.

Horrifically, even now horribly burned and dismembered, some of the bodies continued to crawl toward the living.

Doc could hear the sounds of gunfire from the opposite ridge, as well as the roar of electrocarbine fire and the occasional, mechanised refrain of *"Irwin's Indestructibles!"* that went up as the teslabot unit engaged at the valley mouth. It wasn't exactly the plan they had envisioned, but it was holding together.

The sound of heavy machinery in motion once again rose from the facility and Doc's confidence ebbed a little to be replaced with a creeping sense of dread. The roof of the largest building peeled back to reveal a rising flock of ungainly winged creatures that looked uncomfortably similar to the assailants he had faced the previous day. They rose above the dust and drifting smoke before splitting into two flocks and descending on the soldiers holding the ridges.

"Well, ain't that just peachy?" Doc muttered into his mask.

As if hearing his exclamation, one of the avian monsters broke away from the pack, plunging toward the lawman and his riders. The posse drew their sidearms, firing at the creature, but its erratic flight made for an awkward target as it descended.

One woman, on the far edge of the group looked down as her weapon clicked empty and the distraction cost her dearly. The Hellion swooped towards her, emitting a bat-like screech, with razor talons extended. The claws went clean through her back and abdomen, flipping her from her vehicle in a spray of gore and viscera, leaving her in a screaming, crumpled heap. Her 'Horse wobbled out of control before pitching over onto its side in a spray of dust.

For the second time in a handful of days, Doc chose to put someone out of their misery rather than see them suffer a vile, lingering fate. He turned in the saddle and deftly ended her suffering. He then put a shot through the shoulder joint of the retreating monster. It tumbled, shrieking, from the air and thrashed in wild circles before one of the Indestructibles put an armoured boot on its neck, annihilating the thing with a torrent of shells.

Rage began to well up in the pit of Doc Holliday's stomach. It was an emotion for which he had earned a reputation, some years previously, but which his increasingly delicate health and desire to better himself had tempered. But now, the familiar surge of anger was welcome. He was going to put a stop to this. No more deaths because of that uppity aristocrat. He was going to find her, and he was going to put a bullet clean through her head, consequences be damned.

The taste of anticipation, the yearning to engage in the kill, had always been a bitter one, but now it seemed delicious. Blood pulsed behind his eyes and for several long seconds, he considered testing his 'Horse against the powered fence. Fortunately for him, sanity prevailed, and he was dragged out of his moment of righteous vengeance by a spray of wild gunfire as another weaponised corpse stumbled from the smog. He hunkered down in his saddle and accelerated away with the other riders, guns blazing.

Doc Holliday's sense of fury swiftly vanished, to be replaced by the overwhelming and primal urge to survive that had kept him alive long past his allotted time.

That was when Joe Sweeney arrived, and things began to get seriously out of control.

* * *

"The Hellions have engaged the infantry," observed Lieutenant Mackeye. He and the twins stood on an observation deck located within the central building, observing the battle. "The east ridge is wavering. I estimate... a few more minutes and they will be forced to retreat. The west, however, are making more of a fight of it. Good firing order. Made of stern stuff, those sergeants." Objectively the Lieutenant was more than aware that the embattled Union soldiers were technically his enemies, but the military officer in them could not help but admire such courage.

Annabelle frowned, a delicate expression, and glanced over at him. "Why, Lieutenant. If I didn't know better, I'd swear that y'all are startin' to sympathise with the enemy."

Mackeye lowered the spyglass, offering it in Ben's direction. It was only then that he discovered Annabelle's brother was suddenly nowhere to be seen. "Not at all, ma'am," he said, addressing Annabelle's words. "I was merely observing that the soldiers currently holding the west side of the valley with require more of our attention to dislodge than the east. No disloyalty intended. It was strictly a tactical remark. I..."

Whatever else Mackeye had to say on the matter was cut off by the thunderous boom that reverberated around the valley, eclipsing the sounds of battle and rattled the armoured windows in their frames. Annabelle snatched the spyglass from Mackeye's hand and resumed her own observations of the combat raging outside.

Sarah Cawkwell

A boxy vehicle, huge and lumbering had emerged from the valley mouth and was making its way inexorably toward the facility. It bristled with rotary cannons that were busily spewing lines of fire in all directions and carving up her army with brutal efficiency. The vehicle was capped with a turret that sported a massive cannon. As Annabelle watched, it rotated ponderously toward her buildings.

"The Union have brought an armoured coach!" Annabelle sounded absolutely scandalised at the discovery that her enemies would so much as *dare* to use military science against her.

Further outrage was abruptly curtailed by the cannon firing again. The pressure wave of the blast twisted the drifting clouds of smoke and dust into weird gyres and flattened the shambling horde into the dry earth. Mackeye pushed Annabelle to the floor in a distinctly ungentlemanly way and threw himself protectively on top of her, even as she spluttered in shock and indignation at being so roughly manhandled.

Then the roof of the building was torn off in a storm of sound, fire and flying glass. The platform lurched drunkenly to one side and shattered masonry cascaded past. The shock of impact only lasted a few seconds, but no sooner had it faded than the sounds of battle rushed in to fill the void, loud and immediate.

Mackeye got to his feet and dusted himself down before offering Annabelle his hand. "My apologies, Lady Hamilton. There was no time to warn you."

She took his hand and got to her feet. "They are *shootin'* at me!" She seemed stunned by this revelation, affronted, even. The Lieutenant found that he wondered if, despite the horrors she had wrought, the confidence and surety with which she carried herself, the true reality of war had traumatised her.

"They. Are. *Shootin'* at me," she said again, pointing in the direction of the attacking army, two points of colour flashing high on her cheeks and reflecting the deep-seated anger that she felt.

"Yes, ma'am, they are. I believe..." Mackeye began, but she glared at him and he fell silent as she interrupted him.

"Don't they *know* who I *am*?" She gathered up her fallen rifle and swatted away the Lieutenant's proffered arm of assistance. Then she swept away in a haze of heady jasmine down the stairs. "Benjamin!" She yelled her brother's name into the workspace. "Benjamin! Get out here *right now*, or so help me, I'll..."

Her imperious summons was answered by the throaty growl of an engine and the sudden stench of exhaust fumes. Ben Hamilton emerged from behind something huge that was obscured by a dust cover. He was covered in dirt and grease but gave his sister a huge, slightly manic grin as she advanced on him. "Benjamin! Did ya know the Union had anythin' like that... thing?" She waved her hand vaguely in the direction of the advancing vehicle.

"It seemed likely," he replied, innocently. "But not to worry, Annie. This will give them something to think about." He pulled the dust cover aside to reveal a high-sided wagon covered in armoured plates and sporting a pair of large-barrelled guns. It was crowned with a walled platform and, as Annabelle watched, animated soldiers swarmed up into it from below, carrying cannons of their own.

Her outrage evaporated instantly, replaced by a sweet smile. "Why, Benjamin! Ain't that just *glorious*?"

The machine chugged and growled and then lurched into motion, the heavy ram smashing anything and everything in its path. It crashed through the building doors and plunged into the battle raging through the valley outside.

"Now then. While they're busy playin' with that li'l thing, I need ya to come down to the surgery with me. Help me to finish off a li'l somethin' of my own."

* * *

Willa Shaw leaned into the turn and thumbed the trigger. The guns on her vehicle barked a stream of shells that chewed up the shambling dead in her path. With the arrival of Sweeney and his support, things appeared to once again be getting back under control.

Then something huge and motorised that was definitely *not* the Rolling Thunder burst from the smoke, ploughing directly into one of her riders. The 'Horse broke in half with a shriek of abused machinery. Its pilot span away in a tangle of broken limbs. A pair of K9 units were crushed beneath its heavy wheels and the cannons mounted on its cab obliterated everything in its path, friend or foe. Multiple lines of fire streamed from a platform on its roof and Willa could make out a number of figures with heavy-looking weapons partly concealed from behind an armoured revetment.

Three more riders formed up in pursuit, a pair of her own and one from Doc's posse and began firing. Shells rattled like rain off the vehicle's hull, sending sparks and spent munitions ricocheting in all directions.

The soldiers swiftly realised that their efforts were futile and pulled away before they could draw the attention of the gunners, but the man from Little Beam seemed more determined, or perhaps foolhardy. Willa could not decide which. She watched as he accelerated his Iron Horse until he was alongside the rumbling wagon, then he reached into the satchel and produced a fat canister emitting a tell-tale glow.

An RJ-powered bomb.

Willa bled off some speed and jinked to one side as a line of fire ripped up the earth. She got back into position to resume her pursuit just as the man pressed the activation fuse on the device. Something on the roof of the wagon leaned over the wall and shot the brave man clean through the head. He dropped from the saddle and the bomb feel from his nerveless fingers.

It seemed to bounce in slow motion, the single light on its side blinking malignantly as she passed it.

Then the blast lifted her from the saddle and threw her at the ground and into embracing darkness.

For the briefest time, Willa Shaw dreamed, and in her dream there marched a legion of the dead. The eerie, silent parade of corpses were shuffling endlessly across a polluted, barren wasteland beneath a blood-red sky. Humped, malformed creatures moved among the throng, their swollen limbs dragging in the grey, lifeless dust.

"*Wake up, Willa.*" A gentle, oddly familiar voice cut through the dream, but she did not wake.

A figure in black robes led the macabre procession and though Willa had no sense of herself, some part of her recoiled from whatever it was that lurked beneath the black hood. Two points of crimson light lit the cavernous gloom, the eyes of a predator searching for her.

Something feral woke within her. The inner wild animal that she kept deep within the darkest corners of her soul. Something she knew was there, but never acknowledged.

"Wake up, Willa Shaw!" The voice was more urgent, this time. More insistent. She had the strangest sense of something settling over her, like a blanket. *It's the sky,* she thought in dazed wonderment. *The night sky is covering me. Protecting me. But there is such horror...*

She wanted to run, to hide, to do anything to escape that awful gaze. To be caught by it, she knew, would be to become like them.

"Wake up!"

She surfaced from the dark, suffocating depths of oblivion to a world of smoke, fire and pain. Everything hurt. The sounds of the ongoing battle were oddly attenuated by a tinnitus whine and her good eye was full of grit and tears. She pressed the back of her hand to her nose and observed, without surprise, that it came away bloodied. Someone close by was screaming, a long, persistent howl of anguish that cut through the fog in her brain and restored a small measure of clarity.

She rolled over and saw one of her riders on the ground, his legs pinned beneath the wreck of his machine. One of the Lazarus was hunched over him, slowly and repeatedly stabbing him in the belly with its arm blades. Willa groggily drew her pistol and fired at the thing. The shot went wide but drew the creature's attention. It staggered to its feet and began shuffling toward her, sagging jaw working silently and gore-streaked limbs reaching.

Willa fired again and the energised shot passed cleanly through the thing's torso. It stumbled forward a few more steps and Willa shot it once more. This time, the top and back of its skull exploded in a mist of crimson and it toppled over, blank, dead eyes staring at her.

The Major didn't know how many of her own had fallen, the smoke and the roar of battle made it impossible to tell, but it felt like a lot.

The soldier had ceased his screaming and now lay very still in a slick of his own blood. The Major said a quiet payer for him and pulled herself painfully upright. Her Iron Horse lay on its side a few metres away, its frame scorched and dented but otherwise intact. Beyond it, a wave of the dead emerged from the smoke drawn by the sounds of gunfire. She checked her pistol, already certain that there were more bodies than she had bullets and began firing.

The Lazarus soldiers disintegrated in a hail of fire.

Fresh figures emerged from the smog, angular and bulky, the barrels of their electrocarbines smoking. One of them was missing an arm and the shoulder drizzled reddish fluid and sparks in equal measure. It seemed entirely unconcerned by the injury and braced its weapon against its hip.

"You require assistance, ma'am?" Sergeant Irwin asked as he and his unit approached.

Willa looked around at the carnage, the bodies, the wreckage and then back at the GI Bot. "How are we doing, Sergeant? Have we breached the compound yet?"

"Negative, ma'am! The UR-31E have extremely durable chassis. With your permission, ma'am, the Indestructibles will advance!"

The suggestion was met with a chorus of "*Irwin's Indestructibles!*"

Willa shook her head wearily and immediately regretted. Her skull was still throbbing from the crash. "No Sergeant. That won't be necessary. I need you and your unit to find Sergeant Sweeney and destroy that armoured carriage."

The GI Bot saluted with a clang. "You can rely on the Indestructibles, ma'am!" The unit echoed their sergeant with their ubiquitous chorus.

The Major limped over to her Iron Horse and heaved it upright. It had suffered some superficial damage, but nothing a day in the garage wouldn't straighten out. The engine roared into life and she plunged back into the battle in search of Doc. If they were going to have any chance of salvaging a victory from this chaos, then they were going to have to do it together.

She found him with a handful of the Little Beam posse on the other side of the compound, their vehicles drawn up in a circle. Sergeant Covey and half of his soldiers were also with him and together, the group had been holding their opponents at bay, though with only limited success. A pair of bodies lay within the circle, one of them wearing the chevrons of an officer. Willa drew her 'Horse up beside the embattled survivors and addressed Covey.

"Why are you out of position, Sergeant?"

"Willa..." Doc started to interrupt, but the Sergeant spoke over him. The lawman fell silent, his eyes glinting with annoyance. Allies or not, the militia still treated him and his posse as second-class citizens in this situation and it annoyed him.

"The ridge is lost, Major. Those flying things made a real mess out of me and my boys." He looked over his shoulder at the decorated body. "They got Weis, tore his head clean off. The rest of the troops scattered into cover and I've not seen them since.

We've been holed up down here ever since, doing what we can." The sergeant glanced at Doc. "Without the help of the deputy and his folks here, we'd all be dead."

The moment of unexpected praise quashed the flare of Doc's annoyance and he inclined his head. Willa ran her fingers through her hair and looked around. A pair of dead Hellions lay in the dust near the edge of the circle surrounded by a tangle of bodies, Union, posse and enemy alike. Willa sighed and nodded abruptly.

"Alright. Doc, Sergeant Covey... if we are going to get in there, here is what we're going to do."

* * *

Willa and Doc raced through the smog of battle, their vehicles weaving between the grasping limbs of Annabelle Hamilton's army. The tide of Lazarus soldiers appeared to have ebbed a little now, but they still outnumbered the Union troops many times over. If any sort of victory was to be salvaged from this uncertain battle then it was necessary to take decisive action. Major Shaw could feel events slipping from her grasp, out of control, and she hated it.

"Are you *sure* about this?" Doc's voice was raised to be heard over the roar of their engines.

"You got any better ideas?"

Doc looked around at the wreckage – mechanical and human – and shook his head. "Not really," he admitted. "Just that this feels a lot more like of *my* plans... an' you know how they tend to play out."

She actually smiled at that.

Further discussion on the matter was brought a close by sawing lines of gunfire that poured from the roof of the armoured wagon The Major and the Lawman peeled away to either side of the vehicle, hunkered low on their Iron Horses and accelerated ahead of it. The twin, cab-mounted cannons blazed away above their heads, spewing a continuous rain of spent casings and large calibre fire, while the shambling soldiers above ponderously turned their attention to the troublesome riders. Doc glanced over at Willa, his eyes grim and meaningful and then he turned in the saddle. He pulled one of his pistols and deftly put three shots into the narrow vision that split the cab of the wagon. The guns fell silent and in that moment of sudden reprieve, Willa accelerated off into the smog.

"That's right," the Lawman shouted as the wagon altered course and bounced after him. "It's just you an' me, now!" He opened up the throttle and pulled away, the wagon in hot pursuit. A moment later, the cannons opened up again, whatever abomination that passed for crew clearly having recovered from any damage that had been done. It was now clear that the wagon riders were out to exact their revenge. Doc continued to taunt, unable to stop himself.

"Got y'all riled now, huh?"

A shot glanced from the side of his 'Horse and another plucked at the fabric of his coat, putting a neat hole through the flapping collar. Then he burst from the drifting smoke and drove directly toward the waiting Union gunline. The bulky machine came after him, an unstoppable avalanche of armour plating and bloody determination.

"Open fire!" Sergeant Covey's bellowed command carried clearly across the battlefield.

The air filled instantly with the whine of rifles as the infantry obeyed, shortly followed by the whip-crack of conventional weapons as the Little Beam posse followed suit. The nose of the wagon sparked and stippled with impacts as it was repeatedly struck, but it showed no sign of stopping its wild pursuit. Another volley of shots hammered into it and were similarly dismissed.

"Fire at will!" Covey gave the order and the rifles answered.

A wild shot from the cab guns clipped a man, sending him sprawling, while another went clean through an Iron Horse and the soldier crouching behind. The infantry wavered.

"Fire!" The voice was tinny and mechanical, and heads turned as the Indestructibles rose from cover behind the Union position. Their electrocarbines were held low and without hesitation they fired. The cab of the wagon looked as though it was being struck by the fists of a huge, invisible pugilist. Craters melted and deformed its armour, turning one of its weapons to molten slag and reducing the roof gunners to ragged scraps of flesh. Smoke and fluids leaked from the ruptured grille but still it came on, its remaining weapon defiantly blazing. Doc steered his machine past the Union line, skidding to a halt in a spray of dirt and gravel.

"Come on, Willa," he muttered as the wounded behemoth bore down on them.

A streak of steel and sky-blue burst from the smoke, passing in front of the wagon with barely a hair's breadth to spare It was followed a heartbeat later by the earth-shaking mass of the Rolling Thunder at full tilt.

The Union vehicle ploughed into the side of the wagon with a sound like the Liberty Bell. The enemy machine twisted to a halt, armour buckled and two of its wheels spinning uselessly in the air as it was lifted by the ram. Incredibly, despite the damage, its remaining weapon continued to fire, blazing away at an empty patch of ground. Then the Thunder's turret gun fired, its flared muzzle almost point blank against the side of the stricken vehicle.

The wagon blew apart in an eruption of fire and spinning shrapnel, the two ragged halves of its remains tumbling to a halt in flames a few metres away. The Union troops burst into whoops and cheers and Doc let out a long sigh of relief.

"It's just like I said," he said to nobody in particular. "Just like one of my plans."

* * *

Willa smiled grimly at the sound of the victory cry. It was possible that maybe they could still salvage something from the chaos of the battle, that the Hamiltons could yet be brought to justice for the abominations they had wrought; the lives they had taken.

The thought was arrested by a deep, ululating cry emerging from the smog. She'd heard that sound before, back in Provenance. Her blood instantly ran cold as something huge and misshapen hauled its bulk from the gloom, fixing her with a crimson, cyclopean glare.

Her attention was ripped by an explosion several feet away. Earth and debris pattered against her armour and vehicle and she swerved through the expanding fireball of detonation Heat and choking fumes washed over her, stealing her breath and bringing tears to her one good eye.

Everything in front of her was a misty, indistinguishable blur. More tears spilled down her cheek, stinging the numerous facial abrasions and she swore as the gurgling roar sounded again, closer this time, accompanied by a heavy, awkward treat. She blinked furiously, trying to clear her vision, and barked out her orders in the desperate hope that there was someone – anyone – close enough to obey.

"Move up! Move up! Concentrate your fire on this thing. No cowards on *my* watch!" She was relieved when her vision began to clear a little. Another explosion went off, this time over on her right side and she skidded to a halt. Bodies sailed into the air, rising on a plume of smoke and fire but it was impossible to tell whether they were Union, civilian or the reconstructed. Something awful shrieked nearby, the long horrific wail punctuated by a wet crunch.

Willa cursed for a second time.

"I said fire, damn it!"

This time, when she rubbed at her eye, she saw what it was that had emerged from the gloom. She immediately wished she hadn't seen it. Even with her affected depth perception it seemed distorted and somehow *wrong*.

The thing was huge: easily the height of two, maybe even three men. Bloated, exposed musculature glistened through ragged skin holes where the unnatural growth had stretched the flesh beyond capacity. The chest was broad and muscular but was a mass of puckered scar tissue drooling crimson fluid and corrupted blood. The neck was bull-thick, supporting a head that seemed less part of the original body and more of a gnarled, tumorous growth. Ragged scraps of hair still clung to its scalp, the lines of the skull clearly visible whilst the mouth sagged open in a permanent, idiot scream. The gurgling cry emerged from that gaping maw, and somehow, the ghastly sound conveyed a depth of madness and suffering deeper than any words or fevered dream ever could.

The whole abomination lumbered forward on a pair of absurdly atrophied legs aided by its swollen, muscular arms which dragged it toward her. The whole thing had a peculiar, rolling gait. It left a trail of sticky black residue and ropey strands of gore in its wake and had its one, swollen eye fixed firmly on her. Memories of the beast in Provenance bubbled up, unbidden and unwelcome, and the sheer weight of gunfire she had poured into it.

"Doc!" She shouted as loudly as she could manage. "Sweeney! I need some firepower over here and I need it *right now!*" The distance between her and the Union troops was obscured by the fading smoke, but she hoped that she had not strayed too far from their position.

Brief silence, interrupted only by the sounds of gunfire, the weird howl of the monster and the distant rumble of engines. That meant that at least some of her riders were still up, still fighting. A spark of hope flared. Then she heard the reply, on the very edge of her hearing.

"Be right with you, darlin'. Got a few issues of our own right now."

The spark of hope died. If Doc and the soldiers were pinned down, then there was no way they were going to have the numbers to move on the facility. She had to think and she had to think fast. Even if she used all of her remaining ammunition it was unlikely to be enough to put this thing down for good and if she did not... then it would rampage unchecked through her survivors. She drew her pistol, checked the chamber and fired.

A shower of impacts stippled the abomination's flesh, large calibre rounds driving it back with a ghastly wail. Five Iron Horses pulled up beside her, the barrels of the machines' cannons hot and smoking. Two soldiers and three of Doc's posse. She recognised Mrs. Kelly, but a big man and a youth, little more than a boy rode beside her, their eyes wide and faces smudged with soot and dirt.

Willa had never been happier to see anybody in her entire life. She gave them a fierce, tight grin and levelled her pistol again.

"Well? What are you waiting for? Fire!"

Shots tore into the monster's shoulders, arms and chest, tearing chunks of flesh from its body but apparently doing little more damage than that. A torrent of shells poured into the target and blood sprayed from its wounds. The illusion of blood was quickly dispelled, however, as even that seemed vastly unnatural. Instead of the pink mist of a regular injury, the air was kissed with a spray of a red-black fluid with a familiar smell. Mrs. Kelly lowered her rifle and stared, her rheumy blue eyes wide with shock and disbelief.

"It bleeds RJ."

"I don't care if it bleeds bourbon."

"Our weapons are doing nothin' against it, Major Shaw."

"Not quite true. We're driving it back. Keep up the fire." She didn't want to start arguing tactics, because frankly here were infinitely more important things on her mind. Like the nine foot tall screeching killing machine that was attempting to advance on them, even in the face of overwhelming resistance. The mouth was still stretched open in that horrible wordless scream.

Then the creature bunched its limbs beneath it, the huge muscles of its arms and shoulders knotted, even as they wept poison into the dry earth. It fixed the group with a baleful, burning stare and let out a warbling howl of what Willa could only assume was a mixture of rage and torment.

She took aim at a point in the centre of the thing's forehead.

Then it sprang, its coiled strength hurling it in a high arc toward them.

"Scatter!"

The entire unit broke up, desperate to avoid this new danger. They had dived from their vehicles, letting them fall where they would as the abomination landed among them. The earth shuddered beneath the impact, toppling the vehicles 'Horses and spilling riders to the ground in a tangle. It whirled about, its huge limbs reaching for its tormentors with gnarled, clawed fingers.

In a panic, the big man hurled something from his belt; a crude, metal canister with a fuse jammed into the top. It was way off its mark, but the ensuing blast caught the creature's full attention and it swivelled to face the perceived threat. Without needing to order them, Willa's companions took advantage of the moment and scrabbled further back, putting as much distance between themselves and the beast as they could. Then it turned and focused once more on the living targets. They readied their weapons but instead of a wild charge, the monster reached out and seized the nearest viable projectile. With a heave of effort, it lifted Willa Shaw's trusty Iron Horse and launched it at them.

The machine tumbled through the air in a graceful arc before falling to the ground with a crash of destroyed machinery. Willa threw herself flat and the broken remains of the wrecked vehicle bounced directly over her, showering rivets and abused armour in all directions.

"Oh no," she said, ire taking over. "Oh, no, no, no. "Nobody," and her voice became something low, threatening and deeply menacing. "*Nobody* does that."

The discharge of energy from Willa's gun opened a long, deep wound in what remained of the thing's face and its head snapped back. It screeched and one of its bloated limbs made a swing for her, the massive paw grabbing in her direction. The major dropped and rolled clear of its reach and had her gun up and trained on the enemy within a couple of heartbeats.

"Nothing is taking this thing down, Major." It was one of the soldiers from the barracks and she glanced at him. "We need something bigger than what we got!"

"Yeah, I get that," she retorted. "Only problem is..." She waved her gun vaguely toward the abomination who had now been joined by several of the corpse-like things. "That's between us and them!"

To her immediate left, the teenager from the town – Doc had introduced him as Eli – was fumbling with his shotgun, desperately attempting to load another pair of shells for the next onslaught. This would no doubt be one of the boy's first real battles and she felt a brief moment of pride that he was handling it without any apparent panic, just a little fear – and they were *all* feeling that.

"You got this, kid," she said, and her words brought a brief smile to his face, clearing away the anxiety and enabling him to focus just that little bit better. She turned her attention straight back to the fray. Most of the unit were now firing indiscriminately at the monster before them. Mrs. Kelly was aiming for where its heart should have been, where any natural, living thing would have been vulnerable.

"Damn thing's tougher than stewed boot leather," said the old woman as every shot she fired passed cleanly through its flesh with no effect. "An' my guns sure as hell ain't powerful enough to put it down. Ain't you got somethin' bigger? Better? There's gotta be somethin' else we can try."

Shaw's eyes raked over the creature, assessing it, measuring it, taking in how big it was and how tiny the window of destructive opportunity actually was. The answers to those two questions were 'goddamn huge' and 'ridiculously tiny' respectively.

"We need those cannons back," she said, simply and Mrs. Kelly nodded. Then the undertaker's face split in a mostly toothless grin and she jumped from her mount. "Cover me," she said, without affording any sort of explanation whatsoever.

Before Willa could so much as say a word, the woman peeled away from the group and began running directly at the rampaging monstrosity. It registered her with a strangely childlike curiosity, its lumpen head tipped to one side. Then it took a flailing swipe at her with one of its massive fists. The old woman smoothly dropped into a diving roll that seemed incongruous with her age and passed cleanly beneath it, coming out the other side. As distractions went, it was most certainly effective. Mrs. Kelly ran at full pelt toward one of the other abandoned 'Horses.

"Fire at it!" Willa screamed the order at the top of her lungs. "Keep it off her!" She glanced at the big man. "Is she *completely* out of her mind?"

"Don't look at me," said the man mildly, shrugging easily. "Mrs. Kelly is totally her own person. I ain't gonna start questionin' the whys an' wherefores of what she does now. Besides, she'd take my head off if I tried. Bill Hawkes, by the way, ma'am. Pleasure to make your acquaintance. Doc's sure told me a lot about you."

Willa just stared at him for a moment before shaking her head and returning her attention to the creature.

A knot of six soldiers burst from the smog, led by Sergeant Regan and fired in well-practised unison. The juiced rifles burned craters in the creature's ragged hide, drawing forth fresh screams of outrage from its distended maw. Willa and her group opened fire, but their small arms seemed little more than a distraction, an annoyance the beast attempted to swat away. From behind, there was the sudden roar of Mrs. Kelly's newly-acquired cannons as she emptied the 'Horse's weapons into the bleeding monster.

It sprang again – like some kind of unnatural primate – right over the heads of Willa's group. It landed heavily, crushing two of Sergeant Regan's soldiers and scattering the survivors like matchwood. The men didn't even have time to scream as they were mashed into the dirt. The beast pulled off one of the dead men's arms, holding it up in front of its ruined face for inspection. There was no sign of recognition at all on the terrifying features. It waved the lifeless limb about for a few moments before dropping it and turning its attention back to Willa Shaw and her band of misfits. Once more it screamed its ululating cry.

Moments later, an energy blast from Bill Hawkes's long rifle, striking the thing in the throat, ripping it open and destroying whatever remained of its vocal cords. The scream dissolved into a bubbling wheeze.

"An' *you* can shut up as well," snarled the Fixer who had evidently recovered from the shock of the creature and was already quite plainly sick of it. Despite the desperate nature of the situation and despite her promise to always remain professional, Major Shaw could not help but flash him a grin of camaraderie. She was struck by how these frontier folk were so stoic in the face of entirely bizarre adversity. The thought she might die here today was softened by the knowledge that at least she would be in good company.

Mrs. Kelly roared past on the ancient Iron Horse, the long skis underneath marking it as an early model from the Ore War. She spun the vehicle around in the dust, ready to fire on it again. Willa waved her hands desperately as the abomination lunged again, its head swinging pendulously on its ruined neck.

"Scatter again! Get out of here! We have to find Sweeney!" The group did as they were told, ducking and weaving in all directions. One of the soldiers managed to retrieve his 'Horse and thundered off in search of reinforcements. Inspired by the Union man's fortune, Eli sprinted toward his own vehicle. A huge paw arrested his flight, scooping the boy up into a fatal embrace.

Willa whirled at the cry of alarm and turned to see the boy struggling in the monster's grip. She emptied her pistol into the swollen arm to little effect and then watched in helplessness as the beast, suddenly tiring of its new, squirming toy, squeezed violently. Eli's cries of terror rose several, horrific octaves and then became a strangled gurgle as his body was crushed in a vomiting spray of blood and organs.

It was the grisliest death that Willa had ever witnessed and in a moment of sharp, agonising clarity, she suddenly appreciated what it was that Doc had done for Zach back in Provenance Eli had been a stranger, an unknown quantity to her, but he had followed her – or at least Doc – to this place. He had followed them to fight a battle that was not his, against people he didn't know, all for a cause that he had not lived long enough to understand.

The thought filled her with absolute fury.

The creature shook the ragged remains from its fist and looked at the shocked faces surrounding it. The stench of ruptured flesh and opened bowels was appalling and one of the solders turned and fled, despite the barked orders of Sergeant Regan to hold firm. Desultory fire peppered the monster to little effect, and it once again turned its attention to Willa and her companions.

The Major pressed her last six rounds into the chamber and dug in her heels. She was tired of running. Tired of monsters. Tired of wasted lives. Tired of the Hamiltons and their insane ambition.

The roar of the Iron Horse behind her dragged Willa out of her bleak defiance. Mrs. Kelly sat astride her 'Horse, her rifle cocked against a hip. There was a grim expression on the old woman's face.

"Eli was a good boy," she said, quietly. Willa didn't have the words to reply so she nodded her understanding.

"Do you think you and I can end this thing?"

"I got one round left, Major."

"Make it count, Mrs. Kelly."

"Oh, believe me, honey. I always do."

The world seemed to slow, to stop, to hold its breath and then Mrs. Kelly fired. A spear of scarlet light transfixed the creature through its giant, luminous orb and violently snapped its bulbous head backward. At the same time, a resonant boom echoed once more across the battlefield. A huge shell punched a valley of overpressure through the smoke and then directly through the body of the beast, leaving a ragged and weeping hole.

The Major would never know which of the wounds finished the job, but the beast gave a long, frothing exhalation and then its warped form began to bloat and bubble as whatever insane chemistry that kept it alive went into overdrive. Willa pushed the older woman from her vehicle, diving into cover after her.

Then the monster exploded, painting a wide area with fluid, bile and mucus.

Willa and Mrs. Kelly rose from behind the Iron Horse and then looked back to find Joe Sweeney sitting in the cupola of the Rolling Thunder. He gave the Major a sharp salute before retreating once more into the armoured behemoth.

"You really *are* amazing, Mrs. Kelly."

"Oh, I know that," came the reply. "But this time, I ain't sure I'm gonna be amazin' *enough*, darlin'." She checked over the condition of her weapon and nodded back toward the facility. The last of the smoke was drifting away and only wind-blown dust remained. Out of the dust staggered a horde of deathless soldiers, half a dozen Hellions wheeling above them.

"You know what? I'm done with Annabelle Hamilton." Willa's lips tightened and her face grew hard. "If I have to burn this place to the ground with her and her monsters still inside. I think..."

Then the earth began to tremble, and the air vibrated with the sound of distant thunder.

Willa turned to see what new devilry was upon them and for the first time in a day that had been filled with shocks and horrors, was completely stunned by what she saw.

* * *

Doc unloaded his weapons at one of the Hellions currently circling his little band of survivors. Through a questionable combination of luck and judgement, the shots shredded the joint of its left wing and the vile thing tumbled from the air with a mechanical wail. It hit the ground in a tangle of limbs and thrashed madly for a moment before springing to its feet and slashing wildly at the air in front of it with murderous claws.

Several rifle shots glanced from its armoured torso, but it was clear that the thing would not survive long under the desperate onslaught of all the remaining soldiers and Little Beam posse. Over the course of his comparatively short life as a gunslinger, Doc Holliday often felt some kind of empathy or even sympathy for those who died by his hand. He was not an inherently violent man and on a base level he abhorred killing.

But as he stared into the blank face of the Hellion and he felt no such thing. The person it had once been may as well be dead already, just like all of Annabelle Hamilton's creations were. No matter how evil and corrupt that was, no matter how deeply tragic he knew that it was, he could not bring himself to mourn the passing of the creatures they had become. As the Hellion shrieked its last, ragged and shot through by concentrated fire, he simply turned away.

From his embattled position, he was helpless to send any aid to Willa in her fight against her own grotesque enemy, but he did what he could to keep the foe from her back. At the same time, Hellions and stray creatures would occasionally peel away from the bulk of the force and harass his position. Doc and his team were fast running out of ammunition and he suspected the same would be true for most of the survivors still able to fight. Even Sweeney in his mighty Rolling Thunder was fully occupied controlling the enemy hordes and destroying the greater threats as they emerged.

The sense of impotence at not being able to strike back against the Hamiltons was unbearable. Any minute now, he was going to go against Willa's very firmly expressed orders to hold his position. When the smoke and dust finally began to clear and he witnessed the malformed horror crush poor young Eli apart, he felt sick to his stomach. Still he rallied.

"Everybody with me! We're pushin' forward. Come on, now! We need to take the fight them or they are just gonna bleed us dry. Are you with me?" There were muttered growls of agreement and Sergeant Covey nodded grimly. The officer wore a haunted, hollow expression and it was clear that if he saw this battle out to the end, if he survived to the end of the day, he would be changed man.

"The Indestructibles are with you, sir! The Union stands unbroken!" A tinny recording of *Union, My Nation, 'Tis of Thee* began playing from a hailer grille on Sergeant Irwin's shoulder. The announcement was greeted by the standard Indestructible response, and the automaton soldiers opened fire again, smashing another Hellion in flash and metal scrap.

Doc had been too young to partake in the Ore War and the cacophony of this battle was unlike anything else he had ever experience. The screech of the Hellions, the occasional roar of cannon fire, the cries of the wounded and the dying filled the air with a horrific orchestra of suffering, to which the counterpoint was the near-constant discharge of weapons.

Another Hellion swooped in. Its talons raked the deputy's shoulder and he was grateful that the heavy coat he wore soaked the worst of the damage. Nonetheless, the claws bit painfully into the delicate flesh at the base of his neck and he felt the dampness of blood suffuse the collar of his shirt.

Doc swiftly ducked out of the way of the thing's return swipe and fired into its belly. Stinking, reddish fluid sprayed as it passed, spattering the face of the deputy and those immediately around him. Having missed its initial target, it snatched at a young woman who had come with Doc from Little Beam. She screamed in pain and terror as the monster seized her, but was not able to wriggle free of its grasp. The Hellion sank its talons deep into her shoulders with vice-like tenacity and dragged her from the group. She wailed again as she was carried away and although Doc and his team chased the creature with gunfire, it quickly soared out of range leaving them helpless to watch what came next.

He knew what was coming and still he watched.

Having climbed high above the battlefield, the Hellion released her. The poor victim plummeted to the ground below chased by a long scream of despair. Even above the noise of battle Doc swore he heard the bones in her body crunch as she hit the ground. He closed his eyes, nausea rising once again at the horror he had lead these people into.

We're losin'.

He hated the voice of defeat that was pestering at the back of his mind. He was rapidly falling from the boundless cynical optimism that fuelled him into a black, dark despair. They were losing this fight. Annabelle Hamilton and her army of freaks would be free to wreak havoc on the innocent and it could all have been stopped right here in this nameless valley if only he had possessed the gumption to put a bullet in her skull when he'd been presented the opportunity on a plate.

Is that how you want to be remembered, Henry Holliday? As the no-good, consumptive dentist from Griffin who fell at the feet of a bunch of shufflin' monstrosities?

Hell, no.

It was seconds after this internal monologue that Willa and her companions managed to finally and messily put an end to the beast that had been plaguing them. A ragged cheer went up from his band as the monster blew apart and for just a moment, he forgot the doubt that had been gnawing on his confidence. He forgot the horrors that they faced and he even managed to forget the dead they had already left on the field.

In that sweet moment, victory seemed possible.

Then the last of the smoke and dust blew away, revealing the shambling horde.

"Push forward," he roared. He ignored the sudden burn of intense pain flaring behind his ribs that subtly suggested he might want to re-think his current life choices, and opened fire on the closest creatures. The remaining people in his posse did likewise and their fire tore through the enemy ranks and cut down another Hellion. It tumbled out of the sky, hit the ridge and bounced ungracefully down its side until it came to a crumpled stop at the bottom.

"Some down," Doc said, grimly, looking at the numerous corpses. "Lots to go."

It was at that point that the earth began to shake with rising thunder. The thunder of hooves. A thunder loud enough to drown out the noise of battle. Mounted figures poured over the southern edge of the valley and down the ridge toward them and the sight filled Doc's heart with both hope and dread.

* * *

The noise of the hooves pounding the earth eclipsed all others as a host of Sky Stallions descended into the valley. The warriors on their backs whooped and hollered cries of vengeance and war as the horde surged toward the legion of the dead. Sensing that Doc and Willa were no longer the greater threat, Hamilton's army slowly turned to meet the Warrior Nation force. Rifles crackled and blades flashed as they were drawn.

A huge warrior rode at the head of the wild charge, his heavily muscled body painted for war. He appeared to have his eyes closed, but his lips moved as though he intoned a prayer, or in recitation.

"Look at that!" Sergeant Regan's voice was hushed in awe.

Bright, azure sparks began to stream from the warrior's skin as he rode, leaving retina-scarring contrails in his wake until his flesh glowed with barely contained radiance. Then he opened his eyes, revealing smouldering pits of blue-white fire. Incredibly, impossibly, the big man leapt from his horse but continued to lead the charge, his huge stride pushing him ahead of the mounted host.

Hamilton's army raised their claws and blades to greet him.

There was a blinding flash at the point of impact and a dozen broken, ragged bodies were flung high into the air. Where the warrior had been was now a huge, spectral buffalo. It charged, ploughing through the shambling horde as though they were nothing more than toys. It crushed and rent, trampling everything in its path.

As it burst free of the first rank of creatures, Willa realised that she and her companions were *also* in its path.

"Move," she bellowed as the massive animal bore down on them. "Move!"

The blue, ghostly form of the buffalo took more solid form as it passed and it lowered its head, great horns pointed at the shambling corpses that still advanced in the wake of the wild charge. It gored the first two through the centre, shaking them free as it turned to re-attack the others. Drawn to this new enemy, the corpses lost all interest in Willa and her unit and turned to fight the shimmering blue buffalo.

Their weapons struck its body, but there were no evident wounds that appeared. It wavered with each strike, the form shimmering and re-solidifying with the attacks. A blade-armed horror thrust forward, attempting to pierce the creature, but it moved with astonishing grace for something so large. Willa was completely captivated by its sheer primal beauty and was not even aware she had been holding a breath until she started to see spots dancing before her eyes.

"Warrior Nation," said Mrs. Kelly in a grim tone. She had dismounted from the Iron Horse and was watching the bizarre display with a reserved curiosity. Willa was surprised. Her own encounters with the Warrior Nation had not been plentiful. Most of her business had been conducted far enough into the eastern states that she rarely encountered them. She knew some of the – frankly shameful – history of the first American settlers and the run-ins that they had experienced.

"Well," she said, watching the buffalo performing its individual stampede, a graceful and deadly dance. "Whatever their reasons for being here, they've timed it well. Let's regroup and get back in there."

The blue-wreathed buffalo came to a brief halt in its onslaught, tossing its head with the sort of arrogant pride. Where bodies had fallen beneath it, it began to trample them. Willa could not understand how something so apparently insubstantial was able to manage such an unlikely feat, but she had reached the point where nothing surprised her any more.

Pushing their way across the valley, Doc, Covey and Irwin were fighting a running battle with the remaining Hellions. The men and women had hunkered down beside the Rolling Thunder which was crawling toward Willa's position and which was keeping the airborne monsters at bay with its array of rotary cannons. Joe Sweeney once again rode in the cupola, blasting any stray creatures that came too close with his trusty shotgun.

When the first shimmering blue arrow flew past his peripheral vision and plucked the closest Hellion out of the air, Sweeney thought he was imagining things. Then a flurry of arrows, humming through the air like a swarm of angry wasps followed suit. Some had that same weird azure glow, others were simply regular arrows. It didn't matter. The monster was quickly peppered with the lethal points of the projectiles, the last of which crunched into one of its steel-rimmed eyes and sent it crashing to the ground with the rest of the dead.

Glancing over his shoulder, Sweeney saw the group of Warrior Nation on foot descending from the ridge. At the very front was a lithe young man with a grimly determined expression on his face. In his hands were a pair of wickedly curved daggers, The weapons glowed with a pale inner light and trailed a haze of blueish smoke.

Sweeney, much like Willa, had very little experience of the Warrior Nation. He had heard stories, certainly. He knew about how aggressive and war-like they could be, a hypocritical approach from a nation who claimed to be first and foremost about peace. But right now, rumour and hearsay didn't matter one iota. What mattered was that they were, if only for now, fighting on the same side. He met the eyes of the youth in the front of the archer unit and nodded, speaking unheard words of agreement.

Then the Sky Stallion host broke through the undead ranks and thundered directly toward them. Sergeant Irwin and the surviving Indestructibles formed up in a wedge in front of the Rolling Thunder and levelled their weapons while the Union soldiers and Little Beam posse climbed onto or beneath the hulking vehicle.

"You hold your fire, Sergeant Irwin," Doc barked. "I think we have enough enemies for one day and I for one will gladly tip my hat to anybody who makes such a mess of the Hamiltons' plans in so short a time."

Irwin inclined his head. "Indestructibles, stand down." Sweeney was certain he detected a note of reluctance in the mechanised voice. The musical refrain warbled and died out as the mechanised troops put up their guns.

An optimistic Hellion descended, even as its companions were plucked from the air, and made a swipe for the lead riders. The savage claws opened deep wounds across the warrior's chest, but knives and axes of his fellow riders quickly drove the beast back before it could inflict further harm. Then, something struck one of its wings and it fell beneath the trampling hooves of the throng. Broken and mangled, it still manged to drag itself free of the churning hooves and paw feebly at the waiting braves.

Sweeney stared at the fallen Hellion and shuddered as it was immediately set upon by a Warrior Nation pack, whooping and hollering as they saw to its ultimate demise. A strange silence fell across the gathering. The youth who had brought the warriors to this timely aid stared at Sweeney and then spoke in halted, broken English.

"We are friends in this matter, wagon-rider. We go now. Join the others?" He pointed at Willa's group of survivors. "End this."

"I can definitely get behind that as an idea," Sweeney agreed fervently. The youth spoke to his people in their own language and weapons were sheathed, or simply flickered out of existence. Sweeney had no idea how that even worked, how it was even a thing, but he couldn't help but be impressed.

On an impulse, he offered out his meaty hand. "Sergeant Joseph Sweeney," he said. "Union." The youth tried to repeat the words and Sweeney gave a grin. "Joe," he said, giving the boy an easier option.

"Joe." The word sounded odd in his mouth, but he formed it to an acceptable sound. He stared at the man's hand, then instinct told him what was required. He put his own hand into the soldier's.

"Stone Fur," he said.

"Making new friends, Joe?" Doc's voice was tinged with an edge of amusement as he spoke.

"Honestly, Doc, I have no idea," Sweeney replied.

* * *

"We need to pull the soldiers back inside the compound, ma'am. It's our only chance to hold onto this place now." Lieutenant Mackeye's report did little to calm the furious Annabelle Hamilton. She pounded her fists against her leather-clad thighs, like a child throwing a tantrum.

"This ain't the way this was meant to go! They're takin' out all the foot soldiers!"

"And the Hellions too, I imagine," observed Ben, clearly thinking he was being helpful. His reward was a sharp, stinging slap on the cheek from his twin sister.

"Shut ya mouth Benjamin," she snarled. "We worked hard to prove ourselves an' these *backwater* no-good *hicks* are disrespectin' my skills an' your science! I ain't gonna let this stand. Is Subject Four Thirty Six good enough to go?"

"Four Thirty Six is..." Ben put up a hand to rub his cheek where she had struck him. The blow had not hurt him particularly, but he had certainly been shocked by the suddenness of her attack. "I think we're almost there."

"Then less talk an' more work. I want to get it out here now. It's the best we got. An' I want this ragtag bunch of... fun-spoilin'..."

She ran out of imaginative abuse and focused instead upon the hulking thing that lay on the slab before her. Benjamin busied himself feeding a heavy belt of large calibre shells into one of the weapons while she snapped a thick hose into place. Sluggish red fluid immediately began to ooze through the tube and into the anatomical nightmare. She studied it. The Lazarus blend that was feeding its enforced existential continuity was an older recipe; hearkening back to the earliest days of her research. Fast acting, fast results, minimal longevity. Not the best she could do, but the best she could do *under the circumstances*.

She suddenly felt the helplessness of it all swim over her. She had worked so *hard* for this. Now, she was being beaten and if that wasn't bad enough, then she was having to deal with a sudden, unexpected flare of doubt in whether what she was doing was truly *ethical*.

Perhaps just a tad too late for morality, she thought sullenly. She narrowed her eyes at Mackeye.

"Well, Lieutenant, don't just stand there. Go an' get our troops back inside the compound before they all get wiped out. We're gonna need as much time as we can get to finish up here."

"Ma'am, might I suggest it's time to consider a tactical withdrawal?"

Annabelle stopped working and glared at the Lieutenant. "Ya want me to run scared from a bunch of savages an' misfits?"

"No, ma'am, only that it might be time to..."

"No, Lieutenant, I will *not* withdraw, tactically or otherwise, an' neither will you. Now go an' make sure it takes them a good, long while to get in here so that we can have a *special* surprise waitin' for them."

* * *

Without warning and with their losses mounting, Hamilton's troops suddenly turned, retreating within the boundary of the buzzing, sparking fence. Doc, Willa and their surviving troops were finally re-united at the valley head. Blood had seeped through Doc's shirt and although he looked visibly tired, he still seemed focused enough. He'd removed his respirator and was fastidiously wiping out the accumulated sweat from the battle with a cloth from his coat pocket. Every now and again, he coughed quietly. He waved away any concern about his shoulder claiming that if he was still standing and still walking, then he was surely capable of still fighting. He was still cleaning the mask when a retinue of Warrior Nation led by Stone Fur approached.

"Everyone take a breath," Willa ordered. "Tend to your wounds and your weapons. We're going to attack the compound directly. Keep vigilant!" There were salutes from her people and muttered words of acquiescence from the townsfolk. "And make sure none of those bodies that aren't ours have a chance of getting up again."

It was a horrible thing to call. It was quietly and uncomfortably agreed that the only proper way to absolutely prevent the things from rising again was decapitation and three of her younger soldiers were charged with the less-than-delightful task of roaming across the valley floor and separating heads from bodies. It was grisly and morbid and vile and with each slash of a military sabre, Willa Shaw despised Annabelle Hamilton just that little bit more.

The huge buffalo had ceased its killing spree. She had not seen the moment when the spectral beast had vanished, but the big warrior who had led the charge had returned, suggesting that, for now at least whatever power that lived within him was once again quiescent. Willa knew the stories of those of the Warrior Nation having the capability to shapeshift but had always dismissed it as a ridiculous tale.

Unbidden, she remembered the title of Doc's favoured penny dreadful, *Unlikely Tales.* He'd said that he reckoned many of the stories had a basis in truth and she was left wondering. When the big warrior joined them, Willa addressed her words to him first, not even knowing if he would understand her.

"You came at just the right time. Thank you."

He tipped his head onto one side and considered her. His dark eyes were large and intelligent in his grizzled face and she recognised that same look that the buffalo had given her. Any doubt if they were one and the same was washed away in that exchanged look. He then gave her a smile, displaying remarkably even, white teeth. Willa tried again and spread her hands wide in a greeting.

"Welcome."

The word was obviously alien to him, but Willa pushed on, keen to understand if their goals were aligned. She did not need more enemies in this mix, particularly not if they were capable of the things she had just witnessed. The big man shook his head a little helplessly and turned to look at another warrior, a younger man who stood beside Sergeant Sweeney. He pointed a finger. "Stone Fur," he said. "You speak."

"I think Stone Fur here is in charge of these people," said Sweeney. Willa's eyes widened. The boy could not have been more than eighteen at the most, but he carried himself with the gravitas of a natural leader. In other circumstances, she realised, she might have taken a moment to admire how handsome he was.

In other circumstances.

Sweeney thankfully interrupted her train of thought. "He speaks pretty good English. You shouldn't have any trouble."

"Stone Fur?" Willa repeated the name and the young man nodded and stepped forward.

"Stone Fur," he confirmed and lay a hand on his chest. He touched that same hand to Sweeney's arm. "Joe." He pointed at Willa, and she flashed a smile.

"Willa."

"Will-a. Is good, yes? Yes. I am Stone Fur. Named Spirit Priest by my People, by grace of Great Spirit," he said in that same halting English. "You..." He gestured with a sweeping arc of his arm that encompassed everyone present, "walk close to our lands."

"We have no wish to offend," began Willa but was hushed into silence as Doc stepped up to her side. He spoke a few words slowly, carefully and in a language she did not understand. Stone Fur looked at the deputy, firstly with suspicion and then with apparent approval before replying.

"You speak their language?"

"Don't be so surprised, darlin'. It's hard not to be around folks and pick a smatterin' up. I only speak a little." The deputy was uncharacteristically modest. "Not much. Enough to convey that we only wish to clear this evil from the lands an' then we will be gone." He spoke another few words to the Spirit Priest who answered in kind. Then the young man switched back to English.

"It is not common for the People to... what is word you give me, Joe?"

"Ally."

"Ally yes. It is not common for the People to ally with Incomers. But man with face like..." He made a gesture that suggested thinness, dragging his thumb and forefinger down his own face. "Face with iron. Face shaped like *tokalu*..."

"Fox," murmured Doc. "I do declare the boy means me." Indeed, the sharp planes and delicate bone structure of the dentist's long, thin face – even when he wore the iron respiratory – did have a vulpine air.

Stone Fur nodded. "Yes, the fox. Beneath your iron mask. He speaks from here." He put a hand on Doc's thin chest, above the heart. "I believe you will help us and then you will be gone." His blue eyes, so unusual in a man of the Warrior Nation searched the faces of the Union soldiers and the townsfolk looking for anything that suggested the opposite was true. Willa nodded.

"We will help you, Stone Fur," she said, and she could not help but slow down the words. She had no desire to sound like she was talking to this extraordinary youth like he was a fool, but she also wanted to be sure he understood her. "But my people, all of us, we have our orders. We must follow our own code. The woman who brought war to these lands... we wish to take her alive."

Stone Fur's expression hardened, and she felt uncomfortable.

"These devils took the body of a sacred man. My father, Curved Bear Claw. Took him from holy place. Took him, took all his secrets. Secrets of the People are not for your kind. So... so, we find him, we take him back and we hunt the devils in our way." Doc whistled softly in sympathetic understanding. Willa opened her mouth, but Stone Fur held up a hand to forestall her objection. She fell into startled silence. She could not put her finger on exactly what it was about this young man that made her want to listen. "We respect your wish and if we find the witch that has wrought this evil, then we will give her to the earth. Not yet. Yes?" He looked to Doc. "Iron Fox agree to this?"

"Seems pretty reasonable to me," said Doc, mildly. He was actually deeply flattered to be given a name by Stone Fur. Like Willa, he felt compelled to listen to the young man. It was as though he were being driven by some higher power.

Doc Holliday was not a religious man. He had been raised by a Methodist mother who had converted to the Presbyterian church. She had never forced her religion on him and had been gone before it had been an issue. His hard life and the seemingly endless series of hard knocks had dulled any belief in some sort of supreme being. Now he believed in a bottle of good bourbon, a pair of loaded guns, an acute awareness of his immediate surroundings and loyalty to his friends. But there was a sense of... well, if he was forced to use a word, it would be *holiness* about Stone Fur. Like he had been chosen.

"But here's the thing, Willa, an' I am tellin' you this because I feel that you deserve my honesty in this matter. If my gun should accidentally go off an', say, shoot Annabelle Hamilton in the face, then I ain't gonna feel remotely sorry about it. I do not give one iota of a damn that the Union want her alive. Her foolishness an' greed has cost too many lives. There comes a time when you gotta consider that the only option left is a reckonin'." The deputy nodded at Stone Fur. "In that, I think you and I are agreed, are we not?"

"The Great Spirit guides. It remains to be seen what the Great Spirit wishes regarding the fate of the witch and her kin." He closed his eyes for a moment and when he opened them again, his young face was grave and serious.

"All will be flame," he said, and Doc glanced at him. The major, however, did not register Stone Fur's words. She was preoccupied.

Willa was glowering. She stared at Doc in undisguised fury when he spoke, angry at first that he would defy her so very openly. And then she saw the determination in his eyes. It was a revelation. Willa saw Doc Holliday clearly, perhaps for the first time in her life. Years ago, back in Texas, he had been a man full of hope and plans for the future. Then he had received his diagnosis. All of his hope, all his dreams, ripped from him.

She saw, for a fleeting, telling moment, his whole soul laid bare. She began to understand more about what the hardships of his illness and the added difficulty of life on the frontier had done to him. She didn't see the laid-back, genial man he presented himself as to the world. A man who treated things with humour and often unforgiveable one-liners. In that determination, an expression that showed clearly in his slate-blue eyes, she saw a focused, stone-cold lawman who would do anything to dispense justice in a world that lacked it. She saw a man who was good at what he did.

And finally, after so many years, all of the anger melted away and she found herself – much to her supreme irritation – finally locating a tiny spark of understanding about Henry Holliday and about who he was. He had no hope for himself, so he had instead turned to serving the law as a vessel that enabled him to bring hope to others.

How could you not admire that?

Her scowl dissolved into a smile, and she reached over to lay a hand briefly on his shoulder. His surprise at this unexpected display of camaraderie showed in the raising of his eyebrows, but he said nothing. He reattached his respirator which went into place with a soft click and inhaled the clean air into his aching chest. He was actually feeling pretty uncomfortable. Maybe the time had come for him to consider scaling back his enthusiasm with regards to fighting.

The mask seemed to bring suspicion to Stone Fur's eyes. Doc considered for a moment, wondering how to explain to a man who found dystopian science abhorrent that it was probably the only thing keeping him alive, but found he didn't have to. The hardness went out of the boy's eyes as he pushed what was, after all, a trifling matter to one side. There were more immediate things.

"Then it seems that we are *all* allies," said Willa. Stone Fur nodded, eager to get to the fight. Then he glanced at Sweeney and rather uncertainly held out his hand.

"Is this right?"

Sweeney grinned. The boy certainly learned quickly. "Exactly right, Stone Fur," he said.

Doc chuckled at this, grasping the boy's hand in both of his own, pumping it up and down with enthusiasm. Willa was less energetic but no less sincere as she lay her own hand over those before her.

"Allies," said Stone Fur and his smile was bright enough to light up the valley.

* * *

"We have about fifteen minutes until the portal is at full power," reported Ben, appearing from the back of the facility. He had a drill in one hand and a hacksaw in the other. The leather apron he wore was slick with fluids; blood, oil, grease and he looked harried. "Fifteen minutes. I'm not sure I'm gonna get Subject Four Thirty Six up in that time, at least not..."

"Never mind what ya can't do, Benjamin! I want hear what ya *can* do." Annabelle was in a foul temper. The unexpected arrival of the Warrior Nation and reversal of fortunes they brought with them had both angered her and left her a little shaken. She had not expected the intervention of so many ranked against her soldiers and when it had become necessary to order the remainder of the army to fall back to defensive positions, she had wanted to scream. She considered her army the pinnacle of her collaboration with her brother. The very peak of what they could accomplish together.

And those *horrendous* people in the valley had slaughtered dozens of them without any regard for all the work that had gone into its glorious creation.

Until that point, Annabelle had only assumed that she was cleverer than most of humanity. Now she was certain of the fact. Only idiots would have destroyed something so remarkable without pausing to examine the craftsmanship, the science, the sheer genius of the creation. Yet there it was again, that nugget of doubt eating away at her conscience. It was a revelation that she *had* a conscience and she frankly wished she did not.

She looked over at Mackeye for a moment and her rage lessened. He was still there with her. He still trusted to her intelligence. He was still loyal. Her heart swelled with affection for her closest ally. Perhaps... if they got out of this alive, she would allow him to escort her to dinner. Not as her bodyguard, but...

"What I can do." Ben stared at his sister, hating her because she was so difficult, but loving her because of the sibling connection. "I can get Four Thirty Six off the slab with two of his six weapons up and running." She was grateful that Ben had dragged her thoughts away from Ross Mackeye.

"Two is better than none," offered Mackeye and wished he hadn't. Both twins turned to stare at him. He shifted uncomfortably. "I'll... go check what's going on outside, shall I? I... yes."

He fled. Ben watched the Lieutenant leave and a flicker of a smile ghosted across his face. His head tipped to one side.

"Tell me, sister-mine. Why, exactly, do you keep that strange fellow around?"

"He has his uses. Now shut up, Benjamin and get me my specimen." She was defending him. It was new behaviour, and it wasn't *entirely* awful.

"Subject Four Thirty Six," she urged, pushing Mackeye out of her thoughts once again and trying to get her scatter-brained brother to focus on the present and to stop prevaricating. "What can ya give me, Benjamin? Quickly, now! Our very lives may well depend on it. I don't know 'bout you, but I ain't keen on the idea of dyin' out here in this damned backwater."

"Well... you've given him animation, although he's not doing much in the way of moving right now. I have no idea how your process works, but he looks a bit broken to me." Ben's assessment wasn't what she wanted to hear and she began to scowl. Ben continued hurriedly, hoping to avoid another tantrum. "I've given him means of forward motion and built the most powerful weapon I had in my stock pile. There's been no time to armour him or install shielding. He..."

"Oh, for the love of... Will ya *stop* callin' it 'him', Benjamin?" She moderated her tone, speaking with a little more kindness. "When ya call my soldiers 'him' or 'her', well, truth is, it makes me real uncomfortable. They're not people. Tiny li'l minds like they got? They never really were. Ain't a person, it's an *it*. It. It isn't armoured or shielded. But it can still fight, buy us time so we can get outta here." She gave her brother a supportive smile and squeezed his arm. "Show me, darlin' boy. Let's make the call. The Hamiltons need to live to fight another day, right?"

He appreciated the change in her tone. Petulant Annabelle was hard to cope with for the more mild-mannered sibling. He squeezed her hand in reply and nodded. "There's a lot we still have to offer the world. You and me, against everyone else. Just like the old days, eh?"

"That's the Benjamin I know."

He led his sister through the half-light of the laboratory's rear end to a corner that stank oppressively of rotting flesh and chemicals. His nose twitched at the organic stench that he was simply unused to. Biology was his sister's forte. He was an engineer first and foremost.

"He... it, I mean, is here."

Subject Four Thirty Six was dormant, its upper torso drooping over the massive mechanical undercarriage to which it had been affixed. The visible skin was blistered and sun-burned, the usual mark of a corpse that had been outside for some time. Strips of meat had been flensed from its bones as though someone had picked a chicken carcass of its bounty. Annabelle moved to its side and lifted the head up, although this required her to stand on the tips of her toes. She lifted first one eyelid and then the other.

"Full jolt of Lazarus will have it up and runnin'," she said. "Its levels have been allowed to run too low. Easy fix, but it ain't gonna last for long. Enough to fire the brain synapses back into thought and the harness will aid with the movement." She moved to the cluttered workbench and clicked her tongue against the roof of her mouth in annoyance. "Ya incapable of tidyin' away after yaself, Benjamin? How d'ya find *anythin'* in this pigsty ya call a workspace?"

"I..." Ever since they had been children, Annabelle had been the undisputed leader of the pair. She was bossy by nature, overbearing in attitude and very single and bloody-minded when she wanted to be. His natural inclination was to do anything most people asked of him just so he could have a quiet life and get on with his machines. That was one of the reasons he enjoyed being around Stonewall Jackson. The man just left him alone.

"I know precisely where everything is," he said, standing up for himself for a change. If she noticed, she didn't acknowledge it. "Everything I have is right where I left it and I never have any trouble finding it. Can't help it if you can't look properly, can I?"

"Here it is." She picked up a syringe filled with the reddish fluid of a made-up Lazarus dose. The quantity in the implement was enough to easily cater for three or four normal human specimens. But Subject Four Thirty Six was most definitely not a normal human specimen.

She returned to the creation and handed the syringe to Ben. "Ya gotta do it," she instructed. "In the jugular vein, if ya can find it. I ain't tall enough." Even in that simple statement there was an open challenge for him to dare mock her.

He did not. He had not spent much time with Annabelle in recent months, but he knew all too well just how caustic and spiteful she could be when she was made to feel stupid. If anybody knew how bright and talented, she was, it was her brother – but she had never sought his approval. Maybe, he wondered, maybe if they had spent more time recognising that talent when she'd been younger.

The voice of a late uncle popped into his thoughts. *If you live your life on the back of what-ifs, you'll never move forward.*

He took the syringe with obvious distaste writ largely in his handsome face. She pushed him gently. "Hurry up, will ya? Before those interferin' Union boys an' gals break down my damned front door! All of it. Now."

Spurred by the reminder that war was a mere matter of yards away, Ben nodded and plunged the needle of the syringe into Subject Four Thirty Six's neck. He pressed down on the plunger and injected the fluid into the dormant creature's sluggish system.

Nothing happened for a few seconds.

Then, everything happened simultaneously.

* * *

The voltaic fence sagged in a number of places, the mesh torn by impacts and gunfire, but it still sparked with lethal energy, and behind it waited a mob of silent, deathless soldiers. Under normal circumstances, an assault would have been a daunting prospect. However, circumstances were far from normal and given a little time to regroup, Willa, Doc and their little band of survivors advanced on the Hamilton facility in the cover of the Rolling Thunder. On the other side of the facility, Loud Thunder and Stone Fur lead the horde of the Warrior Nation.

The vehicle's huge turret gun spoke, and a shell ripped a hole in the fragile fence and annihilated the group of waiting creatures on the other side. Now that they could focus on the task at hand, it no longer seemed so insurmountable.

"Don't know how those Warrior Nation folks are going to get in," Sweeney yelled from the cupola. "Arrows and rifles aren't going to cut it."

There was a resounding crash from the other side of the buildings and the fence flared brightly and then died. The chorus of whooping calls and yells and rose in response.

"Oh, I think they'll manage," Doc replied flatly.

Some of the buildings had been damaged during the furious battle in the valley. The large, central warehouse had an obvious, smoking hole where a section of its roof had once been, while the northern outbuildings had been liberally peppered with cannon fire during the initial assault One of the smaller buildings exploded outwards in a shower of broken wood and copper panelling, the debris slicing into the dead soldiers like lethal shrapnel. Out of the carnage stampeded Loud Thunder, once again in the form of a titanic bison, his pale, luminous hide boiling with barely contained power.

"He's extraordinary," said Willa, humbled by the sight. While the battle had been raging, she had not had the chance to truly appreciate what she was seeing. Now, though...

So many native buffalo across the frontier had been slaughtered over the last years, almost to extinction in places. Interventions by the Warrior Nation had called a halt to the mindless killing for pure sport and now herds were once more thriving. But to see this ghostly, perfect animal up so close made her feel a sense of awe and a driving reminder that humans were just a single species among millions.

She had no idea from whence that thought came, but it made her both uncomfortable and respectful at the same time.

Loud Thunder trampled another swathe of shambling monsters as he came about and turned to face the armoured shutter that protected the entrance to the largest building. He paused, one hoof pawing at the dust of the valley floor and snorted plumes of blue flame from his ghostly nostrils, front hoof pawing at the dust of the valley floor.

"That little matchwood shed was one thing. Surely he can't have strength enough to..."

"I'm thinkin' that if he has power enough to turn himself into a creature like that," said Doc, catching her arm and pulling her to one side as the spirit buffalo charged, "then he sure as hell has the power to open a door, no matter how big it is."

He more than had the power. The shutter door, rolled steel reinforced with railway sleepers, did not stand a chance against the onslaught of Loud Thunder's relentless charge. The shock of the impact reverberated around the valley and was greeted by the mixed, victorious cries of Warrior Nation and Union alike. Shards of metal and chunks of splintered wood went spinning across the workshop interior shredding anything and everything in their path. Loud Thunder followed them, a juggernaut of manifest fury.

Instantly, the building was filled with the sounds of gunfire as a neatly arrayed line of Lazarus-infused constructs reacted to the invasion. Lieutenant Ross Mackeye, left to his own devices while the Hamiltons had been squabbling, had taken the initiative and arranged the unfortunates as though there were his own soldiers. He had pointed them at the steel shutter door, anticipating that it would be breached and the second it was, he opened fire. It was enough to spark the reaction in the meat-puppets that they too needed to fire their weapons.

Mackeye had not been expecting a giant, ghostly blue buffalo to stampede through the newly open space and pulverize the first three Lazarus soldiers on its way in. He beat a hasty retreat, because sometimes, a tactical withdrawal was absolutely the right thing to do. And when the very real risk of being trampled and gored by a monstrously sized animal existed, then this was one of those times.

There were still a good ten minutes before the portal cycled up to full power. A lot could happen in that time and he knew that well. As he made his way to the rear of the facility and down into the lower chambers he played through several scenarios in his head. Whichever way he worked it out, this was likely to become a siege, or a last stand and he needed to make preparations.

Loud Thunder exploded from the rear of the workshop and rejoined the Warrior Nation forces. The Sky Stallions were in amongst the lines of the Lazarus soldiers now, their speed and grace easily outpacing their sluggishness. A few riderless horses galloped with the pack, but most of the braves were cutting the enemy down with ruthless efficiency. Stone Fur and his warriors stalked slowly through it all, their long knives finishing any work left undone by the cavalry.

Up on the ridge line, a pair of wagons were drawn up sporting several large rotary cannons. The Spirit Priest let out a long, lilting call and the Fire Bringer crews went to work. A torrent of shells poured into the peripheral buildings, perforating them with fist-sized holes and demolishing anything and everything within.

On the other side of the compound, the Rolling Thunder crunched its way over the remains of the fence and pressed into what remained of the enemy lines. Willa and Doc rode on the rear armour of the vehicle, picking off stragglers with their pistols while Mrs. Kelly and the remaining soldiers and civilians brought up the rear. Several battered K9 units still prowled around the compound worrying at the dead, while Sergeant Irwin and his troops appeared to be having a fine time destroying anything left standing by the Warrior

Nation.

"Once we get past these lines," Major Shaw said, taking overall command with ease, "we have no idea what to expect. Deputy, you and Mrs. Kelly sweep your posse round the left flank. Sweeney, you keep those big guns on that building and you cut down anything that comes out of there that isn't us. Everybody else, you are with me. The rest of the unit can come straight through the middle and Stone Fur can do his own thing. If all goes to plan, we can regroup at the other side and move onto whatever that... *bitch*... has planned for us next."

Harsh language, for Willa Shaw and both Doc and Sweeney looked at her, surprised at the venom. She stared right back. "What? I'm sick of her. I'm sick of this whole thing. I want this done. And I'm confident in that you must all feel the same. Right?" Sweeney nodded, as did Mrs. Kelly. Willa's gaze fixed on Doc, and she raised one eyebrow. He nodded as well. "Good. Then let's do this thing."

Raising her hand, Willa held the moment of anticipation for a fraction of a second and then brought her hand down with a grandiose gesture.

"Company, advance!"

* * *

Subject Four Thirty Six was unfinished and yet even in its uncomplete state there was a haunting, bizarre beauty to it. Its eyes were hidden beneath a skullcap and visor of iron and lenses, but Ben still jumped back the second they flared into scarlet life. The urge to seek, hunt and kill prey washed from the creature in tangible waves and in the face of everything that he had seen since joining forces with his sister, this was still the single most terrifying thing.

What had remained of the torso was mounted on a chassis of pistons, hoses and thick, iron plates. It was bulky and segmented, not unlike a huge, artificial arachnid. But this thing had four legs, like those of a horse. Its gait, as it took its first faltering steps forward, was reminiscent of a new-born foal attempting its first foray into a larger world, but Ben's mechanics were superb, and the pistons fell into line quickly.

"Four Thirty Six will move quickly," he observed, "but because there has been no chance to test it, I have no idea if it will be able to stop as quickly." It was attempting forward locomotion even as he was trying to tighten up the last few bolts. Heavy chains had it anchored to the warehouse floor and realising it could go nowhere, it let out a keening cry that sounded eerily like a hunting hawk. Annabelle was gazing at it in a mix of admiration and thoughtfulness.

"It ain't pretty to look at," she said, "but I gotta say that it's certainly impressive." She moved her attention to the lethal-looking weapons attached where hands had once been. The one on the left was a mass of serrated blades while the right hand was a monstrous, studded wrecking ball. The sheer amount of damage Four Thirty Six was capable of in its unfinished state was inspiring. She looked rather sadly at the other two arms that hung limply by its side, the huge cannon upon its back and the unfinished shoulder mount but there was no time.

They heard the sound of running feet and both looked up in alarm, their own weapons drawn. Lieutenant Mackeye came to a stop by their side. "We have to do something, and we have to do something fast," he said. "They have unleashed that animal again."

"Then it's time for us to unleash ours," said Ben, sounding so grimly determined that his sister looked surprised, then pleased.

"First sensible thing I heard ya say all day, Benjamin," she said, then reached up to stroke Four Thirty Six's arm. "Go an' have fun, my darlin'."

Four Thirty Six gave no sign of having heard or understood her, but it seemed to realise that it was free to move away. Annabelle nodded at her brother who, with obvious hesitation, released it from its chains, unbolting them from the floor anchors. Four Thirty Six powered forward, dragging the chains behind it.

"Ain't that just the most *glorious* thing ya ever did see?" Annabelle sounded completely infatuated with the abominable thing and Ben wondered, not for the first time, just where his sister had gone so very wrong.

"We need to fall back to the portal room," said Mackeye, intruding just for a moment on her adulation. She shot a glare at him, then the expression softened, and she nodded.

"I hate to run away," she said, sadly, "an' I hate that chances are high that they're gonna ruin all this hard work. But we have the important things ready to go, yes?" She narrowed her eyes at the two men who exchanged glances. "I'm waitin' for an answer. Y'all got my Lazarus brewin' kit packed like I told ya?"

"Doing it now," said Ben, hurrying to the bench where her brewing equipment was. Mackeye looked deeply uncomfortable. Annabelle shook her head and moved to push her brother out of the way.

"Ya want anythin' doin'," she said, bitterly, "do it by your lonesome. Get outta my way, Benjamin Hamilton. Ya couldn't treat fragile equipment well if ya life depended on it. Jus' make sure that Four Thirty Six gets some of them before they get him."

Him.

After all she'd said about detaching from the former humanity of her creations, it seemed jarring that she called Four Thirty Six a 'him'. Ben put the thought out of his mind and just got out of his sister's way. It was better than incurring more of her sharp tongue. He moved to Mackeye's side.

"Now what, Lieutenant?"

"Now we adopt an old fashioned position, sir," replied the officer. "We prepare for a final stand and hope to God that we get out of here before the Union descends." The words themselves filled him with renewed vigour and determination. Victory was out of reach now, but that did not mean he could not give a good account of himself before the end. He may not have understood science in the way these two aristocrats did. He may not have his finger on the pulse of society like Annabelle or understand mechanics and engineering the way that Ben did, but Ross Mackeye was certain he knew how to fight the Union. He'd done it before, after all.

Four Thirty Six, free of its restraints and driven by mostly artificial impulse and ancient memories that reminded it how to move forward, surged out of the laboratory and toward the encroaching sounds of battle. In the workshop above, the last of Hamilton's army were once more being laid to rest as the combined assault of the Warrior Nation and the Union pressed into the shell of the building. Despite their progression through the enemy, they were entirely, woefully unprepared for what they were about to face.

The massive creation burst through the floor in a shower of broken boards and debris, its wrecker arm making short work of the relatively flimsy obstacle. For a moment, all eyes turned to the emerging monster, aghast that the horrors which had seemed almost at an end had once again birthed a walking nightmare. The monster struggled free of the wreckage, its torso rotating unnaturally on its quadrupedal carriage as it took in the surrounding forces. The crimson lenses in its helm fasted upon the Rolling Thunder and flickered once as though registering a worthy threat. Then it charged.

There was no transition of motion, not slow build of momentum. One minute it was at rest and the next it was moving, its piston legs driving it forward at a pace that would easily match a speeding Iron Horse.

A K9 unit tore free of the remnants of Hamilton's army and rushed the approaching monster, jaws wide and snapping furiously at the artificial legs. Four Thirty Six didn't so much as break its stride as it stamped the automaton flat. Two Union men were sent spinning aside and a third went flying in a spray of gore and viscera as the blade-limb lashed out. Even the encircling Sky Stallions and their riders were smashed aside by the rampaging juggernaut.

Sergeant Irwin and one of his remaining Indestructibles appeared from the flank, their electro cannons roaring. The bolts seared and pitted the beast's thick hide and burned a charred hole in its flesh, but again the wrecking fist lashed out and the GIs crumpled in a shower of shredded armour and shattered parts. Sweeney fired the turret gun, but the shell went wide and blew the rear wall from the workshop.

Four Thirty Six, with the full momentum of its charge, windmilled the ball of studded iron and swung at the Rolling Thunder. The weapon connected with a sound that could have heralded the end of the world. The boxy body of the vehicle crumpled like paper, and it flipped onto its side, spouting steam, oil and sizzling crimson RJ fluid. The wheels spun uselessly at the air while the frantic gunners that were still capable tried to bring their rotary weapons to bear. Four Thirty Six clubbed the wreck three more times and the guns ceased their movement.

The monster paused and rotated on its chassis again while small arms fire drizzled against its armour like summer rain.

"Willa, I don't mean to sound the pessimist," Doc said, hurriedly reloading, "but I think, in this, we might have met our match. Unless you have another one of those fine plans hidin' up your sleeve."

The monster rotated and fixed on Doc as if drawn to the sound of the Deputy's voice, even over the sound of battle. Willa did not reply, but her expression spoke volumes.

Then Sergeant Irwin stepped up, his armour torso crushed and dented and one arm missing.

"The Union does not surrender!"

His voice was even more distorted. The automata's good arm somehow still held onto the electro-carbine. He fired, the recoil exploding sparks from his damaged body and the bolt slammed directly into Four Thirty Six's face. The glowing lenses shattered, and the helmet broke apart into spinning shrapnel, revealing the scarred and tortured face beneath.

"By the Great Spirit," breathed Loud Thunder, catching Stone Fur's arm. "Curved Bear Claw!"

Stone Fur's head snapped up and he turned in the direction Loud Thunder pointed. His first instinct was to deny the truth of what he saw, but when he saw the face in profile, even horribly abused as it was, he had to concede that his First Warrior was right. The abomination that the Dead Maker had created was indeed forged, at least in part, from the flesh and body of the stolen Spirit Priest.

"I must speak with him."

"He is gone, Stone Fur. The spirit of Curved Bear Claw fled when the last breath of life left his body."

"No. Something of his spirit lingers on!" The youth was passionate in his defiance. "We all know that the life of the People is never truly gone until the last bone crumbles to dust. If there is life in him, even this foul life, then he has not yet returned to the land, the Great Spirit can still reach him. He will know me. I must do this. I cannot..." The Spirit Priest drew a shuddering breath and Loud Thunder's hand settled on his arm. It was easy to forget the young man's age. He had demonstrated such quiet competence and leadership. And now, he was faced with the horror of his old mentor – his adopted father – in the guise of a monster.

"You will not do it alone, my young friend." Loud Thunder hefted the great spear that was his weapon. "I will be right by your side."

"Thank you." Stone Fur inclined his head briefly and then set off at a bound toward the horror that had once been one of their own. Loud Thunder kept pace easily, his superior height allowing him to match Stone Fur's swift pace. As they came closer to the four-legged creature, the stench of death and corruption was strong. What remained of Curved Bear Claw had suffered little from the elements, but was now gigantic with implanted muscle, pulsing hoses and laced with angry scars. He was barely recognisable as the man he had been and yet Stone Fur would have known him anywhere.

The creature raised its razor arm and brought it round in a sweeping arc that Stone Fur barely avoided, springing back and bending his body in such a way that the weapon whistled through the air mere inches from his face. The other hand, the wrecking ball, came down in a solid strike that whispered by the Spirit Priest's ear and smashed a crater into the earth.

"Curved Bear Claw," he impored. He sprang away once more, diving swiftly to the side as the arms came round in another arc that, had it connected, would have torn the young warrior in half. "Curved Bear Claw, it is me. Stone Fur. Look at me, my friend. Look at me and *remember*."

He tried, very hard, to keep desperation out of his voice. To see the once strong, proud and noble Curved Bear Claw mutilated and turned into the abomination before him was the single most horrific thing he could ever have imagined. A flash memory of the visions came back to him.

Dark shapes with red eyes and dead things moving across a bleak and broken plain.

The stab of recognition from the visions made him gasp in horror at the depth of what might await them, what could become of them all if such power was allowed to roam unchecked. Anger, hot and quick followed the revelation. Loud Thunder, standing by his side, was staring at the face of his old, very dead friend with something akin to disgust. For a man who did not often wear his feelings openly, the expression was shocking.

"It is not him, Stone Fur. Curved Bear Claw is gone. This... thing may wear his face, but whatever might have remained..."

"I cannot allow myself to believe that. Curved Bear Claw. Look at me."

Such a tone of command entered Stone Fur's voice that even Loud Thunder was taken aback. Then, unexpectedly, the monster did just that. It turned fully to face the Spirit Priest, the pistons of its chassis grinding and the burning, dead eyes fixed on Stone Fur.

"Curved Bear Claw. Please." He put all he had into those two words.

A simple plea. A child, begging for the attention of a distracted parent. The abomination looked at Stone Fur, looked *beyond* Stone Fur. For a heartbeat, something flashed behind the eyes, something other than madness and fury. Stone Fur's heart jumped with anticipation. He dared to believe that he could reach what little remained of his mentor.

Great Spirit, I have never asked for a thing for myself, he thought as the two, young Spirit Priest and monstrosity stared at each other. *All my work is for those I love, for those I serve. But help me now. Help me reach him. And then, when the time is right... give me the strength to end it.*

A single heartbeat passed, a single, frozen moment of hope and grief and anguish. Loud Thunder could not hope to fathom the depth of the boy's connection to the Great Spirit, but he felt, in that glacial instant, a connection with every living soul in the valley; the others who had travelled with them, the soldiers in their uniforms of blue, the people of the town... there was a sense that Stone Fur was drawing strength from them, from their shared humanity. That in that one, brief sliver of time their collected hopes, dreams and desires were open books. Through them, it seemed, anything was possible.

Loud Thunder stared at the youth, his loathing for the thing that had once been his friend forgotten, at least for that moment. It was as though Stone Fur was trying to remind the husk of Curved Bear Claw what it was to be alive. What it was to be human. What it was to once more feel the breath of the Great Spirit. The chief was only experiencing the reflected glory of what the Spirit Priest was projecting onto the monster, but even that small taste was awesome and humbling.

A spectral blue aura began to coil around the Spirit Priest, an aura which expanded and billowed toward the sky, taking on a hazy, avian shape in much the same way that Loud Thunder presaged his own transformation. But Stone Fur did not possess the heart of a buffalo, or the ferocity of the wolf or bear. No, for the young, gentle-natured Spirit Priest, there was something else entirely.

Curved Bear Claw, when he had lived, had been able to commune with the Great Spirit in the form of a hawk. It had been one of the rarest forms granted to the People. Stone Fur had always yearned for the hawk. But he had something else. Something, Loud Thunder dared to think was more magnificent.

The eagle soars.

For a few moments, Stone Fur was enveloped in the coruscating blue flame of his spirit totem, wrapped in the ethereal wings like a moth in a cocoon. Then those wings unfolded with an ear-splitting screech.

"Curved Bear Claw."

The voice was Stone Fur's but it was also not Stone Fur's. Loud Thunder had to resist the urge to fall to his knees, feeling as he did, the presence of the Great Spirit itself. Stone Fur's first manifestation of this remarkable totem had been impressive but did not compare to the scale or the majesty of what was now unfolding. Loud Thunder was moved almost to tears by the sight of the mighty raptor.

Willa Shaw *was* moved to tears. She caught hold of Doc's arm and drew in an astonished breath. It was so beautiful, so awesome and sublime that she could find no words. Tears started in the corners of her eyes, and she stared at the sight wordlessly. Even Doc had no smart-mouth remark to make, and he laid his hand over Willa's as he too stood mesmerised by the manifestation.

The lumbering monster had come to a complete halt and was now staring, unblinkingly at the youth in its way. But there was...

...something...

The process by which Curved Bear Claw, one-time Spirit Priest of the Warrior Nation had become the creature had been as brutal as it had been horrific. Not much of the original body remained beyond the sutured face, riveted skull and grotesquely altered torso. It had been a thing, a lifeless, abused mannequin. Annabelle Hamilton's introduction of Lazarus had given it life. A horrific, unnatural form of life slaved to impulses that it could neither control nor understand, but life nonetheless. But even the sick parody of life brought with it fragments of who and what it had once been, even though it was buried beneath trauma, madness and mindless rage.

"Curved Bear Claw." Stone Fur repeated the name again and put his hand up, palm facing outward. "It is you. I can see you there, beneath the surface. Come back to us now. Come back to me. Come back to the People and we can make you whole again."

The youth spoke the words, but they came from the hooked beak of the spirit eagle, distorted and changed beyond any recognisably human sound.

Four Thirty-Six could not speak. The tongue had been cut from its mouth and discarded as unnecessary material, but though no words came, the thing that had once been Curved Bear Claw tipped back its head and shrieked, an awful, gurgling sound filled with anguish and despair. It thrashed its limbs about, beating against its own skull with the gnarled wrecking fist while jabbing at the Spirit Priest with its serrated blades.

The eagle screeched once more and Stone Fur took three steps closer. He was near enough now to the monster that it could crush him with a single sweep of its arm. But it did not.

The moment that passed between them, Spirit Priest and horrible, twisted thing, was brief but seemed to extend to an epoch. Loud Thunder could hardly bear the horror of what he fully anticipated happening. Any moment now, he expected the vile thing to simply tear the Spirit Priest in two. It took every ounce of self control the big warrior possessed not to step forward and drag Stone Fur away.

Then, unexpectedly, the monster was completely still. A low keening sound still escaped its tortured lips, but the madness seemed to lift for a fleeting moment. And in that second, the scarlet glow drained from its eyes and Loud Thunder saw instead the eyes of a man. The unblemished, wise old eyes of Curved Bear Claw. The eyes of his friend. Then the ruby veil descended again, like a cloud passing in front of the sun, and the creature screeched. Instead of attacking, however, it charged. It did so falteringly at first as though it warred with itself. But then it propelled itself with increasing certainty back into the depths of the basement from whence it had come.

With another loud scream, the spirit eagle soared from Stone Fur's body and beat its wings powerfully. At first, nothing happened and then the dust on the building floor began to swirl and gather in eddies that gathered momentum, building to a dust cloud that obscured everything from view. Then, the eagle beat its wings again and the swirling dust, debris and wreckage gathered in a cyclone of razored shards and consumed the remaining corpses. It tore them apart, pulled them to pieces and turned their remains into projectiles in turn until nothing remained but a swirling maelstrom of destruction that lifted the wreckage of the roof off and hurled it out of the valley.

Stone Fur drew in a shuddering breath and the huge eagle shimmered and disappeared. When it did so, the storm collapsed. The young Priest fell to one knee, taking gasping, gulping breaths of air. He felt as weak as he had been when he had been carried from the Vale of Sighs, but then there had been time to rest. There was still work to be done here. Loud Thunder took a step or two toward him, but Stone Fur shook his head. He shakily got to his feet and lifted his head to look at the sky.

"When we are done," he said, in a voice filled with love and compassion and which was peppered with a healthy dose of rage. "When we have ended this nightmare, and when Curved Bear Claw is at rest as he should be, then. *Then* I will rest and the Great Spirit will tend my dreams. But while the Witch still dwells below, then there is still a battle to fight."

There was a long, awful moan from somewhere below the workshop and Stone Fur nodded.

"Yes. Now we will end it."

* * *

As it powered, the portal made a noise somewhere between a rumble and a whine. With each passing second, the floor beneath their feet vibrated that little bit more. Between the Hamiltons and Mackeye and the battle that raged upstairs was nothing more than a wooden floor and a handful of basement rooms.

Dusts and wisps of smoke drizzled between the boards as the tempest raged above and then an ominous silence fell.

Then, the distinctive roar of Four Thirty Six bellowed through the basement, far too close for comfort. Ben let out a little yelp of alarm and even Annabelle had the decency to look startled. Mackeye glanced at the portal, then at Ben.

"How much longer?"

"Seventy percent power. It's not going as fast as it should do. Whatever they just did seemed to have some kind of effect on the generators..."

"Make the void engine charge faster, Benjamin, 'cause I ain't wantin' to stay here any longer than we got to." It was fear in her voice and it was both strange and reassuring to know that she could be afraid.

"No, Annabelle, I can't just 'fix it'," he retorted. "I ain't a portal engineer. Best I can do is see if I can pull some power from..." Agitated as he was, more of his accent began to show through his panic.

"Don't give me a lesson in engineerin'," she screeched at him. "Jus' get your idle ass on the case an' do *somethin'!*" For the first time, she was beginning to realise that their time was extremely short and she was experiencing something she had not experienced for some considerable months. It was what had led her to use such language, to slip free of the genteel Southern belle guise that she wore.

Annabelle Hamilton was truly afraid. She was on the verge of tears.

Startled by her sudden bad language, Mackeye stared at her. She stared right back, then hefted the rifle she had taken.

"Guess we have to do all the defendin', then, Lieutenant. On me."

It was so authoritative that Mackeye was briefly taken back to the army. He decided that he would
lose nothing by saluting her order and he did so with
style, grace and genuine respect.

"At your command, ma'am," he said.

They marched into the adjoining room and
stood side by side behind an overturned bench, leaving
Ben to his work. And at last, even if only temporarily, it
felt to Mackeye as though they were the kind of equals
that he had only previously imagined they could be.
He felt his Confederate soldier heart swell with pride
and adrenaline. All the old songs played around inside
his mind and he was compelled to open his mouth and
sing. Softly, at first, but by the time he had reached the
chorus, his voice had gained both in strength and in
volume. His voice was rich and sonorous, if not a little
out of tune, and Annabelle blinked at him before her
own fluting voice threaded through Mackeye's, bringing in a hidden harmony.

"Come tighten your girth and slacken your rein;
Come buckle your blanket and holster again;
Try the click of your trigger and balance your blade,
For he must ride sure that goes riding a raid!"

Mackeye grinned at Annabelle and she returned the expression.

Something crashed through a nearby room
and another howl of madness and anguish rumbled
through the basement. The body of one of Annabelle's
soldiers cartwheeled into the corridor and crunched
into the opposite wall. It crumpled to the ground and
lay still, the body leaking thin, reddish fluid on to the
packed earth of the floor. It was followed a moment
later by the bulk of Four Thirty Six's chassis as the mon-

ster pursued its victim, stamping it into unrecognisable pulp.

Then it turned its gaze on Annabelle and Mackeye before letting out another scream of insanity and terrible, aching loss. The officer reflexively fired his rifle, the shot clipping the creature's shoulder.

"Those *idiots* have broken the control an' regulator system!" Annabelle was indignant, but Mackeye wasn't listening and would not even have cared about an explanation. He aimed for the centre mass of the monster's muscular torso and fired again. The charged shot scorched a hole in the meat but did little more than further draw its attention. It snorted once, a curious, animalistic mannerism, then it accelerated down the hall.

Toward them.

The pair hastily withdrew from their barricade, all their previous bravado erased. They fired a few desultory, ineffective shots and then fell back to the portal room. Mackeye slammed the sliding door shut behind them and retreated to the far side of the room. He was under no illusion as to how long such a flimsy barrier would hold the monster at bay.

A short way behind the rampaging Four Thirty Six came Stone Fur, Doc, Willa and a handful of troops. The youth was taller than the lawman, by a few inches and even though he was clearly exhausted from the effort of summoning the spectral totem, he carried himself with an authority and determination that made the usually egotistical Doc Holliday suddenly feel that his place in the universe was small and insignificant. He pushed his hat back on his head and watched the youth without comment.

"How is it that you managed to stop that..." Willa was going to say 'thing', but some deep understanding suggested that the choice of word would be poor at best, insulting at worst. "...from attacking us?"

"Curved Bear Claw was more than just a friend and mentor. He was a father to me. Some spark of that remains. It will not last. But we will see that he has his vengeance while he is still here, yes?"

"Oh, yes," agreed Doc, and to Willa's ear, he sounded delighted by the prospect. "Oh, yes indeed." He straightened his hat, checked his pistols and nodded enthusiastically. "An' if I might be so bold, I suggest that his vengeance is closer than you might think." He pointed down the hall to where the raging monster was approaching a large, very obvious door.

Stone Fur's head turned to follow Doc's gesture. "I fear you are correct, Iron Fox. Curved Bear Claw's time grows short, and we must soon speed him on his way." The Spirit Priest smiled briefly, but it was an expression tinged with grief at having to once again bid farewell to one who had clearly been very dear to him. To see what remained of him so sorely abused must have been an appalling revelation. Willa found herself thinking of Zach, the young soldier they had laid to rest outside Provenance, and how she would feel if she returned to find him in such a state. Their relationship was, of course, entirely different to that of Stone Fur and Curved Bear Claw, but the idea of having to face a friend in such a state filled the Major with revulsion.

The thing that had been Curved Bear Claw reached the door and crashed into it. Dust and splinters exploded from the impact, but it held firm. Not to be denied, the monster swung its huge, serrated fist and the heavy shutter splintered with an agonising crack. The steel and heavy beams of its construction endured two more thunderous blows before it finally buckled under the assault.

The mass of blades reached through the wreckage and flailed into the more yielding materials beyond. The monster had no understanding or care for the screaming that began as it powered on forward, driving its blade through the flesh, sinew and bone of the unfortunate soul who found himself in the way. One of the blades pierced Ben Hamilton's right shoulder, tearing clean through the meat and muscle and emerging from his back in a fountain of gore. It was a minor miracle that his arm was not instantly severed. He screamed and struggled to free himself from the blade upon which he was now impaled.

Annabelle hefted her rifle and without caring to take any sort of aim simply unloaded through the breach. Most of the shots scattered harmlessly from the monster's chassis, but a few burned into the flesh of its body. Far from slowing it down, the wounds only seemed to fuel its rage and determination to reach them. She reflected, just for a moment, that perhaps this time she had done her work a little too well. Ben continued to scream as he was jerked about on the impaling limb, his blood spattering in crimson drops across the floor and walls.

She never had understood why she cared for him, but there it was. She did and the sound of his suffering cut right through her heart and soul into her very being. "Lieutenant," she said, her voice filled with horror and – damn it all to hell – compassion. "Get Ben. We're leavin'. Right now."

"But he said it had..."

"I don't care!" She screamed the words. "He's my brother and I ain't gonna lose him again. Please, Lieutenant! I'm gonna take my chances with that complicated contraption rather than stay here an' be butchered by my own creations, ya hear me? If you want to make captain, you'll *get my brother!*" She began blasting away through the breach again, but it was increasingly hopeless. The charge on the rifle was depleting fast, the door wouldn't stand for much longer and over it all, her brother's sounds of agony and pain.

Perhaps it was the 'please', but Mackeye felt true sympathy for her in that moment. She had believed in her own creation. Now, faced with the horror of it all, she was finally tasting the sour taste of failure. But her tone remained commanding and there was nothing to do but obey. While Annabelle did her utmost to distract the creature, Mackeye rushed to pull Ben free from the thing's blade-arm. More blood spilled from the wound as he was ripped free and Ben slumped to the ground, half-conscious from blood-loss and agony. He mumbled something which Mackeye did not hear. He gathered the young man up in his arms and looked with no small amount of trepidation at the portal. If it was not fully powered, there was a risk of much unpleasantness. Displacement, dismemberment, death... but it would at least be swift.

Mackeye swiftly weighted those unfortunate potential side-effects to what was likely to occur if they stayed here. Displacement, dismemberment, death... but it was most definitely *not* be swift.

"I'm ready," he said and surprised himself at his own calmness.

"Gonna count back from twenty," she said, not turning to look at him. "An' then we go for it, right?"

"Yes, ma'am."

"The pouch. The pouch! Lieutenant... on the bench beside the portal, there's a leather pouch. I gotta take that with me. It's full of promise. One of us needs to grab it before we jump."

"Ma'am, I don't think we have time..."

"Please. If I get nothin' else outta this, that Warrior Nation medicine bag contains a whole *heap* of mystery waitin' for me to unravel. I'd be so grateful. I promise to put in a word for your captain stripes"

"Alright," he conceded. *Captain* Mackeye sounded fair recompense for all he'd endured.

"Good." She took a breath and began her countdown.

* * *

"Leave."

The one-word command was uttered so quietly as to be inaudible, and it was necessary for Stone Fur to repeat himself. This time, the word cut through the chaos.

"Leave!" He held up a hand to forestall any comments. "The witch is attempting to flee, and I will not send Curved Bear Claw to his rest with his vengeance undone. So you must go. And you must go *now.*" He raised his eyes and Willa was struck, once again, by how piercing and crystalline they were. Loud Thunder, at the back of the group, was staring at the thing that Stone Fur called Curved Bear Claw with an unreadable expression. Then he inclined his head, a last gesture of respect to an old friend, and began to shepherd the People out.

"What..." Willa began, but Doc caught her arm.

"I think," he said, slowly, "we should do as he says, an' hightail it outta here. Like, right now." He let go of Willa's arm and waved his hands at the soldiers who had followed them. "Move," he shouted, his voice brusque and mechanically distorted. "Move!" The urgency in his voice was unmistakable and before Willa could ask another question, she realised just why his need to move had grown so great.

Stone Fur's entire body was shimmering, a blue corona of light spreading from his body and filling the gloomy basement like the like of the sun. All traces of exhaustion had vanished and something otherworldly looked out from behind the white fire in his eyes. She had seen the lambent fire that had taken the form of an eagle, but this looked to be something entirely different and of much greater magnitude. Doc caught her arm again even as she stared.

"Move," he said, simply. She stared at him, at Stone Fur – or at least the column of near-white light that had been Stone Fur a moment ago and back at Doc.

Then she moved.

* * *

"You were my friend. My father. My Spirit Priest. My life. You were given back to the land, as is our way, but the Witch, the Dead Maker... she stole you. Corrupted you. But I set that right, now. Go back to the Great Spirit, Curved Bear Claw. Go back. Rest now and be free."

Outside, Doc and Willa raced from the compound, Willa holding tightly to the back of the Deputy's Iron Horse. The surviving Union troops and Little Beam posse fell back in confusion, not fully comprehending what it was that was taking place. The Sky Stallions and their riders galloped up onto the surrounding ridges, their heads bowed to observe the final parting of Curved Bear Claw. Loud Thunder stood at their head, his face stony and unreadable.

The uncertainty of the retreat dissolved into an earnest withdrawal when the pillar of light burst from the workshop and reached into the sky. It was greeted by the cry of a raptor that shook the heavens and filled the valley with sound accompanied by the beating of unimaginably vast wings.

At the tip of the luminous beacon, a blazing avian shape appeared, small at first but gathering in scale and momentum as it descended. It took only seconds to plunge to earth, but by the time it reached the ground, it was vast enough to fill the valley with lambent flames. It struck the Hamilton complex and detonated, a cataclysmic inferno that ballooned out into an azure dome of soundless, heatless fire. The light became blinding and the ground shook at the fury of the phantasmal conflagration.

Then it was gone.

Little remained of the complex that had stood in the valley, save for a few bits of scattered debris that burned with blue-tinged flames, and the exposed rooms of the basement. A broken half-circle of steel and cables sparked fitfully in one of the rooms, arcs of crimson power crawling across its surface. Then the energy faded and it collapsed into wreckage. The only trace of Annabelle Hamilton's creations were shadowy outlines burned into the earth where their bodies might once have been.

By the time Doc and Willa dared to descend into the silent, empty valley, the Sky Stallions were already riding away, their task complete. A lone figure was walking away when they arrived, a limp body cradled in its powerful arms.

"Is he..." Willa said, leaving the question unfinished. She bit her lip.

Loud Thunder stopped and glanced over his shoulder at them.

"He will live," the chief replied. "But he will not be the same. This..." He cast his gaze around at the scoured earth. "You will not see this again. Only one in many generations may call upon the wrath of the Great Spirit as Stone Fur has done. When he wakes, he may no longer *be* Stone Fur. He may no longer speak with the spirits. He may not know his people at all."

The big warrior gave a small sigh, a tiny gesture that seemed to express a great gulf of regret. "Such is his sacrifice. Only in time will we know the truth of it." He turned to leave.

"It was you, wasn't it?" Doc's question was sudden, the revelation instant. "Provenance. It was you."

Loud Thunder did not look back again, but Doc could tell from the way his shoulder's shifted that he had nodded.

"Yes, it was. Stone Fur was given a vision. That a great evil would begin there. We sought to raze it to the ground, to end it before it began, but we wished to spare the people of the town from punishment. The crimes, after all, were not theirs. In doing so, in taking that approach, the witch was allowed to escape and that led to... this. We will not make such a mistake again."

"What does that mean?" Doc called after the big man's retreating form. "What do you *mean*?"

But Loud Thunder did not reply.

Doc watched the warrior leave, his heart heavy with grief and a sense of foreboding. So many people had fallen here today; Union soldiers, townsfolk and he was even able to muster a small sense of pity for those who had once been human. Before Annabelle Hamilton had sunk her wicked claws into them.

"We're done here," he said, quietly and reached up to remove his hat. He ran his fingers through his sweat-dampened hair. He was exhausted and battered, still in awe and shock at all he had witnessed and all he really wanted now was to down a bourbon or two. Or a bottle would suffice.

Willa nodded her agreement. She too was quiet and thoughtful as she set about the grim task of establishing the military losses on the field of battle. With Joe Sweeney and the severely dented, but remarkably loyal Sergeant Irwin by her side, she stepped away from Doc.

"We're gonna have a hero's burial for each an' every one of our boys an' girls," came Mrs. Kelly's broken and cracked old voice from beside him. The Deputy sighed.

"Mrs. Kelly, I'm so sorry, darlin'…"

"Don't ya be apologisin', lad," she said and she reached out a gnarled, veiny hand and took the Deputy's in it. She patted the back of his hand gently. "We help one another. It's how we always get by. Don't ya *ever* doubt that. It'll be fine."

"I don't know that I can…" Doc could feel his confidence crumbling. To report the deaths of so many townsfolk would surely break him. But Mrs. Kelly was there to bolster him up. She caught the pitch of his hesitation and urged him onward.

"We do it together, eh? You an' me."

She was an old woman, determined and set on her path. He was a young man, aged prematurely by a fatal illness and circumstance, but in that moment, he loved her with a youthful exuberance.

"We do it together."

* * *

Fort Wall, Nightfall

"Colonel Hackett says you're welcome to stay as long as you want," said Willa Shaw, coming up to stand beside him. "He's already planning on having more conversations with Mrs. Kelly about how the barracks and Little Beam can work together more. He's grateful to you for the introduction. Between you and me, I think he's scared of her."

Doc glanced down at the major, amusement in his eyes. "He is a smart man," he said, seriously. "Mrs. Kelly is one formidable lady." Both of them stood in companionable silence for a while, watching the sun sink low and flood the sky with amber hues. After a while, Doc took out his tobacco pouch and began rolling a cigarette.

She felt comfortable in his presence now. All that anger and bile she had directed at him after their first unlikely meeting in Provenance had given way to appreciation of the man he had become. She was also feeling the pleasant buzz of praise from the Colonel and that mellowed her mood considerably. "How's your shoulder?" She looked up at him. He'd not mentioned anything at all about the injuries he'd sustained during the fight, and she knew he'd been in some considerable pain. Still, he dealt with pain constantly and was less likely to complain about injuries.

"Fine, just fine. Doc Taylor's a good medic. Knows not the first thing about dentistry though. Suggested I could stop by some time an' perform checkups on the soldiers here." He was careful to keep his tone neutral. He was still struggling to come to terms with being among the Union. One thing at a time. "He said they would pay for my ex-per-tise." He enunciated the world clearly, self-deprecating and mocking. "I have not done dental work for some considerable time. They would have to be trustin' souls indeed."

Silence fell again and he rolled up the cigarette tightly between thumb and forefinger, squinting up into the sunset. "I think," he announced, slowly, "that I am gonna head off come mornin'. Been invited to a game in the mess tonight an' figured it might just be perceived as rudeness to miss it. An' you know me, darlin'. I do so *abhor* ill manners." He paused in the making of his cigarette, clearly not feeling quite up to removing his mask. He pondered for a moment and then, quite unexpectedly, Willa took the cigarette from him and licked it to provide the seal.

Wordlessly, she handed it back. There was an enormous amount of largesse in that simple gesture and Doc Holliday was, for perhaps one of the few times in his life, completely speechless. He tucked the rolled cigarette into his hatband and watched her for a moment or two, his eyes glittering and impossible to read.

"It's been… interesting working with you, Doc," she said. "And I'm glad we had the chance to… I'm glad to have seen you again." She was so obviously uncomfortable saying goodbye to him that in a juxtaposition from the day he had run from her side, young and scared and full of dread, he decided to spare her the pain.

"Darlin', thank you," he said, softly. "I can see how highly you are thought of among your… among these people, an' I do believe you will go a long way." He caught her hand and squeezed it gently. "I have said how sorry I am for what happened between us, an' that is the honest truth. An'…" He was careful with this, but when he said the next bit, he was rewarded with gratitude in her eyes. "I am real sorry 'bout your husband."

So he knew. Of *course* he knew. He would have spoken to practically everyone in the barracks and something like James Shaw's death would have been easy to find out. His offer of condolence, however, was kind and real and while she appreciated it, she chose not to discuss it further.

Doc studied her for a moment or two, debating whether or not to say anything else and – perhaps wisely – chose not to. "I suppose both of us are changed from back then. Different. We are older people. An' you, at least, are wiser."

She smiled at that, a real smile that lit up her eyes. "Flatterer."

Things that are, thought Doc, just a little wistfully, *and things that never can be.*

"I'll stop by to say goodbye to you when I leave," he said with some hesitance and she knew that he would not. She squeezed his hand back. He understood. It was alright. It didn't matter.

She released his hand and put her hands on her hips, letting her eyes rake over him. "Just do me one favour tonight."

"You name it, Willa darlin', an' I will do it."

"Don't fleece the entire officer's mess by luring them into your ridiculous high stakes games."

"Why, Willa Adams-Shaw! What on *Earth* do you take me for? I…"

"Promise." She pointed at him, but there was a twinkle of laughter in her eyes. He held his hands up in surrender.

"I promise. I will not fleece your officers."

And out of obligation to a woman he had once genuinely loved, he did not.

He only *mostly* fleeced them.

Sarah Cawkwell

* * *

They had enjoyed the journey back from Fort Wall, Joseph Sweeney and Doc Holliday. Despite the discomfort of having to ride pillion, Doc had settled into it after a few miles and begun to relax. Joe set a reasonably hard pace and they had to make only one overnight stop, building a camp and sleeping out under the endless stars of the Milky Way.

Howling Rock came into sight mid-afternoon on the second day. A number of people, recognising the young lawman, greeted him as Sweeney pulled the Iron Horse to a halt outside the *Whistle Stop*.

"You sure this is as far as I can take you, Doc?"

"This is perfect, Joe. Howlin' Rock ain't such a bad little place an' I can set up here for now. I ain't in no hurry to be anywhere else just now. You gonna stop for tonight?" The Sergeant squinted up into the mid-afternoon sun and shook his head.

"No," he replied. "Reckon I should get back to the Major sooner rather than later." He gave the deputy a broad, friendly smile and offered his hand, which Doc shook without hesitation. "It's been... interesting, Doc." It was a delightful echo of the major's own words and it made him grin beneath the respirator.

"I find your choice of words entertainin' to say the least, Sergeant Sweeney," said Doc, pushing his hat back on his head so he could get a good look at the man. "I reckon if – no, *when* we meet next time, you are gonna be somethin' far more important than plain old Sergeant Sweeney. You're one of the bravest men I ever met, an' I know the Earps. Trust me, that's a very high bar indeed."

Sweeney hesitated for just a moment. Then, in a moment of reckless abandonment, he gave Doc

Holliday the advice the deputy did not particularly care to hear.

"Don't regret your choices, Doc. I picked up on some of what you and the Major talked about and I guess you have issues with Marshal Earp – but you should know better than anybody that life's too damned short to bear grudges. I reckon you should find him and sort out whatever it is that is making you mad at him."

"Why, Sergeant, ain't you the philosopher. I thank you for your words, I truly do. And maybe I will give them some thought. After, I think, a good soak in Mr. Lum's bath-house and a good internal soakin' from a fine bottle of Old Overholt. You travel safely now, you hear me?" He winked at the Sergeant. "An' you keep one eye on Willa for me."

"You can count on me, deputy." Joe Sweeney snapped a smart salute, which Doc did not return. But he did tip his hat *most* courteously.

* * *

Doc was the only man who had ever made an effort to learn the name of the elderly Chinese man who ran the bath-house and laundry in Howling Rock. As a consequence, the old man who the locals simply referred to as 'Scrubs' adored the deputy for it. Consequently, when Doc appeared at the door enquiring politely if he might trouble Mr. Lum for a bath of hot water and maybe even a shave after, the laundry owner was more than happy to oblige.

"You still far too skinny, Doc," he scolded as the deputy eased his aching, tired body into the water. "You need to eat more. Eat more, live longer!" He fussed around for a while, making sure the water was fully to the deputy's liking and then left him alone to enjoy the soak. Among his peers, Doc was considered clean to the point of fastidious, enjoying up to three or four baths a week and at one time, refusing to wear a shirt more than once between washing.

Those days felt as though they were a long time ago in a past he had all but forgotten. So many of his memories were tied up with Tombstone, with Wyatt and his brothers that no matter how hard he tried to put them from his thoughts, they always came marching straight back again. He sighed deeply, removing the respirator and setting it down beside the tin tub. He slid deeper into the water and closed his eyes.

Tomorrow, he decided. Tomorrow, he would take Joe Sweeney's advice and he would head back to Tombstone. He'd sit down with Wyatt and they would sort out their differences. Of course, that rather depended on Wyatt being amenable to such a discussion. The Marshal was, without question, the most stubborn, pig-headed creature on two legs that Doc Holliday had ever known.

In the event the Marshal was somehow able to bend his arm and make him agree to come back, he would have to wire Bass Reeves. He'd rather enjoyed the autonomy the other Marshal had granted him, but he'd also come to accept that he was better suited to a deputy role than a Marshal or Sheriff.

And that was just fine.

When he was done with the bath, he stepped out of the tub and dressed himself in the fresh clothing that Mr. Lum had brought for him. He thanked the old man effusively and, as Mr. Lum had anticipated, left a generous tip. He connected his respirator, shrugged on his battered old coat and set his hat atop his head. Feeling a little raffish, even a bit daring, he tipped it at a jaunty angle. He would, he concluded, do. The events of the past days had been bordering on traumatic, but by all the deities of ancient times, Henry Holliday would always bounce back. They bred them for survival in the south.

As the Hamiltons had proved.

He shuddered and put the thought from his mind. Then he headed for the saloon, because no matter how deep and philosophical his thoughts might have been, there was *always* room to contemplate the mysteries of life as viewed through the bottom of an empty bourbon bottle.

* * *

He woke with the mother and father of all hangovers. His mouth was as parched as Fremont Street on a particularly dry day and there was a low, underground pulsing in his temples that suggested he'd had an entirely good night. He'd taken a bed in the hotel above the saloon and had enjoyed the comfort of clean sheets and a comfortable mattress...

...and the girl who was propped up on one elbow beside him, watching his waking moments with a faintly amused expression on her face. He knew her well; she'd kept him company on more than one occasion as he'd passed through Howling Rock. That beautiful, coffee and cream skin and those intelligent eyes that gave away the impressive intellect that he'd always found so attractive.

"Morning, Lawman," she said in a sultry tone. He rubbed at his unshaven jaw and gave her a sickly smile.

"Howdy, ma'am," he said, and gave her a crooked smile. She leaned over and kissed him on the

cheek, a sisterly kiss of affection more than any suggestion that she was after anything more energetic. He
was grateful for that: even sitting up brought a wave
of dizziness and a rush of bile into his throat. He took
a sip of water and leaned back closing his eyes. "I do
declare, Miss Millie, that I enjoyed myself rather too
much last night, did I not?"

"You always enjoy yourself when you're here,
Henry Junior," she said. "One day, you're just going to
put roots down here and stay put." He adored that she
used his given name. He'd grown so used to 'Doc' that
to hear his name spoken meaningfully and not sar-
castically, like Annabelle Hamilton had done, evoked
far-away memories of home. Of family. They'd never
known him as simply 'Henry', because of the confusion
that would cause with his father. Henry Junior was a
reminder of the boy he'd once been before time and
circumstance had changed him.

A pang of homesickness prickled at the edges
of awareness and with practiced ease, he pushed it
back. "That's as maybe, darlin'," he said and turned to
look at her. His gaze met hers and he wondered, again,
at her heritage. She wasn't like any woman he'd ever
known and he had known some great characters across
the years. Millie held herself like a duchess, but was
every inch the soiled dove and proud of it. That she had
chosen to keep him company that night and not given
the task over to one of her girls was deeply flattering.
"An' I probably have you to thank for that."

Somewhat spontaneously, he reached over
and touched her cheek with the back of his hand. Her
skin was soft and smooth, unblemished and untouched
by disease or the ravages of time. She was a rare desert
bloom. "Roots," he repeated, in a soft murmur. "Roots.
To stop movin' about an' stay in one place for more

than a couple of years... ah, Miss Millie, that would be the great dream. But it ain't gonna be today." He let his hand drop and leaned back against the pillows. Very carefully, as he did most mornings when he woke, he did a stock-take of his aches and pains. His dressings were still clean enough that he would not worry himself over them. His chest felt unusually clear this morning. He realised, with that slow dawning wakefulness that comes with a hangover, that he had gone to sleep without wearing his respirator. There was always a real danger in that. He was in danger of haemorrhaging constantly from the cavities in his lungs and to go several hours without the aid of the device was nothing short of daring.

"I do live dangerously," he murmured, to himself rather than to Millie.

She kissed him again. "You had a good night's sleep, Henry Junior, and it was clear that you needed it. You've done a good job over this matter," she said, softly. He narrowed his eyes slightly.

"What do you know about what I've been doin'?"

She laughed, lightly and stuck her tongue out at him in mock torment. "Pillow talk, Lawman. You told me the whole story."

"I did?" Strange how his memory of the night was so very hazy. He must have *killed* that bottle of Old Overholt. "When did I tell you? Before? Or after?" A thought struck him. "Please don't say durin'..."

"After." She laughed, then leaned over him, her lithe, supple body tantalisingly close and took up his respirator. "Here. It'll help with how you're feeling."

The gaps in his memory were frustrating, but he let it pass. It was conceivable that she had simply invited him to her bed for company rather than anything more. It had happened before. For all he knew, they might have just laid down after he had quit with the drinking and talked. What he *did* know was that whenever he spent time in Millie's bed, he slept better than he ever did. It felt like a reward, somehow.

"Thank you, darlin'." He caught her chin between his thumb and forefinger and leaned forward to kiss her, softly on the lips. "Thank you for makin' me feel more like a man an' less like the damn machine I'm turnin' into." He clipped the respirator into position and she was right. He could breathe more easily and the hangover began to abate a little. She ran her hands through his unruly hair and fixed her dark-eyed gaze on his. When she spoke, she did so with complete conviction.

"Henry, you could never be a machine. You have far too much humanity in you." He could not quite put his finger on why, but he found the phrase surprisingly touching. He took her hand and bent his forehead over it. He could not kiss it, his lips encased as they were in the respiratory prison of his mask, but the gesture was unmistakable. Millie smiled at him.

"Thank you, sugar. I am glad someone thinks so," he said.

"I know so," she said, simply. "And I'm an excellent judge of these things."

* * *

It was harder than he had thought it would be to motivate himself to leave Howling Rock, despite all the conviction of the previous night. It was a long trek back to Tombstone, but he didn't mind that so much. He'd considered taking the stage but brushed off the idea. He knew that the walk would give him time to think, to deal with all the emotions that had been stirred since the moment he and Willa had been re-united.

He stopped for a break at a crossroads where a small clump of tenacious trees afforded some shade from the mid-day sun. He leaned back against one, his eyes closed against the bright sunlight and his hat tipped over his eyes. He relished the feeling of the sun on his skin, the very fact of his continued existence still bringing him a simple joy.

He had been there for maybe ten minutes before he heard the sound of hooves on the dirt road and he tilted the brim of his hat back, squinting up at the approaching horses. The one, presently without a rider, was a few steps ahead of the second. It was the figure mounted on the second horse that drew the deputy's attention for a brief moment. A tumult of emotions cascaded through him before he swung his gaze back to the riderless horse. It came to a stop in front of him, before reaching down and biting the hat off his head.

"Well now, Solomon Smith. You sure took your time showin' up, you lazy beast." Without so much as looking up, he greeted the rider as well. "Hey, Wyatt."

"Doc." Marshal Wyatt Earp tipped his hat in greeting and looked down at his friend and deputy who was presently attempting to wrestle his hat back from a smug-looking Solomon Smith. The sight was bordering on the ludicrous. Every time the man got a hold on his hat, the horse would snatch it back, raising his head higher and out of the man's reach. The game went on for a while, but Doc finally won the battle, receiving an unfriendly bite on the arm in the process. He rammed his hat back on his head and then patted Solomon Smith's nose with great affection. The horse whickered in mock-defeat and nuzzled against the young deputy's shoulder, returning the gesture of mutual appreciation. Wyatt almost smiled.

Almost. Smiling wasn't his forte. 'The Frowner', his brothers called him, and it was a sobriquet well-earned.

"When he showed up back in Tombstone without you, I figured... thought you'd want him back. So I followed him." Wyatt didn't add that his initial thoughts had been ones of fear and concern for the safety of his unlikely friend. After all, the last words Wyatt Earp and Doc Holliday had shared prior to the deputy's leaving Tombstone had not been friendly ones, or even remotely civil ones. They had argued. It hadn't been the first time they'd fallen out of one another's favour and Morgan's astute observation that it probably wouldn't be the last was pretty accurate.

Wyatt couldn't even remember what the argument had been about. Something trivial, pointless and definitely not worth losing his only real friend over. When Solomon Smith had trotted nonchalantly into Tombstone minus his rider, Wyatt had been frantic with worry. When the horse had left again, clearly expecting the Marshal to follow, Wyatt had done so readily. Like Doc, he had a certain affection for the old methods of transportation and the ride out into the wilderness had done him good. Given him time to think.

And now, here was Doc. *Larger than life,* as Virgil would say, *and twice as ugly.*

"Well, now that is mighty thoughtful of you, Marshal," said the deputy, putting a foot into a stirrup and swinging himself up into his horse's saddle with casual ease. "But you know Solomon Smith. A horse with a singular mind indeed. I do not doubt for one moment that if you had left him to his own devices, he would still have come back. Nonetheless, here he is, an' here *you* are. As I say. Mighty thoughtful of you."

"I *can* do thoughtful, sometimes, you know."

A silence descended, not entirely uncomfortable, but definitely in possession of teeth. The quiet was long enough that Wyatt, usually silent and taciturn felt the need to fill the empty space with something.

"Gotta say, Doc. There ain't no pretty way of putting this. You're looking a bit bashed about there. Looks to me like you could use a drink."

"That obvious, huh?" Doc turned his head sideways to consider Wyatt for a moment, his eyes glinting with a moment's humour. "I ran into some of Carpathian's folks. I ain't got no idea why you keep on comin' back to those insane people, Wyatt. I really an' truly do not understand it. Suffice it to say... some crazy stuff went down. Met a Warrior Nation Spirit Priest too, an' let me tell you this, Wyatt Earp." The former dentist held up a remonstrating finger and waggled it seriously. "I sure as hell ain't ever gonna be in a hurry to get on the wrong side of *that* kid."

The memory of the azure inferno was still fresh in the deputy's mind, and he shuddered involuntarily. Terrifying and effective it may have been, but it had been difficult to connect the quietly spoken young Spirit Priest with the monster that had destroyed Annabelle Hamilton's production line.

"I'd heard the Enlightened were up to something in these parts." Wyatt nodded but did not pry for information. Doc always gave up the details when he was good and ready to do it.

"Enlightened is an' interestin' choice of name for themselves if you ask me." The deputy thought for a moment. "Knowin' others is Wisdom. Knowin' yourself is Enlightenment."

Wyatt nodded sagely but there was no sign of recognition in his cool blue eyes. *Intellect is wasted on these people,* Doc thought and sighed softly. "Lao Tzu, that one. No? Ah, well, we pretty much shut down their operation." Another pause. "Actually, we destroyed it. The perpetrators, I am sad to say, remain unaccounted for. Could not tell you if we killed 'em or if they escaped. One thing is for sure. If they *did* get away, I imagine we will have to face more of their brand of horror goin' forward."

"We?" One of Wyatt's eyebrows rose. Doc shrugged.

"There was me, an' a fantastic posse I pulled together from Little Beam. Mrs. Kelly was there so I had high hopes we'd be successful." Wyatt nodded at this. Like so many others, he held the indomitable undertaker in extremely high regard. "Then there was Stone Fur – the Spirit Priest I mentioned? And there was a bunch of folks..." The pause was so miniscule that it could not have been measured in any known unit of time, but it felt gaping, nonetheless. "...from the Union. Shut up."

"Didn't say a word." Doc Holliday voluntarily working with the Union was probably the single most shocking thing in his entire statement, but Wyatt wisely chose to leave it. Instead, he focused on other matters. "Look, Doc, I'm sure you have a tale to tell, and we've got a good ride ahead of us. Assuming you come with me, maybe you can fill me in on what's been going on."

There was another of those not-quite awkward pauses and Wyatt didn't let it grow this time. "To be honest with you, Deputy Holliday, I could use your help. Rumours that could use investigating and the like. Outlaw activity for one. I can't think of anybody I'd rather have by my side than you. 'Course, I'd get why you might not want to come with me..." It wasn't begging, wasn't wheedling, wasn't pathetic in any way and something in the honesty and earnestness touched something in Doc's armour of defence. He allowed the annoyance to melt away. As ever, the one question chewed at him.

Why did they have to have such a complicated friendship? Until the day that Wyatt had brought him the respirator, everything had been simple. Since then, Doc had trust issues and Wyatt simply appeared to be selling his own soul piece by piece. A small chunk of that soul had been exchanged for a respirator to keep a feckless dentist alive. It wasn't that Doc wasn't grateful, no sir, he *was* grateful. He just...

He just *cared*.

On the other hand, Doc knew that he was not Wyatt's father. He was not placed to tell the obstinate son of a bitch what he should and shouldn't do. Didn't mean he couldn't worry about it, though.

As he ruminated on the matter, the deputy studied Wyatt silently and with great intent, his eyes filled with a thousand unspoken words and questions and then he reached up to unclick the respirator.

Wyatt tried hard to ignore how pale and drawn Doc looked without the bulk of the respirator masking his face. The old, familiar guilt that he couldn't do more to help his terminally ill friend rose up. He looked away for just a moment and then steadied himself on the horse's back.

Doc coughed, just the once and took a breath of air. Then his gaze hardened.

Here comes the rebuke. Wyatt steeled himself for the inevitable, sneering attack that he'd suspected he might receive from the deputy. Instead, Doc took his hipflask from his belt and had a long pull of its contents. He knew better than to offer the flask to the tee-total

Wyatt and he tucked it away again. When he looked back up, the hint of steel in his eyes had dissipated. He smiled that lop-sided, disarming grin that he was famous for, and Wyatt was momentarily taken aback at the affability. Gone was the iron-clad arrogance to be replaced by the more familiar geniality that endeared the deputy to most people who engaged with him.

"What is a friend? A single soul dwellin' in two bodies." Wyatt knew that one, because Doc had used it before. He'd come to recognise those little quotes across the years. Doc always used it as a mechanism to gauge the level of education of those around him. This time, though, Wyatt suspected he meant the quote with all his heart. He still played the game, though, because old, familiar habits were comforting.

"Aristotle?"

"Aristotle." The deputy beamed a swift, infectious grin, nodded, then continued. "Y'see, Wyatt... I have had a few days to think," he said, wiping his lips with the back of his hand. "A few days to weigh up the pros and cons of where things have been goin'. Oh, I know that I have made some bad choices in my life. But I am also realistic enough to know I cannot change what has gone by. It is tough enough to manage to present some days." He stared out over the frontier landscape in all its wild, untamed glory.

"The future ain't that rosy for me, healthwise, I know that. I gotta keep my eyes on that. You bought me time, Wyatt, but still each day could be my last."

The marshal looked as though he would speak, but Doc didn't let him get a word in edgeways. He needed to say his piece before he let it go quietly unspoken as he had done so many times before. "I thank you for this gift of life, Marshal Earp an' it gladdens my heart that I get to spend whatever time I have doin' the law's work at your side. So... well, I figure, what the hell. If the Fates have decreed that I am gonna die out here in this godforsaken part of the country, may as well go out boots-on, fightin', with my friend by my side." He re-attached the respirator. "I am all yours, Marshal."

The speech had embarrassed him, had maybe embarrassed the both of them and he flushed slightly. He took off his hat, ran his fingers through his hair and reached down to pat Solomon Smith's neck. "Let's go." He set the horse off at a sedate walk and got several yards away.

Suddenly aware that Wyatt was not following him, Doc reined Solomon Smith back in and twisted in the saddle until he was looking back over his shoulder. "You comin', Wyatt Earp? Or have I gotta go save the world by myself? Justice ain't gonna dispense itself, you know."

The deputy's words had been tumbled and awkward and Wyatt knew what it had cost Doc to swallow his pride and offer gratitude. It was enough. The marshal nodded once and as his deputy turned away again, allowed himself the rare luxury of a smile. He grinned at Doc's back for a brief moment before spurring his own horse onward. His own beast drew parallel to Doc's, and he squinted off into the distance.

"Ain't no way I'm letting *you* have all the fun, Holliday."

He kicked his heels into the horse's side and set off at a full gallop. Doc Holliday, despite his best efforts to remain gentlemanly and genteel let out a shout of boyish laughter and followed suit, the two of them racing one another in a manner he thought he might never have enjoyed again. He relished the sheer, simple pleasure of the wind in his face, the thunder of hooves beneath him, the surge of blood through his veins that

368

made him feel fully and truly alive.

For now, everything was fine. It was enough.

* * *

Ben Hamilton's eyes fluttered open. He was lying on a bed, a soft, comfortable bed, in a light and airy room. Daylight streamed through the window, ensuring a plentiful supply of good lighting and after spending so long cooped up in warehouses and manufactories, the natural daylight was welcome.

He went to move, and pain laced through every sinew and a groan came from his mouth. It attracted the attention of the figure standing at the window. Annabelle turned to look at her brother. A look of relief came over her beautiful face, but she smoothed it out quickly and allowed it to become an expression of eternal indifference. He noticed that there was something different about her face; something that had not been there previously, but he was too preoccupied with being in no small amount of pain that he didn't linger on it.

"Benjamin," she said, formally. "Good to see ya could finally be bothered to join us." She moved from the window and crossed to stand beside him. Her eyes studied him carefully. "Ya took a bad wound to the shoulder. Ya should be lucky that ya got a sister who not only cares for ya, but who knows a little 'bout biology and medicine as well."

"The portal..." His memories of those last few moments were hazy and confused. He remembered the screaming with painful, embarrassing clarity: as Four Thirty-Six's blade had hacked through his shoulder. The shame and horror of one of their own creations turning on its masters in that way. Were he not feeling so drained and self-pitying, he might well have been outraged.

"We got off lightly," she said, shrugging her slender shoulders eloquently. "We stepped in at ninety five percent. Mackeye got a few burns, but nothin' that he won't get over."

And that was it. That was what was different with her face. Beneath the carefully applied layers of powder and rouge, his beautiful sister had acquired burns to her face that changed her appearance. She was still as lovely as she had ever been, but if you knew her well, you'd see the changes. His eyes were briefly drawn to the pouch she wore around her neck like a pendant; old, battered, leather, unfamiliar? No, he'd seen it somewhere before...

She took his scrutiny as staring, looking at her injuries and her eyes welled with tears. "Stop lookin'," she said, and he felt contrite. She tugged her hair, which she normally wore done up in a variety of elaborate designs atop her head. She was wearing it loose right now, and the motion cause an artful curl to fall across her face, covering the area that had been burned. "It'll heal. Hopin' the scars ain't so bad. They sure ain't gonna be as impressive as the one that y'all will have when this is done." She flashed him a quick, tight smile. "Ya still have ya arm. Might be stiff and painful for a while but be grateful. I know what it's like ta lose one."

"Thank you," he said and leaned back against the pillow, closing his eyes. Then he opened them again. His brain synapses were not firing at a particularly swift rate and things were sinking in more slowly than they might otherwise have done.

"The portal worked, then? Even at ninety five percent?"

"Obviously," she said – and it was affectionate,

rather than her usual savage retort. "Or we wouldn't be here. You do good work, Benjamin."

His next question was tentative and anxious. "Where is *here* exactly? I knew the portal had made a connection, but didn't know where we'd end up..."

She didn't reply straight away. Instead, she made a big show of checking the bandages on her brother's chest and upper arm, refusing to meet his gaze. "Don't matter," she said, brusquely. "All that's important is that we're all alive, an' that we get to fight another day, right?"

"Where are we, Annabelle?" He was so stern with her that she was momentarily taken aback. Her brother was usually so very quiet and unassuming that to hear such assertiveness from him was nothing short of shocking.

"The Parlour," she replied in a small voice. Ben's jaw dropped open and he stared at his sister in disbelief.

"We travelled *that far*?" He sounded startled at his own achievement. He had made the void engine remain functional without really understanding how it worked. It was only thanks to his sheer brilliance in matters of engineering that he had even managed to channel power to it, let alone get it working so well that they had travelled almost entirely across the country.

"Is she..."

"She ain't here just now. It's been suggested that might be for the best. She's due back later today. Oh, Benjamin, jus' imagine what I could accomplish workin' with a mind like hers!" And there she was once more; the starry-eyed, ambitious girl – no, *woman* – who had once been his petulant little sister. Ben stared at her for a moment, not sure he really understood her anymore.

"Our project was hardly a success," he tried. "We... failed."

"Objectively, we failed. Overall, though, the project was a great success," she countered. "Why, we produced an army. Ain't our fault that the others cheated an' joined forces against us. I tell ya this, Benjamin Hamilton. If *we* were to do the same, to join forces with more of the Enlightened, why, those frontier savages wouldn't stand a *chance*!" Her eyes shone with the passion of her own words and her hands clenched into fists. Ben waited for a few moments, for a natural pause where he could express his own opinion. He anticipated a fight.

"I'm going back home when I'm well enough."

His sister was not tall. But when the words had left his mouth, she seemed, somehow, to diminish further in his sight. Whatever passion drove her to the remarkable achievements she had made left her like air leaving a balloon. She studied him without speaking for an incomprehensibly long time before her fists finally relaxed and her shoulders drooped.

"Stonewall Jackson ain't got what ya need, Benjamin. If ya could only see that... if ya could just take a moment an' see what it is that's missin' from all ya do... the Enlightened can help. Ya got such..." She took a breath and paused. When she continued, it was as though admitting the next thing somehow stung. "Ya got such *talent*, Benjamin. An' I cannot *bear* to think of ya wastin' away in some cave..."

"He doesn't..."

"In *some cave*..." She glared at him, on a roll now. "Jus' tinkerin' ya life away. On the other hand, y'all *are* my brother, an' much as it pains me to admit it, I love ya. I want ya to be happy. I know that stayin' here with me would be better for all of us. But... if ya gotta go, well then. I ain't gonna stop ya."

"Really?" He suspected treachery. What else was he going to believe? She was as changeable as the weather, as unpredictable as a hurricane. And she was his sister.

"Really." She caught his hand in her mechanical grip and ignored the look of pain on his face as the gesture sent a flash of agony up into his shoulder. "But jus' do me the favour of at least *meetin'* the Countess while ya here." Annabelle smiled radiantly, putting just enough wheedling into her voice.

What little colour was in his face drained to alabaster-white. He only knew of Augusta Byron by reputation and frankly, that was enough.

"Maybe just to say thanks," he said, dubiously and Annabelle mercifully released his hand, clapping her own as though she were a little girl again.

"I am *positive* that won't be a decision ya gonna regret, darlin' boy. She has such plans! We can accomplish so much..." Her words flowed into one long wave of noise that he could no longer bring himself to listen to and he leaned back, closing his eyes. He would humour his sister and he would meet the Countess. But then he would leave. He wasn't cut out for this sort of existence.

His hand reached up to the leather pouch at her neck. "What's this?" Her hand closed over it and her smile was radiant.

"The future, Benjamin."

The last thing he heard as he drifted off into sleep was another female voice, this one low and mellifluous, marked by a heavy British accent.

"Your brother's face has the most *beautiful* bone structure, my dear. You are sure he is going to make a full recovery? A pity..."

* * *

Stone Fur had always found the most inner peace during the hours of dusk. There was a brief period of absolute silence; when the animals and birds of the day crept to their quiet hideways and before the creatures of the night came out to begin their own cycle anew.

In this time, he would retreat to the very edges of the settlement, sometimes even as far afield as the Hollow of Sighs and quietly reflect on the day's activities, or simply meditate, enjoying the silence and calm the desert night carried to the turmoil of his soul. Those early hours on their return from battle had been critical; when he had finally regained consciousness, he could not even recall his own name. But the universe – or at least the Great Spirit – clearly felt the boy deserved a reward and memories had returned. Halting at first, but recall followed soon.

This night, he remained within the settlement, taking a strange kind of comfort from the fact that his People remained safe from the horrors he had experienced in the last few days. There were any number of questions that Stone Fur needed to answer, but he was lost as to exactly where he should start.

"You are troubled, Spirit Priest." Loud Thunder, his near-permanent shadow was never far from his side. Since the battle, the big warrior had been bordering on the very edge of awe for his young companion. Some months before his death, Curved Bear Claw had confided that he believed Stone Fur's ascension to Spirit Priest would result in a shift in the balance of power. He had firmly subscribed to the understanding that the Great Spirit would imbue the youth with a power unlike anything the People had seen in recent years.

He had been correct in that assumption.

"I am always troubled, my friend." Stone Fur smiled at the other warrior and ran his fingers through his tangled hair. "I am simply less troubled at this hour of the day."

"Do you wish to be alone, Spirit Priest? I do not wish to interrupt your meditations..."

"No, please stay." The answer was quick, suggesting that Stone Fur welcomed the company and Loud Thunder settled his bulk down on the ground beside the younger man. They sat together in companionable silence for some time, Loud Thunder not in any rush to extract conversation. Eventually, Stone Fur spoke.

"I had a vision, earlier."

"Should I be concerned?"

"I do not know." The youth stared out over the horizon, watching the bands of blue gradually fade into a deep, rich amber. Soon, red streaks would join them and finally, night itself would swathe the world in its velvet embrace. "I felt calm at its conclusion. I feel that we have served the Great Spirit's will. That we have done a great deed by ending these terrible things before they could infect the world. And our meeting with the Incomers. The warrior woman. The man of the law. That may yet prove to be a blessing or a curse. I cannot yet tell."

"They fought well," observed Loud Thunder. "But none of them will ever be Warrior Nation."

"No, that much is true. Their hearts, though." He placed a hand across his chest and nodded. "Their hearts beat with the same fire. Even if just for that brief time. I am grateful they were there to assist us."

Loud Thunder passed no comment. As far as he had seen things, the Warrior Nation had assisted the others, not the other way around. "Your vision?" He pressed for further details and Stone Fur nodded.

"Yes," he said. "It is ever impossible to fully describe these things, but I can relate the feelings. Joy that we have seen victory in this matter but... trepidation. That this is just the beginning. That this was just one battle and that truly, we must prepare for war." He looked at Loud Thunder, his face serious and thoughtful. "There is a darkness on the horizon. A storm yet to come," he said.

"Then we will prepare," said Loud Thunder. He put a hand on Stone Fur's shoulder. "With you to guide us, to shine the Eagle's light upon us in times of strife, Spirit Priest, we will overcome." The big warrior got to his feet. "We will weather this storm and we will emerge victorious."

"Yes," said Stone Fur and watched the big warrior amble away. He waited until he was sure Loud Thunder could not hear him. "At least, it is good to believe that we will."

Sarah Cawkwell

EPILOGUE

Another place.

The Order considers the actions of humanity. They watch, they assess, and they judge.

"Her skill is remarkable, the corruption evident." The first voice is female, a husky tone to it that suggests that it is as capable of barbed cruelty as it is of honeyed praise.

"Yes." The second voice is male, much older, with the faintest hint of what might be the accent of someone not native to the New World. "Remarkable and accelerating at an unprecedented pace. The Influence is strong with her. And with her sibling, too." There is a long, thoughtful silence, the kind that is tinged with the impression that the speaker would far rather engage in discussion and contemplation of something far more important.

There is a creak of leather, a rustle of a softer, more delicate fabric and the woman shifts her position. Her hands run over the weapon, the ancient artefact that she wears at her waist. Her tongue flickers over the surface of her lips with unconcealed hunger.

"Intervention is necessary, before they can further spread their pollution." There is an eagerness in her voice and the man turns, studying her thoughtfully.

"It is a tempting prospect," he says, after some consideration. "But you know as well as I that our directives require subtlety unless open confrontation is unavoidable, at least until events escalate. Regardless of how strong this woman, this Hamilton becomes, she is merely a symptom of the greater sickness, a divergent branch of the rotting tree. Better to follow the flow of poison back to its source so that it might be cut or burned out before it can spread to the farthest reaches. We must not lose sight of our mission of salvation, however tempting the prospect of purification may be."

"As you say, High Sircan," acknowledges the woman, but she does nothing to hide her disappointment. "What of the others? The lawman..."

The man lets out a sharp bark of a laugh, devoid of humour. "The chaos of Holliday is no threat to our cause. He brings trouble enough down upon himself." Long, elegant fingers steeple together beneath his chin and he stares out once more across the reddening western skies. "I predict he will be dead before long if he continues to explore that which he does not fully understand. The mask he wears is keeping him alive, but he knows that his pattern has been changed, even if he does not appreciate what that truly means. There is a subconscious understanding in that one. A realisation, even on the most basic that the very thing that gives him life is somehow altering him."

"He does not trust it." The woman smooths down the front of her tunic. "That much is obvious, even to one as... unsubtle... as I."

"You do yourself a disservice, my dear Elita." The man reaches out a hand and lays it upon the woman's shoulder. "You observe well. And you are correct. Holliday does not trust this new age of progress, although he grudgingly works with it. His instincts serve him well. But as is true of most of his kind, he wants to live."

"A selfish human drive. Particularly when it comes at such great cost." She clicks her tongue in a noise of disapproval, shaking her head at the arrogance of mankind.

"Indeed. But is that not what drives all life? The will to survive against all odds? Even our ancient enemy understands that most basic of instincts. No, my dear, it is not selfishness. Not in this case." The answer does not satisfy her and her arms fold beneath her breasts. Her stance is defiant, her attitude rebellious. He does not mind. All children must learn.

"That man should be dead, but he is not. His gamble has ensured that he cheated his pre-ordained destiny." Again, that click of disapproval. "The universe rarely settles for such imbalance. He has evaded his fate."

"And his fate will catch up to him, my dear, just as it does for all, in their time. No, leave Holliday be. He serves us better alive. For now, at least. As to the military woman..." A ghost of a smile flickers over the man's face, an expression rarely seen on him. It does little to dispel the severity of his aging features, although a light shines momentarily in the pale blue eyes. "As to her, she may well be of use to us."

"What would you suggest then, my lord? If we are not to intervene?"

"Monitor their activities. If events are in danger of escalating beyond their ability to contain, report to me. Otherwise... continue with your investigations."

"Yes, High Sircan." She inclines her head to him with gracious respect and with the lithe, easy gait of a predator, she leaves his presence. Abner watches her go and returns his attention to the setting of the sun over the plains of the western frontier. The amber and burnt orange hues in the sky are quite lovely. Even the aloof Cor Caroli had remarked on occasion that, despite its many flaws, this world is one of the more pleasant ones that the Order has been forced to take up residence on.

It will be a true tragedy, High Sircan Abner mused, that if this world burns, for none will remain to appreciate its beauty. The board will be swept clean with fire, and the game began anew. This RJ-1027 and the taint it brings to humanity must be stopped. He must prevent the Exodus or humanity will be just another civilisation sacrificed in the Allshard's sacred crusade.

ACKNOWLEDGEMENTS

This book has been a while in the making. It's a privilege to write tie-in fiction of any kind and this has been no exception. I adore the Wild West Exodus setting – and I am an avid student of frontier history. Being able to bring the two together has been an utter joy.

Getting to write an acknowledgement page brings a strange sort of insecurity with it. Many people who were present in my world during the writing of this story, or who have had some hand in shaping it are going to be missed off the list that follows. Don't take it personally. You're all there in one way or another. And even if you don't see yourself in this list, be reassured you're in my thoughts. Yes, even you.

To Stuart and the team at Warcradle for bringing this beautiful game into my life and letting me run rampant in the toy box – thank you. Thank you also for putting up with my occasionally wild ramblings during the process. You bring so much love to this game and the wider Dystopian World and it is seen and respected by many.

To Darren Dale, Steve Boland, Andrew 'Dudge' Dudgeon and Jeff O'Brien, who left this world before this book was finished. My brothers-in-arms whose friendship and wise words I will cherish to the end of my days.

To Colin, for the inexplicable joy of throwing chocolate brownies at me at four in the morning.

To Rob, Chaz, Jordane, Janice, Dave, Laura and Baz – the tabletop crew who kept me sane throughout lockdown.

To everyone from Weird West – particularly Jamie, Dave I, Chalkie and Andy for pushing me so far out of my comfort zone that I nearly fell off the planet. You all challenged my confidence and gave me something beyond who I am.

To Kyle (my own personal Doc Holliday who gave me away during the renewal of my wedding vows at the OK Corral in Tombstone), Nicole and little Henry for showing me the true meaning of grit and resilience. May the rainbow always touch your shoulder.

To Rikku and Yuna, the best cats that ever were and who have both crossed the rainbow bridge.

To my long-suffering dad, Mike, and to my patient brother, Stephen – you guys are the best.

And finally, to my son Jamie and my husband Ben. Told you I would finish it.

Look for more books from Winged Hussar Publishing, LLC – E-books, paperbacks and Limited-Edition hardcovers. The best in history, science fiction and fantasy at:

https://www. wingedhussarpublishing.com
https://www.whpsupplyroom.com
or follow us on Facebook at:
Winged Hussar Publishing LLC
Or on twitter at:
WingHusPubLLC
For information and upcoming publications

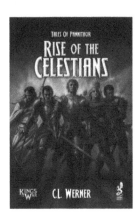